CHARBONNEAU

Old men should be explorers?
I'll be an Indian. . .
                —THEODORE ROETHKE

CHARBONNEAU
MAN OF TWO DREAMS

A NOVEL BY WINFRED BLEVINS

*To the memory of James Crawford, master woodsman,
who went to the wilderness always as a pilgrim*

TO THE READER

It is our pleasure to keep available uncommon
titles and to this end, at the time of publication,
we have used the best available sources. To aid
catalogers and collectors, this title is printed in
an edition limited to 300 copies. ——— **Enjoy!**

To order contact
AMEREON HOUSE, the publishing division of
Amereon Ltd.
Postal Box 1200
Mattituck, New York 11952

Manufactured in the United States

Contents

Rocky Mountain Fur Trapping Area, 1806—1843

Preface

All that is known about the historical Jean-Baptiste Charbonneau could be printed in a few pages: That he was born to Sacajawea and Toussaint Charbonneau and was carried as an infant across the continent with the Lewis and Clark expedition; that William Clark brought him to St. Louis as a child and arranged his education by a Baptist preacher and possibly a Catholic priest; that at eighteen the youth met Prince Paul of Württemberg by chance; that he then went to Europe with the Prince, traveled extensively, was further educated, and returned to St. Louis after six years; that he became a mountain man and rode with such trappers as Kit Carson and Jim Bridger; that he guided the Mormon Battalion to California in 1846; that he was one of the first to join the California gold rush. From there the historical evidence stipulates that he spent his remaining years with his mother and her Shoshone people.

But this is a novel, not a rendering of history. And from the first I saw the material as redolent of a larger theme: Charbonneau was by blood and by breeding fully a member of two cultures that were in conflict. Almost alone of both the Indians and the whites, he might have been able to choose freely between the life-styles and the values of his two peoples. I wrote *Charbonneau* to discover what his choice would be, and why he made it.

So I have played free with history where it suited my dramatic and thematic purposes. Much of the material here is authentic—the material, for instance, from the journals of Lewis and Clark, Clark's letter, the visit of the Flathead chiefs to St. Louis, certain episodes in the mountains, Washakie's speeches in my Prologue, and so on. Likewise most of the principal characters are historical. But I have invented, elaborated, and even made small changes in history, changes that scholars will recognize.

1

The happenstance of life sometimes does not meet the needs of art.

One liberty is large: I have devised a conclusion to Charbonneau's life-long conflict that fits neither of the two historical versions. Probably I have also made the character more sophisticated and more cultured than the historical personage.

For both liberties, and all the smaller ones, I plead Henry James's celebrated edict that a novel can be held to no rule except one—that it be interesting.

WINFRED BLEVINS
July 1974

Prologue

AUGUST, 1876: The old man awoke in the pre-dawn light. He felt it, sometimes, like this; he could sense that in a few moments the sun, like a bubble of air that has risen from the bottom of a lake, would burst silently over the ridge to the east. He got up quietly from his buffalo robe, not disturbing the two squaws who slept nearby, and walked to the flap that always faced the rising sun and looked out at the eastern sky. His sense had been right, as it had been right on most mornings since he had come to live here in this wide grove beside the Salmon River. He looked at the distant ridge across the river where the sun would appear this time of year to the right of three juniper pines just below its flat top. The sky was not yellow or red—the sun had been above the earth's horizon for more than an hour already; it was instead the crystalline, corn-flower blue of mornings in the mountains. The spot where the sun was aiming turned a brilliant white, and then the first edge of the yellow globule flickered above the ridge.

The old man stood facing it, as he did every morning, naked in the cool air. His body was slender and hard. If he showed the effects of seventy-one years on the earth, it was in his stringiness. His arms, his trunk, and legs were unwrinkled; the skin looked weathered from exposure to sun and wind. His face was crinkled, particularly around the narrowed eyes, and his neck looked like creased paper that has been wadded up and pulled flat again. It was a dark face, as dark as any Indian's, but the body was no-ticeably lighter.

He did not pray on this August morning. It would have been good Shoshone custom to utter a small prayer to the sun, the giver of life, but he did not even remember the prayers clearly. He observed the event each morning sim-ply by standing there, naked, and looking.

The older of the two squaws joined him—she was as

3

ancient as he—and made the soft sound of a song in half-voice. Always she rose a little after he did and took part in his salute; always the young squaw—young enough still to be handsome—slept on in the sleep that the young are granted. The old man liked them both. The older one had lived alone with him for thirty years, the younger he had bought ten years ago, mainly for more company. His two children had for ten years been living with the tribe, many sleeps to the south in the Wind River Mountains. The squaw made a ritualistic gesture to the medicine bundle hung from a tripod in front of the tent, and another to the painting on the lodge.

He walked to the river and dashed cold water into his face. A little way upstream a tiny creek flowed into the river; it was smoking. Further from the bank a pool steamed more heavily, and the cool breeze carried the familiar sulphur smell to his nostrils. He went to the pool, stepped in, and let his body sink into the hot water. For several minutes he lolled and luxuriated there.

This hot-spring bath was also part of his morning ritual, and this morning it felt especially good. His legs and arms were not any stiffer than usual, though during the last ten years they seemed to loosen more slowly. No, it felt especially good because he would not be able to lie in this hot, spring-fed pool again until the aspen had begun to turn gold and the chill of autumn was in the air. Last night, in the tipi around the stew pot, he said to the squaws, "We have not tasted the meat of the buffalo in too many seasons. Far too many seasons. Tomorrow we start to cross the mountains and go down into the land of the buffalo."

He lived in a good place—it had good water, good wood, good meat. He pitched his lodge most of the time here on the Middle Fork of the Salmon River, not far above its mouth, in a wide, tree-studded meadow. In the winter the deep gorge made its own climate, so that while the mountains all around were deep in drifts, the snow never stayed on the ground at the floor of the canyon. In the summer he moved upstream into the high mountains to avoid the heat. No area he knew had more meat—grouse, deer, elk, mountain goat, bighorn sheep, and bear; the river provided plenty of trout and salmon, when he wanted them. All winter, the snow kept the animals penned up deep in the gorge, so that hunting was easy. In the summer he followed them to the high peaks, the stony ridges, the alpine meadows, the tiny, swift-rushing mountain streams. His territory was a Garden of Eden of a place, and he loved it. It had everything he wanted, except buffalo. They stayed on the eastern side of the Continental Divide in Montana. So once in several years he would journey across the mountains to kill one.

Lying back in the hot water, he could see smoke wafting out of the top of the lodge and knew that his young squaw would soon have the meat hot. The old squaw was packing what they would need for the trip onto a travois. The dog, having noticed, was stirring, curious to see where they would go. The old man decided to relax where he was a while longer.

Friedrich thought he had a fever. In fact he was sure of it. He had been trying for two days to reconcile himself to dying in this awful, awful country—Godforsaken was truly the word for it—but now that he felt the fever he was angry and dyspeptic, unwilling to be taken away ignominiously.

"*Gottes Wille wird vollführt werden,*" Jurgen said to him again, making a point of sounding sympathetic.

Friedrich supposed that was true. He could feel an edge in himself, though, an edge ready to be angry at God as well.

They were riding down the South Fork of the Clearwater River—Friedrich, Jurgen, Kurt, and the boy, Willy—and they were lost. They had left Salt Lake with a guide, a scurrilous-looking fellow named Elkanah, to ride north, strike the Salmon River, cross over to the Clearwater, and follow it to the Snake and the settlement of Walla Walla. That way they could have preceded the rest of their party, all German, which was hauling wagons bought from the Mormons over the Oregon Trail toward the settlement, and they could have gotten the work started. But Elkanah, as unreliable as he looked, had been seized with a fever and died abruptly two days before. Which left them, as Jurgen insisted, to rely on God's will.

Friedrich didn't like the look of it. The country was not merely wild, it was savage. The earth was hard, dry, and rocky. It rose into spiny ridges fit for nothing but an unfamiliar tree or two, trees shaped by a hostile wind and parched by a merciless sun. Friedrich could barely imagine game living here, and could not imagine man inhabiting the place at all. Not only its stubborn dryness, hardness, and stoniness, but its sheer size militated against man. The scope of it alone seemed anti-human to him.

As solid family men with a major stake in the outcome, Friedrich and Jurgen were the leaders. Willy was just a boy, and Kurt—well, what could Friedrich say about Kurt? He was a young no-good. Jurgen had spoken for going on and trusting to God. Kurt had said they couldn't find the way back, and would probably kill themselves anyway, so they might as well try to go on. Friedrich had consented to try to get down the Clearwater less out of Jurgen's faith than out of fear Kurt was right. How could a man trust to the will of God in a country that God so clearly had cursed? They did not even know for a fact that they were on the Clearwater River. The wrong river might take them, as far as they knew, straight into hell.

Friedrich sagged in the saddle, let his horse meander along, and strayed in his thoughts. He checked his forehead again for the fever, and found it hot. At least today was an improvement on yesterday. All afternoon Kurt had chosen to be contentious and answer disrespectfully, so that the three adults disputed while they rode. Friedrich hated disputation, especially when he stooped to it himself.

"Pay attention," said Kurt. He had stopped his horse a few yards back. Friedrich heard before he saw—a wheezy music floating on the hot, motionless air, the strangest music he had ever heard. A few phrases sounded like something familiar, something he might have heard in Swabia; another bit sounded like the rhythmic, chanted Indian music they had heard after they got off the train at Salt Lake; and another part of it might have been a jig tune. An unholy alliance, an impossibility, perhaps a tease of the devil's.

Then he saw his devil—an old Indian, dressed in buckskin, coming through the trees toward the river on a horse and leading two squaws, a packhorse, a broken-down horse dragging a travois, and a dog. He was riding toward them.

"I'm scared, Pa," the boy said. Jurgen nodded. "Will he scalp us, Pa?"

"He'll more likely beg from us," said Kurt. "He looks pretty scruffy."

"If he's friendly," Jurgen observed, "he could be our salvation."

Jurgen switched to his broken English: "Good morning, friend. Where do you go?"

The old Indian moved his hands away from his mouth—Friedrich saw in some surprise that he had a mouth organ—and rode slowly up to them. *"Guten Tag, verehrte Herren,"* he said. *"Wo gehen Sie hin?"*

"Im Gottes Willen!" said Jurgen. Friedrich shivered with a terrible chill, despite his fever. His hands flinched on the reins, ready to flee the agent of Beelzebub.

The Indian asked, still in unaccented, rather formal and courtly German, "Are you lost? May I be of service to you?"

Friedrich spoke up and explained their dilemma.

The Indian considered. "You are white men." He looked at them flatly, as though expecting them to acknowledge their fault. "You do not belong in this country. The Lehmi Shoshone have lived here for centuries. Also the Nez Percés. The Sheepeaters have made their abode here since time immemorial. This is their land. You are trespassers."

Friedrich hurriedly explained that they wanted only to cross through to Walla Walla.

"All right. Pass through. Do not come back. Stay out. Tell your friends at the settlement to stay out, and that if they come, the Indians will drive them out. Tell them one old man will be happy to kill them." Friedrich wondered what the old man had in store for the four of them right then. Kurt put his hand on his Colt .45, but Jurgen stopped him with a hand wave.

"What is the route, sir?" Jurgen asked.

"You are on the way. Go down the river. In three or four days you will see the forks of the Clearwater—you cannot miss it. Go on downriver about six more days to the mouth, where it comes into the Snake. Cross and follow the Snake eight or ten more days to the mouth, at the Columbia. There you will find the settlement and the mission."

Friedrich was getting more scared. The man's German was perfect, even elegant. He had not learned it from immigrants.

"I am willing to help you move through this country," the old man said. "I would never help you if you wanted to stay here." He looked at them directly.

"Where did you learn to speak such excellent German?" Friedrich spoke up.

The Indian grinned. "That is a long, long story for a better place than a dusty trail in the hot sun. By the way, how goes it in Württemberg? Is Paul, Duke of Württemberg, still at Karlsruhe?"

"Paul is dead fifteen years," Jurgen stammered.

"I'm sorry to hear it." He thought a moment and smiled a little. "Did you ever hear of Madame Sophie Hoffman, the novelist, of Stuttgart?" he asked. "Is she well?"

She was a scandalous figure. "She achieved a fame of a kind," Friedrich said, "and is Baroness von Webern."

"I'm pleased for her," the Indian said.

"By the way," Friedrich dared, "what was the music you were playing?"

"A composition of my own," said the Indian. His face turned serious. "Be on your way now. Travel fast. No one will be pleased to see you here." He started to kick his horse on. "Do you have enough food? You will see very little game at this elevation."

"Enough for perhaps four weeks," said Friedrich.

"Good. I must go." He smiled. "I have an assignation with a buffalo." And he spurred his horse upriver, his squaws following in silence.

"Papa, what was he? Was he a spirit? Papa, I'm scared."

"He may have lied to us," said Friedrich. "I don't believe a word of what he said."

"Nonsense," Jurgen exclaimed. They rode forward and he thought a while. "It is the clearest indication of God's providence I have ever experienced. It is a miracle." No one spoke for a little. "We must tell everyone," Jurgen said. "I do not understand the miracle. Perhaps he spoke in his native tongue and God led us to hear in German. Perhaps he was an angel. No mere man can explain this. But God has sent us a message, even as Paul received the message on the road to Damascus."

No one dared disagree. "Willy," said Jurgen after a little, "you will learn to believe now, and to trust. You have seen with your own eyes and heard with your own ears."

"Yes, Papa," the boy said solemnly, and full of wonderment.

Even Kurt kept his mouth shut.

Chapter One

1804

1803, APRIL 30: The United States, paying about $15 million to France, effected the Louisiana Purchase.

1804, MAY 14: The Lewis & Clark Expedition, commissioned by President Thomas Jefferson to explore the Louisiana Territory, set out from St. Louis.

1806, JULY 15: Zebulon Pike initiated his exploration of southwestern plains, mountains, and deserts.

1806: Noah Webster's *Compendium Dictionary of the English Language* achieved compromises between British and American English that later became standard; some of the dictionary's Americanisms were attacked as "wigwam" words.

Eighteen Hundred Four

MAY 14, 1804: The Lewis and Clark Expedition embarked from St. Louis. Clark wrote in his journal: "Rained the fore part of the day. . . . I Set out at 4 oClock P.M., in the presence of many of the neighbouring inhabitents, and proceeded on under a jentle brease up the Missouri to the upper Point of the 1st Island 4 Miles and camped on the Island which is Situated Close on the right (or Starboard) Side, and opposit the mouth of a Small Creek called Cold water, a heavy rain this after-noon."

JUNE 26, 1804: The expedition reached the mouth of the Kansas River, the future site of Kansas City. The summer was in full strength, which meant oppressive heat broken by violent thunderstorms. Various diarists remarked on the beauty of the countryside, and on the ferocity of the ticks and mosquitoes.

JULY 21, 1804: The expedition reached the mouth of the Platte River, the traditional line of demarcation between the upper and lower rivers.

AUGUST 27, 1804: The captains made their first contact with the Sioux, who had closed the river to trade from St. Louis almost completely and might be the expedition's most formidable obstacle. With a great display of bravado, and after some tense moments, Lewis and Clark maneuvered the Sioux into letting them pass.

OCTOBER 26, 1804: They got to the Mandan Villages clustered about the mouth of the Knife River in modern North Dakota, nearly the furthest point upriver seen by white men. There they decided to stay the winter and constructed Fort Mandan.

FEBRUARY 11, 1805: She felt it first as no more than the

gentle tensing of a muscle—the flexing of a calf muscle, maybe—so she paid no attention. She was squatting on the dirt floor of one of the huts, stitching buffalo hides together into the conical shape of a tipi. Her left hand gripped the edges of the hides tightly, and her right darted quickly and surely, the awl carved from bone pulling the deer sinew through the skins and binding them together. She made sure of the stitches. She and her husband and their child would be sleeping in this tipi in the Moon when the Ponies Shed and for many moons beyond on the long westward march, sleeping in it with the Long Knife Chief and the Red-Headed Chief. She noticed that the tensing came every once in a while and that it stayed for a moment. But it did not hurt, it was only there. She kept stitching.

She was a slight girl, slender and lithe, but frail-looking. She was plain except for her eyes, which were too wide for her small face and looked as though she were constantly surprised and often delighted. Anyone would have thought her a healthy, supple girl with the promise of a healthy woman, except that the size of her belly signified that she was already a woman, and she seemed too slight for that. The belly bulged hugely and comically, making her look like a bulbous root tapered at both ends or a snake that had swallowed a bird. The men made jokes about that because she was a Snake Indian and her husband said that her name was Bird Woman.

The tensing came again and rose to pain, like the pain of her every-moon-bleeding. She stared at a log wall as she felt it and decided that her time had come. She wished that some of the older women of her tribe were here. They would shut her away in a tipi and tend to her and tell her what to do and help her when the final time came. But they were many, many sleeps away. The only other woman at the fort then was Otter Woman, her tribeswoman and another wife to her Frenchman. And Otter Woman was younger than she, and childless. When the pain eased, she stood up to go and tell someone.

The morning was clear and bitter cold. The sun, an hour off the eastern horizon, made the Dakota prairies shine a brilliant white, but the wind off the river cut its warmth away. Icicles pointed down from the door sill where the girl came out, and the branches of the trees were circled with clear ice that sparkled as the limbs waved in the wind. The girl squinted her eyes against the harsh glaze and held her buffalo robe tight at the throat. After a warming, the Moon of the Cold that Split Trees had returned.

She found Jessume, the French-Canadian interpreter, and told him. The Red-Headed Chief was away hunting, he said, and no one knew where her squaw man was, but the Long Knife Chief was there, and Jessume would help her. The girl felt shy about speaking to the Long Knife Chief, but Jessume said he would do it for her. She went to the log pile, picked up an armload of sizable fire sticks, and stepped into the darkness of the hut. As she was making the fire grow, the pain grabbed at her again. She lay down, as Jessume had said to do. It was like the clenching of a fist in her belly, and it got stronger as it held. Then suddenly it was gone. When the next pain came, she went back to squatting. That was more comfortable.

Jessume could see, early that afternoon, that the pain was severe. The girl tried to chatter amiably with him in Minataree between pains, but the seizures cut her off cold, and her smile in between looked wan. She said everything was well, using the Minataree when she would have usually exercised her few words of French. He had come to offer her some meat and broth from a stew made of poor, scraggly elk. But she turned it down. He was getting her to sip the broth a little when Charbonneau came in.

"Cq va?" he asked his squaw lightly, sure that cq va. She looked at him blankly, not understanding. Charbonneau put a hand on her belly then sagged against a wall, half sitting and half sprawling. Jessume could see he had gotten a little whisky from someone. Just as well. Jessume crossed the yard to see Captain Lewis. "The squaw she too small," he indicated, hands touching hips, "maybe hard."

Lewis stood over the girl smiling slightly. He seemed far away. The pain came and held and gripped harder, and for a long time they all—Jessume, Long Knife, and her man behind her—went away. When it went, Lewis was looking at her strangely. Is something wrong? she wondered. It couldn't be. She reached for the cup the captain was holding for her, and smelled it. Whisky. Lewis gave another cup to Charbonneau, and she set hers behind for him as well. She didn't like the smell, and thought it would make her throw up.

Outside, the wind was up, and the sky was half-clouded.

"Want Bluster Bear drunk enough to be out of way,"
Jessume said in his heavy accent. They called Charbonneau "Bluster Bear" because one of the several derisive
names the Mandans had for him was Forest Bear, and the
word for *forest* sounded like *bluster*. The men of the expedition thought it fit. Jessume and Charbonneau didn't get
the joke, and thought they were mispronouncing the word.

She had been running for hours. She had never felt so
tired in her life. She kept running. She had the terrible
ache in her gut from running too long. The silver leaf of
an aspen darkened, and falling off the tree, blackened. She
knew before she saw the change, before the black leaf
struck the ground, that it was a NunumBi. She clutched at
her belly, saw his arrow huge before he shot it, and bolted
in another direction. She turned downhill through the
sparse fir, toward the wide meadow. More light there. She
could hear many NunumBi behind her. A rock jumped
and clawed at her ankle. She screamed.

She saw the door open, and Jessume appeared against
the reddened sky. He crossed and stooped down beside
her. "It is soon now," he said softly in Minataree. She
didn't know what he said but knew he meant well. Her
arms and chest hurt from tightened muscles. She clamped
down on her stomach, holding against when the pain
would come again, trying to control its long surge.

She remembered the Long Knife Chief shooting the
wind gun to show the Mandans. He set a melon on the
ground at fifty paces, aimed, and pulled the trigger. Only a
sound of sudden wind. But the melon jumped and rolled
over with an awful splatting sound. She saw it all split
apart, its pulp and seeds smeared the grass, the rind in
little pieces. She laughed without knowing why.

The cold settled in now. She sweated terribly, and
shivered at the same time. Between pains once she rolled
to one side and vomited. Then she lay back, legs spread
wide, tired beyond caring, unable to go on. She thought
she was going to die.

She heard the voices above her, but even when the pain
left, she did not try to understand. Lewis had asked four
or five times whether nothing could be done. Jessume
smiled a little at him. The captain had big medicine. His
mother was said to be an herb doctor, and Lewis administered herbal medicines to the Indians. Yet in the face of so
simple and common an event as this, the captain was

helpless. Jessume thought Lewis felt his helplessness, and berated himself for it.

"The Minatara say the rattle of a rattlesnake broken in water will help," he told the captain. He himself did not know whether to believe it.

"I have a big rattle for a souvenir," Lewis said. "I'll get it." Lewis left quickly. Jessume wondered whether he only wanted to be away from there.

The girl pushed. All that she was she gathered from her head and shoulders and chest and knit it together and sent it down to her groin in a push. She was nothing else. She knew that she would die, that the thing inside would tear her like a deer being gutted and she would die. She didn't care. She felt nothing but an overwhelming want to push the thing out. Something in her bowels seemed to be in the way, and she was pushing it out too. Everything in the middle of her she was forcing out.

Jessume made her drink something. She took it only to get him away by the time the next push came. She felt it rise in her and she gave herself to the push. She had never worked so hard in her life.

With the next one she was sure the time had come. Now it would split her as a bullet splits a melon, but it would be gone. She was no longer afraid. It would happen. She pushed and felt her body relax and lost herself in the push. That felt right. She felt an immense stretching. Now, she thought, now I am coming apart.

"*Pousses!*" Jessume yelled. "*Pousses très fort. Maintenant, encore.*" She heard nothing over the roar in her mind. Jessume could see the baby's head.

In three more pushes it was over. Jessume held up the baby for her to see. A boy. She pushed again and felt something follow. Yes, a boy. She was pleased. She supposed she was alive. She felt peaceful. She had never imagined such a feeling of peace.

Jessume woke Charbonneau against the wall. "*Regards ton fils,*" he exclaimed. "*C'est un garçon. Un beau garçon.*"

"*Garçon,*" muttered Charbonneau. "*Evidemment un garçon.*" He passed out again.

When Jessume put the child on her chest, the girl realized she had fallen asleep. She looked long at the child's head lying just below her chin. At length she felt the strength to pick him up and inspect his arms and legs and belly and eyes—light eyes, she noticed—and gaze at his tiny face, shiny wet and wrinkled as a dried grape. She set him down and the child sucked at the buckskin. She opened it and put him to her small breast.

She looked at Jessume squatting beside her. His face showed how worried he had been. "*Ça va,*" she said, and smiled. "*Ça va, merci.*" Within an hour she was carrying wood to the fire.

The next morning William Clark and George Drewyer, the interpreter, were straightening out the chaotic aftermath of the elk hunt in a hut, Drewyer knocking the ice off clothes and hanging them to dry, Clark treating a man's frostbitten toes.

Charbonneau lumbered through the door with a swagger, the girl on his heels with the child smothered in blankets. Clark sprang up to look, touched the baby's cheeks with a huge forefinger, and grinned broadly. "*Garçon,*" Bluster Bear kept proclaiming, "boy, *garçon.*" He started to open the blankets to show Clark the unmistakable evidence, but the Red-Headed Chief put a hand on his wrist.

"What's his name?" Clark asked the girl.

"*Comment s'appelle-t-il?*" helped Drewyer.

"Jean-Baptiste," interjected Charbonneau. "Jean-Baptiste Charbonneau."

The girl said something rapidly to Charbonneau in Minataree and smiled broadly at Clark. "*Aussi Paump,*" she said, "*aussi Paump.*"

"*Paump?*" Clark raised his eyebrows at Charbonneau. The French went much too fast for him.

"First-born it means," said Drewyer. "It is a Snake word. It means first-born, or leader, or head man. The man."

Clark looked a long moment at the girl. "It is good," he said, and waited for Drewyer to translate. "He is named for a great leader, a great man of religion, a great medicine man of the white people of his father." Again a wait. "And he is named for a chief of the people of his mother. It is good. May he be a great leader to both peoples." The girl beamed.

"Sah-kah-gar-we-a," Clark lettered it phonetically into his journal weeks earlier. He mumbled the sound of the name to himself two or three times while he inspected the letters he had made. The captain had not had much schooling, and knew he didn't spell well. He wasn't sure that he had the hang of the Shoshone girl's strange-sounding name, but he had sounded it out the best he could, so he was satisfied. He had taken to calling her "Jawey" for short. Charbonneau said her name meant Bird Woman, but then he didn't speak Shoshone. Drewyer, the expedition's specialist in sign language, said that Sacajawea signed to him that the name meant "canoe launcher." Hell, Charbonneau didn't speak any language very well, and probably didn't know his own wife's name.

Wife—and mother. Those words seemed strange for such a slip of a girl. Clark judged her to be no more than fourteen or fifteen; Lewis, who was given to amused cynicism, said she might be twelve or thirteen. For she was a slave girl. Though Clark didn't like to think about it, he knew that she must have been used by any fired-up brave or pubescent boy who had a mind to. Jean-Baptiste was her first child, and clearly she would have conceived him as soon as she was physically able. Clark was glad that he and Lewis had at least maneuvered Charbonneau into marrying her a while before she gave birth. But the squaw man treated his fahms, as he called them, as Indians treated their women generally. "She'll still be a kind of slave," Lewis had said. "We can't help that."

The captains had gotten her story from the girl herself, in her combination of broken French, Minataree, and signs, with Charbonneau and Drewyer interpreting. Her people, the Shoshone, lived in the mountains, on the side where the waters flow to the west, the land of the thunder and the setting sun. Each summer they made a journey across the mountains to the headwaters of the Missouri River and the buffalo plains. They needed to get meat for the winter and to break their meager diet of fish and roots. But they went in stealth and never stayed long, fearing the warlike Blackfeet. Five seasons ago, during this annual hunt, they had camped on the most westerly of the three rivers that flowed together to form the Missouri. A far-ranging band of Minatarees had raided them there. In the general flight, Sacajawea and several other children had been captured. The Minatarees had brought them here to their village, a thousand river miles from their homeland and their people. Here where the great river was brown and muddy, where the plains stretched away flat in all directions, where men saw no mountains, here where the earth was parched. Some children had escaped, but not

Sacajawea and Otter Woman. A season ago Charbonneau won Sacajawea from her owner. And he bought Otter Woman. So he had two child-slaves as fahms. Sacajawea had now borne him a son—she was proud that it was a son—and Otter Woman was with child.

The girl told this story matter-of-factly, even brightly. The captains detected no sorrow in her, merely acceptance. But her story had roused an interest in her that Sacajawea could not have guessed. She was from beyond the Continental Divide. Her people crossed the mountains to the eastern watershed every summer. She might help them pass some of their most formidable barriers. Did she remember the way across the mountains? Yes, but the way was hard and long.

Maybe the girl could guide them across the mountains. More important, maybe her people would give them horses. They knew that although their assignment was to find a waterway to the Pacific Ocean and thereby open possibilities of trade with the Orient, they would have to make a land portage of indeterminate distance from the eastern to the western watershed. For that, horses would be crucial. Perhaps with Sacajawea to ease the way they would get their horses and learn something of the route to the ocean.

So they talked it over in their tent that evening. Each man had sentimental reasons for wanting to take the girl along. Lewis, of Welsh stock, was a reflective, melancholic, romantic man; the notion of having an Indian girl on the first crossing of the United States and the rest of the continent to the Pacific Ocean appealed to the romantic in him. Clark, of Scottish stock was a sensible, practical, and fatherly man, though unmarried; he felt protective of the girl and her infant son. Besides, both men liked the slender wisp of a girl-woman. She was plucky, full of fun, always cheerful. But both were also officers of the United States Army on an enterprise of high seriousness and grave danger. They were battle-tempered Indian fighters. So they didn't speak about sentiments.

"We don't know when she'll drop," said Lewis with a wry smile. "We can't afford to wait for the baby." The plains were full of boasts that the Sioux would attack their Fort Mandan and massacre the invading white men as soon as spring came. The captains were planning to move their boats upstream even before the river was clear of floating ice.

"She'll give birth in a month or so," said Clark—this was about Christmas—"but she may not be fit to travel for a while."

"The woman we could handle. But I don't see how we can take a newborn child."

"Though Indian women always travel with them," Clark said. "During a march they go to the bushes, have their babies, and catch up with the tribe a couple of hours later."

Lewis mused a moment. "Hell, old Bluster Bear might be more trouble than she'd be. He's no good for anything."

"I'd bet on it."

"Still, she says she knows the pass. She says her people will trade us horses." Lewis looked straight at Clark. "It's too good a chance to pass up." Clark nodded.

Lewis stood up. "Maybe we'll create another Pocahontas," he grinned. And he stepped out to check the watch.

Later, the captains decided to get Charbonneau to marry Sacajawea. That might make it easier to keep the men away from her. The last thing they needed was an amorous squaw, rivalrous soldiers, and a jealous squaw man. Sacajawea seemed as uninhibited as any Indian woman, and a lot of squaws would have liked being community property, if the community was white.

APRIL 7, 1805: The expedition set out from the Mandan Villages for the mountains.

APRIL 9, 1805: Lewis noted in his journal that the Indian "squar," poking in some driftwood with a sharp stick, had turned up some roots for the stew. They looked like Jerusalem artichokes, and tasted like them too.

MAY 14, 1805: The white pirogue, bearing the expedition's crucial instruments, was making its way upstream under the charge of Pierre Cruzatte. Charbonneau was at the rudder, though he was a timid waterman and steered capriciously. A sudden gust of wind ripped the sail out of a man's hands, Charbonneau turned the rudder the wrong way, and she tipped until the sail hit the water. With Cruzatte threatening to shoot Charbonneau unless he brought her around, and both captains screaming from the

shore, she shipped gallons of water. Sacajawea, in the turmoil, calmly plucked boxes of equipment from the river
back into the boat. And Charbonneau, screaming to God
for mercy, finally righted the boat. Lewis ascribed to Sacajawea "equal fortitude and resolution with any person on
board."

MAY 20, 1805: Lewis's journal: "The hunters returned
this evening and informed us that the country continued
much the same in appearance as that we saw where we
were or broken, and that about five miles ab[ov]e the
mouth of the shell river a handsome river of about fifty
yards in width discharged itself into the shell river on the
Stard. or upper side; this stream we called Sâh-câ-ger we-
ah or bird woman's River, after our interpreter the Snake
woman."

MAY 31, 1805: The expedition had passed into the Missouri River Breaks. Lewis's journal: "The hills and river
Clifts which we passed today exhibit a most romantic appearance. The bluffs of the river rise to the hight of from
2 to 300 feet and in most places nearly perpendicular;
they are formed of remarkable white sandstone which is
sufficiently soft to give way readily to the impression of
water. . . . The water in the course of time in decending
from those hills and plains on either side of the river has
trickled down the soft sand clifts and woarn it into a thousand grotesque figures, which with the help of a little immagination and an oblique view, at a distance are made to
represent eligant ranges of lofty freestone buildings, having
their parapets well stocked with statuary; collumns of various sculpture both grooved and plain, are also seen sup-
porting long galleries in front of those buildings; in other
places on a much nearer approach and with the help of
less immagination we see the remains of ruins of eligant
buildings; some collumns standing and almost entire with
their pedestals and capitals; others retaining their pedestals
but deprived by time or accident of their capitals, some lying prostrate an broken othes in the form of vast pyramids
of connic structure bearing a serees of other pyramids on
their tops becoming less as they ascend and finally termi-
nating in a sharp point. nitches and alcoves of various
forms and sizes are seen at different hights as we pass. the
thin stratas of hard freestone intermixed with the soft
sandstone seems to have aided the water in forming this

curious scenery. As we passed on it seemed as if those scenes of visionary enchantment would never have an end."

JUNE 21–JULY 15: The expedition portaged the eighteen miles of the Great Falls of Missouri, brutally hard work done in blistering heat and abrupt thunder and hailstorms. Sacajawea was sick, and the captains feared for her life.

JULY 4, 1805: The hauling finished, the captains declared a celebration. In the evening they got out the last of their whisky and gave each man a gill. Pierre Cruzatte played his fiddle. John Potts called some square dances, and the men allemanded each other. York, Clark's black, was the most enthusiastic dancer, rolling his lank frame smoothly to the tune, letting his arms fly, carrying on 'in the way that always titillated the Indians. Paddy Gass chorused Potts in his sing-song Irish, and for once didn't resent even York. The Fields brothers, as partners, took turns aping feminine wiles. Drewyer, the French-Canadian interpreter, good-naturedly ribbed Bluster Bear, who didn't know the steps but shuffled along by himself anyway. The captains stayed to one side, and asked Sacajawea to sit with them— no sense reminding the men how attractive she was. Sacajawea studied Paump. The child, five months old now, seemed transfixed by the dancing, or the music, or something.

JULY 28, 1805: They pointed up the most westerly fork. "Yes, my people come to the plains along that river," she said. The captains nodded at each other. That fork had to be it. So they named that southwest fork of the Missouri the Jefferson Fork, after "the author of our enterprize"; they called the middle fork the Madison, and the southeast fork the Gallatin, after two members of Jefferson's cabinet.

They had been traveling—hauling their cottonwood dugouts against the current—south up the Missouri from the Great Falls. They were standing at the landmark the Minatarees had told them about, the Three Forks of the Missouri. If the Indians were right, or if Lewis and Clark understood them aright, the pass to the tributaries of the Columbia River lay due west. And Sacajawea confirmed it. They had come to the crux.

Lewis went ahead, and Clark stayed with the canoes to

supervise the hauling. His ankle was infected and swollen, so he was no good for walking. Sacajawea and Charbonneau stayed back with their adopted uncle, Clark.

The river began to batter the men now. It was in transition from a plains river to a mountain river, falling more swiftly, colder, rougher. The brush forced them into the water to haul, and the water was bone-cold. Soon the Jefferson forked again, into three tumbling mountain creeks. Lewis had left a note to take the middle fork. Clark forced his way up with grim persistence, making a shorter distance every day, encouraging his men and cursing the ankle that kept him inactive.

Sacajawea pointed out to him the spot where she had been captured five years earlier; she'd been crossing the stream at a shoal place. She seemed singularly calm and equable about the incident. Lewis commented that she was of such philosophy that she did not permit her feelings to extend beyond having plenty to eat and a few trinkets to wear.

Sacajawea looked high into the mountains now, in the long twilight when the sun was behind the Bitterroots but not yet down, thinking of her people up there, of her family. Charbonneau noticed her looking westward, wondered if she might be thinking of deserting him, and made up his mind to assert his authority over his property, to fight the bastards if he had to. Lewis noticed her looking westward but had no idea what the simple girl might be feeling—he guessed she had no strong feelings about her return. Another instance, to him, of the inscrutability of the Indian mind. Neither man knew her.

AUGUST 10, 1805: Fifteen days after the party reached Jefferson Fork, Merne Lewis came to the junction of two creeks. He decided that it was the highest navigable point of the Missouri River, and wrote Clark a note to leave the canoes. With McNeal and Drewyer he struck west, looking for a pass.

AUGUST 12, 1805: Lewis reached "the most distant fountain of the waters of the Mighty Missouri in surch of which we have spent so many toilsome days and wristless nights. thus far I had accomplished one of those great objects on which my mind has been unalterably fixed for many years, judge then of the pleasure I felt in allying my thirst with this pure and ice-cold water." Just below,

MacNeal stood triumphantly with one foot on each side of the rivulet and "thanked his god that he had lived to bestride the mighty & heretofore deemed endless Missouri."

They walked across Lehmi Pass, where Lewis looked westward toward the Pacific and saw high mountains partly covered with snow. Drewyer stood across the fountainhead waters of the Columbia and ceremoniously pissed into them. "And may God speed your message," intoned Lewis, "to the great Pacific Ocean."

AUGUST 17, 1805: Sacajawea was walking through a high alpine meadow in the forenoon, Charbonneau alongside her and Clark, still lame, trailing a little behind. Small rivulets of creeks, only a stride across, crisscrossed the meadow, making the earth soft and the grass lush. Lodgepole pine, slender and straight, rose tall near the hillsides. The air was cool and abnormally clear, the sky the unnaturally deep blue of high-mountain country, the sun-glow light and wispy on the land. Clark was thinking that the girl did not so much walk as prance, playing her way across the meadow. Then she began to bounce up and down. She whirled around to Clark, dark eyes gleaming, and stuck her fingers in her mouth—sign language for Shoshone—and pointed to the high end of the meadow. Indians, Clark saw. Sacajawea ran to meet them.

When Clark came up, he found a large group of Shoshones with Lewis, Drewyer, and MacNeal among them dressed as Indians. Sacajawea was embracing everyone, laughing and weeping at once. Suddenly she let out a great cry: She had found another teen-ager who was captured when she was, but had escaped. The two girls could scarcely stop babbling long enough to hear each other. The Shoshones greeted Clark exuberantly, hugging him and nuzzling cheeks until he got more than tired of the ritual.

Lewis explained the native garb: He had met the Shoshones a couple of days earlier and, after initial fright, they had been friendly. When he tried to get them to come down the mountain to meet Clark and help with the baggage, they had been afraid of a trick, an ambush. They were scared of all their enemies, Lewis explained. They stayed high in these mountains, living on only nuts and fish, to avoid the other tribes. When Lewis's men shot deer to provide food for everyone, the Shoshones thought they were being attacked. Finally, to reassure the chief, Cameahwait, the three white men had given the Indians their hats and other white clothes and had put on the Indians' clothes.

The captains had duty to attend to. They followed Cameahwait to a shade of willows, removed their moccasins, and began the pipe-smoking ceremonies. Taking off the moccasins was important for both sides: It said, symbolically, "If I am not sincere, may I ever go barefoot"—a stern penalty in the mountains. Cameahwait offered the pipe to the earth, the sky, and the gods of the four winds, puffed reflectively, and passed the pipe left. Clark knew that there was no hurrying the smoking.

When they were ready to talk, the captains sent for Sacajawea to be interpreter. She slipped in, took the humble place at the far right of the circle, and sat down. Abruptly she jumped up, threw her arms around Cameahwait, wrapped her blanket around him, and began to cry. She had recognized Cameahwait as her brother. The chief was visibly moved, but not so expressive.

Lewis and Clark then made the necessary speeches about the Shoshones' dependence on the government of the United States for items of trade, and that government's friendliness toward them and willingness to protect them. This trade could not begin, Lewis went on, until the long knives returned to their home country. In order to return they needed many strong Shoshone horses, guidance toward Salt-Water-Everywhere, and help in transporting their goods across land. Cameahwait regretted that he must give horses now in return for promises rather than rifles—the British were already giving his enemies, the Blackfeet, rifles—but he would do so. And so the council ended.

That was when Sacajawea, already overcome by the rejoining, was told that all her family was dead except for two brothers and a nephew. She burst into tears again. Immediately she adopted her nephew, Bazel, as her own son.

Outside the tent was bedlam. The men had not seen any Indians—especially any Indian women—since they left Fort Mandan over four months before. And the squaws were making over them, exclaiming at the marvelous whiteness of their bellies, their faces were dark as any Indians, oohing at tiny pieces of mirror, aahing at blue beads and strips of ribbon, toying with belt buckles. The braves were distracted with rifles and pistols.

The biggest sensation was York. They were awed by his hugeness, his kinked hair, his black-all-over skin. None of the long knives had painted themselves black for war except this one. He was painted black all over—a powerful warrior—and his color was permanent. A man who feared nothing. The squaws were fluttering and chattering like wrens around him, touching him, poking at him, smiling and giggling like children. York was basking in it. He was surprising them with the places on him that were blackened. The display was about to become indecent, though the Shoshone would consider nothing indecent. Clark found himself hoping that York would stop assuring his sexual future and head into the bushes to enjoy his sexual present. The Shoshone teen-age girls, not yet worn by hard work, were quite handsome, he had to admit.

"Nothing to do about it, Captain Clark," observed Lewis.

"These Indians haven't seen many white men, maybe none," said Clark. "Maybe they don't have Louis Veneris."

Lewis made a noncommittal sound. They were worried about a further breakdown in the expedition's health. Lewis took some braves off to demonstrate the air gun, a rifle that worked on compressed air which he had had made and brought along and of which he was inordinately proud. It drew the appropriate amaze. Clark noticed that York had gone into the bushes.

After an hour a new clamor got started. Colter had killed a deer, and these people had almost no meat to eat. A train formed behind him as he dragged the carcass into camp. Braves, squaws, and children tore at the raw flesh as soon as Colter stopped, and stuffed it down. They shrieked and picked like crows. One young brave, evidently of strong stomach, Lewis thought, took the small intestine aside, put one end in his mouth, and sucked it down inch by inch without biting or chewing, squeezing the contents out the other end with his hands as he swallowed.

Several older squaws were fussing over Paump. They scrutinized his dark hair, his light eyes, his light brown skin. They looked from the child to his father, very white, and a chief among the long knives. They touched the child, wondering whether he had the big medicine of the

Frenchmen (as they called whites) coursing in his veins. Would he bring the medicine to them? They looked at Sacajawea, holding the child on one arm, head cradled in the palm of her hand, and wondered whether she could give them the medicine. They doubted it. One old squaw, stooped with years and her face crevassed, shaded the child's squinting eyes with her hand and looked long at his face.

"Your first-born?" she asked.

"My Paump," Sacajawea affirmed.

"Will Togowata give him a name?" Shoshone children were named by wise old men or medicine men, usually when they were much older.

"He has been given his name by my Frenchman and the Red-Headed Chief," said Sacajawea, and beamed. "He is called Jean-Baptiste, after a great medicine man of the whites."

The old woman looked at her long and smiled a slow smile. Sacajawea knew that it was good.

While Lewis stayed to bargain for horses, Clark set out to check the water route to the Pacific. Cameahwait, making mounds of sand for mountains and finger-lines for rivers, indicated that this river, the Lehmi, flowed into the Salmon River, which cut steeply through the mountains and emptied into the Snake, which emptied into the Columbia. Could they take canoes down the Salmon? Cameahwait shook his head no. Clark went into the deep cut to make sure. A week later he confirmed that the Salmon was as rough and turbulent a river as he had seen. They would have to travel on horseback until they found smoother waters. President Jefferson's dream of a transcontinental water route was dimming.

At length, with fine promises, more than the dwindling trade goods, they persuaded Cameahwait to part with twenty-nine horses, many of them Appaloosas. An elderly guide, Toby, led them across the pass, down the Bitterroot River to a wide, handsome meadow with a creek joining the river from the west; they named the spot Traveller's Rest and camped there for two days, gathering food and repairing clothing. Game was scarce, and the men were getting thin. It was September 9, and they had been snowed on once already. Here they would strike directly west across rough mountains. Cameahwait said the

Pierced-Nose Indians used that way to go to the buffalo plains, but that it was almost impossible. Lewis and Clark decided that if the Pierced Noses could do it, so could they. And so they came out of the Bitterroot Mountains, having passed the Great Divide.

SEPTEMBER 11, 1805: The expedition set out across the Lolo Trail, an arduous route through high mountains barren of game.

SEPTEMBER 26–OCTOBER 10, 1805: The expedition, wearied from severe cold and hunger and suffering from dysentery, made recuperative camp with the Nez Percé Indians on Wieppe Prairie. From here the Clearwater River was navigable, so they made canoes.

OCTOBER 31–NOVEMBER 2, 1805: The expedition passed around and through the two sets of great falls on the Columbia.

NOVEMBER 14, 1805: The captains saw, for the first time, what they took to be the Pacific Ocean, at the mouth of the Columbia.

CHRISTMAS DAY, 1805: Clark's journal: "at day light this morning we awoke by the discharge of the fire arm of all our party & a Selute, Shouts, and a Song which the whole party joined in under our windows, after which they retired to their rooms were chearfull all the morning. . . . The Indians leave us in the evening all the party Snugly fixed in their huts. I recved a presnt of Capt.L. of a fleece hosrie Shirt Draws and Socks, a pr. Mockersons of Whitehouse a Small Indian basket of Gutherich, two Dozen white weails tails of the Indian woman, & some black root of the Indians before their departure. Drewyer informs me that he saw a Snake pass across the parth to day. The day proved Showerey wet and disagreeable.

"we would have Spent this day the nativity of Christ in feasting, had we any thing either to raise our Sperits or even gratify our appetites, our Diner concisted of pore Elk, so much Spoiled that we eate it thro' mear necessity, Some Spoiled pounded fish and fiew roots."

NEW YEAR'S DAY, 1806: Hungry, restless, and tired of the relentless rains, the men completed Fort Clatsop.

MARCH 23, 1806: Clark's journal: "This morning proved so raney and uncertain that we were undetermined for some time whether we had best set out & risque the [watęrs] which apeared to be riseing or not. the rained seased and it became fair about Meridian, at which time we loaded our canoes & at 1 p.m. left Fort Clatsop on our homeward bound journey. at this place we had wintered and remained from the 7th of Decr. 1805 to this day and have lived as well as we had any right to expect, and we can say that we were never one day without 3 meals of some kind a day either pore Elk meat or roots, notwithstanding the repeated fall of rain which has fallen almost constantly since we passed the long narrows."

MAY, 1806: The expedition camped and relaxed with the Nez Percés on Wieppe Prairie, waiting for the snows to melt in the high mountains ahead. Later, half the Nez Percé tribe claimed members of the Lewis & Clark expedition as their forefathers.

JULY 3, 1806: After a short stay at Traveller's Rest, the expedition divided and moved out. Lewis went due east to find a short route through the mountains to the Great Falls. Clark, with Charbonneau and Sacajawea, took the previous year's route in order to pick up caches of supplies, and then swung south to explore the Yellowstone River.

JULY 24, 1806: Late afternoon. A stand of cottonwoods alongside the wide, lazy Yellowstone. The sun glistened yellow on the clear water and glanced up at the faces. Clark and George Shannon were squatting on logs on a sandbar, the captain looking toward the far rise of the Rocky Mountains, the private whittling at a stick and unconsciously humming an old hymn. A small fire of dead fall burned between them, almost unnoticeable in the glow. Sacajawea was moving around the fire, roasting hump ribs slowly, the fat dripping down and firing spurts of flame. She poked quickly at the tongue cooking under a pile of coals become ashes. Charbonneau was stretched out sleeping on the sand to one side. Except for the soft sizzle of the ribs, the late afternoon was perfectly quiet.

Paump was playing near Clark. The child picked up a driftwood stick and poked it into the sand, flicked some up, touched the grains with a finger. He picked up a small stone and slung it in an awkward half throw. He toddled over to Clark, jabbed the stick into his right palm, and rubbed it around. He wanted to play tug. Clark tugged lightly, then picked the boy up and set him on one knee.

The air, cool with the coming of evening, stirred gently. Clark looked over the child's head toward the Rockies. The sun was almost on the ridges now, half behind the clouds that hung on the high peaks. It had reddened perceptibly. The river glowed rose, the cottonwood branches beyond blackened against the sky, the buffalo grass on prairie was rose lights and rose shadows, as though glazed with alizarin crimson. Captain Clark looked west but thought east, thought of the girl named Julia he wanted to marry, a girl twenty years his junior—Sacajawea's age, in fact.

The Shoshone girl, slight but hardy, as Clark well knew, was cleaning currants and gooseberries to go with dinner. Clark put his big hands on Paump's belly, aware of the softness and warmth of the child's skin. Paump smiled big-eyed at Sacajawea. Bending over, she looked up at Clark and smiled lightly and easily. The soldier drew in the night air deeply, and caught the good smell of ribs with it. His eyes settled toward the Rockies. He would be glad to be back in the States. But he would miss the mountains.

A few days later, Clark spotted a huge stone monolith rising up on the right bank. Examining it more closely he found Indian paintings on it; he climbed up, surveyed the countryside, and decided to cut his own name into its face. He named it Pompey's Pillar.

AUGUST 12, 1806: Clark's party waited for Lewis a few miles below the mouth of the Yellowstone, uncomfortable in the windless heat and plagued by mosquitoes. They had waited for nine days when Lewis showed up, an invalid. The day before he had gone with Cruzatte into the underbrush to kill an elk. Cruzatte, an expert hunter and boatman, was blind in one eye and dim-sighted in the other. When Lewis raised flintlock, Cruzatte shot him straight in the backside, the ball passing through one buttock and grazing the other. "Damn you, you've shot me in the ass," Lewis howled and laughed at once. But that night the wound got very painful, and Lewis could neither sit nor stand the next day. Sacajawea giggled when she saw the wound, Charbonneau guffawed, and Clark cleaned and dressed it, wondering aloud whether the men had been creative in their jokes about their bad-assed captain.

That night the company celebrated its reunion. They feasted on ribs and boudins—the buffalo intestine they had learned to like—and beaver tail. John Collins distributed some beer brewed from bread made from roots, and it was judged toluble. Late in the evening, a fine, clear, warm evening with unnaturally bright stars, Cruzatte hauled out his fiddle and scraped some tunes for dancing. The men partnered each other and kicked up their heels. Paump was fascinated. He stood on his small, fleshy legs and wavered and bumped unsteadily. Cruzatte leaned down and rolled his good eye at the boy, and Paump gave a comical, sucking laugh. At length Clark offered him a thick finger to hold onto, and the eighteen-month-old boy began to dance, hopping up and down somewhere near the rhythm, stomping, shrieking with glee. He danced for some ten minutes, fell down, and collapsed into sleep. Sacajawea picked him up and wrapped him in his blankets.

"Isn't he something?" Clark exclaimed at large. "Sich a child."

The talk around the fire that night was of home—of white women, of whisky, of proper American food, of their families, of the stories they would tell. Then it was of the plains and mountains behind—of the hugeness of the country, the strangeness of the Indians, the lust of the squaws, the fierceness of the grizzly bear, the stupidity of the buffalo, of the pure clearness of high-mountain streams, of the hungry and feasting times they'd seen.

"They're going to bust with bragging," Lewis observed to Clark.

"They've got it coming," Clark answered.

AUGUST 15, 1806: The expedition arrived at the Mandan villages. Clark's journal: "Colter one of our men expressed a desire to join Some trappers who offered to become shearers with and furnish traps &c. The offer a very advantagious one, to him, his services could be dispenced with from this down and as we were disposed to be of service to any one of our party who had performed their duty as well as Colter had done, we agreed to allow him the privilage provided no one of the party would ask or expect a Similar permission to which they all agreed that they wished Colter every Suckcess. . . ."

AUGUST 17, 1806: Clark's journal: "Settled with Toussaint Chabono for his services as an enterpreter the price of a horse and Lodge purchased of him for public Service in all amounting to 500$ 33 ⅓ cents. . . . at 2 oClock we left our encampment after takeing leave of Colter who also Set out up the river in company with Messrs. Dickson & Handcock. we also took our leave of T. Chabono, his Snake Indian wife and their child who had accompanied us on our rout to the pacific ocean in the capacity of interpreter and interpretes. T. Chabono wished much to accompany us in the said Capacity if we could have provailed the Menetarre Chiefs to decnd the river with us to the U. States, but as none of those Chiefs of whoes language he was Conversent would accompany us, his services were no longer of use to the U. States and he was therefore discharged and paid up. we offered to convey him down to the Illinois if he chose to go, He declined proceeding on at present, observing that he had no acquaintance or prospects of makeing a liveing below, and must continue to live in the way that he had done."

Sacajawea had received no pay, but Clark had something in mind for her. "Your son," he said to the two of them, "is a beautiful, promising child. Let me take him to the United States. I will see that he is educated. I will raise him as my own son."

"Yes," said Sacajawea tentatively, *"mais pas encore."* Frustrated, she spoke rapidly to Charbonneau in Minataree. They exchanged several sentences.

"She likes it," explained Charbonneau, "I not. Besides, the child yet. . . ." He smooched his lips to imitate suckling. "When next the ice breaks on the river, he comes, maybe." Sacajawea spoke firmly to Charbonneau. "We come him then," the squaw man said.

"Charbonneau," said Clark formally, "he is a fine child and does you credit. Do not fail to send him. I will be as his father."

Sacajawea and Charbonneau embraced Clark and walked toward their canoe. For the first time Clark could remember, Bluster Bear picked up his son, tossed him gently in the air, and caught him. From the stern of the canoe he waved to Clark, and gave a self-important little bow.

Three days later, at the Arikara Village, Clark wrote a letter and gave it to traders to take to Charbonneau and Sacajawea:

Charbono:

Sir: Your present situation with the Indians gives me some concern—I wish now I had advised you to come on with me to the Illinois where it would most probably be in my power to put you in some way to do something for yourself. . . . You have been a long time with me and have conducted yourself in such a manner as to gain my friendship; your woman, who accompanied you that long and dangerous and fatiguing route to the Pacific Ocian and back, deserved a greater reward for her attention and service on that route than we had in our power to give her at the Mandans. As to your little son (my boy Paump) you well know my fondness for him and my anxiety to take and raise him as my own child. I once more tell you if you will bring your son, Baptiest, to me, I will educate him and treat him as my own child—I do not forget the promise which I made to you and shall now repeat them that you may be certain—Charbono, if you wish to live with the white people, and will come with me, I will give you a piece of land and furnish you with horses, cows, and hogs—if you wish to visit your friends in Montrall, I will let you have a horse, and your family shall be taken care of until your return—if you wish to return as an interpreter for the Menetarras when the troops come up to form the establishment, you will be with me ready and I will procure you the place—or if you wish to return to trade with the Indians and will leave your little son Paump with me, I will assist you with merchandize for that purpose. . . .and become myself concerned with you in trade on a small scale, that is to say not exceeding a pirogue load at one time. If you are disposed to accept either of my offers to you, and will bring down your son, your fahm Jawey had best come along with you to take care of the boy until I get him. . . . When you get to St. Louis write a letter to me by the post and let me know your situation—If you do not intend to go down either this fall or in the spring, write a letter to me by the first opportunity and inform me what you intend to do that I may know if I may expect you or not. If you ever intend to come down, this fall or the next spring will be the best time—this fall would be best if you could get down before winter. I shall be found either in St. Louis or in Clarksville at the falls of the Ohio.

Wishing you and your family great success, and with anxious expections of seeing my little dancing boy, Baptiest, I shall remain your friend.

WILLIAM CLARK

It was a big mouthful for a reticent man. He spent more than an hour by the fire that evening scraping it out. He showed it to Lewis.

"Think it'll work?" asked Lewis.

"It'll go to Bluster Bear's head," said Clark. "Though he doesn't need more of that."

"And Sacajawea will admire your English style," smiled Lewis.

"She does respect writing."

The Red-Headed Chief had thought about it since he'd left the Mandans, and a dim idea had been taking shape in his mind since the wintry day Paump was born. East of the Mississippi, whites and Indians were always fighting. They did it because they didn't understand each other. Clark himself liked Indians, always had. Whites and Indians just needed to understand each other.

Maybe it would be a different story west of the Mississippi. Paump might make a good start. If the boy was white and Indian, if he had a white upbringing and an Indian upbringing, if he spoke English and French and Mandan and Minataree and Shoshone, well, at least he would be a fine interpreter. And maybe he would be a beginning toward two races' being able to live together. He could explain them to each other.

So William Clark, offering Paump the great medicine of the white man, sent back to the Mandan villages a sample of that medicine—the marks that made words to tempt his mother, and an offer of prosperity to tempt his father.

Paump settled with Sacajawea and Charbonneau in the Minataree villages, and for four years lived the daily life of any Minataree child. The family lived in a wickiup during the winter, its entrance facing the rising sun in tribute. The child saw the ritual decorations of the lodges, the signs that placated or implored the forces of the earth. He saw the medicine bundles, with their magical feathers, claws, and stones, and noticed that the boys of the Lumpwood Society carried nobbed sticks onto the prairie to fast, where songs were revealed to them that would allow them to lure the buffalo into the pens they had built. He heard the war song of the Stone Hammer Society, made up of boys only a little older:

> *I am on the earth*
> *just for a little while;*
> *when there is a fight*
> *I must die.*

He learned that the members of the Dog Society behaved backwards, walking backwards, saying yes when they meant no and no when they meant yes, charging the enemy when told to flee, shouting when told to be quiet; for such was the oath of their society. In the summer, when the braves went on their sacred buffalo hunts, Paump stayed with his mother to tend the corn and sing the prayers that made it grow. In the evenings he heard the tales of the Shoshone—about NunumBi, elfin spirits that lurked in the woods and shot arrows of misfortune at passersby, and about the elders of Dinwoody, the dead braves of the Shoshone who lived in a cave in Dinwoody and would one day reappear. Most of all Paump learned what cannot be communicated in words: the way in which the life of the Minatarees and the Mandans and the other tribes they visited was governed by ritual, by revelation, by fear and reverence for the elements of the earth—sun, water, winds, growth, fire, death, the march of the seasons.

Chapter Two

1814

1807, MARCH 2: Congress prohibited further importation of slaves into the jurisdiction of the United States.

1808: Robert Fulton's steamboat made its inaugural voyage.

1809, MARCH 4: James Madison became the fourth President of the United States; Thomas Jefferson retired to Monticello.

1812, JUNE 18: Congress declared war on Great Britain.

1812: A representative of two missionary societies traveled through the territories between the Alleghenies and the Mississippi River and reported a lamentable want of religious instruction.

1814: The first factory in the world to make cotton cloth with power machinery opened in Waltham, Massachusetts.

1815, DECEMBER 24: The United States and Great Britain signed a peace treaty at Ghent.

1817, APRIL 11: America's first Negro bishop was appointed head of the new African Methodist Episcopal Church.

Eighteen Hundred Fourteen

MARCH, 1814: The Reverend J.E. Welch was festering. He walked along the mud track bumpily, a heavy wooden bucket in each hand, the fester jerking his hips about, his boots skating a little in the wet. He skidded at the fence and cracked a split rail with a bony knee. For a moment he glared at the black, white, and mud-colored hog, the one sidling over slyly and looking impassive. He dumped the buckets of slop into the pen. He drew himself erect for a moment and stared over the rolling hills toward the west. The sun was setting an apocalyptic red over the patchy snow. Welch was bareheaded, his hair sandy and thinning, his forehead split into red and white by forty years in the fields, his eyebrows bushy, his face knotty and cedar-colored. He was thin and bony and hard. He had a face of a certain mad intensity, and might have looked as imposing as an Old Testament prophet, had he not stood five-feet-four. His eyes fixed westward, as though he were trying to out-eyeball the sun. When his right eye shifted a little north, the left kept challenging the west.

"And these vittles to the nourishment of our bodies, amen." Welch, his shabby frock coat slipped on over his slopping clothes, looked magisterially around the table, carefully taking in each boy, then sat down. All was in order, save Benjamin, and that required no comment. Dishes piled high with food were set in front of him. He spooned peas onto his own plate and handed them to the right. *"Des petits pois,"* he said flatly. He started each dish thus, and they worked their way back to him slowly. Five boys were seated around the plank table, ranging from perhaps six to fourteen years. A roundish woman of about thirty sat at the far end on the edge of her chair, as though forever about to rise. She was pretty in her soft, plump way, her eyes large and brown, her glance gentle as she watched

36

the boys. She was timid, and almost never spoke at table. None of these boys were hers—four were Indian pupils and one, the oldest, was her stepson.

"Yves," Welch spoke up, meaning the second Indian boy to his right, *"Dépêche-toi."* Welch permitted French at table because it was *la langue du pays* and the boys were most accustomed to it. It was also his wife's mother tongue. He insisted on prayers and Scriptures in English. The Bible in French sounded like papism to him.

Baptiste, on Welch's immediate left, clanked his fork against his glass and looked studiously at his turnip greens. "Baptiste," challenged Welch, "was that you?"

"No, Sir, not me," Baptiste answered with a smile, looking straight at Welch. Just then Yves tapped a responding clank on Welch's right. Welch glowered at him. Then he decided to ignore the whole thing. He knew what was going on. He heard the third clank.

Baptiste, who was now nine, always sat on Welch's left. The Reverend's left eye was glass. Since it didn't move, Baptiste had nicknamed Welch Dead Eye. Each night he started the clanking ritual, and each night it eluded Welch. Baptiste had even gotten Welch's teen-age sons to join in. If he didn't hear five answering clanks on any given evening, he would find the culprit and assign him the duty of emptying Welch's chamber pot the next morning. Tomorrow morning it would be Benjamin who drew that duty. Baptiste wasn't big enough to force Benjamin, but he had his ways.

The Reverend J.E. Welch did not persecute the boys. He believed himself to be a good man. He also believed that he was one of the elect, and had spent his fifty years waiting for the laying on of hands. It had not come. As a boy in Virginia, on his father's hillside farm, he had shown a knack for book-learning and, almost alone of the boys he knew, had learned to read and write. He could speak twenty or thirty verses of the Bible by heart before he was twelve. He had known early that God had chosen him for a mission in life—something special, something that others were not called to. He found a great thrill in the hymns that raised praises unto the Lord, and a special beckoning in the invitation at the end of preachment. He was saved at the age of ten. His mother said he would be a great Baptist preacher one day, and everyone marked him down as different. He hired out as an extra hand in the

country, saved money, and sent himself to missionary
school in Roanoke.

But the high functionaries of the Baptist Church Missionary Board were blind to the light the Lord put in him.
Though they trained him to carry God's word to the
French-speaking Indians of the St. Lawrence River, and
though he spoke the language to a fare-you-well, they
never called him. He kept working on his father's farm
until he was thirty. He married, got his wife with child,
built a second cabin on the place, annexed some more
acres, and expanded the farm. Instead of cultivating souls,
he cultivated tobacco and corn and beans and hogs.

In 1804 his wife died in the birth of their third son. In
1807 his father, long a widower, also died. J.E. Welch sold
the old place, added Reverend to his name, and headed
for St. Louis. It was new, it was American, there was
room; he would let his light shine at last.

He set up a boarding school in St. Louis for Indian
boys, Indian boys whose only white language was French.
At forty-five he remarried, and his wife—a young French-
woman—knew a woman's ways and a woman's work. He
was selected now—by himself, it was true—for even the
eminent William Clark had sent him an Indian boy, Jean-
Baptiste, for schooling. But somehow the coals still burned
in him. J.E. Welch had three hatreds in this world—the
sound of Latin in God's house, the smell of tobacco in
leaf, and the snort of a hog.

He was, nearly enough, what he thought himself—a
good man, by his own lights. He was saving the heathen;
he liked and understood heathen boys better than most of
his contemporaries, though he knew that his temper was a
failing. He meant to teach them to read and write, to wash
and dress like civilized men, and then—if their heathen
nature didn't reassert itself—to till the land. He had no
higher hopes for them: After all, they were what they
were. But if they could not become merchants, teachers,
and lawyers, or even carpenters and mechanics, they could
learn obedience to civil and divine authority; they could
learn to grow crops and stay put in one place. If their understanding of divine will was limited, that was as it must
be. Perhaps their children could be taught to be white
men. In the meantime, the key to their temporal and spiritual salvation was discipline, the fear of the Lord, and the
fear of the Lord's representative, J.E. Welch. Welch held

onto hope for them: he remembered, always, that his God was a God of miracles.

He was reading Scripture aloud after dinner to the boys—the story of Abraham's sacrifice of Isaac—when he heard Benjamin's step. Welch looked as though that step had turned loose a spring in him. He jumped up, knocking his high-backed wooden chair flat, and bolted through the door to the parlor where Benjamin was creeping toward the room he shared with James. Baptiste heard Benjamin's back crash against the wall.

"It's divil whisky on your breath, is it?" screamed Welch. He took a hand off the boy to slap his face. But Benjamin, who was sixteen, and half a foot taller than his father, shoved and sent Welch sprawling backwards over a table. Benjamin shot out the door and back toward the riverfront. Before he got ten yards down the muddy street, Welch was within two strides of him.

"Ye've been drinking," shouted Welch. Boot slaps while he caught his breath. "I kin smell it." Slaps again. "And I'm gonna smell"—pause—"for your other evils." Pause. "Been to the harlots, have ye?"

Benjamin's groin, recently warmed, ran cold. Welch's two big hands hit him flat on the shoulder blades and sent him headlong into the mud.

Welch dragged him into the house with mud all over his hands and face and back, his pants half off, and a big strawberry on one cheekbone. Mrs. Welch and the boys were gathered around the front door.

"He's drunk and he's been to the Frenchy whore," Welch bellowed at no one in particular, and disappeared into the bedroom with Benjamin.

He was apoplectic. Baptiste had never seen so fine a rage before. He knew enough to stay out of Welch's way at times like this: In his first five years he had caught some of Welch's anger. Now he grinned at Yves. That night the boys swore that they would find a way to get out of Welch's school before they started with whisky. Before they started with French whores, too, though they weren't sure what you did with whores.

Baptiste didn't mind Welch. He had been scared of him at first, less because he was violent than because he was strange. A six-year-old cannot understand the terrors of hell-fire-and-damnation as rendered in full plumage by a

Baptist preacher, but he has easy access to terror. Baptiste, in the first couple of years, had been terrified of something, he didn't know what. His mother hadn't been able to help. She was in town sometimes, but she only told him that the white man's god was most powerful and the revealer of the white man's great medicine and that Baptiste must know this god and learn his medicine. She had taught him about the gods of the four winds, and he had seen the Thunder-being come from the west and unleash its power, so he knew that gods were awesome.

He had quickly learned how to pacify Welch. He memorized Scriptures easily and repeated them back. "The wages of sin is death," he would enunciate carefully to Welch after dinner by the fire, getting his English and his Bible right at once. "Repent, O ye of little faith." "For God so loved the world that he sent His only begotten son. . . ." He could remember the words with no effort, and he discovered that he only had to parrot them. He had nothing he could connect any of it to, but he knew that his diligence, his quick grasp, and his smile pleased Welch.

Mrs. Welch—the Reverend always called her Mrs. Welch as far as Baptiste could tell—had taken him under her wing when he first arrived. He had been too young to help out around the farm, so she kept him in the kitchen. And she sang as she worked—sang the songs of Aix-en-Provence, where she had been born. In a good mood and out of earshot of Welch she would throw in a saucy Creole song or two that she had heard in New Orleans; Baptiste didn't get them entirely, but he loved the jaunty tone. While she did the lunch dishes, she would sing rounds, getting Baptiste started on the first round, then carrying the second while the boy sounded out his in a small, brave unsteady voice. When he would get lost, he would stamp out the rhythm with his feet while she finished. One afternoon the two of them were dancing in a circle in the kitchen to "Frère Jacques," Mrs. Welch with broom in hand and her skirts picked up, when Welch walked in. The Reverend sent Baptiste to bed without any supper and scolded Mrs. Welch roundly in front of him. He didn't expect his own wife to teach Indian boys, who had the divil in 'em anyway, the divil's recreation of dancing. The next day they were dancing again in the kitchen anyway. Mrs. Welch was a French Protestant and had become a Baptist by marriage; this she didn't understand, so they defied her husband on the sly.

Days on the school-farm were long and strictly regimented. Everyone got up in the pre-dawn light and ate a big country breakfast, eggs from the henhouse, pork they had slaughtered, milk from one of their two cows. First the boys of ten or older, including Welch's sons, did chores until mid-morning, then had lessons until lunch, each boy working on his own level. Welch drilled them in reading and writing both English and French, read aloud to them in French the history of the world, told them stories of great men, and infused them with American patriotism. Mrs. Welch, who had a knack for figures, took over for arithmetic. It was a program, Welch reminded them constantly, remarkably advanced. A lot of whites didn't read and write, and almost no Indians did. They were getting a headstart in life, for which they should thank the Lord.

After lunch came more chores and, at mid-afternoon, more lessons. After dinner he read the Scriptures to them—always in English—and told them the great Bible stories, Daniel in the lion's den, Jonah and the whale, Jesus walking on the water and changing the water to wine (which was really grape juice, he explained), Paul being struck down on the road to Damascus. Baptiste loved these stories. And after an hour or so of Bible, they would sing hymns. Mrs. Welch played on one of her prize possessions, a clavichord. Her family had crated it over from France before they lost their modest fortune, and she had brought it to her marriage. It marked the Welch home, she thought, with a gentility rare to St. Louis, even if the Welches didn't have any money. She didn't know the hymns of the American Protestant backwoods, but she had a quick ear. And so "Amazing Grace" and "Nearer My God to Thee" resounded through the dusk of the Welch parlor every evening. Baptiste loved the singing. And to bed at sunset, as there was no sense in wasting candles.

FEBRUARY, 1815: Baptiste fretted all day on February 5. It was a warm winter's day with ragged clouds and fitful, spitting rain, and it was his tenth birhday. He smelled something special in the air. He mooned about, hanging around the kitchen with Mrs. Welch, dawdling through his lessons, looking at Mrs. Welch with big eyes. He had to wait all the day through dinner and through the Scripture readings.

When Baptiste heard the rapping on the door, Welch was praying aloud. Mrs. Welch crept away to let their guest in. William Clark stood in the doorway while Welch continued his conversation with God for some ten minutes, for the blessing of more funds to expand his work on the Lord's behalf. Reverend Welch wanted the Brigadier General to know that he didn't come before the Lord, or an American citizen's right to talk with the Lord. Baptiste slipped to his feet when he saw Clark, but Clark solemnly lowered his head and Baptiste stood fidgeting the whole time, looking at Clark from under his eyebrows. At the words "In the name of our saviour, amen," he sprinted across the room, coolly stopped, and stuck out his hand. Clark shook it with a smile. He had two packages in the other hand.

Mrs. Welch introduced Clark to the other boys, who were duly impressed by the large, robust man in the resplendent dress uniform. He had a friendly face and a smile that said he liked to have fun too. Welch was polite but not deferential. The first package opened, the big one, held a birthday cake, and Clark produced ten candles from a coat pocket. The second he handed to Baptiste.

The boy didn't know what it was. It was made of shiny tin and nickel and polished wood, half a foot long, shaped like a tiny box, with a lot of square holes on one side. Baptiste looked at it a long time, then up at Clark.

"Paump, my boy, it's a mouth organ." He took it and blew through the holes. It made a clash of unmusical tones. "Mrs. Welch, maybe you can operate this thing better than I," and he handed it over. She toyed with it tentatively for a few minutes, then produced something that Baptiste could recognize as a not-quite-right melody.

Clark handed her a piece of paper with a name and address on it. "This gentleman will call before the end of the week," he said, "to show Paump how it makes music. I have no skill at such things, though I like a good tune. If you want him to," he nodded at Mrs. Welch, "I'm sure he would come by from time to time to give instructions." Mrs. Welch was pleased. It had been her idea.

Clark stayed after the boys had eaten their cake and

been sent to bed. "And how is Paump progressing?" he asked Welch.

"Baptiste applies himself, and he's a quick learner," answered Welch. The Reverend didn't like to hear Clark using the boy's heathen name. "He's a bit of an unbroken colt, though. Could cause trouble later if he doesn't learn discipline."

"Spirit is troublesome in a boy, but helpful in a man," Clark observed. He was fond of saying such things.

"I hope this machine," meaning the mouth organ, "doesn't encourage his waywardness." Welch considered a moment and put it diplomatically. "I think Indian boys should be at what's useful."

"But he loves music so," his wife put in boldly. Welch ignored her.

Clark didn't want to be party to a domestic disagreement, so he stood to take his leave. It was not his custom to involve himself in matters of strong feeling—they made him feel unclean. "You'll let me know, I'm sure, if Paump needs anything."

Welch shook his hand. "Baptiste don't need but what the other boys have," he said. He thought better of it. "But we'll let ye know if he needs a doctor or some such." Clark nodded gravely.

Baptiste's aptitude for that mouth organ amazed them all. In a couple of months the boy was playing the hymn melodies that he heard every night; in a couple of months more he was adding simple harmony to them. Mrs. Welch, impressed, asked Welch for permission to give him some musical tutoring. "He can learn to play the music," Welch said, "that praises the Lord." So she taught him the names of the notes and what the black spots on the lines meant, and the rests, and the differences between the clefs, and other musical paraphernalia. Quickly he was playing with both hands—one note for each hand—on the little clavichord, and before he was eleven he could play the simple four-part harmony of the hymns. When he learned a hymn well, Mrs. Welch even let him play accompaniment for the nightly singing.

But Welch predicted that the thing would lead to trouble, and it did. Baptiste picked up by ear the French provincial songs that Mrs. Welch sang and danced with him. Then he added the music of the streets. When he went to market with Mrs. Welch—the large open-air carnival of cart peddlers that focused the city's commerce—he heard all sorts of fascinating sounds. The Americans had their robust backwoods songs; the Negroes, who were French-speaking, had their exotic, rhythm-driven songs; the French-Canadian riverboatmen had their lusty, bawdy working songs. Baptiste would beg the peddlers to sing for him, holding back the marketing, and the peddlers were amused by the little Indian boy who could imitate their tunes on the mouth organ with scarcely a mistake. As they walked to and from the market Baptiste played the mouth organ all the way, sounding out the song he thought he remembered from the last time or the new one he had just heard. Mrs. Welch indulged him, but warned Baptiste not to try that music on the clavichord. Reverend Welch might not like it.

"Baptiste," said Mrs. Welch, "go tell Reverend Welch that a letter has come." Welch and the older boys were slaughtering, out behind the barn. Baptiste couldn't resist playing a tune as he walked. It was a Spanish fandango, a lively thing, and it made him lilt as he moved. He deliberately didn't quit playing until after he was within Welch's hearing range.

The Reverend glared at him. "There's a letter for you," Baptiste said, growing afraid. Welch didn't answer. He ripped the instrument out of the boy's hands and stuck it in a hip pocket. Then he marched off toward the house. Welch was not a man to beat boys; he thought that punishment should be mental and emotional because that counted for more. He took the mouth organ away for a month, and called off Baptiste's keyboard lessons for a week. When he let the lessons start again, he told Baptiste bluntly that he was to play only hymns, and no music for dancing or the divil's other fancies.

OCTOBER, 1815: One morning after Baptiste angered Welch—he was expecting a stern regimen of chores and an after-dinner lecture—Baptiste got pulled off duties to go see William Clark. Clark lived clear across town—from the outskirts on the southwest to the northeast corner near the river—but Baptiste was ten and could go alone. He took the mouth organ to play on the way; he wasn't allowed out often, and could take the occasion to wander around without Welch's knowing.

Baptiste liked to visit Clark. Welch's house was a primitive affair, made of posts that supported cross-ties, filled in with a paste of mud and straw, and covered with whitewash. It was only one story, had a big fireplace, and uneven slat floors. There were four rooms plus the detached, lean-to kitchen—the parlor, the dining room (which served as schoolroom and study as well), and two bedrooms, one shared by Welch's sons and the student-boarders. In the winter it was drafty, dark, cold, and damp. But Clark's place was handsome and elegant. The main house was of stone. It had joined walnut planks for floors, waxed and polished, with an immense center fireplace of stone in the parlor. Clark also had a separate building for the kitchen, a stable and yard, a blacksmith shop, a gunsmith shop, and a dram shop. Baptiste loved to watch Clark's blacksmith work with the bellows and the fire, sparks flying and hammer clanging and the metal white turning to red. He also loved the parlor where Clark had collected memorabilia of the Lewis and Clark expedition—stretched hides, horns of elk and buffalo and big-horn sheep, Indian pipes, and the canoe that carried Baptiste, his mother and father, and Clark floating down the Yellowstone. When his mother and father came to St. Louis, Baptiste spent hours in that room, listening to stories of old times and the things he had done as a child.

It was a clear October morning, cool, with a hint of autumn in the air. He could smell leaves burning somewhere, for the maples had turned to red and begun to shed. As Baptiste walked he played "All the Way to Shawnee Town Long Time Ago," a tune he had picked up from a boatman. When he grew up, he thought he might be a boatman himself. He had seen them bring the keelboats up to the levee. The boatmen had long poles that they socketed under their shoulders and drove into the river bottom. Then they walked backwards, downriver, along a cleated running-board, pushing the boat up against the current. It was hard work they did, and they sang all the while.

A tall, solemn black man opened the door for Baptiste. "Brigadier-General Clark, please," Baptiste said politely.

"Governor Clark," the black man answered without expression. Baptiste knew that, but he'd forgotten. "Governor Clark," he said meekly. The black man led the way toward Clark's office. Baptiste thought he looked strong just to be answering doors for someone. He knew that

Clark owned the man, and wondered what it felt like to be owned. He couldn't see anything in it.

Clark stood up behind his big walnut desk and walked slowly toward Baptiste. He said nothing, and his face looked strangely solemn. Baptiste stuck out his hand. Clark ignored it, stepped close, and without bending over put his hands under the boy's shoulders, lifted him, and hugged him. Pressed against Clark's cheek, Baptiste could not see his face. He was puzzled, and a little frightened. Clark drew back a little, and Baptiste could see tears in his eyes.

"Paump, my boy," he said, "your mother is dead." Baptiste looked straight into his eyes for a long time, but Clark said nothing more, and there was nothing more to see. Clark set him down. Baptiste slipped out of his encircling arm and sat down in front of the desk. Clark sat behind it.

The boy would not look at Clark. The big man fingered a piece of paper for a while, waiting for the boy. "This letter," he finally said, "came down from Fort Atkinson. It says that Charbonneau has sent word from west of the Arikara villages that your mother is dead. It says nothing else, nothing about how or why."

He pushed the letter across the desk to Baptiste. The boy didn't pick it up, didn't look at it, just kept staring at his knees.

"She was a fine woman," Clark said. "Christ, she was." He grimaced.

Baptiste kept looking down. At last he stood up, walked around the desk, and offered Clark his hand. Clark shook it. Baptiste turned and marched out of the office, through the parlor where the black man was polishing something, and out the front door. Then he slowed down and wandered along the street.

He spent the afternoon on the bluff above the river, at the far end from the levee. He could see the keelboat and the workers far down, loading and unloading, out of hearing range. He looked at the water for a long time, thinking of nothing, just watching the brown water move slowly down the river and sometimes curl into a long eddy and straighten out again and flow down. The river was quiet except for the faintest lapping sound on the sand. A hawk came over his head, soaring high. Baptiste wondered whether it was looking down for something. It seemed just to hover there, high above the earth, unconcerned. It flapped its wings once, abruptly and briefly, and floated on toward the Illinois side.

Most of the time he just sat and looked. He did not think of his mother. After a long time he slipped his mouth organ out of his pocket and began to play softly. It didn't matter what he played. He sounded out every tune he knew. Sometimes memories of his mother rose in his mind as he played, not thoughts, just sense memories—the warmth of her hand on his back, the smooth feel of her cheek, and the vibration in her throat when she held him there and talked to him. He would have played one of the songs she sang to him, but he could not remember the sounds clearly, and the ones he remembered didn't fit the mouth organ. He played hymns, soft and plaintive, and liked them:

> *Nearer, my God, to Thee,*
> *Nearer to Thee.*
> *E'en though a cross it be*
> *That raiseth me,*
> *Still all my song shall be,*
> *Nearer, my God, to Thee,*
> *Nearer, my God, to Thee,*
> *Nearer to Thee!*

> *Though like a wanderer,*
> *The sun gone down.*
> *Darkness be over me,*
> *My rest a stone;*
> *Yet in my dreams I'd be*
> *Nearer, my God, to Thee,*
> *Nearer, my God, to Thee.*
> *Nearer to Thee!*

Late in the afternoon thin clouds covered the sky, the river turned gray, and a slight, chill wind freshened. He got up—his legs were stiff—and started walking home.

He went straight to bed, without seeing Welch. In the middle of the night he woke up, touched his cheeks, and realized he had been crying.

Mrs. Welch had nothing to say about Sacajawea's death—just a hand on the cheek and "I'm sorry"—but she started using Baptiste every day to go to the market with

her and tote things back. The market was a building and
the plaza in front of it, on the south end of the levee.
Carts rumbling and peddlers crying and chickens squawk-
ing turned it into bedlam every day. Baptiste got to know
some of the peddlers: There was a German Baptiste liked
to tease who sold milk. When Mrs. Welch would ask how
much, he would answer, "It ish a bit" or "It ish a picayune." Missouri, and the Louisiana Territory generally,
had almost no U.S. coins or currency, so everyone used
the old Spanish coins. A picayune was a half *real,* worth
about six and a half cents; a bit was a section of a coin
that had been primitively quartered, and it was worth
twelve and a half cents. Baptiste discovered that the poor
German, a worn, suspicious, middle-aged man, knew no
other English. So if he asked the fellow, "Are your children yours?" or "Is your wife a witch?" and pointed to the
milk, the German would answer uncertainly, "It ish a bit."

An Irishman was sometimes there selling butter. Baptiste loved his blarney, and wouldn't let Mrs. Welch pay
until they had heard it. "I'd like to see anny butther in the
whole market like that, I would, faith. 'Tis illegant i' 'tis.
That butter ull be making ye rise in the mornin' now, it
will."

An Illinoisan came to peddle chickens. He was a tall,
strong-looking, slouchy fellow with an air of obstreperous
independence, sullenly proud to be an American and a
free man. His hair signaled his independence by waving
through the ripped crown of his straw hat. He stood with
his hands in his pockets and looked about dourly, as
though ashamed to be a mere chicken-peddler. Mrs. Welch
asked, pointing at the sign on the homemade, two-story,
cart-mounted chicken coop, "Is that the lowest you'll
take?"

"Well, yes, ma'am, it's thar at that price." He shrugged.
"I couldn't take a mite less—the old 'oman says they're
futh it, and she knows, she does." He always took less of
course, looking mightily offended as he took the change.

Sometimes Baptiste would stay with the Irish butterman
while Mrs. Welch shopped and haggled. Baptiste would
play his repertory of songs on the mouth organ—avoiding
the hymns, which once made the Irishman curse at him—
and if the fellow had been supping the profits from the
butter, he would join in. Then he'd switch to old Irish
songs in a vigorous, scraggly, wretched tenor, and Baptiste

would follow along, learning whatever was new. Hearing
Baptiste fumble, the Irishman would curse. "Mither of
God, don't ye know anythin'?" He'd look fiercely at the
boy. "Heathen, a damnable heathen."

Mrs. Welch gave him a final sprucing. Baptiste turned
his head around to look at the tails of the new coat Governor Clark had bought him. It was a miniature imitation, in
dark brown, of just the sort of frock coat that gentlemen
wore. He also had light brown pants and a fine-bosomed
shirt decorated with a paste roseate stud. Baptiste thought
he had never seen any clothes quite so elegant.

The black man was waiting in Welch's parlor to escort
him to Clark's house, for it was almost dark out. Baptiste
couldn't remember when Welch had allowed him out after
dark, but this was an occasion. Baptiste walked fast
enough to make sure he didn't slow the black man down.
The man admitted that his name was Isaiah, but had nothing else to say.

The company dazzled Baptiste. Here was some of St.
Louis's first society: Clark and his wife Julia, the "Judith"
he had longed for on the expedition and named a river after, Manuel Lisa and his wife Polly, Auguste Chouteau
and his wife Thérèse. Lisa was a native Spaniard, a dark
impulsive man, and spoke French with a thick accent.
Chouteau, dressed quaintly in knee breeches with silver
buckles on his shoes and his hair *en queue,* was the
wealthy patriarch of one of St. Louis's most distinguished
French families. Baptiste had heard of both men. They
had been involved in getting St. Louis's fur trade started,
and Clark had been one of their partners. There were also
Bernard Pratte, the fur-trader, and his wife Emilie; Pierre
Chouteau, Jr., and Bartholomew Berthold, partners in a
store, and Berthold's wife Pélagie, who was Pierre's sister.
Baptiste never got the other four children connected with
the right parents.

Clark introduced Baptiste to M. and Mme. Lisa. "He
has been to the mountains many times, Paump," Clark
said, "and has stayed at the Mandan and Minataree villages."

"And I know your father—a fine man—and was acquainted with your mother, God rest her soul," Lisa said
in French. Lisa gave Paump the recent news of Chief
Shehaka and Paump's childhood friends. Charbonneau and

Otter Woman and Toussaint and Lissette, he said, were doing splendidly. He thought they would be down to St. Louis before the river froze.

Clark insisted that the children sit at the main dining table during dinner. It was a sumptuous meal, full of fishes and meats and rich sauces. Chouteau pronounced it exceptional, but Baptiste found it too strange to eat. He was not permitted to talk to Bernard, the boy next to him.

After dinner they adjourned to the parlor. The ladies talked in one corner—Baptiste caught snatches about the Labbadie boy, who was gone east to school, and about the brazen behavior of the Cousteau girl, and something about extraordinary gowns brought up the river for Victoire Gratiot. The men assembled in another corner and talked about the prospects for reopening the fur trade, the new Bank of St. Louis, currency problems, and the advantages and disadvantages of statehood for Missouri. (Clark, hoping to become state governor, was avidly for statehood.)

Baptiste fidgeted. He was self-conscious in his new clothes, and aware that his French didn't sound just like the other children's. Jefferson Clark, the youngest, was sitting with his hands pinned between his knees. Bernard was boasting to the little Pélagie: "My pa," he said in French, "says I can go to the States for school if I want to—to Virginia. He'll take me on his next trip if I want to go."

"But it's so far." Pélagie was a bright, pretty child, all done up in frills—lace on her bodice, ribbons around the bottom of her full skirt, her hair in long, shining curls.

"Yes," said Bernard, striking the pose of a young man, "but it's important for us to get an education. St. Louis will need leadership."

"Yes," said Pélagie softly.

"My pa wants me to take over his business. But we have a lot of money already. I think, I'd like to be a lawyer."

"What's a lawyer?" Baptiste put in.

"Lawyers memorize the law," Bernard answered decorously. "They represent clients in court cases. Sometimes they become judges. Or they represent the people in government." He stopped, needing to say nothing more.

Baptiste had been wondering whether the girls of prominent families went to school: "Will you be going east, too?"

"Such an idea," Pélagie giggled.

"I'd like to go," Baptiste said. Bernard and Pélagie looked at him strangely. "But I don't think I can," he backed up. "I have to do what Governor Clark says." He hesitated and then jumped in headlong. "I'd like to be a soldier, like Governor Clark, or a governor. Or maybe a lawyer."

"A governor? A lawyer? But. . . . Papa," he laughed across the room to Pratte, "this boy wants to be a governor or a lawyer." Pélagie tinkled with laughter.

Baptiste roared with hatred for Bernard. "I can—"

"Bernard," Clark interrupted, "Baptiste is an extraordinary young man." He stepped over, put a hand on Baptiste's shoulder, and turned to the group. "You know his background," Clark began, "and you can hear that he speaks French and English well. He also speaks Mandan, Minataree, and some Shoshone. Paump is the most accomplished linguist among us. And he reads and writes well.

"I think you will be of service one day, Paump," he said turning back to the boy. "To commerce. To the government. Being Indian, you see," Clark said at large, "he understands Indians. Being white, he understands whites. Our country and our businessmen need youngsters like him."

Baptiste was catching on. He rattled off several strange phrases. "That's how the Minatarees say 'I give you my deepest respects and pledge my everlasting sincerity,'" he said with a smile and a slight bow. He sat back down and glared haughtily at Bernard.

When Baptiste was leaving with Isaiah, Clark saw him to the door. "Governor Clark," Baptiste asked looking up, "can't I be a lawyer if I want to?"

Clark looked at him seriously for a long moment. "I hope so, Paump, if you want to. Remember, though, some whites are not as Christian as they ought to be to halfbreeds. But don't fret," he said with a clap on the back. "We'll find something suitable."

Clark did wonder, as Baptiste stepped out, what would prove to be suitable. He was a little afraid for the boy—afraid that Paump might not be satisifed with his lot, that education and exposure to the way of the white world might raise yearnings in him the boy would never be allowed to fulfill. But that was far in the future, and Clark did not trouble himself unduly about it. For William Clark was above all a practical man, a man who worked within realities as they were given to him, never one to dally with fantasies, speculations, might-have-beens. He had a will, within that context, to work good, and he did. He was a responsible husband, father and civic leader, an appropriately ambitious politician, a well-wisher for his adolescent country. He was also a man concerned for the welfare of the Indians, whom he understood better and cared about far more than did most white men of his time. He loved Paump as a kind of godfather, and intended to do as well for him as was possible. Further than that the matter was out of his hands.

Reverend Welch's Bible lessons ran to four subjects—the amazing sacrifice of Jesus, the terrors of the Last Judgement and hell, the insidiousness of sin (which he saw creeping and clinging everywhere around him, like poison oak around a tree), and the long-suffering virtue of Job. Welch had a colorful, even lurid, imagination, so he was able to make his stories vivid. Baptiste didn't know what to make of Jesus, he delighted in the terrors of hell just as he delighted in ghost stories, and he was uneasy about the insidiousness of sin. The one that made no sense to him was the story of Job: He thought Job shouldn't ·just have stood there and taken what was dished out. He should have fought back.

Welch never talked about Sacajawea's death to Baptiste, but the boy noticed that his evening teaching ran considerably more toward death in the days after.

He took as his text one evening, for their devotional time, *Isaiah* XXXIII, 12-13-14: "And the people shall be as the burning of lime, as thorns cut up shall they be burnt in the fire. Hear ye that are far off what I have done; and ye that are near acknowledge my might."

" 'It is a fearful thing to fall into the hands of the living God,' *Hebrews* X, 31," he expounded, "yet when we die, we all must fall into his hands and stand before his terrible judgment.

"Death is God's curse upon man for his disobedience, for the sin that through Adam is born unto all men. And for that Original Sin must we all answer. No man may think to escape it. For him who does, lo, there shall be wailing and gnashing of teeth. Nothing on earth is to be feared as the day when all sinners shall find themselves in the hands of an angry God.

"On that day all men are equal in the sight of God, the mighty and the low alike, and all who are not washed in the blood of Jesus, cleansed by the blood of Jesus of their sins, shall tremble before His awful and inevitable judgment. 'As thorns cut up shall they be burnt in the fire.'

"For the Lord sees all, the sins committed in the shadow of the night, the sins committed in the darkness of the closet, the sins committed in the closeness of our very beds"—Welch looked at his sons to see if they were squirming—"and the sins committed in secret thought. At Judgment Day some of us, the few, shall be white as snow, and others, the many, black as tar. Some shall be saved unto life eternal, and the others shall hear the dread words 'Depart from me, I know ye not.' And they shall be plunged into everlasting torment. 'For behold, the Lord will come with fire, and with chariots like a whirlwind, to render his anger with fury, and his rebukes with flames of fire,' *Isaiah* LXVI, 15."

Yves was asleep now. Baptiste was still, looking at his hands. They kept jumping oddly.

"For the body is but the shabby house of the soul," Welch went on. "The body carries, even in life, the insidious disease of mortality. In time the putrescence which is native to the body shall overthrow it. In time, it shall creep like a fog through the limbs and render them still, it shall creep through the blood and make it black, it shall cloud the brain and still the tongue. And in time the body, surrendering the soul, shall pass unto the earth whence it came. It shall be placed in the grave, and dirt shoveled onto its face—dirt that is the same as the face, which shall become dirt." Welch paused a moment and considered. His silence made Baptiste even more jittery than his talking. "Dirt to dirt, ashes to ashes—such is the fate of all mankind, the curse of Adam.

"And the earth itself shall dishonor the body. The flies shall feed on its blood. The worms shall crawl into the flesh and eat thereof. As the flesh rots, it shall reveal itself by its very smell as the excrement it is. At last it shall become nought but mud and slime.

"I pray," Welch perorated, "that Christ may come again in my lifetime to take the saints to be with Him in glorious light in heaven. I pray that we may not pass through the decay of the grave. I pray it fervently." Welch stared into space, his right eye divergent from his left. "But the

time of the second coming is known only to almighty God,
and it shall be as the twinkling of an eye. Let us therefore
be prepared to meet Him. Let us now call on His holy
name, knowing that all ye who know Him not must surely
perish. Let us be prepared for the destruction of the body
and the judgment of the soul."

He closed his eyes for a moment of silent meditation.

"Reverend Welch," Baptiste burst in when Welch
opened his eyes, "what about those who don't know about
Jesus and can't call on his name?"

Welch looked at him solemnly. "They must surely perish."

"It isn't fair," Baptiste said.

"It is not for us to question the Lord's infinite mercy,"
Welch reprimanded him.

"I don't see how it's fair," Baptiste repeated.

"You are arrogant to think to judge God."

He marked that evening down, years later, as the beginning of his unconversion.

NOVEMBER, 1815: Isaiah came unexpectedly to Welch's
house to take Baptiste to Clark. And sitting beside Clark's
big walnut desk was Charbonneau. Baptiste dashed up and
hugged him. "What happened to Mama?" he asked in
French.

"She was lost on the plains. No one knows what happened to her." Charbonneau had told Clark a fuller
story—that Sacajawea had been jealous of his new wife,
that he had lodgepoled her and that she snuck away onto
the plains and disappeared. Clark knew that no woman
could survive alone on the plains of the Dakotas.

The boy looked at his father a long moment, bit his
lower lip, and then looked down.

"Baptiste," Charbonneau called him back. He was holding something out to the boy, a necklace of some sort.
Baptiste examined it. "Your mother made it for you, and I
thought to bring it as a gift now."

It was a rather large hoop, probably made of stripped
willow twigs shaven very thin and bound alternately with
strong grasses and hair—it would be Sacajawea's own hair,
Baptiste knew. It dangled from a hide thong. In the center
of the hoop, suspended tautly with strips of hide, was the
strangest stone he had ever seen. It was a single stone,
peculiarly heavy, yet it seemed to be a stone made from

many stones. From a distance it would have looked gray, but up close he could see that it had sworls of strong color—streaks of gray with streaks of crimson, bright green, black, white of a blue cast, and pure alabaster. A very strange stone. He rubbed it with a forefinger. She had polished it as smooth as marble.

"It is a stone of signs," Charbonneau cut in. "It is the piece of a star, one says, that fell to the earth a long time ago. One saw it blaze through the sky on fire, attacking the earth like a cannonball. It boomed to the earth many miles to the west and to the south of the Missouri, and one traveled many sleeps to see it. It came from beyond the stars, and some people said it was a message from the One-Who-Created-All, but others said they could not understand the message. People took the pieces of it because they were sacred, and for many years the small stones have been traded from medicine bundle to bundle.

"Your mother believed all this, though I not, and she traded two pairs of mokersons and two buffalo robes so that you might have it. She made the hoop, which she said is both your peoples. They and you shall be well so long as the hoop is never broken. The stone made of different stones that do not go together is you. She said that it was a traveler from strange places, and that you are a traveler to strange and far places. She said you should wear it always so that it will give its strong medicine to you, and keep you well in your wayfaring."

The boy put it on. It felt heavy around his neck, but it was beautiful. He decided to wear it even in his sleep.

Baptiste spent the day playing with Toussaint and Lissette and talking in rusty Minataree with Otter Woman. (The new wife had not come downriver.) They confirmed Charbonneau's story. Clark watched the boy quietly, and concluded that Paump had weathered his mother's death well. He seemed very grown-up, very even-keeled for his age.

After dinner that evening, Clark called Baptiste into his office. Charbonneau was sitting—uncomfortably, for he wasn't used to chairs—in the leather chair opposite the walnut desk.

"You must change your schooling," Charbonneau told Paump. "Your mother wanted that for you to learn to read and write. *Bien,* though your father cannot, nor his father before him, and had no need. But you must not learn to be a heretic Protestant. Your mother said leave it to the General, I say *bien*. But she is gone. You must be learned by the priests of the Mother Church."

Baptiste looked at Clark. "It is his right," Clark said simply. "He is your father."

"It is good. Charbonneau says it must be so," his father exclaimed. That simply, all was changed.

Baptist was surprised that he felt disappointed. He didn't dislike the Reverend, though, and he liked Mrs. Welch.

"I will see that it's arranged," Clark said to the boy.

Baptiste stood up first. *"Bien,"* he said, shook hands, and went to find Isaiah.

He made a boast of it at Welch's house. Charbonneau became the *deus ex machina* of Baptiste's elevation to a new world, to French Catholic society, to the domain of Bernard and Pélagie, M. Lisa and M. Chouteau. Isaiah helped him move his belongings the next day. It pleased Baptiste just a little to see that the other boys were envious; he promised Yves that they would get together often. The Reverend spent the day in a mood. He said good-bye with a grave finality, as though the boy were about to cross the River Styx. Mrs. Welch hugged him and kissed him, and almost made him cry.

DECEMBER, 1815: "Who made you?" asked the priest.

"God made me," intoned Baptiste and the rest of the boys, "to know Him"—here some started mumbling, hoping the priest would not notice—"and serve Him in this world"—now most of the class was mumbling—"so that I may be happy with Him in heaven," Baptiste finished loudly and alone.

"Drop out, Baptiste, and let the others try it bit by bit." He spoke in French—all the instruction was in French— and began to rehearse the others. "Who made you?"

"God made me," they started in an unintelligible rumble, "to. . . ." It was a mixed class of boys. Besides the half-breed Baptiste, there was one Indian, Jacques, a German Catholic who spoke almost no French or English, several mulatto boys who spoke French with a funny accent, and the sons of some of the town's first families—the Chouteaus, the Lacledes, the Prattes, the Lisas, the Bertholds, the Gratiots, a mélange of French, Spanish, and Swiss *cum* American frontier aristocracy.

The priest amused Baptiste. His name was Francis Neil, and he wore long black robes which he treated fastidiously with delicate hands. In spite of his Irish name, he identified more with his French mother than his Irish father, and his English was halting. He was a light young man, refined-looking, gentle, mild, and in Baptiste's opinion a little intimidated by his playful charges. Being naive and sincere, he was an easy set-up for practical jokes. But Baptiste, the ringleader, felt sorry enough for him that the jokes were gentle.

Father Francis Neil rather thought he had missed his calling. He might have been a monk who spent his hours reading devotionals and singing a half-dozen masses daily within the quieting walls of a cloister. Or, since he loved music and thought music the noblest form of praise to God, he might have been organist and choirmaster at a great French cathedral, perhaps Notre-Dame de Paris herself. Instead, by an infelicitous stroke of fate, he had been born into a crude frontier town on a brawling young continent more concerned with the ways of mammon than the ways of devotion. And, in an additional maladroit gesture, the town had been removed from the sovereignty of two old European Catholic cultures to the sway of an upstart Protestant nation, and had recently been filling up with merchants and rivermen and tradesmen and woodsmen and farmers who—Father would have put it delicately—did not share his own predilections. He walked through the streets of St. Louis with a faint air of disconnection, his skirts slightly hiked from the dirt streets.

He was at home in the cathedral, though. He liked its dark recesses, the soft light from its windows, its awesome height, its burnished pews, its peace. He reveled in its ceremonies. Though he knew that some people dreaded the confessional, he took to its intimacy, its humility. He found in the Holy Eucharist a moment of quiet epiphany. He felt uplifted every morning when he intoned the first chanting sounds of the mass. And he loved the hours he spent alone, every afternoon, practicing on the great organ.

For Francis Neil, in the thin and therefore overburdened hierarchy of the diocese, was the cathedral organist and the inculcator of the faith and of learning in the boys of the parish; in addition, he carried out his priestly duties of taking confessions, performing baptisms, administering other sacraments, and frequently singing mass. He knew

that he would never rise higher in the hierarchy of the
church, and at thirty-four he was resigned to that. He
knew that the Bishop had many duties that were more
practical and worldly than he would take to.

Baptiste's lessons had changed tenor now—not only
reading and writing in French and some English, but the
catechism, Church history, stories of the saints, Latin for
the boys over twelve, and lots of singing. Baptiste liked
these lessons better: The catechism was easy, and he
learned it as a game. He adored the stories of the saints.
Father Neil's favorite seemed to be St. Francis of Assisi,
but he struck Baptiste as a little soppy, mooning over flowers and birds. Baptiste liked St. Maria Goretti, who chose
at thirteen to be killed rather than to be touched in sexual
intercourse; Baptiste liked to tell that story because the
privileged white boys didn't know just what sexual intercourse was, and he did. He also liked St. Januarius, who,
on his saint's day every year for hundreds of years, had
wrought himself up and bled from the head and hands and
feet where Christ had bled. Baptiste loved fantasy, and he
would repeat this story to Father Neil so luridly that the
good father wondered if the boy was too much affected.
Baptiste took no interest in his namesake, who struck him
as a madman, and a boring one.

During the Christmas season, Baptiste's first weeks with
Father Neil, the students were absorbed in singing. Father
Neil taught them "Silent Night, Holy Night" in French,
"Adeste Fidelis" in Latin, "Panis Angelicus," "Good King
Wenceslaus," and dozens of other Christmas carols and
songs. Some of them seemed a little too mournful or
soupy to Baptiste, and he sang them in nasty little paro-
dies. But he tried them on his mouth organ when he was
well away from Father Neil, and they sounded nice. The
harmony was simple enough for him to figure out, and
soon he had the melodies pat.

One afternoon at the cathedral he slipped the mouth organ out of his pocket and played softly along with "God
Rest Ye, Merry Gentlemen," one of his favorites. Father
stopped conducting and stared. "Baptiste," he asked,
"what? . . . Play this song for me." Baptiste did, this time
loud, fast, and jauntily. Father Neil came and knelt down
by the boy. "Why didn't you tell me?" His puzzlement
turned to beaming. From then on the class had its own ac-
companist. Neil spent half an hour three days a week

teaching Baptiste new music—all sacred music, of course. He promised Baptiste more lessons on the clavichord after he had learned his catechism and been confirmed. Father Neil was pleased. Here, for once, was an Indian boy with possibilities. For the Father believed that music revealed the soul.

After Baptiste's eleventh birthday the work on the catechism got serious. He had been baptized as a matter of course when he came to the school. (The sprinkling made him smile when he thought how Welch would have hated it.) But now he was to be confirmed within a year and he had a lot to learn. He was quick, but Father Neil wondered whether he was too quick, wondered just what God meant to a boy born heathen, and sometimes suspected that Baptiste treated the catechism as a joke. Neil made him stop showing the heathen emblem he wore around his neck, though Father knew the boy kept it on under his shirt, and instructed Baptiste to keep a diary recording his spiritual progress. Nevertheless Baptiste and the other boys his age drilled and drilled. Soon the big occasion would come: the first confession, the first communion, and confirmation. Father Neil intended to make himself proud of them.

Baptiste was boarded with an elderly Frenchman, M. Honoré. He was told that M. Honoré was kindhearted to take him in, but Baptiste thought the old man just wanted the boarding money for wine. In the first three months he hardly ever spoke to the boy, and seemed never to get out of his ancient, battered robe and slippers, appearing always slightly drunk, Baptiste wondered what strange world he lived in as he lay on his sofa doing nothing all day. But he didn't care, really, because Honoré left him alone. For the first time, Baptiste could wander around the city unrestricted.

It was a good city for an eleven-year-old boy to explore. The river, except during the spring rise, left a dirty, sandy beach where the keelboats put in and unloaded. Behind the beach, limestone bluffs rose from twenty to forty feet—good places to scramble and climb. The levee stretched from the bluffs to the tall, narrow, elegant houses that lined Main Street. At the north end of the levee squatted Battle Row, a long block of buildings first built as stores but then allowed to decline into boarding houses, taverns, and gambling places for the boatmen and their rough women. At the south end stood the Market House, where farmers and gradesmen plied their wares. On the levee the storage sheds of the fur trade were erected.

On any given day the levee was likely to be the center of the action. A keelboat would be unloading its sugar, tobacco, coffee, molasses, cloth and other staples from up the Ohio or from New Orleans, French-Canadian boatmen doing the heavy work and singing their rowing songs. Merchants would be weaving in and out of the sacks and barrels, making sure of their shipments, paying the keelboat captain, the clerks counting and checking; one farmer might be hawking apples cradled in his arms, another just gawking; French-speaking Creoles might be lounging or mixing in, making fun of the high-born French dandy who ignored them; rough fur trappers, scarcely used to such civilization, would be toting their skins to the warehouse, or heading from there to a tavern with their deerskin notes, the most reliable form of currency. Altogether a place to strike a boy's fancy.

The town itself was going through severe growing pains. It had been a remote outpost of the French and Spanish, maintained for nothing but its prime location for trading in furs. It was becoming the principal city of the entire Western area of the United States, the hub of commerce and transportation. Within a little more than fifteen years from the time of its purchase, American storekeepers, farmers, tradesmen, merchants, fur traders, lawyers, and preachers flooded westward to St. Louis and made it the business capital of a new state of the Union. Even then it was a mélange of aristocratic and wealthy French, ambitious and rambunctious Americans, Creoles, mulattoes, French-Canadians, freed blacks—a pastiche of people, languages, customs, attitudes, prejudices, hopes.

Baptiste was just starting up Market Street from the levee one afternoon when a rock skittered past his leg. Baptiste wheeled: Two boys, one tall and gawky, the other short and stocky, both older than he, were leaning against a wall. The tall boy was casually tossing another rock up and catching it.

"What in hell you think you're doing?" Baptiste challenged them.

"Chunkin' rocks at a redskin," the tall boy said. The

stocky one snickered. He was fingering rocks in the street to find another one.

Baptiste was uncertain. "You think that's fun, huh?"

"He's a chickenshit redskin, too," the tall one said sideways.

Baptiste doubled his fist and took a few hesitant steps forward. He was just about to yell back at them when the tall one bolted toward him at full speed.

Baptiste turned and ran like hell. He stumbled once and almost fell, and was mad at his legs before he got to the corner. Just as he turned onto Main Street, he saw a black boy standing there.

"They ain't comin'," he said simply, "they laughin'." Baptiste stopped and looked back. "They laughin' they fool heads off 'cause they skeered a breed and made him run."

Baptiste glared at him. "Don' put it on me," the boy said, "I ain't chunkin' at ya'. 'Sides, I ain't so white myself."

"Yeah," Baptiste said, and grinned. "I guess I let them scare me." He looked around the corner. The boys were gone.

"They hate you ass 'cause you ain't nice and white like them."

Baptiste eyed the boy. He seemed angry and amused at once by the episode.

"My name's Jean," he said, giving it its French inflection. He had used that first name before.

"John," the boy stuck out his hand. "I'm Jim."

Baptiste shook it. He thought a moment and sized up Jim. "You want to get them?"

"Why not?" Jim grinned.

They circled the block the other way, picking up rocks as they went. "I live just off the Row," Jim volunteered. "My ma takes in washin', and she's real perlite to the white folks she works for. Real perlite. She was so perlite to my daddy that me and my sister come along. He's white—owns a tobacco plantation in Virginia."

"He owns a plantation?"

"Yeah, he's done rich. He freed us. Then he sent us all the way to St. Louy. To get us outa' sight, my ma says." He laughed.

They were just coming back to Market Street. Baptiste

stuck his head around the corner and saw the two boys walking away.

"If anything happens," Baptiste said, "I'll meet you at the far side of the Market House."

They walked up behind the two quietly, and from about fifty feet heaved their rocks. The boys started yelling and grabbing for their own rocks. Baptiste threw three, but as far as he could see, they all missed. He ran, Jim was alongside, and both were laughing. They scooted up an alley and hid.

Later they skipped stones on the river and talked. Baptiste told Jim about Charbonneau and Sacajawea and the expedition. Jim was impressed. He wanted to go up the river, he said, and trap them beaver. And he wouldn't ever come back. He wondered why John had come back.

"My ma wanted me to learn to read and write," Baptiste answered.

"Kin you?"

"Sure."

Jim considered that. " 'S fancy," he decided, "but they ain't nothin' in it. They ain't never gonna let you near 'em. Ain't never. Now they might let my sister near 'em," he grinned, "but they got a special notion for her. You and me, no way."

Baptiste considered that he'd better not say anything about his benefactor, Clark.

It was dinnertime, time for whatever pickings Honoré would have for him while the old man sipped wine.

"See you tomorrow?" Baptiste. "At the levee?"

"Down to the levee, John, about the same time. I ain't got nothin' better to do. Some time we can get them two bastards again, one at a time. I knows where they live."

APRIL, 1816: "Bless me, Father, for I have sinned. This is my first confession."

"Yes, my son, what have you to confess?"

Baptiste was well prepared. "I have taken the name of God in vain three times, Father." He shifted slightly on his knees in the dark confessional.

"Yes, my son."

"Once I had a good reason, Father."

"There are no good reasons to curse God, my son. He is our creator and our saviour."

"But Yves threw something at me, Father, and it hit me

in the eye. I yelled ... I took the name of God in vain. It was a piece of cow-shit, Father."

A long pause. "Have you other sins, son?"

"I screamed at my father once, Father."

"Yes, my son?"

"I stole a chaw of tobacco from Governor Clark, Father. It made me sick."

"Any other sins, my son?" A long pause. "Remember, you have the sins of a lifetime to atone for. This is your first confession."

"I'm not certain about something, Father."

"You may ask a question."

"What are impure thoughts, Father?"

"They are thoughts of lewdness, my son." No response. "Thoughts of sex."

"I think I've had impure thoughts, Father. Impure thoughts about Saint Maria Goretti."

"About whom, my son?"

"Saint Maria Goretti, Father."

A long pause. "What is the nature of those thoughts?"

"Well, when she was thirteen, Father, she chose to be killed rather than to be touched by a man in sex, Father." Pause. "I imagine that I'm giving her the choice, Father, and I have a sword, and whenever she chooses death instead of sex, I strip her, Father, and I. . . ." Baptiste heard a rustling on the other side of the window. He wondered if the priest might fly out of the confessional and pounce on him.

"You know, Father."

"Yes."

"And sometimes," Baptiste plunged on, "she chooses sex and I run her through."

"Are these thoughts willful, my son?"

"Father?"

"Do you will these thoughts, my son, or do they just come on their own?"

"They come, Father, they just come. I don't want them. I fight them. They come when I'm in bed, Father."

"Are you sure, my son?" A long pause. "It is much more offensive in the sight of God if we will such thoughts, my son."

"I'm not sure, Father. I don't think I do."

"Do you wish to confess anything more, my son?"

"No, Father."

"Teo absolvo," the priest began. Baptiste crossed himself and said a rapid Act of Contrition, as carelessly as though he had been saying it for years. The priest gave him ten "Hail, Mary's" to recite as penance and suggested that he think, before coming back, about whether he willed his impure thoughts.

Baptiste flung back the heavy cathedral door and ran into the sunlight. He jumped across an imaginary mud puddle. He had this priest set up. He would think up some good stories for him.

MAY, 1816: When the days were getting long and the evening light lay in a soft glow on the wide river, Jim and Baptiste lounged on the sand beach in the late afternoons. They were watching the rivermen unload a keelboat one afternoon, hauling sugar and molasses from New Orleans and coffee from South America, when Baptiste decided to ·check out an idea. He went up to two men who were taking a huge barrel across a gangplank.

"Hey," he yelled. No answer. The men kept working. "Hey, how can a fellow get work around here?" The taller of the two workers looked at him oddly. Then they dollied the barrel onto the levee, ignoring the boys. After a moment they came back.

"Work ye'd like, would ye? And what sort of work?" The man speaking was about forty-five, tall, heavy, dark, and sallow, as though he had been raised on ague and fever. He looked grave, and he moved and spoke very slowly. He was not smiling.

"Any work," answered Baptiste, feeling a little scared now.

"Hang around," said the tall man in an accent that was Kentuck', "and we'll see what we can do." The shorter man grinned.

Baptiste was thrilled, and Jim impressed. They waited.

An hour later, just at dark, the workers quit. The two men came over. "I am called Mike," said the tall one, "Mike Fink. This is Bill."

"Jean," said Baptiste distinctly, offering his hand. "And Jim," he indicated with a nod. They shook ceremoniously all around.

"Boys," said Mike, "we've nothing for ye now.. But come back tomorrow before dusk and we'll think of something."

"I mean boat work," said Baptiste, realizing Mike misunderstood. "I want to be a boatman and go to New Orleans and Pittsburgh and Ohio."

Mike grinned. "À *demain*, Jean," Mike waved, and walked away. A man of wide travels, he had a few words of the boy's language to show off. "Meet us in front of the Row," he called back, pointing.

Battle Row was a flank of two-story buildings at the north end of the levee. Intended as stores, the buildings were also serving as lodging houses and taverns for the deckhands; the limestone buildings, with high-peaked roofs and dormer windows with heavy double shutters, were getting disreputable. Welch, showing his pupils the levee, had pointed out the beams projecting from the tops of the windows. They were meant, he explained, for holding hoisting tackles, but they ought to be used for hoisting the thugs of Battle Row by the neck.

Baptiste and Jim arrived two hours before dusk. They had never met anyone who lived on the Row before. It was a quiet afternoon there. Most of the hands were not working—they were waiting for the next job—so they were playing. Some were pitching quoits—flattish iron rings that they tossed at sticks jammed into the ground, trying to see who could pitch the ring around the stick or get it closest. Some were playing euchre outside the houses. Some were wrestling—matches of throws. Most were drinking.

They found Mike and Bill down by the river just north of the Row, watching some men shoot at planks stuck in the sand. "Hallo Jean, Jim," Mike cried with a toothy grin. He was stretched out. Between him and Bill was a girl of about 17, dirty and tough-looking. Mike nipped at her ear with his fingers, and she brushed his hand away half-impatiently. She was fixed on the shooting match. Everyone watched for a moment. The rifles of the day were huge—they shot lead balls half an inch in diameter—but not accurate in amateur hands. The Kentucky long rifles looked slender and graceful; some of the others, much heavier, were thick and short. It took a good man, a fellow who could judge the arc of the ball and the effect of the wind, to hit much of anything. These three men were hitting the boards regularly. "They some'p'n, ain't they?" said the girl.

"This be Blue," said Bill to the boys. "Pittsburgh Blue.

She just come down from Pittsburgh with us, and she don't know nothin' yet."

Mike lay back and looked at the sky unconcernedly. "Blue's a good woman," said Bill, and looked at Baptiste and Jim. "But you boys look a mite young to check that out."

Mike looked at them with interest. "How old you be?" he asked.

The boys said "twelve" at the same time. Both were lying by a year.

"Then you are now men," Mike said, "or soon men." He put a big paw on his crotch. "You have balls," he said. "Soon you have a man's cock." He looked at them straight on, seriously. "You have a man's cock," he said, "you are a man. Take no shit from no man." He was making the French-Canadian accent thick for Baptiste's benefit.

The boys just looked back at him. Mike was looking at the sky again. Everyone just lay there for a while.

Mike yawned and stretched. "Ah, you wanted to work. You ready?"

"Sure," the boys said in unison.

"O.K. Bill, you ready to die?"

"Sure."

"I am ready to die," Mike declared easily, and stood up.

"Your job," Mike said, "is to fill a cup with whisky. Can you do it?" The boys nodded. "Afterwards maybe you carry one of us to the cathedral and dump the body on the Bishop's doorstep. That is if we miss."

Mike and Bill picked up their long rifles off the sand and began loading them. They poured powder down the barrel, patched, rammed the balls home, primed the tiny hole between the flint and the powder, checked the flint. Bill handed Baptiste a stone jug. It reeked. Mike grabbed it and swigged deep. "You kill me first," he said to Bill, and handed him the jug. Bill swigged. Blue was sitting up now and looking from man to man intently and with a slight smile.

Mike walked fifty slow steps away. Bill handed the jug back to Baptiste along with a tin cup. "John," he instructed, "you fill this cup with whisky. Then carry it down to Mike—don't spill any now—and put it on his head. Then stand back."

Baptiste tiptoed toward Mike, holding the cup with both hands and staring at the sloshing liquid. When he got there, Mike was squatting down, ready for the cup. Baptiste placed it carefully, and Mike slowly stood up. The cup stayed.

Mike began to bellow a boatman's song in French. Baptiste stared at him. Mike was singing at the top of his lungs, and looking about to grin.

"Stand off, John," Baptiste heard Bill yelling. He had forgotten. He jumped back a little. Bill raised the rifle at the other end, and spent a long time sighting. Baptiste wanted to run and hide. He was about to cry when he heard the roar, and the cup went zinging off Mike's head.

Mike grinned hugely, wiped the back of his neck with his fingers, and licked the whisky off. "It always gets me wet," he told Baptiste, and they walked back.

Jim got to go down with Bill with the whisky and put it on his head. Mike made a ceremony of the shot. He stuck a finger in his mouth, tested the wind, and wiped the finger on his pants. He held the rifle straight for a long time. "Damn barrel's crooked," he said. He squeezed slowly, there was an explosion, and the barrel flew up over Mike's head. Mike saw Baptiste staring at him. " 'It's O.K.," he said, nodding. "Look down there." Baptiste saw Bill picking the cup up from the sand.

They all lay down again, and Mike, Bill, and Blue swigged from the jug. Blue was lit with sass now.

Baptiste smelled in the air that he and Jim might have to leave. He got his mouth organ out of his pocket.

"That's some'p'n," Blue said to Mike.

"Next time you have the cup," Mike said.

"I can go it."

Baptiste started playing one of the rivermen's songs he knew. No one said anything. He played it all the way through, and then put the mouth organ back without looking at Mike.

"That's fine," said Bill.

"You got a job as a boat band one day," said Mike. "But now you gotta go. We're gonna fuck."

The boys walked silently across the levee in the half light. At the far end of the levee Jim said, "That's some'p'n, all right."

Chapter Three

1821

1819: Financial panic caused the closing of banks, fore-closing on Western lands, and the slowing of westward immigration through most of the 1820s.

1820, MARCH 3: The Missouri Compromise admitted Missouri as a state and prohibited slavery in most areas of the Louisiana Territory.

1821: William Becknell pioneered the Santa Fe Trail.

1821: Over the next decade coffee became a popular beverage in America, despite temperance efforts against it; some people considered it an aphrodisiac.

Eighteen Hundred Twenty-One

MARCH, 1821: Baptiste, Jim, and Winney ran to see where the singing came from. It was a Canadian boat song lifted by a lot of voices, blocks from the river in a middle-class French section. The house had tall windows and sat almost on the street, so they could see inside well. The parlor was jammed with people—a lot of girls elaborately decked out, some fashionable older men and women, and a lot of young bloods. Winney, who was two years older than her brother Jim and had been around more, said, "It's their damn pancake frolic."

"They do that during Lent," Baptiste added, "when they can't dance."

> High row, the boatmen row,
> Floatin' down the river, the Ohio!
> The boatmen dance, the boatman sing,
> The boatman up to ev'rything.
> When the boatman gets on shore,
> He spends his money and works for more.
> Dance the boatman dance,
> Oh, dance the boatman dance,
> Oh, dance all night, till broad day light,
> Go home with the gals in the morning.

> When you go to the boatman's ball,
> Dance with my wife or not at all,
> Sky-blue jacket, tarpaulin hat,
> Look out, my boys, for the nine tail cat.
> Dance the boatman dance,
> Oh, dance the boatman dance,
> Oh, dance all night, till broad day light,
> Go home with the gals in the morning.

The song was sung in French, and everyone was roaring, led by a fellow who didn't care about prohibitions and danced alone. The girls and the older adults were French society, but the young men were of every class and nationality. They paid to get in, to cover expenses.

When the song ended, a rough-looking fellow dressed like a fur trapper started to tell a story about his adventures among the Indians. But then someone cried out and everyone gathered around a long table, the young men and girls in couples. An old man flipped a pancake, paper-thin, into the air and caught it, done side up, in a frying pan. With the other hand he flipped another one, managing the two pans with marvelous dexterity. Neither the cook nor the diners were allowed to touch these pancakes with a knife, fork, or spoon—fingers only. The young men grabbed the pancakes out of the hot pans, handed them to their ladies, who held them by an edge and dashed to be the first to dip into the molasses and start the whole process again. In a few minutes molasses was running down the fronts of shirts and dresses. It made Baptiste hungry.

"C'mon," he said, and started for the door.

"They ain't goin' to have nothin' to do with us," Winney said sharply. She always talked like she knew best.

But Baptiste would try anything in front of Jim. He took out his mouth organ and stood by the front door playing as loudly as possible the Canadian boat song they had just heard. He played it all the way through, and nothing happened. No one came. He started playing it again, and rapped on the door. Jim and Winney fidgeted.

A matronly woman of about fifty swung the door open with a smile. Then she scowled. "What do you want?" she asked. Baptiste kept playing, but since he was the closest, she pulled his hand away from his mouth and repeated the question.

"We just thought the pancakes looked good," said Baptiste in his most polished French.

The woman simply closed the door.

"You see," jeered Winney," we niggers. And you breed. Ain't no white folks gonna invite us."

"Maybe it's just because we're too young," said Baptiste.

"Humphf," Winney sounded.

It spoiled the evening, and they split and went home.

Winney always jeered at Baptiste for thinking he was smart, and for not knowing how those white folks were taking him in just so they could throw him out. Baptiste was tall, though too thin, and graceful, and had a winning flash of smile. He thought Winney noticed, despite her air of superiority.

He found her walking toward the Row one afternoon without Jim.

"Where are you going?" Baptiste used his high-falutin'-style English to tease her sometimes.

"To the Row, boy." She kept walking.

"What for?"

"Gonna get some'n'." He fell into stride with her, but she stepped ahead. "You ain't man enough to get it. Or give it." She flared her nostrils.

Baptiste was ready for her this time. "I'm man enough to whitewash your tonsils," he said, trying to fix her in the eye.

"You dirty mind," she said, and laughed. She was still walking backwards in front of him. "I'm goin' after whisky. Man I know down there's got some for me. Just whisky, that's all." She turned and ran off, laughing.

MAY, 1821: Baptiste sat down and leaned against the outside wall, to the side of the swinging sign that read Green Tree Tavern. He was lonely—Jim and Winney seemed to have disappeared, Clark was away on government business, and he was too shy to go to the Row for Mike and Bill and Blue.

There was always fun inside the tavern. Warren Ayres, the municipal politician who owned it, made everybody welcome. It had a big yard in back for wagons and it was filled every night with farmers and drovers and traders. Besides boozing, they sang heartily and told tall stories. Baptiste had never been inside. He put his mouth organ to his lips and began to play "All the Way to Shawnee Town Long Time Ago." It was Mike's favorite, and if Mike was in St. Louis, he would be in the tavern.

He felt a hand on his head. Blue was smiling sassily down at him.

"Evenin', John." She looked at him a long minute, and then decided. "I'm goin' to join the party. Why don't you come with me?"

She stopped inside the door, ran her eyes around the

room, and headed for a corner table. Baptiste, sixteen now and taller than Blue, put an arm around her waist and made to guide her. "Mike and Bill are to cards," she said, nodding toward the back, "and I don't feel like socializin'."

Baptiste waved at a waiter. "Who's your friend, Blue?" the waiter asked, with a suspicious eye at Baptiste. Baptiste started to order something but Blue cut him off. "He's O.K. Whisky, and sassafrass for him."

Baptiste looked at Blue, wanting to catch her eye and then say something clever to her and get things going, but her eyes were flitting past him and around the room. The drinks came. Blue hadn't said anything, and Baptiste was feeling confused. Finally she looked at him and smiled, realizing. "You make some fine music on that thang. Give us a tune."

So Baptiste blew "Shawnee Town" again, the verse bouncing, the chorus wailing plaintively but prettily. In the chorus he got up his courage and looked at Blue. She was staring into her whisky. He kept looking, hoping she would raise her eyes. Then he realized that she was avoiding someone. When he finished a heavy hand clapped him on the shoulder.

"I lof that song, boy," he heard, and a big man drew a chair beside him and thumped down. The hand clapped him again. The man was huge—pot-bellied, thick-legged, with a chest as big as his stomach and biceps the size of hams. He stood way over six feet and must have weighed, Baptiste thought, 250 or 300 pounds. He was Baptiste's idea of a giant.

"What news, Blue?" the big fellow asked, his huge arm around Baptiste.

"It's trouble, Dutch," Blue said flatly.

"Dutch Krieger, boy," the fellow said, and offered Baptiste a hand.

"John." Baptiste shook it.

"How come you think the lady doesn't introduce us, huh?" Baptiste recognized the accent as like the German market peddler's. Dutch called for drinks. Baptiste thought Blue eased a little closer to him.

"Who is this boy, Blue?"

"He's a breed, and he ain't no boy." Her eyes played over Baptiste's face. "At least I don't think so." She rubbed his knee.

"You a lot off woman, Blue." She avoided his eyes.

No one said anything for a while, and Blue left her hand on Baptiste's knee. A shout came up from one of the tables in the back, and Baptiste recognized Mike's angry voice. Dutch ordered another round and chugalugged his. He was getting flushed.

"You go with me tonight, Blue?" Dutch asked, trying to grin.

"Mike and Bill just got in this morning."

"But they do not come to you. They play all day here, and they lose."

Blue ignored him.

"Also they drink." Dutch clapped Baptiste again, and hit Blue's hand on his knee. He didn't seem to notice. "Do not drunk too much, boy. A man no good for woman when he drunk."

Blue stood up, taking Baptiste by the hand, and said, "Let's watch the game."

They drew up chairs. Dutch hulked behind them. Bill acknowledged them with a quick look. Mike ignored them. Blue warned Baptiste with a finger to say nothing.

The game of euchre went on endlessly. They took cards, put out money, raked in money. Baptiste didn't understand it. Occasionally someone would curse quietly. Otherwise nothing was said. A lot of glasses were filled and emptied. Bill seemed to be winning, Mike losing. Baptiste noticed after a while that Dutch had draped his big paws over Blue's shoulders, his fingers nearing her breasts. Bill, on the opposite side of the table, glanced up. Baptiste judged that Mike, sitting just in front of them with his back turned, didn't notice. Baptiste started getting sleepy.

He woke up when Blue touched him on the knee. He was conscious of the words Mike had just spoken: "Women need a delicate touch, *nicht wahr*, Bill?"

"I believe so."

"Some men are oafs, *nicht wahr?*"

"Yup."

A man leaned forward and slid coins off the table. Another edged back in his chair.

Mike lunged backward, knocking Blue one way and Baptiste the other. He hit Dutch in the chest with the flats of his hands. The big man lost his balance. Baptiste, crawling away on the floor, saw Mike club Dutch on the shoulder with hands locked together, then with an elbow to the mouth. Dutch reeled against a wall. Mike kicked him in the stomach, and he fell. Mike pounced on him, but Dutch flung him off. As Dutch got onto his knees, Bill kicked him in the ribs. Dutch twisted Bill's leg, and Bill toppled. Mike butted Dutch from the blind side, and the big man fell sideways. Mike grabbed his head with both hands, and bit Dutch's ear. Dutch screamed. Baptiste saw blood around the ear.

Then Baptiste felt Blue pulling him away. "C'mon, quick," she said.

They ran through the cold evening air toward the Row. Blue, in the room where she boarded, piled blankets on Baptiste's arms, and hurried him out. Then they sat down on some rocks at the far end of the Row along the river and waited. For a long time they just sat.

"Was it because of you?" Baptiste asked.

"No, Mike just wanted to." She looked at him, and her eyes got softer. "You don't have to stay," she said.

"I'll stay."

"Right. Hope they get here quick. If not, they in jail."

Blue stood up when she saw them. They were walking, not running, but moving loosely and fast. The four walked up the river a quarter-mile in the dark—Baptiste couldn't see, and wondered that they didn't pick their way more carefully—and spread their blankets. Mike handed Blue a bottle.

"Lew"—Lew was the bartender—"was glad to let me steal it to get us out," he grinned. The three drank for a while in silence. The moon rose, and Baptiste could see better.

"I feel good," Mike said, and stretched. "God, I feel good."

"And I left Levi some'p'n to remember me by." Mike grinned toothily and swigged long and deep. He was half horse and half alligator, as the saying was.

Baptiste thought that Mike and Bill would have something to remember the fight by, too. Mike had a long, nasty gash running out of his hairline halfway to an eyebrow. Bill's face looked puffy and bruised.

"How big's the furniture bill?" Blue asked.

Mike fixed her sharply. "Don't matter, woman." He looked at her a long time. "I feel very, very good," he said, and gestured with his head sideways. Blue took a blanket in one hand, put the other around Mike, and they walked off into the dark.

Baptiste's eyes felt very dry. He rubbed them and looked around. The sun was several hours high. It glanced off the water and hurt his eyes, so he turned away. Blue and Bill were gone. Mike was snoring loudly next to him.

He sat cross-legged and watched Mike for a long time. Then he discovered Mike looking at him. "You missing school," Mike said.

"Doesn't matter."

Mike looked up at the sky for a long time. Finally he stood up stiffly and awkwardly and picked up his blankets. Baptiste fell in beside him, walking back downriver.

"How come it felt good, Mike?"

"Ah," exclaimed Mike, "it always feels good. Don't you ever feel that? Want to hit a man? To kick him, to bite him? Sometimes a man busts open with that." Mike was shaking a fist and grinning. "You ever feel that?"

"Yeah, I guess so," said Baptiste.

"Sure, Jean, it feels good."

"I am disappointed in you, Paump." Clark was looking at him somberly across the big walnut desk. Clark said nothing more, so Baptiste stood up to leave. Clark had gotten word from Honoré that Baptiste stayed out all night and hadn't gone to school the next day, worrying everyone half to death. So Clark had announced his decision. Honoré does not supervise you adequately, he said. You are hanging out with low friends. I must go against your father's wishes in this instance. I have made the arrangements. You must go back to Reverend Welch.

Clark called him back before he got out of the room. "Don't take it too hard, Paump. I think this is best for you anyway. You are just finding yourself, and I know that you will make us all proud of you."

"Yes, Sir." Baptiste didn't give that much of a damn about what school he went to. He knew, though, that Welch would be hard to slip away from. And he was hurt at Clark.

Isaiah went to Honoré's later that day and packed his belongings over to Welch's house.

Mrs. Welch greeted him happily. Even Welch seemed pleased, though Baptiste thought the Reverend might just be gloating over the failure of the papists. Mrs. Welch got him started on his clavichord lessons again, and Baptiste liked that. Welch was irksome, but Baptiste got even with him by littering the Bible lessons with words like "sacrament," "eucharist," "confession," and "indulgence." Within a week he had some of his freedom back. He got permission from Clark to clerk at the gunsmith shop Clark owned. That gave him an excuse to stay away from the Welch's. He spent part of his time learning to play euchre and seven-up with Jim and Winney. Jim was apprenticed to a blacksmith now. Winney had turned into a nice-looking girl, all willowy, and she was still a tease.

He got back down to the Row after about three weeks.

"Hi, Good-lookin'," Blue greeted him.

"Hello, Jean," Mike bellowed, and grabbed him by the top of the head and shook him. Bill, stretched out on the bed of the cheap room, lifted a hand lazily.

Baptiste told them about his bad luck in getting sentenced to Welch's school.

"Ah, it's not square," Mike exclaimed. "They push you around because you're Indian. You gotta stomp 'em. Let'em know you're yer own man."

"Injun kid's damn lucky to larn readin' and writin'," Bill muttered. "I cain't read nor write. I don' know nothin'."

Silence stopped them for a moment.

"You're jest drunk, Bill," said Blue. "And jealous. This boy's sexier 'n' you are."

Bill humphed.

Everyone sat quiet, waiting for the breeze to come up or the sun to go down or the river to flow backward or someone to get a card game started. It was late afternoon, a lazy and restless time of day before the evening's play got started. Mike, Bill, and Blue, bored, were getting tanked. Baptiste plopped down next to Blue, who was sitting on the floor propped against a wall. She leaned her head against his shoulder. After a moment Baptiste wondered if she were asleep.

"Bill, she's rough with you. And now look at her scrunched up." Mike nodded at Blue and Baptiste.

"Woman needs to have fear put in her," said Bill. But he didn't sound like he cared.

Mike was getting antsy. The minutes slipping by were

pricking at him one by one. Someone rapped on the open door.

It was a gangly, warped-looking young man—slightly humped in the back, slightly splayed out in the hips, his muscles odd bumps on his arms. He smiled fatuously, showing his buck teeth. " 'Lo there. You Mike Fink?" Mike nodded. He could tell by the smell that the fellow was a farmer, and he held farmers in contempt. "And Bill Carpenter?" Bill looked sideways and grunted.

"Well, my friend and I hear tell"—a bent old man, his hide well dried, made himself seen behind the young man—"that you fellers do a cup shootin' trick that's fancy. Mighty fancy." He showed his buck-toothed smile again, and looked like he wanted to paw the doorsill. "Well, we'd sure like to see it, we would, yessirree."

Mike scowled and turned away. "We know that to do some'p'n like that, that's real dangerous and all, you got to be paid. And we got five dollars. Five dollars in gold."

Mike went to the door and looked out, nearly bumping the young man out of the doorway. He could see fifty to seventy-five people on the levee—some boatmen lounging around in front of the Row, some others unloading a keelboat, some merchants and clerks, some farmers hanging around to watch.

He turned to Bill. "Some àction, maybe." He grinned. He and Bill had been stone broke for two days.

He sent the young farmer and the old man to the boat to spread the word. He and Bill told a couple of the boatmen on the Row. They needed to stir up the action both ways. Then Mike and Bill whispered for a moment, looked at Blue, and laughed.

Mike bet the five dollars twice. So did Bill. They were sure about this first part. The crowd was gathering and murmuring, men were gesticulating, some men were accepting money to hold. Several small boys were crowding to the front. Baptiste stayed close to Mike and Bill until they took their stances and Blue filled the whisky cup.

Mike shot first—off-handed, without a rest, as was the bargain—and the crowd cheered when he sent the cup spinning. Then Mike insisted on collecting his bets, asserting that if he had to die, he wanted to die rich. Bill plunked the cup off his head just as easily. Everyone hurrahed again, even the losers.

Mike shouted for attention. He would offer everyone a

chance to win his money back, he said. He and Bill would attempt something much more difficult and much more dangerous. The crowd murmured. Mike strutted over to Blue. He lifted her skirt and put the cup between her legs just above the knees. Snickers ran through the crowd, but Mike shushed them with a scowl. He and Bill, he explained, would shoot the cup at the same time. At the same time. Difficult, because if either man shot first, the cup would fly out and would be hit only once. Then the bets would be lost. For this trick, he announced, the odds would be five to one, he would take five dollars to cover one dollar of his own. The crowd roared.

Mike and Bill circulated, taking bets. They now had twenty-five dollars between them. Mike bet all his share. Bill held back five dollars.

Baptiste had seen Blue stand for them several times, and knew that they had tried this trick in practice. This was their first time to put money on it. Whenever she stood for them, Blue's eyes seemed to get blacker, and she stood straight and shook her hair in the wind. Baptiste liked to see it.

Blue held her skirt up, higher than necessary for the trick, and looked defiantly at Mike and Bill. They stood fifteen or twenty feet apart, looking very relaxed. When they raised their long rifles, Baptiste called out the count.

The rifle barrels jerked toward the sky at the same moment. The cup tore from between Blue's legs. Mike frowned at Bill. "You a little quick," he said.

"You were a mite slow," Bill answered.

They were right. Just one hole in the cup. Mike paid off slowly and sullenly, fingering the coins.

When they had paid, Blue eased between Mike and Bill and took both their arms. They walked along for a moment, then Mike jerked his arm away and walked ahead. He spun around. "Bill," he said, smoldering, "let's get drunk."

Blue stopped and Bill walked on. Baptiste slipped up beside her, knowing better than to touch her now, and reached into his hip pocket. When Blue saw the flask, she took it, sniffed, and flashed him a big smile. Baptiste could still see the anger behind it.

The light had faded in the room, so that blue-gray shadows fell on the walls and the day bed and the cot and the pot-bellied stove. Blue had not lit the candles—she had

no camphene lamp—and she didn't seem to be thinking
about it. She was stretched crossways on the bed, half bol-
stered by the wall, and Baptiste was next to her. For an
hour or two they had sipped slowly, nursing what liquor
they had. Baptiste had never drunk more than a taste before, and he felt a bit giddy. Blue stood up abruptly,
stepped to the stove, and chunked a couple of pieces of
firewood. As she walked back, the half-light from the window caught her blue calico frock and made it seem to
bristle as it swished. She jutted her back against the wall
again beside him, tipped the flask high and held it for a
long moment, then let it drop onto the bed between them.
"That's the bottom of it," she said. Baptiste could see a
glint of eyes in the shadows of her face. She held his eyes
a while.

She reached across and put a hand on his flat belly. She
was facing him now, and close. Her hand slipped down to
his crotch. One firm squeeze and she felt him come hard.
She smiled into his face. "You ain't afeerd of me, are ya?
You ain't afeerd of any woman." She kissed him on the
lips, and her hand moved faster and harder. In his ear she
squeezed out, "Let's fuck."

Lying on the bed naked afterwards, he could feel her go
restless. Half-asleep or passed out, she was twitching and
tossing. He could never have slept. He could feel his heart
pounding, and his mind was racing calling up odd images
of his mother bending over a pot and of the taste of the
whisky and Welch's bad eye and the smell of burning
buffalo chips and the sound of *"Panis Angelicus"* and the
feeling of Blue warm and tight around him, images going
nowhere but just spinning out into the darkness. He wanted
to pound his chest or jump into the air or chop wood until
his arms fell off.

He got up, dressed, and slipped out into the cool night
and walked for a couple of hours. He sat on the sand. He
tried to play something on the mouth organ, but he was
too restless. After midnight he sneaked back into Welch's
house and went heavily to sleep on the floor of the detached kitchen.

He heard Mrs. Welch stirring at about dawn and
cleared out, grabbing some food on the way. He sat in
front of the Beckwourth house, the skimpy half of a du-
plex, and ate a roll. He had an idea. After an hour or so
he saw Jim leave for the blacksmith's shop.

"Picnic," he said to Winney at the front door, holding up the sausages and bread and grinning impishly.

She cocked her head sideways at him. "Why not?" she answered. "Take me a while," she said, glancing back into the house.

"At the bottom of the cliff path."

An hour later she came down the path to the bottom of the cliff that guarded the river below the levee, looking at him a little warily but with a big smile. He stood up and took her hand and started leading her along the bank downriver. She started to pull her hand back but looked at him oddly and left it.

"Got an idea," he said.

"Probably trouble, knowin' you."

"Goin' to Carondelet."

Half a mile down the river some heavy wooden flatboats were tied to crude docks, boats used for taking the big catfish out of the channel. Baptiste helped Winney in, pushed off quickly, and paddled slowly down under the cover of the high bank. He passed her last night's flask, now filled with snitched apple brandy, and she took a tentative pull, testing. He could feel her watching him when she thought he wouldn't notice.

He put in on a sizable point most of the way to Carondelet, the village of French poor who survived on odd jobs and booze. It was a well-wooded point, with deep, prickly grass, some brambles, and a thick stand of oak. They stretched on their backs in the sun, knees up like children, and munched the sausages.

"What do you do all day, Winney?"

"What can I do with myself?"

"You got do somethin'."

"Some'p'n ain't much if you a nigger." He let it pass. "My pa, he send some of his white money sometimes. Not much I can do but keep goin'. I do washin' once in a while, like Ma, but I hate that. I could wipe they kids asses for 'em in they fancy houses. But I don' wonna do that. Shit."

"You'll get married, I guess."

"Shit."

After a while he got out the brandy again. She drank without seeming to like it. She just lay there in the sun, watching him once in a while.

He got up on one elbow, leaned over her, and kissed

her on the lips. She didn't kiss him back, so he moved his lips around a little. She still didn't stir.

He drew back and looked at her. She said nothing, made no gesture, no move. He thought from her eyes that maybe she was laughing at him a little. He put a hand on her small tit and rubbed it. Still nothing. He reached under her skirt and felt and rubbed. Now he could see play in her eyes.

When he came to her, she was wild—bouncing, grabbing, clawing, daring him with her eyes to do more and do it harder. He did. He did her and rested and did her again. She never encouraged him or led him, always responded strongly, always dared him with her eyes. Much later, when he came at her again, she said " 'Nuff," turned onto her side and got up. "What's that?" she asked. Baptiste's hoop had fallen out of his shirt.

"Something my mother gave me."

"Stand for somp'n'?"

"Wards off evil spirits," he grinned.

"How come you keep it hid?"

"It's my secret medicine."

The wind and the current pushed at the boat and made the two miles back slow, tedious, and hard. Halfway, he put in and left the boat. They walked back in the settling dusk.

At her door Winney said only, "So long, John," and smiled.

He reflected, on the way home, that he was not her first. That dropped out of his mind, washed away by the thought of what he had done. He imagined himself coming over her. He felt the power again. He shot one arm in the air and yelled, for the whole street to hear, "Damn, I feel good."

Welch did beat him that night. He took off his heavy leather belt and strapped Baptiste on the legs with it. He did it in front of Mrs. Welch and the eight other boys, them just gawking. Baptiste felt himself hating Welch as the strap cut into his calves, but he just stared at the Reverend coldly. Welch turned the belt end for end and hit him with the cinch, which hurt deeply. Baptiste thought of hitting the bastard back, but he felt humiliated at being watched, so he couldn't hate completely.

He went straight to bed and lay there rubbing the welts

on his legs. He made up his mind that next time Welch beat him, he would lambast the bastard.

Baptiste was surprised the next morning that Welch did not send him to Clark. Welch intended to show that he could handle discipline by himself. Baptiste was glad he meant to try.

JULY, 1821: The next time Baptiste saw Blue, she was with Mike and Bill, and Baptiste felt uncomfortable around them. He drank some whisky sociably, to show that he knew how and to let them see something of a mysterious new air in him. He left before long. Blue had given no hint of what had happened, or what might yet happen.

He went down to the levee with Jim and Winney a couple of times and watched the keelboats being unloaded, joshing with the boatmen. Winney was as relaxed and easy as if they had never made it together. A couple of weeks later, though, he found her alone late in the afternoon. They screwed in the dark on the deck of one of the boats. Winney told him that she had done it on the deck of a boat before, but she wouldn't say with whom. She hinted that she had done it more than once.

He did take Blue again when Mike and Bill were gone up the Ohio, twice. The second time she said she didn't reckon he had any money. He answered that he didn't, so she said to bring her some whisky, or some'p'n anyway, next time he came.

SEPTEMBER, 1821: Welch had been sniping at Baptiste for a week: He was loafing, Welch muttered, or he was dawdling, or he was hanging out with low people. No telling what all he was up to, or rather he would stoop to. Baptiste knew perfectly well that "what all" meant boozing and whoring, which were so evil that Welch could only bring himself to hint darkly at them. Welch angled these grumblings at him obliquely. Baptiste turned a deaf ear.

On Thursday he was late for dinner—he'd been down to the levee. "It be disrespectful, boy," Welch said loudly, "not to show up here when you're supposed to." (*En famille* the language had by now switched from French to English, since St. Louis was, increasingly, an American city.) Baptiste just circled the table and took his accustomed place; he avoided Welch's eyes, and was careful to sit properly and not slouch. He doubted it would work this time.

Welch glared at him. "I'll see ye in private after dinner." Baptiste nodded; he didn't want to throw fuel on the fire.

"Why don't ye mind me when I speak, boy?" Welch said in the kitchen when the others had left. He was already starting to unhitch his leather belt.

Baptiste held up one hand pacifyingly. He held Welch's eyes for a moment. "I'd like to tell you," he said in his most adult tone. Welch was taken aback.

"Ordinarily I would listen to someone with more experience of the world than I have," Baptiste went on. "But I have good reason not to. You have told me fairy stories since I was small. You have misrepresented the world to me." He was surprised at how easily the words came out, and how measured they sounded. "You told me fairy stories about a God, Mr. Welch. Fairy stories about heaven and hell. About me being born sinful and rotten. About my mother being damned to hell."

He felt that he might explode with exhilaration: He was getting away with it. "You taught me to see things that aren't there. You taught me guilt and fear. When I wasn't old enough to question you, much less know better. That's a crime against a child, Mr. Welch. And I resent the hell out of it."

Welch looked stupefied. Baptiste wheeled and marched out of the house. Safe on the street, he started running. He walked evenly into Clark's house and asked permission to stay a couple of days.

Clark judged the situation shrewdly. From Welch he got hints of Baptiste's debauchery; from Baptiste he got exaggerated, passionate stories about Welch's tyranny. So Clark offered Baptiste a proposition: Paump could go to live with Honoré again; after all, he was nearly seventeen and didn't need chaperoning, and Clark wanted him out about the town to learn its ways. In return, Paump was to apply himself to lessons from Father Neil every morning, and was to start learning the fur trade in the afternoons. Clark would secure a position for him, and Paump might even get some pocket change from the job. Agreed.

The position, apprentice clerk, was with Berthold & Chouteau, merchants and fur traders. The company had three buildings—the Berthold house, which was a store on the first floor and a dwelling on the second, and two storage sheds east of the house close to the levee. Sometimes Baptiste would spend the afternoon bundling deerskins or beaver pelts (called "plews") for storage, or counting furs brought in and issuing warehouse receipts for them, or taking care of the stock at the rear of the store, or clerking for the buyers of linen, flour, clothes, nails, and other miscellaneous goods. He much preferred working in the front of the store. He found it easy and pleasant to chat with the ladies who came in, and to banter with their children. They seemed to like him: He was affable, quick with a quip, charming, and nice-looking—altogether a curiosity for an Indian.

Baptiste was learning something of the nature of power with Berthold & Chouteau. Bartholomew Berthold was an immigrant merchant. Born in the Italian Tyrol, he had made his way to St. Louis with some salable provision which the isolated frontier town needed and put himself into business. A few years later he married the daughter of Pierre Chouteau, Sr., a member of the landed French family headed by the patriarchal Auguste Chouteau. A little later, Berthold formed a partnership with Pierre Chouteau, Jr., and expanded into fur-trading.

The fur trade was the nerve center of St. Louis commerce. It provided the goods that the town traded to New Orleans (and to the eastern United States) for cloth, hemp, tobacco, whisky, screws, nails, molasses—everything needed for daily consumption. And it supplied the money for St. Louis and all of the Missouri Territory. Coined U.S. currency was scarce in the territory. Spanish *reales* and French *livres* were common, and had been accepted means of exchange for years. But that still left money, a commodity you could carry in your pocket and trade for goods, altogether short. Some banks had issued paper money, but it was of dubious value; merchants had, on their own, issued pieces of paper valid for exchange at the stores—but some of them took the liberty of handing out far more than they could redeem. So the fur companies issued "money" that gained wide circulation and confidence in the Territory—deerskin notes, or *bons*. When a trapper or hunter brought his skins to the warehouse, the clerk gave him a receipt for so many *bons*, good at St. Louis for so many *reales* or *livres* or *piastres*, and the trapper traded the receipts for goods. The fur merchants became the community's bankers.

Besides, the U.S. government intended to encourage the fur trade. Fur-trading in the great area of the Louisiana

Purchase would secure the claim of the U.S. to the vast territory, it would establish relations with the Indians—the hope was for peaceful relations—it would diminish British influence in the area and keep John Bull on his own side of the 49th parallel. So the names of the most influential men in St. Louis attached themselves to the trade: Chouteau, Berthold, Pratte, Lisa, Clark, Lewis (Meriwether's brother Reuben), Labbadie, Henry. Within two years General William Ashley would launch a major fur-trading enterprise, and not long after, Pratte, Berthold, and Chouteau would join hands with the biggest name of all, John Jacob Astor and his American Fur Company. The trade was patriotic, it was profitable, and, most of all, it was powerful.

Baptiste assembled hints and glimmerings during his afternoons with Berthold & Chouteau into a shadowy but large picture of power and influence in the world of the white men. His mother wanted him to discover the secret of the white man's big medicine. The first secret was knowledge; the second was enterprise; the third, subordinate but crucial, seemed to be social influence.

Baptiste was pleased one afternoon when he overheard one of the customers, the wife of a prominent American merchant, remark of him to another woman, "I wish more of our own young men had as much decorum." He was taking care to make himself charming to his customers, asking about their children, telling them what Mrs. So-and-so had said, and what the Such-and-such boy was doing. He dressed smartly, though he had to press Clark for money from the Bureau of Indian Affairs for his clothes. He was aware that he carried himself well and had certain social poise. He bided his time.

Baptiste still dropped around to see his friends—lazing with Jim and Winney, drinking with Mike, Bill, and Blue. He was popular among the trappers and the boatmen, and a welcome figure on occasion at the Green Tree Tavern, where he entertained everyone with dance music from his mouth organ. Sometimes, when Mike and Bill were away, he went to see Blue for the night on the Row, but his welcome there was unpredictable. Winney grew a little cold; she talked scornfully about his dalliance with the fashionable white world. Besides, she let him know she was mostly interested in putting out for pay. He and Jim also made a new friend—a tall, muscular, shy, awkward boy who was apprenticed to another blacksmith, Jim Bridger. They liked him, but he was slow and oddly serious, so not much fun.

Baptiste cleaved this part of his life cleanly away from the other part. He would work late at the store and then accept an invitation to dinner with the Bertholds upstairs before wandering over to the tavern for a late-hour drink. He contrived a couple of times to be invited to call, with the Bertholds, on Auguste Chouteau on Sunday afternoon. Chouteau claimed to remember their meeting at Clark's house some years ago, and complimented the young man expansively on his self-cultivation. Baptiste paid attention primarily to the men at these gatherings, because he felt a touch of frost when he attended the women and the girls. When he went to a few dances—dancing was the favorite pastime of the French community—he was careful to dance amiably and courteously with as many women as he could, including women old enough to be his mother. They invariably remarked on his politeness and deport- ment. But he scrupulously showed no personal interest in any eligible young woman. Sometimes, after dances, he went to the Row to sleep with Blue, or with Blue's friend Kiki.

JANUARY, 1822. On New Year's day, Baptiste made several resolves, among them to keep a diary. Father Neil had in- sisted that he keep a daily record of his moral progress for a long time—a log of achievements and lapses after the model of Ben Franklin—and Father had inspected it regu- larly. Now Baptiste started his own private record of progress by his own standards, which were social and material:

JANUARY 2: "Madame Berthold, having found me late at work in the store, invited me to accompany her upstairs to dinner, as indeed I hoped she would. However, made no headway with M. Berthold's reserve, but some with Mme. Berthold, by an effort (subtle, I hope and believe) to be entertaining."

JANUARY 5: "Worked late to no avail; found Kiki at the Green Tree. I told her (falsely) it was my birthday and she afforded me an unmentionable present. Drank too much and stayed too late; was listless all day at the ware- house; must maintaine caution."

JANUARY 7: "To the Bertholds again for dinner, a good evening: Talked at length with Coco, naturally under the eye of Mme. Berthold. Coco has the promise of a splended woman at 17—a full head of flambouyantly red hair, a slight but attractive figure, and a face that, if not beautiful, is always full of impishness and fun. Laughs rather too heavily; Mme. Berthold, I believe, would like to refine away that laugh and touch of the hoyden which remains in her character. She has a quick mind and is widely read, for a girl, and talks avidly about books. I wonder."

JANUARY 12: "At dinner with the Bertholds again (also on the 9th) which I hope and I believe will be an on-going event. Coco was pleased, I had almost finished the Plutarch's *Lives* which she lent me, and we had a lively discussion about the models it presents. Mme. Berthold was surprised, charmed, and amused that I had actually read it; I think she cannot quite believe that half-breeds can read, or else she takes their reading as an engaging parlor trick. Coco otherwise."

JANUARY 16: "General Clark comended me on my deportment today, and gave me $12 for new clothing of which I find myself truly in need."

JANUARY 16: "Told Coco that *Paradise Lost* was not to my liking; a declaration which may have marked me as somewhat barbarrous. Had not the courage to admit that I had even less regard for *Pilgrim's Progress*. This connection seems to be working out. If I succeed here, I believe it will prove an entrée to St. Louis's social world. A grand opportunity which I must not muff."

JANUARY 18: "We read Racine's *Phèdre* aloud tonight, Coco as Phèdre, myself and Francine the rest in some confusion. Mme. Berthold, kniting as she attended, was much amused by our performance, but complimented me on my French, perhaps condescendingly. I cannot sleep now for remembering what transpired during the evening, and perhaps more for dreaming of what may yet transpire between myself and Coco. Am I falling in love with her? I fear that. If I am to approach her, I must maintain complete poise. The ramifications could be most dangerous, and I must not permit myself to be transported on these waves of strong feelings, like a love-sick fool."

JANUARY 21: "Took *The Tempest*, which was not familiar to Coco, to read tonight. Hearing her quaint English reciting the bard's Ariel and Miranda was most droll; I myself rendered a vociferous Caliban which made Francine laugh."

JANUARY 22: "Rummed the plews in the warehouse today and got somewhat inebriated. The others rummers chuckled at my expense: They had not informed me that in rumming plews, as an antitoxin one must first rum oneself. Went to the Row in the evening for the first time in a long while."

JANUARY 24: "May have made an arse of myself at the Berthold's last night. After dinner, Coco and I converssing on the sofa, and I kept breathing the smell of her (some fine parfum no doubt bought from a Paris house, light, delicate, and sweet). She was most coquettish. I lost my tongue to the fool smell. I fear that Mme. Berthold may have opined that I comported myself like a doltish boy. Berthold always is down stairs at his ledgers. I *am* enamored of Coco. Would she lead me on just to spurn me? She appears to be too good-hearted for that. I cannot be sure, though; a *breed* cannot be sure."

JANUARY 25: "Fr. Neil reprimmanded me today that I have not applied myself 'accidously' (sp.?) to my lessons at the clavichord and the organ and to my studies. A just charge. I have the ability to go far, to be as cultured as any Frenchman in these parts, and I must not neglect the advantage."

JANUARY 27, 1822: His eye caught Coco through the window, heading into the store instead of going upstairs to the family apartment. "Call Louis from the back and come to the bookstore with me. It will be all right." He slipped his apron off and she gave him a big smile. "Canady told Papa my books are in. That's the Byron *Poems* and the *Ivanhoe*."

When they started back from the bookstore, it was in the half-light of an unseasonably warm day. They walked in a roundabout way to stay on paved streets. (The new paving made the old French residents curse because it broke their wooden cartwheels.) A thaw was on. There was no sense in getting muddy or getting splashed by passing wagons. There was also no reason to hurry.

Coco was leafing through the Byron. She stopped to read a short lyric aloud to Baptiste in her chirping English. He stood close so that he could see the page. When she looked up at him to say with her eyes how fine the last line was, he slipped an arm around her waist and kissed her tentatively. She pulled away and looked seriously at him. Then she kissed him back, and she meant it. He was kissing her more eagerly when she broke it off. She took his hand, touched his shoulder with her head for a moment, and they walked home. Baptiste was rampaging with elation and confusion and fear and eagerness. He was also embarrassed. His pants bulged like they were trying to hide a wagon tongue.

During dinner and in the parlor afterwards they were most discreet, sitting well apart and permitting themselves no more than sly looks. Baptiste did lapse into long silences a couple of times, awkward, ungracious, uncharacteristic silences. He was looking at Coco and wondering whether she was a virgin. He was afraid that would be a barrier. By the time Mme. Berthold proclaimed herself tired, he had made up his mind that she was a virgin, and that it would be a barrier. Coco managed to squeeze his hand quickly in the hall as he left—there wasn't time for more—and he didn't care about barriers. He was in love.

JANUARY 31: Baptiste's diary: "Am I the tinker's lame-brained, hare-lipped son? Four straight evenings have I been late at the Bertholds dallying with Coco—dallying because I have scarce more than kissed her *sweetly* on the lips. Why do I tap timorously on the *door* when I ought, like the intruder at Macbeth's gate, to cudgel it until it swings wide? I play the lackey in this affair, when I should be playing the knight gallant. If I try that, I may end up playing the knight errant. But I must, must, must try."

FEBRUARY 2: "A day of mixed clouds, foreshadowing nothing—*rien*. A splendid evening: No especial progress with Coco, though I think she turned away my explorations less promptly than before. Still I am transported. With her and her alone do I feel and believe that I can be happy, for the present, with stolen kisses; such extraordinary kisses they are. And there is her strict background to consider. Altogether I am a happy man, supremely happy when I can touch her and hear her voice."

FEBRUARY 4, 1822: Thinking it over, Mme Berthold reached a conclusion. Doubtless the flirtation was innocent, though looking at the Indian boy she sometimes wondered how innocent. She liked the boy, liked his adolescent graciousness and his obvious desire to please. But if the children intended to go beyond innocent play—Coco was no longer a child, really—she would have to put a stop to it. So when they went to Coco's room on the transparent premise of finding a book, she delayed for a few minutes and walked in on them.

They were only kissing, standing up by the bookcase. Not bad. They didn't notice her. "Coco," she said calmly, "this is out of the question." They sprang apart awkwardly. She ordered Baptiste to the parlor and stayed to talk with Coco. After five minutes she walked in magisterially and said, "Baptiste, we invited you here out of our generosity. You have betrayed our trust. What you've done is understandable, but improprietous. You must not return."

"Damn it," Baptiste started.

"I'm surprised," she cut him off, "that you've lost your sense of decorum. If you do it again, or if you try to see Coco in the future, I will speak to M. Berthold about your dismissal. Good night." And she stepped out of the room.

Baptiste was split by hurt and loss and fury. After a sleepless night, he sneaked a note to Coco: "I love you," the first time he had used those words. "If you love me, write to me through Fr. Neil."

For two days he heard nothing from her. On the third he marched into Berthold's office at the back of the store. "Monsieur Berthold, I wish to resign my position as clerk."

Berthold, who had not yet assimilated the hints of what had happened, looked stunned. "But Baptiste—"

"I was having an innocent romance with Coco. We were fools enough to believe that caring about each other mattered. Madame Berthold found us out and forbade us to see each other again." Berthold was too stupefied to speak. "One day," Baptiste said, "this continent will change. It will have to. Indians are just as good as whites."

On the street he felt good, really good, until he thought

of Coco again. That night he went to the Green Tree and got roaring drunk.

FEBRUARY 13, 1822: An advertisement published in the *Missouri Gazette & Public Advertiser*—along with the usual offerings of merchandise like liquors, mackerel, boots, bar iron, Indian goods, and cigars, and announcements that certain husbands would no longer be responsible for the debts of certain wives—created a hubbub in the frontier town of 5,000 souls:

TO
Enterprising Young Men

The subscriber wishes to engage ONE HUNDRED MEN, to ascend the river Missouri to its source, there to be employed for one, two or three years.—For particulars enquire of Major Andrew Henry, near the Lead Mines, in the County of Washington, (who will ascend with, and command the party) or to the subscriber at St. Louis.

Wm. H. Ashley

The subscriber, as everyone knew, was the lieutenant-governor of the state. General Ashley did not have to spell out the duties of the enterprising young men at the source of the Missouri: They'd be trading for the Indians' beaver. After a dozen years—since Manuel Lisa and the same Andrew Henry got chased out of the mountains by the Blackfeet—Ashley intended to push the fur trade again beyond the plains to the Stony Mountains.

The next day, in response to a note brought by Isaiah, Baptiste went to dinner at Clark's house. As he expected, it was a small birthday celebration. (Because Clark was out of town, and because of the upset with the Bertholds, his seventeenth birthday had passed unobserved on the 5th.)

"Paump," Clark began over his after-dinner brandy and cigar, "you saw General Ashley's offer yesterday?" Baptiste nodded. "It is an important enterprise, commercially and politically. Establishment of the fur trade in the Rockies proper is inevitable, and highly desirable. Those who get an early footing will reap the advantages later. I can secure a place for you if you'd like to go along."

Baptiste was already squirming. Iron traps and greasy skins were a long way from the clavichord, Byron's poetry, and attractive ladies. "I don't think so."

Clark raised an eyebrow, drew on his cigar, and blew the smoke out slowly. "The fur trade offers great opportunities for you. You have the background, you have the languages, you are familiar with Indians. Eventually the trade will penetrate even to the Shoshones, who would make you welcome. You don't have to trap—you can clerk, making use of your education. Some day I hope that you will become an Indian agent. The government needs men of understanding to help the Indians adjust. The fur trade would be an auspicious start."

"I feel that I have a great deal to learn here, Sir, for the present."

Clark considered. "I understand. If you continue with Berthold, will you agree to go up to the lower Missouri this summer to learn the operation of the posts?"

"Yes, Sir."

"Splendid." He relit his cigar.

"Sir, I must tell you that I am working for Pratte, not Berthold."

"What?"

"I resigned a week ago. Monsieur Berthold gave me a recommendation to Monsieur Pratte."

"Why'd you resign?"

"It was just over a little flirtation, Sir, entirely innocent, with Coco. Madame Berthold found us out and declared me unwelcome in their house." He just let the words sit there, bluntly. Clark waited for an explanation.

Baptiste's voice sounded harsh to himself, and he was afraid it would break. "Sir, I love Coco, at least I did love her. Now she doesn't communicate with me, but I think she loved me as well. Truly, I believe that Madame Berthold liked me. She ran me off, Sir, because I'm a breed. Nothing more. It's stupid, Sir. I hate it."

Clark cut him off. "You want to ask whether prejudice against Indians and breeds will change. Yes. Slowly. I will not see it. You may not see it. Baptiste, don't kick against the pricks. Don't. And engaging yourself with young white girls—particularly young white girls of standing—is not the way to make the peace that must be made."

For a moment Baptiste hated Clark. Then he wanted to cry. He kept it back.

He flung himself into his studies, amazing Father Neil with his ardor, staying up into the wee hours with books propped open, his eyes struggling to focus. He stole hours of practice on the clavichord at the rectory and sometimes to play the great cathedral organ. Father Neil noticed that he played with more expressiveness than Neil had previously heard from him, and thought the boy had a special gift. Despite Baptiste's ardor, Neil found him growing remote and impersonal, a strange contradiction.

Pratte found him the very model of correctness, with a formality odd in such a young man. Baptiste worked on the stock meticulously, and with the customers graciously; he seemed less conscientious in the fur-storage shed.

Baptiste took what invitations he could get to socialize, and occasionally sat in the parlors of the fine houses. Sometimes he visited his friends on the Row, sometimes had a drink with Jim, though the friendship had cooled. He dressed smartly at all times, and spiced his conversation with Latin proverbs and quotations from Shakespeare and Lord Byron, which amused the social set and the tavern bunch alike. Underneath all that, he concealed his rage.

Chapter Four

1823

1823: Charles J. Ingersoll defended American culture against criticism by British intellectuals in a lecture before the American Philosophical Society.

1823, DECEMBER 2: James Monroe proclaimed the Monroe Doctrine.

1824: Jedediah Strong Smith discovered South Pass, the gateway through the Rocky Mountains.

1824: Weavers in Pawtucket, R.I., held the first recorded strike in the U.S.

1825: Eight Northern legislatures proposed the emancipation of all slaves at federal expense; Southern states rejected the proposal.

1825, MARCH 4: The sixth President of the U.S., John Quincy Adams, was inaugurated.

1825, OCTOBER 26: The Erie Canal was officially opened to shipping.

Eighteen Hundred Twenty-Three

SEPTEMBER 1823: It was a lazy afternoon, an afternoon spliced between the dog days of late summer and the cool days of October when the maples, elms, and the great oaks turn color, an afternoon of Indian summer. Baptiste was sitting cross-legged on the east bank of the Missouri, his back against a cottonwood tree, enjoying his next-to-last afternoon before going back down the river to the city and to his job. He watched the muddy river ease by, lazing its way toward the Mississippi so slowly that it looked still. In places it eddied around and pushed up current for a moment, resisting the quiet but awesome force that took it to St. Louis.

Baptiste's mind was far away. He was practicing a song, one of the songs taught him by Broken Foot, an Osage medicine man, the summer before. He learned some of the old stories of the Osage and the Pawnee and the Sioux in his first summer, and he tried to learn the songs. They were difficult, because they were sung by men who had been given them in dreams. To sing them truly a man must have had the dream, must believe in the songs' sacred power to change events through incantation, must transform himself into a trance of belief that puts him in touch with the magical powers of the world. They were also difficult to sing because they were against the forms of the music that Baptiste knew; they ignored the mathematically measured rhythms and seemed to play devilishly with the twelve known pitches.

Baptiste took no stock in their magical powers, but he responded to the feelings in some of them. He had gotten them down in singing pretty well. He was trying, now, to transfer their sounds to his mouth organ.

The song he was playing, "The Song of the Maize," might be rendered into English like this:

Amid the earth, renewed in verdure,
Amid rising smoke, my grandfather's footprints
I see, as from place to place I wander.
The rising mist I see as I wander.
Amid all forms visible, the rising mist
I see, as I move from place to place.

Amid all forms visible, the little hills in rows
I see, as I move from place to place.

Amid all forms visible, the spreading blades
I see as I move from place to place.

Amid all forms visible, the light day
I see as I move from place to place.

In this song, the medicine men explained to him, the spirits of the dead were speaking of the coming of spring, the reawakening of the earth from the deadness of winter to fertility. In the morning mist they see the planted rows, the tiny blades of growing corn, the day itself and, most of all, the signs of the Great Spirit—grandfather's mysterious footsteps—whose power makes things grow.

Baptiste liked the simple appreciation of this power fundamental to life. But try as he might, he could not get the mouth organ to render its sound. The notes didn't fit the instrument, and his playing sounded like an approximation of the song without sounding like the song.

It had been a good summer, the first time in Indian country that he thought of himself as a grown man. He spent part of it moving with his father around the plains of the lower river—meaning below the mouth of the Platte—from tribe to tribe, and had spent a lot of it at Fort Kiowa and Fort Recovery. Old Charbonneau, who was now over sixty, found work mostly as an interpreter and errand-runner for the traders, and sometimes for the U.S. troops led by Colonel Leavenworth. Baptiste had met some of the Plains Indians and was mildly intrigued by them. He observed them as an outsider rather than as their blood kin: He liked their openness about sex—one chief was known for walking about the village naked and perpetually tumescent; most Indians told jokes for which "ribald" was too mild a word; and plenty of women were always available for a man who had the urge. He was amused by their emphasis on honor and the manly virtue of making war; he was appalled by their brutal violence, including their custom of dismembering the bodies of dead enemies. He was puzzled by their treatment of women, making drudges and beasts of burden of them generally, offering their bodies to other men for baubles, but punishing them severely if they committed adultery without permission. He was amused by their native spiritualism, their custom of seeking spirits behind all natural forces, their passionate belief in dreams, their serene trust in totem objects, their conviction of the magical power of word and song.

Yet it was the word and song that enchanted him most. He remembered hearing and seeing a rain dance:

> Hi-iya naiho-o! *The earth is rumbling*
> *From the beating of our basket drums.*
> *The earth is rumbling from the beating*
> *Of our basket drums, everywhere humming.*
> *Earth is rumbling, everywhere raining.*
>
> Hi-iya naiho-o! *Pluck out the feathers*
> *From the wing of the eagle and turn them*
> *Toward the east where lie the large clouds.*
> Hi-iya naiho-o! *Pluck out the soft down*
> *From the breast of the eagle and turn it*
> *Toward the west where sail the small clouds.*
> Hi-iya naiho-o! *Beneath the abode*
> *Of the rain gods it is thundering;*
> *Large corn is there.* Hi-iya naiho-o!
> *Beneath the abode of the rain gods*
> *It is raining; small corn is there.*

As he listened Baptiste had to smile at the singers' faith that the rumble of their drums would bring the rumble of thunder, that the cloudlike eagle down would bring the clouds, that the rain would fall and help the corn grow. But he did not smile at their singing. He listened to the chanting, the wailing, the high-pitched screeches, the plaintive calls, and he thought they had power. They were music. They were no more superstitious, he thought, than "Amazing Grace," and much more beautiful.

But he wasn't thinking of all this by the cottonwood tree. He was only trying to torture his mouth organ into making the corn song.

He heard the cloppings and stopped. Two horses, he thought. On the plains it could be important to know from the sound. He stood up to look.

"Did I hear what I thought I heard?" asked the young man. "An Indian song on a mouth organ?" He spoke English with a heavy German accent. He was wearing riding breeches with leather trim, expensive knee-length leather boots, and a proper riding coat. The other fellow, older, dressed similarly. Baptiste had never seen anything quite like them on the plains.

"You did, Sir. Jean-Baptiste Charbonneau," he introduced himself and shook both men's hands.

"You have the honor of standing before Paul, Prince of Württemberg," the older man said stiffly. "I am Heinrich Düsse." The younger man—the prince?—seemed amused by the proceedings.

"*Est-ce que vous parlez français?*" Baptiste wanted to make it easier for them.

"*Bien sûr,*" smiled the young man. "And do Indians of America," he went on in French, "speak perfect French and English?"

"I have," Baptiste nodded deferentially, "English, French, Latin, Mandan, Minataree, some Shoshone, Sioux, and Pawnee, figures, history, theology, a General as my benefactor, a derelict as my father, a squaw as my mother, and a great respect for Your Highness."

It worked. Paul laughed.

"We are on our way to the house of Messieurs Woods and Curtis, fur traders. Is this the way?" asked the prince.

"It's less than a mile downstream, up the hill. I am staying there. May I show you the way?"

"With pleasure. And will you give us more of your Indian song?"

Baptiste walked and played the "Corn Song." His mind was working furiously. A prince. And perhaps for himself, a *deus ex machina?*

Over dinner the two exchanged their stories. Baptiste, at his most fluent and entertaining, told of being carried on Sacajawea's back on the Lewis and Clark expedition, of his early years among the Indians, of his education in St. Louis (which he exaggerated slightly), of William Clark, of his experience in the fur trade.

Prince Paul was inclined to be reticent about himself. He was the second son of Duke Eugen of Württemberg, the brother of King Friedrich I of Württemberg. He had fought on the side of Prussia in the post-Napoleonic Wars of Liberation, but he was by preference a naturalist. He had come to North America to observe the flora and fauna, and to make notes about the peoples and their ways—strictly a scientific expedition, he assured Baptiste. But Baptiste gathered that he was a hardy and venturesome traveler: He had been to Cuba, New Orleans, up the Ohio, and to St. Louis. He had come up the Missouri with a boat provided by the Chouteau brothers, bound for Fort Kiowa. He was riding downriver among the banks ahead of the boat though, with only three retainers, a countryman, a Creole guide, and a half-breed who liked his liquor. So he was running some risk from the Osages, the Kansas, and the warlike Iowas. Baptiste judged him to be in his mid-twenties.

The prince spoke carefully and formally, always as though he were at some official meeting. He was curious about Baptiste, about his mixed blood, about his education, about his acceptance in St. Louis, about his plans for the future.

Baptiste, trying to answer, was becoming more and more aware that he was talking to a prince, an actual prince. He had never heard of Württemberg, and wasn't sure whether he remembered Stuttgart, its capital. But this was a king. His mind, slightly intoxicated with exotic, regal perfumes, swam with fragments of memories of Queen Elizabeth and Julius Caesar and Napoleon. A man to put the mere Chouteaus, Prattes, Bertholds, Ashleys, and Clarks to shame. He wondered, as he spoke hesitantly of rising as a clerk in the fur trade, what the odds would be of a half-breed boy becoming first the protégé of William Clark, United States Superintendent of Indian Affairs, and then meeting a prince. Baptiste wanted to laugh crazily.

Paul listened politely, then withdrew to talk to Curtis before dinner.

Grand Louis strutted up in time to eat. Louis, a big French-Canadian with a Creole wife, was the head man of the area. Of course, the area was small. There were a half-dozen cabins (including Louis's) five miles below the mouth of the Kansas, hunters with squaws, who lived by their rifles and by raising a few cattle, hogs, and chickens. The nearest settlement of any size was Liberty, in the state of Missouri, several miles below the cabins. Louis was a braggart, a daredevil, a man who loved to raise hell with whisky and women, and a damned good hunter. Paul had stopped at his place earlier, and Louis clearly intended to pursue the acquaintance, very sure that he himself was the most interesting natural phenomenon of the territory.

"D'ye hear tell of John Colter?" Louis began ceremonially after dinner. They had their chairs tipped back around the cookstove, and Baptiste saw that everyone was in for a spell of yarn-spinning. Louis recited the Colter yarn with some flair and more than a few embellishments: How Colter didn't go home with Lewis and Clark, but stayed in the mountains. How he lived with the Crows and crossed the Continental Divide alone. How he wandered into strange b'ilin's around Yellowstone, and seen clay and b'ilin' water throwed into the air, and smelled hell-fire just beneath the ground, and saw flames, and cleared straight out lest he run into the Old Gentleman himself. Also the time he got caught by the damned Blackfeet and they stripped him jaybird nekked and give him a start runnin', and he run six miles and outrun 'em all and hid in a beaver dam, near freezin' to death, and got away. It was a handsome tale, but Baptiste had heard it before. Besides, he was feeling edgy, left out.

Woods told a story about two *voyageurs* who had come up the river the spring before. He heard that the prince was a fine shot, Woods said, and won the prizes at the shoot down to Liberty. Wall, these fellows was some shots, this Fink and Carpenter. (Baptiste paid attention now. He'd had no news of Mike and Bill since they went to the mountains with Ashley the year before, and Jim Beckworth went with them.) Woods told how they amazed some Kansas Injuns, who looked a little like they'd a mind to fight, by shooting cups of whisky off each other's heads. They'd won buckskins and mokkersons and two women for each for the night, too.

Baptiste decided to risk it. "The Osage have a story about the origin of creation," he ventured. "It doesn't have the drama of Genesis, but it's curious." He saw that the locals were impatient with him, but Paul and the other German looked interested.

"Way beyond," he started, "some of the Osage lived in the sky. They wanted to know their origin, how they came to exist. They went to the sun, and he told them that they were his children. They went to the moon, and she told

them that she gave birth to them, and that the sun was
their father. Then she told them that they had to go down
to the earth and live there.

"They came to the earth, but it was covered with water.
They couldn't go back, and they didn't know what to do.
They wept. They floated around in the air, hoping that
some god would send them an answer, but none came.
The animals were floating around too, and one of them
was the elk, the most handsome and stately, who inspired
all creatures with confidence. So they asked the elk for
help. He dropped into the water and started sinking. Then
he called out to the winds, and they came from all quar-
ters and blew the waters up into mists.

"At first only rocks showed, and the people and animals
walked on rocky places where nothing grew and they had
nothing to eat. Then the water went down and exposed the
soft earth. When that happened, the elk was so happy that
he rolled over and over on the soft earth, and all his loose
hairs clung to the soil. The hairs grew, and from them
sprang beans, corn, potatoes, and wild turnips, and then
all the grasses and trees."

The prince clapped his hands. "Marvelous, *wunderbar!*
Do you know more?"

Baptiste thought for a minute. "I can sing you a song,"
he offered. "I heard it from a priest who came up from
Santa Fe, and he got it from the Indians." Baptiste wasn't
ready to try the mouth organ yet and, throwing back his
head, he went into a wailing chant:

> Tsegihi.
> *House made of dawn.*
> *House made of evening light.*
> *House made of the dark cloud.*
> *House made of male rain.*
> *House made of dark mist.*
> *House made of female rain.*
> *House made of pollen.*
> *House made of grasshoppers*
> *Dark cloud is at the door.*
> *The trail out of it is dark cloud.*
> *The zigzag lightning stands high upon it.*
> *Male deity!*
> *Your offering I make.*
> *I have prepared a smoke for you.*

Restore my feet for me.
Restore my body for me.
Restore my mind for me.
This very day take out your spell for me.
Your spell remove for me.
You have taken it away for me.
Far off it has gone.
Happily I recover.
Happily my interior becomes cool.
Happily I go forth.
My interior feeling cool, may I walk.
No longer sore, may I walk.
Impervious to pain, may I walk.
As it used to be long ago, may I walk.
Happily may I walk.
Happily, with abundant dark clouds, may I walk.
Happily, with abundant showers, may I walk.
Happily, with abundant plants, may I walk.
Happily, on a trail of pollen, may I walk.
Happily may I walk.
Being as it used to be long ago, may I walk.
May it be beautiful before me.
May it be beautiful behind me.
May it be beautiful below me.
May it be beautiful above me.
May it be beautiful all around me.
In beauty it is finished.

Baptiste thought that Paul was about to compliment him again, but Grand Louis busted in. "Damn, I hate to hear them Injun screechin's here. In a white man's house." He looked sharply at Baptiste. "Remembers me you're half Injun, boy." Baptiste started to flare, but shut up.

So Louis told a story about when he ran into a grizzly bear with her cubs—she was tall and broad as two oxen—in a thicket, and she chased him into the river and he hollered for help and it took eleven balls to bring her down. Everyone but the guests knew that he was borrowing the story, since grizzlies didn't live this far down the Missouri and it was an old story anyway. After a while Baptiste suggested that Grand Louis show everyone a dance, which Louis was pleased to do, and Baptiste cut a tune for him on the mouth organ. Finally the prince excused himself, pleading fatigue. Baptiste said he would like to speak with the prince in the morning, with the prince's permission.

After breakfast Baptiste spoke casually about his education, about Clark's benevolence, about his future as a fur trader. Maybe he would work for General Clark, he said, as a U.S. government Indian agent. He had come upriver even now, he claimed, to improve his knowledge of Indian culture and to learn Indian languages and sign language, the *lingua franca* of the plains and mountains.

Finally he quit stalling. "Sir, I believe you are traveling to St. Louis on horseback, staying in contact with the Chouteau boat?"

"That is so."

"I am to return by the same boat. May I ride with you instead?"

"Of course," the prince said, and then seeing the look on Baptiste's face, added, "but why?"

"Because, Sir, I wish to have time to persuade you that I can be of service to Your Highness. I want you to employ me, in whatever capacity you see fit. I will save my *apologia* for myself for the trail."

Paul nearly laughed out loud. "Of course, join us, by all means."

Within a few days it was settled. Baptiste's arguments ran to his languages, his wide education and sophistication, his knowledge of the country, his unique position as an urbane half-breed. He did not have to advance them insistently, since Paul was disposed to hire him anyway. Paul's reasons had little to do with Baptiste's arguments.

"Yes," Paul said on the morning of the fourth day, "yes, I will employ you. That is, I will if you are willing. Because when I get to St. Louis, I am moving on to New Orleans. And then by ship to Germany, your new place of employment." He gave that a moment to sink in. "Among other things, you can help me with my book about North America. You might also attend the university. You will live at the castle as a member of the royal household. I promise that you'll be well taken care of, and that you may return when you like." The prince seemed vastly amused. "Will you go?"

Baptiste thought for a moment that the words wouldn't come out: "I will."

NOVEMBER 3: Baptiste's diary: "Embarked early this afternoon on the steamboat *Cincinnati* for New Orleans.

Much fuss filling Paul's many trunks with Indian and natural *memmoribilia* and carrying them on board and stow'd, in contrast to my own few poor things. All appears promising: Gen. Clark most heartily gave blessings and a sum of money. Everyone impressed and pleased for me. Coco seemed still distant but sincere and perhaps even moved in her well-wishing, and I promised a suitable surprize from Europe. It is very grand. I really cannot quite believe how grand it is."

JANUARY, 1824: The wind was in his face. He felt it cold on the bridge of his nose and on his cheekbones and against his forehead, where it had stretched the skin tight as a tautly stretched tanning skin. He was looking past the bow, toward the western coast of Europe out there somewhere, toward Le Havre-de-Grâce, at the far end of several thousand miles of ocean. He could see nothing in that direction, only a night blacker than any he could remember. Just on the port side of the bow the water flared out in phosphorescent foam, flickering iridescent white and violet. He kept his back to the cloudlike billowing of sails and to the moon that hung behind them. Above the blackness of the ocean glimmered pin-pricks of cold light, tiny jabs from stars millions of miles from the earth and serene in their remove.

He rubbed his eyes with his sleeve. It was 14 degrees below zero, the captain had informed him, that night off the coast of Newfoundland. The wet air was crusting to ice on his eyebrows and the bone in his nose ached from cold. He looked forward again. He had not climbed up here to think—about Paul's formal and impenetrable benevolence, about the captain's fatuous cordiality, about the endless lessons in German, the coaching about Napoleon and the Hapsburgs and the tsars, the well-wishing of General Clark, the interminable delays at St. Louis and New Orleans. He had come to be alone. He sat looking out at the sea for a long while, and admitted to himself, "I am afraid." Then he turned his back to the wind and walked the foredeck back toward his cabin. He had to work on German syntax.

FEBRUARY 14, 1824: Baptiste disembarked at Le Havre-de-Grâce, and set foot in a Europe in a state of transition. Napoleon had been quelled less than a decade earlier, and old regimes had reasserted themselves. The Congress of

Vienna in 1815, intending to reestablish the old order in a chaotic Europe, introduced once more an era of oppressive regimes; Charles X brought the monarchy back to France, and with it various forms of repression, including control of all books and newspapers; Metternich, the majordomo of the Austro-Hungarian Empire, set out to increase the power of the Hapsburgs; in the German federation of small, quasi-independent states, royal families who had been subject to Napoleonic rule now picked up the reins again and aligned themselves with Metternich. As they will after a period of revolution, conservative forces were waxing, and often reawakened an *ancien régime* decadence.

Yet the powerful impulses that gave rise to the French Revolution were still at work. The new ideas of government, of religious freedom, of the worth and equality of all men, of freedom of expression, of the importance of the individual, the non-divinity of monarchs, would not be unseated. The Industrial Revolution was pushing its way into politics. In 1822, King William of Württemberg, uncle of Prince Paul, had given his small, southwest German kingdom the first constitution granted to a German state. In France, in 1830, Charles X would fall in the July Revolution and Louis-Phillippe would rule: in 1848 Louis-Phillippe would give way to another Republic. The forces of royalism had won the battle of arms but lost the war of ideas.

In the arts, all Europe was agog about the doings of George Gordon Lord Byron, who wrote verses brilliantly and behaved scandalously. Huge audiences awaited new historical romances by Walter Scott. The iconoclast Beethoven was at the height of his fame, though Haydn and Mozart were more revered. Within months of Baptiste's disembarkation, Alexandre Dumas, *père*, would stand Paris on its head with his first play. Before the 1820s were out, Victor Hugo would do the same; and Frédéric Chopin would captivate Paris salons with his compositions for the pianoforte, which was new enough that middle-class families could not yet own one. In 1824, the year of Baptiste's arrival, Lord Bryon would die fighting for freedom for Greece, and thus give the revolutionary spirit a celebrated martyr. Romanticism was burning at its most intense.

APRIL 1824: Baptiste was transfixed. He was sitting between Paul and the Queen Mother in the royal box, but he had long since stopped noticing where he was. He was listening to the orchestra and swimming in the sounds. He had no idea what he was hearing. He had been given a program that listed eight or ten pieces; since he spoke little German, neither the names of the pieces nor of the composers meant anything to him. He only listened, without thoughts, and lived inside the sounds.

Baptiste would not have been able to put any words to the music or to what was happening to him. Having slight literary education, he did not think the music noble or tragic or pastoral or passionate or whimsical. He took in the sounds themselves simply, naively, amazed. At first he was taken with the sheer sound of an orchestra; though he had read about orchestras, he had never heard one. Then he began to recognize in the music feelings of his own—he did not identify them, but he experienced them as his. He felt as though someone had stepped inside him and rendered his own responses into sound and played them back for him; or, rather, had taken his glimmerings of feelings and had amplified them and played them back on a grander scale. But he would not have known how to say any of that.

At intermission he was relieved that he could not yet speak German well enough to understand the talk in the box. It seemed unduly light. He himself wanted nothing but for the orchestra to begin again. He sat through the concert, nearly four hours of it, entranced.

After the concert Paul and one of the guests tried to tell Baptiste about the music in French. He tried to be polite in paying no attention. He was absorbed in his strange state, an exhilarating sense of being clean. He interrupted to ask Paul if he could resume his music lessons. Paul promised to assign him to the *Kapellmeister* himself, the man who had just conducted the orchestra. Baptiste quaked with excitement. He let his mind drift back to the music. He could not hear the sounds as clearly as he could remember the feelings. It was as though someone had knocked down one of the four walls of reality and had shown him another world.

That night in bed, he reflected that if he had doubts about coming to Europe, about discovering more of the

white man's world, the concert alone had made the journey worthwhile.

OCTOBER, 1824: Karlheinz he liked. Karlheinz, having noticed him in the lecture hall, ferreted out his rooms and
simply appeared late one afternoon with two bottles of
Rhein wine, several cigars, and Hamlet, his Great Dane.
"Would you permit me to introduce a personage of some
distinction?" he said when Baptiste opened the door and
looked on Karlheinz for the first time. "Hamlet, the Dane,
the descendant of the most eminent attendant of this fair
university." Karlheinz tapped his leg and Hamlet rose on
his hind legs to an awesome height, right paw extended.
Baptiste shook it. "I am his retainer, Karlheinz Ehrlich-
mann, last son and black sheep of the family of the youngest son of a family obscurely related to the House of
Hanover. May we join you?" Blue eyes gleaming and
small red beard flaming, he brandished the whisky and
cigars.

The talk had broken an afternoon of tedious and frus-
trating study, for Baptiste was lost with his curriculum at
the University of Württemberg. In fact it had broken the
year's studies, because Baptiste only dabbled in his courses
after that afternoon.

Karlheinz had a flair for living. He did it without
money, of course, because the last son of a cousin of the
head of a royal household was relatively disenfranchised.
Karlheinz supposed that he would eventually enter the
military as his only way of advancement. In the meantime
he went forth in style, thanks to the ingenuity and arro-
gance with which he begged and borrowed. He knew the
people who counted, not the royal family of Württemberg,
Baptiste's patrons, but the young who lent some brilliance
to the salons of Stuttgart, the men of fashion, the poets,
the intellectuals, the musicians, and the beautiful young
women. Beside them, the royal family was stuffy.

It was Karlheinz who nicknamed him *"le sauvage naïf"*
and introduced him to everyone thus. It was Karlheinz
who pointed out that the clothing Paul had brought him,
though expensive, was boring and *bourgeois* and gave him
the look of a banker's son. Karlheinz picked out some
smarter outfits for him—frock coats fitted tightly at the
waist, trousers of fawn or pearl gray that showed the
shape of his legs, lace white shirts that opened deep onto

the chest. It was Karlheinz who made him familiar with
the taverns of Stuttgart on all-night carousals. Their invari-
able companions were Hamlet and Émilie, Karlheinz's ser-
vant-mistress who lived in his rooms, whom Karlheinz
liked to disguise as a boy.

And it was Karlheinz who introduced him to Sophie
Hoffman. She was, to put it mildly, different from anyone
he had met in Europe.

Baptiste's first months in Württemberg had been spent
in relative seclusion. After their arrival at Stuttgart about
March 1, 1824, Paul installed the two of them in a well-
appointed apartment in the castle of Stuttgart. Paul
wanted to catalog his various specimens and memorabilia
from North America for a permanent collection, and for
that he chose the help of Dr. Lebret, his old teacher and a
distinguished professor of natural sciences at the University. Besides, Paul, having been educated under the aus-
pices of his royal uncle at Württemberg University, felt at
home in Stuttgart as with his own family in Karlsruhe.

Baptiste's days were largely given to the tutor Paul as-
signed him—improving his German, learning something of
the French Revolution and Napoleon and Lord Byron,
and Herr Beethoven—simply learning something of the
world he now moved in. His evenings were spent in quiet
dinners with Paul, who did not care for society, or sometimes with the royal family at performances of chamber
music. King William loved Haydn and Dittersdorf and
Hummel, and tolerated the assault and battery of Beethoven. Twice Baptiste went with Paul to the opera, an event
he understood not at all.

One evening, after an intimate dinner with the royal
family, two young ladies, nieces of the king, undertook
some musical entertainment with voice and pianoforte.
Baptiste had never heard a pianoforte before, and it made
Mrs. Welch's clavichord sound puny. The songs were by
Mozart, and he found them pretty, with sweet and mobile
lines, charming. He burned with an idea.

The next afternoon he persuaded the nieces to play for
him again. He astonished them by following along on the
mouth organ, reading from the sheet music only a little
awkwardly. Then he fumbled through one of the songs on
the piano, but the keys felt clumsy under his fingers. The
girls were delighted. They rehearsed all afternoon and
presented Baptiste in his musical debut that evening to the

king and to Paul. The king applauded loudly, though Baptiste suspected that he was more amused than musically gratified. Then Baptiste gave them a raucous rendition of "Voyageur's Song," and the king seemed a good deal less gratified. But the next day Paul arranged for his lessons with the *Kapellmeister*.

Through the spring and summer, though, the royal family had not brought him out. He met with them only *en famille*. He prepared for his entrance to the University that autumn. In October he took lodgings there, Paul went home to Karlsruhe for a while, and Baptiste emerged from his cloister.

NOVEMBER, 1824: Karlheinz took him to one of the Sunday-afternoon gatherings for which Sophie Hoffman was noted—an ensemble of the witty, the dashing, the literary, an ensemble at once suitably fashionable and riskily Bohemian. It was at gatherings like Madame Hoffman's weekly affair that the young of provincial Stuttgart cultivated and affected the attitudes of the cosmopolitan centers.

A pop version of Romanticism was coursing through Europe like a fever. After the defeat and exile of Napoleon in 1815, the old power structure reasserted itself: Kings returned to their thrones, Metternich consolidated power for the Hapsburgs, commerce thrived, the bourgeoisie grew, the press and rebellious youth were curtailed. But radical ideas survived, even as they had under the old order. Young men and women of fashion, esthetes, and intellectuals fastened on Romantic heroes—Faust, cosmically arrogant and damned; Werther, swamped in youthful sorrow; Manfred, tragic, passionate, noble, proud in his moral isolation. They admired Goethe, Beethoven, Napoleon, and, above all, Lord Byron, himself the apparent ideal Byronic hero. They spoke out for freedom from oppression, rebellion against the old order, libertinism, atheism.

The young women circulating through Madame Hoffman's spacious rooms that afternoon said little but looked much. They pined, they looked wistful, they looked melancholy, they looked consumptive. These effects they achieved with some care: They avoided the sun to get the pallor, they sucked lead pencils, they drank vinegar. The lucky ones with dark hair made it lustrous with belladonna, and circled dark eyes with bistre. Any one of

them might have been Ophelia, gravitating from pining
sorrow toward madness, weeping from unquenchable anguish beside their favorite symbol, the weeping willow.

The more ambitious of the men adopted the attitudes of
creatures of the damned. They dressed like dandies—
trousers skintight, frock coats snugly tailored to show
form, hair in shoulder-length curls, page boys, or even
frizzed. They had sallow skin, burning eyes, brooding and
surly glances. Every man of them seemed tortured by a
noble anguish that only he could know.

Baptiste was struck, just after he came in, by a young
fellow dressed entirely in black, with very fair skin and jet
black hair. He sported a crimson vest beneath his black
frock coat, and looked like a stage version of the devil, or
of Don Juan. Karlheinz was steering Baptiste in his direction, murmuring about introducing him to their hostess.
Baptiste was astonished that their hostess proved to be the
young Don Juan.

"Sophie Hoffman," he made out from Karlheinz in his
confusion, and he bent toward her hand. "Jean-Baptiste
Charbonneau," Karlheinz went on, *"le sauvage naïf."*

She gestured that he was to shake her hand rather than
kiss it. He muttered "Madame Hoffman," entirely flustered
and certain that he seemed a fool. She looked at him for
too long a moment. She was pale, with gleaming black
eyes that seemed unnaturally large in that pale face, with
high cheekbones, a finely shaped nose, hair cut shorter
than the men's.

"I'm pleased to meet you. Karlheinz has spoken of you
often. Perhaps we can talk later." Baptiste, not knowing
what to say, bowed. He felt it to be more a dismissal than
an invitation.

As he retreated, he took her in. Tall—very tall for a
woman—slender, with a small high bosom covered by her
man's shirt, of aristocratic but careless bearing, smoking a
Turkish cigarette in a long black holder.

" 'Friendship is love without his wings,' " the tall, husky,
blonde fellow was saying to her.

"Will you ever tire of Byron?" she remarked off-hand-
edly. Baptiste immediately felt the blonde fellow a fool,
and was jealous.

Karlheinz was watching Baptiste watching Madame
Hoffman. "Are you enthralled by Sophie, then? You

might do worse," he mused. "She has a taste for the exotic."

NOVEMBER 13, 1824: Baptiste, beginning to be comfortable with German after nearly a year, determined to keep his journal in that language. He was making frequent entries in the diary: The long days at school were lonely since he had quit going to classes almost completely. He turned his diary into full little essays when he could; he even toyed with the idea of perhaps turning his diary into a book—*An American Indian Sojourns With Royalty,* or some such. Thus his tone:

"*Le sauvage naïf* met today with Madame Sophie Hoffman, divorcee and social luminary among the literati. She is a striking woman, not only in her considerable beauty but as well in her demeanour: She comports herself in dress, in manners, in conversation, in all behavior as a man. About her the people of her circle know but little, yet speculate much. Reputedly, she is the natural daughter of an Italian count and a Norwegian gentlewoman, but this story may be held in the suspension of doubt. Several years ago she came to Stuttgart to live with her husband, a painter, with whom she is said to have had a torrid romance at the seashore at Genoa. She tired of him before long and caring nothing for conventions, left him to set up house nearby. Attracted to herself are the principal young intellectuals and artists of Stuttgart, who invade her salons each Sunday afternoon. She has also friends among men of arts and letters over all of Europe, including Henri Beyle, known as Stendhal, a French novelist of some note. Report is that she takes from among all these acquaintances a variety of lovers—painters, writers, Bohemians, aristocrats. Apparently she *lets that be known,* but *will not say it is so.* Such, presumably, is the concession that even so independent and autonomous a woman must make to convention and public opinion. Madame Hoffman seems most worthy to figure as a character in these pages and in the life of *le sauvage naïf,* who confesses that he might like to number himself among the variety of her lovers."

NOVEMBER 20: "The afternoon again at Madame Hoffman's. I am ashamed to say that our hero today made an arse of himself. In the sophisticated company at the salon he was acutely struck with his own lack of sophistication—with his mere nineteen years (though nearly twenty), with his accent, with his halting German, and with his ignorance of the books and pieces of music which everyone else was talking about. As a result, though he dearly wanted to make an impression on Madame Hoffman, he spent the hours clinging to a bookcase and looking nauseated. At my own apartments I then consumed time contemplating my visage in the mirror; I was cheered by the thought that in dress, bearing, and features I seem equal of most and the superior of some.

"Karlheinz, noticing his *savage*'s sickly withdrawal, suggested that I render some of the Indian songs which so pleased Prince Paul and King William. One hesitates to play on the mouth organ some primitive piece of music—in front of women who play Mozart and Beethoven and men who invent their own pieces. Yet Karlheinz may be right, and I may try it."

November 23: "Dinner with the prince at his apartment in the castle this evening. He is, as always, pleasant, benevolent, and removed. Though he provides everything I need or want, I could scarcely call him a friend. Tonight when he gave me a letter of credit for three months' allowance, I found myself oddly irritable. No matter."

November 27: "Madame Hoffman is away, so Karlheinz, Hamlet, and *le sauvage naïf* passed the afternoon *chez* Herr Weiskopf, a banker who collects paintings and plays somewhat at the violoncello. I believe that Hamlet made eyebrows raise in the company, which was musical but more proper and *demure* than the other circle. The *Kapellmeister* himself rendered a new composition at the pianoforte. Hearing a professor of music comment softly that the *Kapellmeister* is a musical fuddy-duddy fifty years behind the times, I offered a piece that is hundreds of years behind the times, a song of the Sioux Indians. That prospect aroused great curiosity, and so came about the amusing and ironic spectacle of our *sauvage naïf* singing a Sioux morning prayer. Despite the fact that I could not remember many of the Sioux words, I believe it was quite well received. I imagine that they view it as a curiosity, and not as music, as indeed I suspect they view *le sauvage naïf* as a curiosity, not a person. But we shall make them discover their mistake. I met a handsome blond woman, a Madame Strasbourg, who seemed interested."

NOVEMBER 30: "A note from Amalie Strasbourg invites me to join her party at the opera on Saturday. The Prince urges me to accept; she is the wife of an army officer presently in Prussia, and a lady of independent means. I should have accepted anyway."

DECEMBER 3: *"Le sauvage naïf* did appear at the opera—a music-drama about a girl who kills herself for lost love, entirely too melodramatic—in the Strasbourg box. The company was Madame, her brother, and his wife, neither of sufficient interest to enliven these pages. Our hero, thinking to make an impression, even a minor sensation, wore *memorabilia* of Paul's—a totemistic headband with two feathers, a pipe decorated with a chief's sacred signs, and my own hoop necklace. The combination was dubious medicine, but abutting my frock coat and lace shirt, they made excellent stage sense. The effect through the house was as I had hoped. At Madame Strasbourg's home after the opera, we fell into a discussion of Indian names, and I ended by giving each of them an appropriate name. For Madame I chose *Mourning Dove,* which seemed to delight her. I thought *Wounded Bird* more apt: she is thin and wan, which gives an impression of height, with yellow hair piled high on her head and a reed-like neck. She creates an air of frailty, both by her appearance and by clinging always to some gentlemen's elbow. *Le sauvage naïf* finds her interesting, or at least moderately challenging: and he will abandon modesty for a moment to say that she finds him *fascinating.*"

DECEMBER 4: "Called late this afternoon on Amalie Strasbourg with flowers, stayed to dinner, and after dinner succeeded in all his hopes and designs. The very idea that she was in bed with him seemed to throw Amalie into a swoon, and what she did in bed was mostly to *swoon.* Both before and after the fact, the lady much protested helplessly, 'I cannot, I cannot,' but she did and she will. Her enthusiastic protestations had equal fervor."

DECEMBER 9: "Ever when I am abroad in society, my necklace is the center of curiosity and comment. People gaze at it, ask about its totem meaning, and sometimes even finger it as though it had power transmittable by touch. Karlheinz because of it has sometimes introduced me by yet another familiar name, *Sternenstein,* or Star-stone. In our incognito carousals I now adopt that name; it even gives the illusion that I am German, denied by my skin, my accent, and the necklace itself; strangers are much surprised by the name. I give no one the true answer as to why I always wear the necklace and its star-stone publicly: The stone makes visible what is ever in my heart."

DECEMBER 23: "Amalie's husband is home on leave for the holidays; she claims to be simply eager to see me, but what she seems is unconsciously eager to flaunt her affair before her husband, which I find embarrassing and distasteful. In addition, her *clinging* is becoming *cloying*. As I am returned to the Prince's apartment for the time and obliged with a busy holiday season here, I think it better to let the affair drop. It was only a passing dalliance, pleasant enough, in the life of *le sauvage naïf*."

JANUARY 1, 1825: "Sternenstein left the grand celebration at the castle yesterday evening before midnight, in a minor transgression against my host in this country, to attend Madame Hoffman's assembly. She, dressed in black coat and trousers, as is apparently her custom, looked most striking with her pale skin and jet hair. I feigned indifference to her for an hour before admitting—to myself only—that I am as entranced with her as before. She engaged in a substantial discussion of a painter whom I know nothing of. Once again I was thinking that I behaved like an awkward, retreating boy: but whether or no, I am invited to tea on Thursday. She says she has a friend who is most eager to meet me. Our hero's single resolution for the New Year is to cultivate Madame Sophie Hoffman, and amorously."

Just as Baptiste was chiding himself for sitting there frozen, and wondering whether hot coffee might loosen his arthritic tongue, Sophie launched in.

"Johannes"—that was the portly professor of music in the leather chair—"is interested in Indian music," she said. "I understand that you play. Will you?"

He apologized for not having his mouth organ and for being inept at the pianoforte. (Damn! She must have heard about my demonstration at Herr Weiskopf's.) Johannes lent him his churchwarden.

"The Sioux begins his songs by offering his respects to the gods," Baptiste started, the pipe in his hand. He mimed blowing smoke upward, downward, and to all four sides. "He honors the sky, the earth, the west, where the thunder-beings live, the north where lives the white giant, the east whence comes the morning star, the south whence comes the spring." Johannes looked fascinated. "He takes his time about all this. It does not do to hurry the sacred powers.

"He holds up his medicine bag as he sings. It holds some object—a bear claw, a jay's feather, a black stone—that has been revealed to him in a dream as his private, sacred emblem and protector. The song is holy as well, and it is his personal song. Songs often come in dreams, and are handed down from father to son. A man who does not dream a song or inherit one, must buy a song from a man who has one. Songs are sacred personal property. An elementary notion of copyright, sanctified.

"This is a song that a holy Sioux heard the sun sing at daybreak one day:

> *With visible face I am appearing.*
> *In a sacred manner I appear.*
> *For the greening earth a pleasantness I make.*
> *The center of the nation's hoop I have made*
> *   pleasant.*
> *With visible face, behold me!*
> *The four-leggeds and two-leggeds, I have made*
> *   them to walk.*
> *The wings of the air, I have made them to fly.*
> *With visible face I appear.*
> *My day, I have made it holy.*

He sang it in the Sioux tongue, knowing that he was getting half of it wrong. He sang with his eyes closed, try-ing to bring back some of the rapt intensity of the old medicine man who chanted it.

He was damned uncomfortable, but Sophie and Johan-nes were eager for more. He gave them two of his favor-ites and tried to quit. Then he gave them three or four more that he knew well, plus a couple that he might be misremembering. Johannes had taken out a notepad and pencil and asked if Baptiste would play them on the pi-ano; he wanted to transcribe one or two. So Baptiste picked them out with one finger—he had some idea of the pitch equivalents from his mouth organ.

In the middle of the "Corn Song," Karlheinz came in with a stranger, Hamlet trailing. "So you have him," the fellow said at large when the song ended. Sophie presented him as Jacques Balmat, professor of philosophy. He was a tall man with a red face, strong bony features, and a strange air of energy about him. He was Baptiste's idea of what a revolutionary would look like.

"You are more than fashionably late, gentlemen," Sophie chided them.

"I delayed Jacques because of a most engaging barmaid," Karlheinz grinned.

The maid served more coffee and cakes. "I am curious what you see as the central differences between white and Indian cultures," Jacques started.

"Jacques, must you be so blunt?" asked Sophie.

He ignored her. "Some philosophers have the idea that man left alone in his natural state, untouched by civilization, has an innate nobility. The traditional idea is that the savage grovels in benightedness."

"I have been exposed to Monsieur Rousseau," Baptiste said uneasily.

"Jacques," interjected Karlheinz, "must you philosophers always play chess with ideas? If you want to play chess, then, let's play. Sophie, have the board brought." He gave Hamlet a small cake.

"Baptiste," Sophie said quietly, "how much did you live with your Indian people?"

His own tribe he scarcely knew, he answered. He had lived until his sixth year among the Mandans and Minatarees, and five summers among various tribes—Sioux, Osage, Arikara, Iowa, Kansas, Pawnee. And how long among the whites? He'd gone to school in St. Louis for twelve years, he said, and then had come to Europe. He was twenty years old.

"You are a white man, then, with red skin," inserted Jacques. "Your mind is white." Jacques seemed to be very sure and definite about everything. It made Baptiste uncomfortable.

"The first six years can be formative," Sophie said.

She led him into talking about Indian music and white music and the difference between them. Baptiste explained that all Indian music is sacred. It is all, in effect, prayer. The Osage "Corn Song" he had sung for them, for instance; it is a tribute to the force—the god, if you like—

that makes things grow, and was intended to produce the effect of a healthy and abundant crop.

Amid the earth, renewed in verdure,
Amid the rising smoke, my grandfather's footprints
I see, as from place to place I wander,
The rising smoke I see as I wander,
Amid all forms visible, the rising smoke
I see, as I move from place to place.

Amid all forms visible, the little hills in rows
I see, as I move from place to place.

Amid all forms visible, the spreading blades
I see as I move from place to place.

Amid all forms visible, the light day
I see as I move from place to place.

Baptiste translated the song into German, line by line, pointing out that the new greenness and the growth-bringing mist are the visible forms of the great spirit, his footprints, and pointing out the tone of reverence and thanks. The incantation of these powers, he explained, would make the corn sprout from the earth. The Indian perceived a magic power not only in natural forces, but in the words of his song that named them. The making of the sound of the word, this act itself, has a magical power. So it is with a death song, he said. An Indian sings his death song and clutches his medicine when in ultimate danger. The object would have been revealed to him in a dream, as protective against death, and the song with it. He believes that if he invokes the powers implicit in the object and the words of the song, they will defend him against insuperable odds. So it is with a rain song and rain dance, a buffalo song and buffalo dance. All call on mysterious forces in nature to make something happen. Indian music in that way is sacred.

Baptiste was talking animatedly. He had not quite known he knew these things.

Johannes asked if the white man's music seemed sacred to him as well. Baptiste considered. He thought not. He did not see a religious attitude in a boatman's song or in a square-dance music or a polka or a drinking song. But in some European music, yes. He thought of the orchestra concert he heard when first in Stuttgart. That had a serious tone, maybe a sacred tone. The words were elusive here, he thought, the meaning of "sacred." He mentioned Beethoven and Mozart. Some of their music was not frivolous like a drinking song. Still, young ladies performed their music in salons to demonstrate their personal accomplishments, with no sacred motive. That was frivolity. The white man had a different attitude toward music.

Jacques asked what the words "visible forms" in the "Corn Song" meant.

Some Indians have the idea, Baptiste said, that things, objects in the world, are visible representations of their true forms, which reside in the center of the earth and are sometimes revealed to men by the gods in dreams. Thus "renewed verdure" is the visible form of the principle, the force, that brings spring back to the earth. The principle is permanent and true, the greenness its manifestation.

"Plato among the primitives," Jacques exclaimed, amused.

Baptiste remembered something of Plato's metaphor of the cave from a lecture at the University, but he was impatient of metaphysical speculation. He remembered also that the lecturer pondered whether individual men exist or only the idea Man, or whether all men and all existence might not be an idea in the mind of God, and have no independent existence at all. Baptiste thought that sort of questioning the silliest thing he had ever heard. Only a white man, he had thought, would ask whether hunger pangs were real, whether he had a belly to be empty. A sensible man asked only where the pantry was.

So Baptiste was annoyed at the prospect of the conversation's taking a metaphysical turn.

Just then, Karlheinz fortunately suggested a supper at his favorite small restaurant, which served squid, and they all accepted.

When the supper broke up, Jacques insisted to Baptiste that they must meet again and talk. Jacques was terribly urgent about everything, Baptiste thought, but he accepted. Johannes thanked him. Baptiste noticed that Jacques took Sophie home, and was jealous. He noted in his diary that night that he had not made any small gesture toward starting his campaign to become her lover.

JANUARY 9, 1825: Baptiste's diary: "Sophie, myself, Karlheinz, Johannes, and Jacques to the ballet this evening. Boring, boring, boring. We left at the interval."

JANUARY 12: "Sophie, Helga, and Sternenstein to the river this afternoon for a long walk. A splendid day: The temperature was down, and kept the snow hard; it shone almost blindingly in the sunlight. Cold enough to require warmed brandy after. Helga, a middle-aged gentlewoman who was once mistress to a duke, is the only female friend Sophie has, so far as I know."

JANUARY 15: "Visited Sophie's salon this afternoon, but found her much preoccupied with her friend Giovanni, a Florentine sculptor who arrived today and is apparently her houseguest. Tavern-crawling with Karlheinz and Hamlet most of the night, with the result of too much wine and a groggy head."

JANUARY 19: "The morning with *Herr Kapellmeister*: My playing has improved greatly since I dropped classes and started practicing with a modicum of regularity. Consequently, he has offered to teach me musical theory as well, which promises to be interesting. I was writing out some exercises when Sophie and Jacques appeared by surprise at my rooms. (She really cares nothing for the proprieties!) The afternoon spent amiably in their company, they talking about novelists; *le sauvage naïf*, regrettably, could do little but listen. She and Jacques are invariably together; I wonder what she sees in him, as I find him mildly interesting but abrasive."

"Are you religious?" Jacques asked over the rim of his brandy glass.

"Sophie," said Karlheinz, "if we are teetering into this sort of talk again, I will need much more brandy than this."

"I'd like to talk about it," Baptiste said. He had been given three religions, in fact: the first by his mother and the Minataree Indians, wordlessly; the second by a hell-fire-and-damnation Baptist preacher—here Baptiste gave a short comic digression on Welch's lurid imaginings; the third by a withdrawn, effete, intellectual Jesuit. The three freethinkers were amused by the tales of the confusion these religions caused in Baptiste. Until he was fourteen or fifteen, he said, he had simply believed all of them without questioning. He was aware of no contradiction.

"And which would you choose now?" Karlheinz asked. Baptiste was taken aback at Karlheinz's asking.

"None," he replied promptly. "Religion is a way of putting order onto what should remain chaotic."

Sophie asked him to describe the Indian attitudes toward their gods.

The principal difference between the Indian gods and the Christian god, Baptiste answered, was that Jehovah was a defined sort of person, a kind of superman, and the Indian gods were natural forces, power of the water that makes it flow, the power that brings rain, the power of the winds, the power in the elk, the power in grass. The Indians saw power in every animate and inanimate thing —the secret power that made it what it was—and he revered and solicited that power, the hardness of the rock, the ferocity of the bear, the warmth and light of the sun. That was the essence of his religion.

Jacques judged that it sounded more sensible to him than Christianity. At least the object of worship was, in a sense, real.

Karlheinz disagreed. It was not real. If the Indian understood that gravity makes water run downhill, that rain comes from the ocean and is brought by winds whose motion follows natural laws—if he understood that the phenomena he worshipped were natural and not supernatural—he would have no religion.

Jacques said that was why it was more sensible.

Sophie asked Baptiste what he thought.

He reflected a little before he answered. "The religion sounds more attractive than it is. The Indians I've seen are craven in their worship. They are dominated by fear of the powers they appeal to. Since they don't understand natural forces, they believe the powers are whimsical, arbitrary, malicious. Why do the rains abandon them for long periods? Why does thunder come and strike their forests with fire and deluge them with water and swell the rivers until they are impossible to cross? It makes no sense. So the Indian quakes before his gods. I hate that."

"I like you, Baptiste," Sophie said abruptly. Baptiste, who had never gotten a compliment from Sophie and normally would have hung on every word, was now merely pleased and interested. "You have an original mind. You consult your experience for your answers—what you've heard and seen yourself. You contemplate your experience and answer from that. First-hand."

Baptiste took what she said seriously. After a moment he said, "I have been deceived by both and have learned to distrust them. From very early I had to figure out things wholly by myself."

"What are you, Baptiste, an Indian or a white man?" Jacques asked.

Baptiste said nothing. He thought of saying that he was a white man who used his Indian blood to attract the attention of those who would otherwise ignore him. Finally he said, "I am neither. I am simply me." And he shrugged, embarrassed.

"Why, then, do you wear that totem object about your neck?" Jacques asked. Baptiste always wore it showing, now.

"In memory of my mother, who gave it to me. I have my own meaning." He explained Sacajawea's message relating to the symbolism of the hoop and the fragment of meteor.

"What is your meaning for it?" asked Sophie.

"Like this stone, I am an alien."

JANUARY 27: Baptiste's diary: "The afternoon with *Herr Kapellmeister,* who is pleased with my progress in learning the chords; soon, he says, I will start at elementary counterpoint; I can now play the little Beethoven *andante* at the pianoforte with a reasonable facsimile of musicality; it is all great fun. Though I was at the castle, I did not see Prince Paul, who is much absorbed in making his notes on North American flora, fauna, typography, inhabitants, customs, and commerce into book form. The king lets his minstrel run free."

FEBRUARY 2: "My tutor—at least he is officially my tutor—suggests strongly that I make an effort at the University; else why, he asks, did I matriculate? I answered that I am most given to the study of music. Sternenstein is also given, we know, to interesting people, stimulating talk, and good wine."

"Oh, don't tease us, Karlheinz, tell all, tell," Sophie laughed.

He had been casting about amusing hints of the charms

of a Viennese whore he had once known. "If you are intrigued by the ways of little Anna," Karlheinz offered in
his most courtly tone, "perhaps you would be intrigued by
the real thing. I know a reputable sporting house in town,
one where gentlemen of means can imbibe, gamble, and
take their pleasure with the ladies if they like." He smiled
wickedly at her and Baptiste.

Sophie slipped out of her parlor. Twenty minutes later
she came back dressed completely as a man, in fact in a
rather conservative man's costume, her short hair looking
perfectly male under her beaver hat and her make-up
stripped off. Baptiste laughed, because she looked exactly
like a green youth going out to examine the doings of the
sophisticated world. She announced that she was ready to
go.

At the house she was quiet and intense at first, following Karlheinz and Baptiste from table to table as they
rolled the dice. When they found a table and ordered
some champagne, she relaxed and became gay. The ladies
of the house, who were splendidly dressed—as fashionable
and handsome as ladies of a court—flirted with the three
of them. Sophie, in the middle, was infinitely amused. She
asked in a whisper whether Karlheinz or Baptiste did not
intend to go upstairs with one of them. They had a brisk
talk about which would be the best, Sophie pooh-poohing
the men's notions and picking out entirely different ladies.
Finally the men declined the opportunity. At that point
Sophie got up and flirted with one, an elaborately feminine, auburn-haired girl full of giggles and sighs—just the
opposite of Sophie. After a few minutes the two of them
went upstairs. Sophie came back much later looking perfectly composed. She refused absolutely, on the way home,
to say what had gone on upstairs. Baptiste had never seen
her so full of fun.

FEBRUARY 10: Baptiste's diary: "Our hero is beginning to
suspect that his friend Madame Hoffman is trying to im-
merse him in culture. She has led me (always in company,
so that I am frustrated in my desire to make her a licen-
tious proposition) on a furious round of theatre, opera,
and museums for the last ten days, and has given me a
slim volume of the verses of Heine. She walked through
the museum today at a terrific pace, spending half-hour in
front of whatever she liked and dismissing the rest with

scarcely a glance. She cannot be described as tolerant: She is contemptuous of all in art that she thinks is sham, imitative, the work of *poseurs*. With decorative and *roccoco* she has only a little more patience. Yet when she sees something that strikes her as original, or 'first-hand,' as she is fond of saying, she is full of enthusiasm for it, and most articulate about her reasons. I saw her one afternoon at salon firmly slap down a professor who criticized Benvenuto Cellini, one of her favorites. *Le sauvage naïf*, being in such matters precisely *naïf*, has only an inkling of what she is talking about."

"Why do Europeans have such strange, rule-ridden notions about sex?" Baptiste asked. For once he had called by surprise and had found her alone. He was trying to slip up on the subject of her own romantic life.

"Why?" Sophie smiled. She let a beat pass as she settled her demitasse of coffee next to the silver service in front of her. "Are Indians superior in their attitudes?"

"Well, they're natural. They do whatever they feel like doing."

"For instance?"

"They copulate without embarrassment in the tipis next to their children, sometimes even in public view. A chief in a tribe where I stayed made a habit of walking around camp naked and tumescent. They're open about it."

"Don't they have customs, restrictions, taboos?"

He thought a moment. "I don't know." He smiled sheepishly. "I guess so." Women are property, he explained, as horses are property. When a girl comes of marriageable age, her father sells her to a brave who wants her. He may sell her again, or trade her for a while, or lend her to another man. She is property, and a rich brave accumulates wives as he accumulates all the trappings of wealth.

Romantic love doesn't enter into it. A man marries out of practical considerations—to have his clothes and lodge made, his food cooked, his household arranged, his belongings toted on long trips, his lust appeased, his family increased in numbers. Women are useful. Of course, the Indian notion of honor assigns the woman the drudgery and the role of beast of burden. (Sophie was making faces through all this.)

Jealousy is almost unheard of. Adultery is censured,

sometimes mildly and sometimes severely, but that's because a squaw belongs to a brave, and he has as much right to her usefulness as to the usefulness of a horse. He can and does lend or sell her, but she has no autonomous rights on her own. Adultery violates a principle of property. Some tribes don't take adultery very seriously, their ideas about it notwithstanding. But the Blackfeet cut off the noses of adulterous squaws, or kill them.

Otherwise there are no sexual taboos. Girls are expected to take their pleasure where they find it until they are sold to their husbands. Men are expected to take pleasure where they can get it all their lives. That way of doing things is obvious to the Indian, and the white man's restrictions are simply incomprehensible to him. (Baptiste looked for an expression of approval about this, but saw nothing in particular in Sophie's face.)

They do whatever feels good, he said. They are sensualists, and experimental ones. Indian teen-agers do in bed what respectable European couples have barely heard of. (He couldn't help smiling.) Homosexuality is acceptable; homosexuals are thought to be following the way revealed to them in a dream in childhood. You can copulate with an animal if you want to, it's common enough. Sometimes braves rape their dead enemies to humiliate them one final time.

And with all this, the Indian just doesn't make a big thing of sex. That most of all.

He looked at Sophie expectantly. "It sounds awful," she said. Baptiste was puzzled. "There's no room for feeling."

"They don't have any hopeless, pining longings," Baptiste said, "or all-absorbing passions."

"It sounds like they have no room for feelings," Sophie repeated. "They're just masters and slaves."

"They stay away from fairy tales," Baptiste answered, uneasily.

"Baptiste, forget storybook romance. Haven't you ever felt really strongly about anyone? More excited and more alive when you're with them? Haven't you ever been enthralled by anyone?" No answer. "I couldn't stand to live with someone just from duty and habit. I want. . . ." She broke off with a playful smile, her eyes hinting at whatever it was she wanted.

Baptiste didn't know what to say. If he had ever felt strongly about a woman, he thought, it was Sophie.

She rescued him by asking him to take her out to dinner. They dined quietly and leisurely at a small restaurant that was one of her favorites. They reminisced. He spoke tenderly of his mother and tolerantly of his father. She told him stories about her childhood, which had been spent in the Tyrol and at the sea. She had come to love the sea more than she could love people, she said. She seemed softer than usual. She also seemed, he thought, amused about something, but he didn't know what.

When they got to her house, he had made up his mind to speak to her, not to tell her that he loved her, which never occurred to him, but to say that he wanted to sleep with her. He held the violence of the word he would use for it in his mind. He turned around different ways to say it, most of them blunt, some of them witty. But there in the foyer, as he helped her off with her heavy coat, he could say nothing.

So he turned her around and kissed her. After a long moment she began to pull away gently. He held her with one arm and tilted her head back firmly with the other. "I want you," he said. She looked at him for a long time, then turned a playful smile. She slipped out of his arm before he knew what happened, walked down the hall and started up the stairs. He followed her.

They made love all night. She had a long, slender body, smooth like a swimmer's, wide shoulders, small breasts, willowy arms and legs. He thought she was beautiful. They said almost nothing. He was afraid to speak, afraid he would sound foolish. He had the impression that she was laughing at him inside, laughing with delight, perhaps, but laughing. When he came at her again, and again, she laughed aloud. It was the only sound that passed between them. When they made love, they kept their eyes open and looked at each other hard.

As they were finishing breakfast, still without having talked, she said, "You're in love with me."

He shook his head no, and was conscious of her watching him.

She let it go. "Come tonight," she said. "Not until midnight. And don't think that you own me."

He went to her often the next few weeks. The University had gone into its spring recess. They saw none of their friends together, meeting late, alone. He could not have described his feelings about her. Nothing that he had heard or read fit, and he thought the words people had invented for it excessively foolish anyway. He knew that it felt very serious to him. Their lovemaking was a strange mélange of solemnity and play. He talked to her intimately sometimes, not about his feelings for her, but about himself, stray thoughts and feelings he hadn't known he had, but that seemed important. He had never spoken to anyone openly about himself.

At the end of three weeks she said that she was going for a while to the seashore near Spezia. Some friends had loaned her their cottage. She had in fact planned to leave before now. He was invited for a week. Five days after she left, he followed. They spent six days walking on the shore, musing, talking, being quiet, or lying in front of the fire. On the fourth day he thought seriously that he had never been so happy. But he said nothing to Sophie.

She got back to Stuttgart nine days after he did. He wondered where she had been, what she had done, but she was mysterious about it. They did not see quite as much of each other now. Some nights seemed extraordinary still, and on others she seemed a little distant.

One night, when they were lying in bed and she was smoking her Turkish cigarette, she asked suddenly, "What will you do, Baptiste? It's very well for me—I have my father's money—but what will you do?" He had not thought much about it. He would stay at the University for a while and something would come up. Perhaps Paul would secure him a place. He could get along as well as anyone. Sophie herself, lying naked next to him, was a sign of that. "I'll do something," he said, "later. For now, I'm doing Madame Hoffman."

Then, in early May, she had a houseguest for five days—a Dutch mathematician she said she'd known for many years. She introduced him at her Sunday salon, and people said he was celebrated. He was a man of perhaps forty-five with a severe face and a hawklike nose, the kind of face that has seen and been through too much. Baptiste disliked him. At the salon Baptiste whispered to Sophie that he wanted to come over late that night. "Not until Henryk leaves," she said simply, "on Tuesday." Baptiste left the house in a pique.

He could not believe he was jealous. He would not believe it. But he did wonder whether they were lovers. She told him nothing of her other involvements, would never speak of them, he knew. He supposed he was jealous.

On Tuesday night, though, everything seemed the same. From then on he felt when he was with her as he always had, and nothing else mattered. When he was not with her, when he saw her at the theatre with someone else or watched her talking with a man at her salons, he felt a kind of helpless rage. It was as though he had two separate sets of feelings, unrelated. But he would catch himself, walking down a street on an errand, inexplicably angry without knowing why.

One night in bed he said to her bluntly, "Let's marry." She waited, but he said nothing more.

"Don't spoil it," she said.

He started to answer, but she put her hand over his mouth and then kissed him. Later that night, for the first time he could remember, lovemaking was painful and left him edgy.

JUNE 2: Baptiste's diary: "A note from Paul today requesting my company for dinner and mentioning a proposed trip to England for some weeks—he is related to the Royal House there in some way, a puzzle I have never been able to unravel. It is an invitation which leaves Sternenstein little choice, as there is something of the *well-loved slave* in his position. I will miss Sophie—if indeed Sophie and I are still lovers by then; I sometimes wonder what future we have."

JUNE 5: "Prince Paul presented me with a most handsome gift, another birthday present which he said had been some time in the making: a harmonika of teak, mahagony, and silver, with Jean-Baptiste Charbonneau engraved in florid script on the silver. The new ones were introduced in Vienna only three years ago; mine has a button which changes the key of the instrument and thereby augments the tonal possibilities. I was highly gratified. I played for him some American and French-Canadian folk tunes, and we talked of old times in America. I *do* think of it sometimes. We're off to England in three weeks."

JUNE 9: "*Le sauvage naïf* seems to be spending less time courting Sophie, which is probably just as well. Today I drank the afternoon away with Karlheinz in a *Schenke* and drank the evening away in the company of high-class whores. Karlheinz loves to dally with them even when he doesn't feel like bedding; tonight their presence spurred him to one of his finest mock-philosophical orations, this time in the style of Descartes. He and Sternenstein drink too much, but in that particular company we are still favored."

JUNE 14: "An accomplishment: *Le sauvage naïf* today gained an earnest compliment from *Herr Kapellmeister* for his application to his musical studies. I have the rudiments of harmony, and demonstrated today that I can harmonize certain hymns, songs of the common people, and drinking songs. I now try my hand at small compositions—rounds, canons, short songs. What a surprise I would be to General Clark, to Coco, and to the awful Mme. Berthold."

JUNE 22: "This afternoon Sophie and I went walking to the river to see the steamboat. Standing on the high bank, I asked her again to marry me. She said no; the answer seemed quick, firm, light. She smiled slightly when she said it, and I thought looked a little sad; then she took my hand. On the way back we stopped at a cottage to talk with an old man who was working in his garden. He gave us a short lecture on the plan*s—their roots, their tubers, their sproutings, their leaves, their pollen—far more than I ever wanted to know about plants. He seemed completely absorbed with the fact that they struggle to live and thrive, and that, with his help, they succeed. As we moved on, Sophie pronounced herself touched. A moment later she put her head on my shoulder and her arm around me and said seriously, 'Baptiste, this is everything there is. This happiness. This *now*. Take it, and don't look for possession.' That, I suppose, is all the answer I shall have to my proposal. I feel on the edge of bitterness."

JUNE 26: "What do you think, wise reader? Is Sophie playing *le sauvage naïf* for a fool? Does she not mean for us to play like healthy young animals while we are in the flower of life so that she, when a little faded in bloom, can marry some fellow who is rich, respectable, titled, and *white*? Or have you known this already for many pages?"

JUNE 28: "Sophie invited me to the house today, took me most tenderly, lovingly, and later passionately to bed, and then told me it was the last time. What else is there to say? The Prince and I leave for England day after next."

Sissinghurst Castle
August 7, 1825

Mlle. Coco Berthold
Main Street
St. Louis
State of Missouri
United States of America

My dear Coco—

I beg your forgiveness for having been so long delinquent in writing you; I am, you may be sure, ashamed not to have sent you a letter these eighteen months when I promised periodic accounts of my adventures.

I am now some four weeks in England, and at present am a guest with the Prince in this castle in Kent. I well know you and your family have no great love for the English, and I have learned to have none as well: They are tedious. The days in England are an endless procession of gray skies and muggy heat. The best one can say of the people is that they are careful, measured, and dignified. They have neither dash nor style, no sense of fun; but cut all their feelings in half: Never fascinated, they are only *curious;* never outraged, they are merely *miffed;* never exultant—merely *gratified.* Do you remember the impertinent fun and gay times we used to have? They would think it unseemly. It is precisely the sort of country to have led the fight against Napoleon and to have driven Lord Byron into exile, and perhaps to an untimely death.

They understood so bold and heroic a figure as Napoleon not at all. Of the English only Byron has caught him on the proper scale—do you know the verses?: *"Whose game was empires, and whose stakes were thrones,/ Whose table earth—whose dice were human bones."*

Paul spends his time here either consulting with professors of natural history or having leisurely chats with his various royal relations. I have been bored,

but have used the time to grasp something of English
history: I am fascinated by Sir Francis Drake and Sir
Walter Scott, but don't understand the reverence for
Elizabeth, and I find Cromwell quite distasteful. Byron interests me ever more; *Don Juan* seems a mas-
terwork, and I am posting you a copy when I post
this letter. In it are two of my favorite couplets:

> *Society is now one polish'd horde,*
> *Formed of two mighty tribes, the Bores and*
> *Bored.*

> *Oh, you lords of ladies intellectual,*
> *I know your wives hen peck you all.*

The words apply to the English most aptly.

In Stuttgart I did attend the University of
Württemberg; though I confess that I did not apply
myself to the Roman history, Latin, military theory,
& etc., I have, however, labored assiduously at my
musical studies: I have been playing the musical compositions of Mozart and Beethoven (Germany's most
celebrated living composer) at the pianoforte, which
to me is much superior in sound and expressive range
to the harpsichord; I have also composed a song or
two, and look forward to testing their worth against
your discriminating judgment if I may be allowed to
play and sing them for you in the future.

It has been my privilege to be in the company of
some of the luminous figures of the two countries in
which I have been living: King William of Württemberg, naturally, as I lived in the castle, and the Queen
and Queen Mother; here in England most of the
royal family, though that was a mere presentation out
of courtesy and I did not speak much with them. I
have made some friends in Stuttgart, including a fellow student and a young woman several years our
senior. She fascinates all who know her: Manners being less *restrictive* here, she dresses and comports herself in somewhat masculine style, and is not retreating
and *obsequious* in the way women are taught to be.
She is now engaged in writing a satiric novel, normally
the province of a man. As she counts among her acquaintance many of the principal artists and intellec-

tuals of Württemberg, and indeed of Europe, so I have been privileged to meet them as well. *Romanticisme,* as it was named by the brilliant Mme. de Staël, is all the rage in Europe; it is sure to have its foolish aspects, but I believe that it is a powerful force and liberating, and one day it will change all of the Western world; even in St. Louis it will make people more nearly *free men* than they are, and I look forward to that day.

I have spoken enough of myself for now, and eagerly await your response. I hope (and believe) that this letter finds you well. Is your family prospering? Are you engaged or married (do not be coy with me, good friend)? Please send all the news *post haste.* I am, mademoiselle

Yrs. respectfully

Jean-Baptiste Charbonneau

Stuttgart, September 30, 1825

General Wm Clark, Superintendent
Bureau of Indian Affairs
St. Louis
State of Missouri
United States of America

Sir:

I have just received your letter on return from a journey to England; my most humble apologies for my failure to send you an account of myself and my activities long since.

I matriculated at the University at Württemberg, the University of Shakespeare's Hamlet, a year ago, and have made some progress in my studies, especially my musical studies, of which I am very fond. You have often recalled to me that you named me "Dancing Boy" when I was but an infant on the great Expedition; perhaps you then perceived my predilection for music, which now evinces itself so strongly.

In England this summer, where Prince Paul was kind enough to present me to the royal family, I witnessed an event that may be of considerable interest to you: The British opened the first locomotive-powered Railway line, between Stockton and Darlington. This railway employs cars that run on tracks, as in the coal mines; but rather than being drawn by mules or horses, they are pulled by a *Locomotive,* an engine car that is powered by steam. In this manner the cars may be moved much more rapidly than before; and the British carry passengers on this Railway. It is much anticipated here that before the lapse of many years the Railway will become a principal mode of transportation for people and goods through all of Europe. The drawback, which does not apply to the steamboat, is the necessity of putting down metal tracks on which the cars may run; but the Railway may go *anywhere.* This invention may become of importance to U.S. commerce, and I imagine that you will be interested to hear of it, if the newspapers have not heretofore carried the news.

The main gratification of my eighteen months here is the numerous friends whom I have made, both in intellectual and artistic circles and in *society.* I do not find my *blood* a hindrance here; perhaps it is an advantage, in that many people of consequence wish to meet me, at least for *curiosity,* which I confess can be loathesome. Society is not strict in Europe, however, and men of color seem to be regarded as men. I was even able to initiate an *affaire of the heart* with a prominent young woman; alas, it has come to naught, but I do not believe its termination had to do with my race. Therefore I see opportunity here from which ignorant prejudice bars me in St. Louis.

I regret, then, that I must answer your question about my possible return to the U.S. negatively for the present. My feeling at this time is that, as long as Prince Paul wishes me to reside as his guest in Stuttgart or his companion in his travels, I will stay on here and try to discover a place for myself in the world.

I remain deeply grateful to you, the single person most responsible for my being given opportunities seldom afforded to members of my race. I look forward to hearing from you, Sir, about the welfare of your family and yourself, and the news of the city where I passed twelve significant years. Your most humble and obed't. svt.,

Jean-Baptiste Charbonneau

FEZ, 30 August 1826

Karlheinz von Sternberg
University of Württemberg
Stuttgart
Württemberg

My Dear friend:

Your *Sternenstein* has some leisure just now here
in Fez; the Prince is busily engaged in final preparations for our caravan to the interior. I know nothing
of the real North Africa as yet; we have not approached the Atlas Mountains nor the Sahara Desert,
neither have we met with the primitive tribesmen
who inhabit those places. I am but slightly acquainted
with this city, the capital of the Sultanate but am
more acquainted than I would wish to be with the
Moorish city of Tangier. However, I must write you
now or not at all for some months, as the interior is
quite beyond reach of postal services.

Tangier is a city twice conquered. Centuries ago,
the native Berber people held sway in this country;
but Moorish sultans took dominion from them. These
Sultans still rule, and the vast majority of the people
are Moors, Berbers making up an oppressed class. (I
have not yet made the acquaintance of anyone of
mixed blood, to discover the fate of half-breeds in
this land!) Effectively, however, the French have
great influence here; for what small commerce there
is, the French govern; there is report of approaching
French rule.

One cannot imagine that it matters who governs
here and who is governed; the people are desperately
poor and ill, and Tangier is the most repugnant city it
has been my ill luck to visit. Beggars line the streets
endlessly, sitting against the walls, seldom if ever
moving, and ignored by everyone. They sometimes
seem to be shadows or spirits instead of people. When
they do move, to cry out for a small coin, they plead
their case by pulling back their robes to show the
most grotesque sores and deformities. Some have no
noses, others neither mouths nor hands nor feet; lep-
rosy has maimed them. Many are missing hands that
were chopped off in punishment for theft; many have
syphilitic sores; I have seen one old man with a scro-

tum swollen to the size of his head, and swinging
between his knees. Altogether this place is a phantas-
magoria of the grotesque, far more bizarre and
gruesome than the pale imaginings of our Gothic
novelists. Removed from the land on which they must
have once sustained themselves, gathered into cities
that yet have not the employment that European cities offer, these wretches live in the worst of two
worlds. The North American Indian, regarded as
"backward," has a life that makes sustenance, responsibility for oneself, and dignity possible. These backward people have no hint of the worthiness of their
own persons.

They do gravitate toward a certain way out:
Hashish, when they can get it; delirium from their
illnesses also provides a kind of relief. In either case
many live in lotus land, and are said to fade into
death scarcely noting a change. Also their near neigh-
bors oft do not heed their departure from life—not
until they smell the bodies.

Surely the tribesmen of the interior, hunters and
goatherds, cannot be so abject as the swellers of Tangier.

Day after tomorrow we set out, if all goes ac-
cording to plan. Paul and I will be mounted on drom-
edaries, light, fleet camels bred especially for riding;
with us will be several of the Moors, an interpreter, a
guide, plus drovers; and we shall have some camels
and burros as pack animals. Perhaps it will be like
many expeditions I have made on the Great Plains of
the American States.

I anticipate with great eagerness seeing you next
winter, and sharing a bottle of a vintage that will help
me to forget the local potions.

Yours ever in friendship,
le sauvage naïf

SEPTEMBER 20: Baptiste's diary: "We have been riding
for some days now on high plateaus of grassland, with
mountains sometimes visible to the southwest. It is an odd
country, and has a strange effect on the mind. One moves
as through an illusion of time. Every morning the sun
rises, a sun identical to yesterday's in a cloudless sky over
a featureless plain; every noon it stands overhead and

scorches even the shadows away, raising waves of heat that blur the horizons; every evening it sets behind high mountains to the west. During the day we pass a few words, mostly the same ones; Paul notes in his journal that the vegetation is the same; we take three meals and a noon rest; the camels and burros plod so many steps forward. Yet nothing at all has changed. We might be on some vast treadmill, creating the illusion of movement in a landscape that moves by without any shift in its character, an endless repetition of the same hills, ravines, and far-stretching grass; a sort of cosmic joke."

ABOUT OCTOBER 1: "Still no change. I have been bored with this arid land; I have been awed, perhaps even frightened by it; I have been intrigued with it: It is a place where men are made to feel that they count for little, a place too mammoth huge for human beings."

ABOUT OCTOBER 5: "Gradually, grassland has been transformed into the greater aridity of high desert. We are moving down an immense, high, flat valley flanked by mountains running parallel on each side, the ones on the south edging the great Sahara itself. The terrain has shifted from the gray of parched grass and shrub to the red, tawny, and yellow of desert earth and rock. Grass grows in occasional clumps, like camel droppings, at random. The mountains on either side just straight up; looking at them, Sternenstein tried to feel the gargantuan force of their life toward the sky; he failed but the idea excited him.

"They have a kind of poetry, these mountains, a poetry utterly unlike anything in books. Its rhythm is the hard, firm rhythm of rock itself, drawing lines against the sky; its feeling is austere, harsh, serenely distant, enigmatically itself. I hesitate to put more words to it. In the last two hours before the sun fades, the red and yellow rock radiates a violent glow of pink, as though it, and not the sun, is the source of that rose light. It makes one *marvel*."

ABOUT OCTOBER 20: "We encountered some Berber nomads today. They had removed high onto the slopes of the mountains on the northern side of the valley, where there is grass at this time of the year. In the winter they will graze their herds at lower elevations, and we saw stone terracing there that evidences the growing of certain grains.

These nomads were utterly unlike other denizens of Northern Africa we have met: They are said to be fiercely independent, proud, utterly self-sufficient, and sometimes unfriendly. Some of this they showed in their disinclination to converse with us, limiting themselves to terse answers to thrice-put questions. *Sternenstein* liked them. We have come upon no Touregs, nor are likely to; the guide says that if we did, we would probably pay toll with our blood."

ABOUT NOVEMBER 1: "Have long since lost track of time, and am glad of it. The white man's time matters not at all out here; only the time of the sun and the seasons speak for ought. Paul talks volubly of his great love of this wild place; so volubly that I think he scarcely is able to take the time to look, listen, and smell."

PERHAPS NOVEMBER 10: "We are camped on a boulder-strewn plain near the top of a high pass through the Grand Atlas Mountains. Three days ago we turned back toward the sea, riding into what seemed an impassable massif; we are near what is said to be the highest point of the Atlas range. The wind has lashed at us for two days, and the steep grade has fatigued the animals brutally. The mountains to either side are barren and wind-swept, the dark rock plastered with snow, jaggedly austere. We are above the realms where either creatures or plants can live. These mountains are at once great nay-sayers to life, and yet awesome and grand. We men only scurry through their austere immensity.

"Some Berbers on their way to Market at Marrakesh are likewise encamped here. This evening I had an exchange with a Berber boy of perhaps 13 or 14, though we could not converse: I showed him something of how to play my harmonika, and learned from him to make sounds on his Jew's harp. Then we shared a dinner of warm goat's milk, cheese, and bread. I have enjoyed being in this strange land and look forward to Europe."

OCTOBER 21, 1827: Baptiste's diary: "I cannot see Sophie these days; I would probably be reluctant to attend her salons, anyway, from mixed feelings, but she is not holding them. The report is that she is working furiously on her novel, and that it will be a satirical lampooning of *Society;* perhaps, if she disguises her fictional characters but thinly, she will have a *succès de scandale*. Paul is immersed once again in the preparation of his *ms.* about North America for publication; I have seen him and the royal family but twice in the month since our return. So I occupy myself in the morning with *Herr Kapellmeister,* applying myself musically with some diligence; in the afternoons with my tutor, Herr Doktor Professor Steinhaus, attempting to learn something of philosophy, and in the evenings with Karlheinz, drinking ourselves toward *Götterdämmerung.* Since I allow myself no other diversions, it is a program of some austerity. *Le sauvage naïf* is, in fact, in jeopardy of turning into a scholar; he is engaged, at the behest of Herr Steinhaus, in the composition of a small paper in philosophy to be called 'The Spectacles of Mythology.' Sometimes I become so that serious about it that I chide myself against becoming an *enthusiast.*"

Karlheinz waved at him from the other end of the *Kaffeehaus.* He was setting up the chess pieces before Baptiste sat down. "Two hours, and not a single game," Karlheinz complained mildly. He dropped a bishop, which was not like him, and his fingers jerked at the pieces. Baptiste had known him to hold the chess table against all comers for an entire evening.

"Is this still your idea of sport?" Baptiste demurred. He leaned over and gave Hamlet an affectionate pat on the rump; the Dane would lie quietly under the table for hours while Karlheinz drank wine and talked.

"No, it is my addiction. Besides, you are bait. And I do have to concentrate against you. Sometimes." When he couldn't find a game, Karlheinz would harass Baptiste into playing him. Baptiste understood how the pieces moved, but nothing else of chess, and he played lackadaisically. Karlheinz's entertainment was in trying to checkmate Baptiste's king without losing a single piece of his own.

"I've worked it out," Baptiste said, advancing his king's pawn the mandatory two spaces. "It's in my head, but not on paper. Do you want to hear?"

Karlheinz gave him a mock-hateful look, opening with a knight move.

"Never mind. It's the price you pay for humiliating me on this imitation battlefield. This chessboard, in fact, may be a symptom of the illness I'm writing about."

"Far be it from me to claim health," murmured Karlheinz. "I am quite mad." He shot Baptiste his mad look and went back to the chessboard. Baptiste moved a piece pointlessly.

"The world is encrusted with mythology," Baptiste started. "The natural world is so thick with accreted mythology, like pigeon shit on the façade of a cathedral, that no one can see the original through the myth.

"In fact the white man's particular mode of thought may be described as myth-making. He refuses to see a thing simply as a thing. It is a revelation, a manifestation, a symbol. The rainbow is not a meteorological phenomenon I don't understand; it's God's promise of fair weather to mankind. The lily is not simply a plant that grows in certain places; it is God's example to mankind of the foolishness of laying up riches. The very mustard seed is an incipient parable. The key is that nothing is itself; everything is a manifestation."

Baptiste noticed that Karlheinz's knight had forked his castle and his king. He ignored it and moved a pawn; Karlheinz put the pawn back, moved Baptiste's king out of check, and took the castle.

"Some of this is all right, and has a certain poetic beauty. But a lot of it is dangerous. What happens is that we get handed ready-made ways of seeing and understanding. That's what religion is—a fabricated way of seeing the world. It converts everything from what it simply is into a metaphor of a divine plan, divine will, divine love, or whatever. Christianity holds that simple, observable fact like the coming of spring is a symbol of God's benevolence.

"I say it's dangerous. Some of it puts destructive ideas in our heads. As children we are given the notion of Original Sin, of fault transmitted genetically that makes us evil. Thus, when we err, or misbehave out of anger or desperation, we don't say we did something we wish we hadn't done. We take the error to be a manifestation of inherent evil. A simple deed becomes a cosmic one."

Karlheinz was proceeding with some care. Baptiste guessed that he was not merely trying to get a checkmate, but to capture every one of Baptiste's pieces first.

"But it isn't just that they've given us wrong ideas. It's that they've put spectacles on us, spectacles that *a priori* change existence. The world, for instance, is not simply the physical world. It's an arena in which man plays out his drama of good and evil. And man is not simply one organism among many on the earth, he's the zenith of creation, the completion of God's plan. Life is not merely the finite event of my existence, it's an elaborate moral trial. Witness here the transformation of all that is physical into the metaphysical.

"The problem is teleology. The search for a divine plan, for final causes, for ultimate reasons—where there are none.

"Religion, though, is not the great culprit."

"Check," Karlheinz gloated.

"Religion is not what makes the white man mythologize the world, it's the result of that impulse. Observe how we are governed by an ideal of courtly love. When a modern gentleman approaches a lady, he is not simply his particular self coming to a specific lady, he is in atmosphere and imagination Pelléas coming to Mélisande, or Lancelot to Guinevere. These trappings, of course, may make his actions entirely inappropriate to the actualities at hand, may make him absurd, and must lead to romantic delusions with disastrous consequences. But unless he can see himself in those terms, he is not satisfied.

"Today, young men cast themselves in the aspect of the late and tragic Lord Byron, cultivate melancholia, put on airs of grandeur, and walk to bed with a limp. To be less than that—to be themselves—would be petty and inconsequential. Ship captains embarking for Corsica strut the deck as they think Magellan did; junior French officers learn to stand with their fingers inserted between the buttons of their coats. None of them are willing to see themselves or others simply as what they are. All is colored with myth, with the ideal. Everyone is a figure in a cosmic drama—an imaginary drama."

"Checkmate," Karlheinz announced with satisfaction. He beckoned toward a girl at another table. "Do you mind?"

"No, but I'm not finished. The result of all this mythologizing is of course that we miss life. We miss our own lives as they pass. That can be dangerous. The modern Magellan strutting the deck and imagining for himself the fierce winds off Tierra del Fuego may put his little bark on some mundane local rocks. But whether or not it's dangerous, we lose the experience of our own existence, we miss

the beauty and ugliness of our surroundings, we pass
through the world without noticing it."

"Anna Jurgen," said Karlheinz, "Baptiste Charbonneau.
You've heard me speak of him." She was pretty, but had
the face of someone perpetually injured. Baptiste remembered Karlheinz's descriptions of his amorous delights with
her. "You may see Anna's lovely legs," Karlheinz went on,
"at the ballet. May we have a moment?" he asked Anna,
seating her. "Baptiste is coming to his peroration."

"The lover likewise moves through a dream," Baptiste
went on. "Meeting a lady at the ballet, he converts her
and himself into idealized figures—demonic or angelic, it
makes no difference. Later, if he is successful, he makes
love to a dream, and does not touch the actual lady he is
with."

"I find the flesh more stimulating than the gauze of
imagination," said Karlheinz. "If Hannes is making love to
dreams, that will explain his impotence. He will be glad to
know."

"The list goes on and on. We are living, most of us, in
an elaborate myth, far from the feeling of the dust under
our boots and the hardness of the wooden chairs we sit on.
We cannot see or feel the world we walk through, for the
haze of myth that engulfs it. We live in a God-damned
dream world. The pun is deliberate."

"So what would you do?"

"I wish we could see the world as Adam saw it. Purely.
Without encrustation. For the concrete, physical thing it is.
To him a snake was an animal of a different shape. To us
it's a symbol of evil. I'd like us to see a snake as a snake
again. Somehow we ought to learn to see the world with
our eyes, first-hand, and not through the eyes of a thousand teachers, poets, priests, and myth-makers."

"Anna would like to know," Karlheinz tossed out with a
smile, "whether the Indian is a better lover than that."

Baptiste scowled at him. Anna was watching Baptiste
with amusement. "I make love to the woman I am making
love to, in my own person." Anna's smile acknowledged
his poise.

"Does the Indian live any less in a dream world?" Karlheinz poked lightly.

"Not much. His life is based on dreams in a sense. In
his favor, he does not devise the elaborate metaphysical

schemes of an Aquinas, or debate about how many angels can stand on the tip of a porcupine quill."

"Will you return to your people?" Anna asked.

"No," Baptiste started, and then hesitated.

"Consider the difference between the primitive and the European," Karlheinz offered. "The primitive lives at the mercy of things, the European masters them. Because he thinks about the world differently, the Indian accepts it as he finds it—and lives in fear and supplication. The white man considers how he can change the world, and reshapes it to suit his purposes, to make his life safer and more comfortable. Where the Indian appeases natural forces, the European studies them, discovers how they work, and puts them to this service. He uses running water to grind grain. He cuts trees into planks for houses. He converts boiling water into energy that drives machinery. He shears the sheep, weaves its wool into cloth, and sews warm clothing from it. The Indian hasn't the knowledge for that; the knowledge comes from a European habit of mind, the inquiry for the causes of phenomena.

"That's why, in the end, the European will take the rest of that vast New World for himself and push the Indian off. The European will be master because he has the mastery."

"He'll leave the Western lands alone, I think. They're useless—vast empty plains, mountains, and deserts. Useless."

"Anna and I believe you," Karlheinz smiled, "on all counts. An interesting thesis you have. Shall we go now," he turned to her, "and make love in our own persons?"

Baptiste walked with them into the cold November twilight. Karlheinz beckoned to the setting sun with a finger, saying, "Come, sweet one, come, you are leaving us to cold once more." He wrapped his other arm around Anna. "A good day to be indoors in the warmth, a good day to fornicate, and a poor day for too much thinking. Let's leave that to philosophers with troublesome stomachs in dark, dusty rooms."

Just then, his eyes glazed and he humped over strangely. He put a hand to his chest, and his eyes stabbed up at Baptiste, as though calling for help from a great distance. Then he pitched hard to the sidewalk. Hamlet whined loudly, circling his master's form.

Rolling him onto his back, Baptiste tore open his shirt.

Karlheinz gave a squeaking, wheezing moan. His arms were rigid, fingers pushing stiffly at the sidewalk. His face was contorted horribly by pain. The thought crossed Baptiste's mind that he had never seen such an ugly face. He was barely aware that Anna had run for the doctor. He could feel no beat at Karlheinz's heart. He pressed and eased upon Karlheinz's chest, pressed and eased up. He did not know if it would help. Baptiste was shaking all over.

After a minute Karlheinz's face softened a little and did not look so horrible. His hands and arms relaxed. Baptiste could still feel nothing at his heart. He sat back on his heels and stared at the face, with its traces of surprise and pain and fear. He was sure that Karlheinz was dead.

"He always had a weak heart," the doctor said later at the office. He had no more than that to say.

Karlheinz's face picked up soft light from the satin that framed his head. His hair was ridiculously red. The closed eyes, the still mouth, had taken from the mortician's hand an air of unrufflable repose. It made Baptiste damned uncomfortable. He forced himself to stand by the casket longer than he wanted, looking down at his friend's body; he was trying to figure out why the thing in front of him did not remind him of Karlheinz. At last he realized that he had never before seen Karlheinz's face when it was fixed, when expression was not moving, flowing, on into another expression. He tried to plant Karlheinz's amused, curling smile on this face; it wouldn't work. Anna tugged at his hand.

At the cemetery Baptiste was not aware, amid the strangers and watching the shovelfuls of fresh dirt pitch into the grave, of feeling sorrow, just a peculiar hollowness. He heard nothing of what the priest was chanting. He was held by a single thought, which seemed luminous: So this was in him all along.

As they walked back toward the carriage, Anna murmured, "Why? Why? It's senseless."

Baptiste let a flicker of anger pass. No reason, he thought. There are no reasons. He was here, alive. Now he's gone, dead. Damn.

Chapter Five

1829

1826: Various Northern states passed laws forbidding state help in returning fugitive slaves; colony Nashoba founded to train Negroes for colonization in Africa.

1826: Jedediah Strong Smith led the first overland expedition to California.

1828: The U.S. and Great Britain agreed to joint occupation of Oregon territory.

1828: Construction began on the Baltimore & Ohio Railroad, first to operate in the U.S.

1828: MARCH 4: Andrew Jackson was inaugurated the seventh President of the U.S.

1830: The 1830s witnessed a sharp increase in immigration from Europe and in American prosperity.

1830, APRIL 6: Joseph Smith founded the Church of Jesus Christ and the Latter Day Saints.

1830: The forced march of Eastern Indians to Indian territory in the West gained the name "The Trail of Tears."

Eighteen Hundred Twenty-Nine

AUGUST, 1829: "I left you," Baptiste smiled, "at the age of eighteen an innocent much in need of your tolerance for my transgressions. I return to you at twenty-four a widely traveled, modestly educated, modestly cultured innocent, much in need of your tolerance for my transgressions."

It was nicely done, and Clark proposed yet another toast to Baptiste, which Pierre Chouteau, Jr., again seconded loudly.

It had been Clark's idea, a small dinner party with two Chouteau couples, the Bertholds, along with Coco, Father Neil, and Prince Paul. Clark had also persuaded one of the local newspapers to mention in passing that Jean-Baptiste Charbonneau, half-breed protégé of General William Clark, had returned to St. Louis after nearly six years in Europe. Baptiste was pleased, though he was aware that the homecoming celebrations were kept to a modest scale, and he knew why. He displayed his most gracious manners.

Mmes. Berthold and Chouteau and Coco were most curious after dinner about European society and fashions. Baptiste described, in circumspect terms, Princess Victoria, a lively young woman with whom he had passed a pleasant time, Charles X of France, to whom he had been presented only briefly, King William of Württemberg, the Marquesa du Breslin (he had not had the honor of meeting the Marquis), and other celebrated and high-born personages. He praised their beauty, their deportment, their qualities.

He offered as well something about his studies at the University, his devotion to music—he had brought back reams of sheet music which he would be pleased to lend them—and his reading, but they seemed only politely interested in that. Paul sat aside, somewhat to the ladies' chagrin, and let Baptiste dominate the conversation. Baptiste was amused that they did not ask him whether he had met any attractive and suitable young ladies; he wickedly let a hint or two drop about his delight at European womanhood.

He was being generous because he could afford it: He had a plan.

On his arrival in New Orleans Baptiste had posted a letter to Harper & Brothers in New York:

New Orleans, July 17, 1829

Gentlemen:

I propose to write a book that will I believe be of uncommon, indeed *unique* interest. Since it concerns myself, I must give here a brief account of my own life:

I am a half-breed, son of a Shoshone woman Sacajawea and the French-Canadian interpreter and guide Toussaint Charbonneau; both, you may recall, are somewhat celebrated for their role in guiding the Lewis & Clark expedition across the Shining Mountains and to the Pacific Ocean. That I was carried as a *papoose* on my mother's back on the journey has changed my life and brought about events that defy expectations and credibility; yet they are fact.

William Clark generously offered to have me educated in St. Louis and to treat me as his own son. From my fifth year, when I left the Minataree Indian tribe with which my parents and I lived on the upper Missouri River, until my eighteenth year, this General Clark generously and faithfully did. I was trained at some times by a Baptist minister and at others by a Catholic priest; my schooling included reading, writing, figures, world history, theology, *belles lettres,* and music, for which I showed a special aptitude. I also added to my native languages (French, Mandan, and Minataree) English and Latin. In two summers in Indian Territory, I was able to append some Sioux, Pawnee, Osage, and Mandan to my linguistic *repertoire.*

By good fortune, when I was employed in the fur trade on the lower Missouri in my eighteenth year and apparently gravitating into a career in the fur trade, I met Prince Paul of Württemberg, now Duke of that German principality: he was gathering botanical specimens for his collection and learning something of this continent for a book which he subsequently published in German. Being ambitious of greater things than guiding, interpreting, and trading in Indian Territory, I persuaded Prince Paul to retain my services and thereafter he took me with him to Europe. In Württemberg I lived for four years as Paul's protégé and virtually as a member of the royal family; I attended the University of Württemberg, which Shakespeare's Hamlet attended, and added greatly to my knowledge; I deepened my study of musical history, theory, composition, and performance at the *pianoforte;* travelled widely in France, Spain, England, and North Africa, venturing to the Atlas Mountains and the impenetrable Sahara Desert. I am now returned with Paul to St. Louis at the age of twenty-four.

The success in this country and abroad of many romantic books and plays about Indians evidences the great popular interest in the native inhabitants of the North American continent. Yet these *oeuvres* are precisely *Romantic*; their representation of Indians is very fanciful indeed. As a member of both the white and red races, familiar with both cultures, and as a widely travelled and experienced observer, I believe that I can made a unique contribution to the knowledge of Indians, and to the attitudes that each race has toward the other. My experience, which is that of being regarded as an Indian in white society and as a white in Indian society, gives ground for observations that I believe to be original.

You may apply to General Clark at St. Louis and to Prince Paul (in care of General Clark) for an account of my character; and I have confidence that both of them might be persuaded to write notes of foreword for my book, which would add substantially to its interest.

In two months the Prince and I shall leave St. Louis for the upper Missouri and the Rocky Mountains; the Prince wishes to make more observations of Indian life; because of his generosity to me, I am

obliged to accompany him on this journey which was
the purpose of our taking leave of the continent of
Europe; I shall take the occasion to reacquaint myself
with the country and the people to which I was born.
We shall return to St. Louis next spring, at which
time I plan to begin to transform the journals, which
I have kept scrupulously since the age of sixteen, into
a book. May I suggest the title *An Indian Abroad,*
using *abroad* to mean not only "in foreign places"
but "in alien places"?

I beg you to write me in care of General Clark
about your interest in my undertaking.

Your humble servant, &c.,
Jean-Baptiste Charbonneau

AUGUST 7: Baptiste's diary: "Coco remains in the situation in which I left her, but there is irony in that: She has
been married; her husband, whom I never knew, took employment with American fur, went upriver for a single trip
to learn something of the field end of the fur trade, and
managed to get himself killed by an irate Sioux. Careless-
ness? Jealousy over a woman? It matters not. At 24, Coco
was a widow and again living with her parents. Invited to
dinner *chez* Berthold (a pleasant development, the result
of my small *celebrity*), I rendered "Für Elise" on the *pianoforte*, which is one of only three in the city. Coco pronounced it exquisite, and I believe Mme. Berthold was
duly impressed. They were intrigued to hear more of
Beethoven—his deafness, his virtuosity as pianist and vio-
linist, and his titanic compositions, all of which they had
only by vague report. Coco having been too impatient ever
to learn to play, Mme. Berthold and I fumbled our way
through the slow movement of Beethoven's *E-Minor Sym-
phony* in the four-hand arrangement which I have
brought. The reception much flattered the performance,
and the entire evening was a grand success."

AUGUST 9: "General Clark approves my scheme of writing
a book, though the persuasion of Prince Paul added to my
own was necessary to move him. He emphasizes that I
must now make my own way in the world, and still talks
much of my entering government service as an Indian
agent. My further ideas of opening a shop to sell musical
scores and musical instruments and to give music lessons he

dismissed with the silence that with him means impatience. Nevertheless, he consents to write a foreword for my book. He also gave me a curious document, just published in *The Western Review,* that relates the life and violent death of Mike Fink. No one seems to know anything of Jim Beckwourth since he went with the Ashley men for the mountains some years ago. Winney is reported gone to New Orleans, doubtless a whore."

Mike Fink: The Last of the Boatmen

In 1822, Mike and his two friends, Carpenter and Talbot, engaged in St. Louis with Henry and Ashley to go up the Missouri with them in the threefold capacity of boatmen, trappers and hunters. The first year a company of about sixty ascended as high as the mouth of the Yellow Stone river; where they built a fort for the purposes of trade and security. From this place, small detachments of men, ten or twelve in a company, were sent out to hunt and trap on the tributary streams of the Missouri and Yellow Stone. Mike and his two friends, and nine others were sent to the Muscle Shell river, a tributary of the Yellow Stone, when the winter set in. Mike and company returned to a place near the mouth of the Yellow Stone; and preferring to remain out of the fort, they dug a hole or cave in the bluff bank of the river for a winter house, in which they resided during the winter. This proved a warm and commodious habitation, protecting the inmates from winds and snow. Here Mike and his friend Carpenter quarrelled a deadly quarrel, the cause of which is not certainly known, but was thought to have been caused by a rivalry in the good graces of a squaw. The quarrel was smothered for the time by the interposition of mutual friends. On the return of spring, the party revisited the fort, where Mike and Carpenter, over a cup of whiskey, revived the recollection of their past quarrel; but made a treaty of peace which was to be solemnized by their usual trial of shooting the cup of whiskey from off each other's head, as their custom was. This was at once the test of mutual reconciliation and renewed confidence. A question remained to be settled; who should have the first shot? To determine this, Mike proposed to "sky a copper" with Carpenter; that is, to throw up a copper. This was done, and Mike won the first shot. Carpenter seemed to be fully aware of Mike's unforgiving temper and treacherous intent, for he declared that he was sure Mike would kill him. But Carpenter scorned life too much to purchase it by a breach of his solemn compact in refusing to stand the test. Accordingly, he prepared to die. He bequeathed his gun, shot pouch, and powder horn, his belt, pistols and wages to Talbot, in case he should be killed. They went to the fatal plain, and whilst Mike loaded his rifle and picked his flint, Carpenter filled his tin cup with whiskey to the brim, and without changing his features, he placed it on his devoted head as a target for Mike to shoot at. Mike levelled his rifle at the head of Carpenter, at the distance of sixty yards. After drawing a bead, he took down his rifle from his face, and smilingly said, "Hold your noodle steady, Carpenter, and don't spill the whiskey, as I shall want some presently!" He again raised, cocked his piece, and in an instant Carpenter fell, and expired without a groan.—Mike's ball had penetrated the forehead of Carpenter in the center, about an inch and a half above the eyes. He coolly set down his rifle, and applying the muzzle to his mouth blew the smoke out of the touch hole without saying a word—keeping his eye steadily on the fallen body of Carpenter. His first words were, "Carpenter! have you spilt the whiskey!" He was then told that he had killed Carpenter. "It is all an accident," said Mike, "for I took as fair a bead on the black spot on the cup as I ever took on a squirrel's eye. How did it happen!" He then cursed the gun, the powder, the bullet, and finally himself.

This catastrophe (in a country where the strong arm of the law cannot reach) passed off for an accident; and Mike was permitted to go at large under the belief that Carpenter's death was the result of contingency. But Carpenter had a fast friend in Talbot, who only waited a fair opportunity to revenge his death. No opportunity offered for some months after, until one day, Mike in a fit of gasconading, declared to Talbot that he did kill Carpenter on purpose, and that he was glad of it. Talbot instantly drew from his belt a pistol (the same which had belonged to Carpenter), and shot Mike through the heart. Mike fell to the ground and expired without a word. Talbot, also, went unpunished, as nobody had authority, or inclination to call him on account. Truth was, Talbot was as ferocious and dangerous as the grizly bear of the prairies. About three months after, Talbot was present in the battle with the Aurickarees in which Col. Leavenworth commanded, where he displayed a coolness which would have done honor to a better man. He came out of the battle unharmed. About ten days after, he was drowned in the Titan river, in attempting to swim it. Thus ended "the last of the boatmen."

AUGUST 12: Baptiste's dairy: "At breakfast Paul indicated that I must press forward with my St. Louis business so that our expedition upriver can begin; he has completed what preparations are needful, but can profitably spend more time conversing with General Clark about Indians and perusing Clark's large collection of *artifacts*. I much impressed upon him that all my hopes rest on my book—otherwise I may end as only another buckskin-clad interpreter, scorned by civilized people—and that I wish to wait a while in anticipation of a reply from Harper & Brothers. He has given me until September 1. I have the $100 per month Paul will pay me for my services as an interpreter and guide, probably a sum of $900; and Gen. Clark has generously offered me $250 to carry certain papers to Fort Leavenworth, Fort Atkinson, and Fort Union. On my return, that much will I be able to count on for sustenance while setting down my story for the public."

AUGUST 14: "Now *le sauvage naïf* has apparently gained the place of an acceptable young gentleman about town. Today I took Coco riding to see the convent below the islands of the Missouri, borrowing Gen. Clark's handsome roan for myself. Mme. Berthold may not have been entirely pleased with Coco's choice; but she is now a young widow and therefore of status where she may be neither directed nor chaperoned; and she could see no objection to her riding with her "old childhood friend." Did Mme. Berthold know what transpired between us, she would be most displeased, volcanically displeased. For when Coco

spread the cloth for our picnic luncheon, I gently untied
the bow of her chapeau, unfastened her elegant white
dress (which took so much time that she very nearly
recovered her resistance), and in full daylight under the
hot August sun, put it to her. As it happened, when I gave
her my *love*, it was full of anger and therefore of energy. I
have the distinct impression that she had never been loved
quite so actively before. It seemed to surprise her, but
from her reaction I can only judge that she wishes thus to
be loved again and again. That causes me to regret that
my time in St. Louis, on this occasion, is no longer than it
is. A happy event, a happy day."

The next morning Isaiah appeared at the hotel to summon Baptiste to see General Clark immediately.

Baptiste found Clark in the big Council Room with five
Indians—chiefs, he guessed, from the elaborateness of
their dress. Clark asked him to sit down. No one knew the
chiefs' languages, and maybe Baptiste could help out.

They were Flatheads and a Nez Percé, Clark explained.
Ashley's crew had directed them to St. Louis from the
trappers' rendezvous because they wanted to see the Red-
Headed Chief. Clark did not remember any of them, but
the Lewis and Clark expedition had camped with both
tribes crossing the Rockies westward in 1805. And he'd be
damned if he knew what they'd come for. General Clark
was evidently a bit out of patience. Had they been a tribe
of the Great Plains, any number of trappers, boatmen, and
interpreters might have spoken their language. But this
bunch was from Oregon.

Baptiste didn't speak their languages either. He could do
nothing but confirm for Clark that the ambiguous sign language conveyed what it seemed to convey, though with
signs you could never be absolutely sure.

Right now the chiefs were again going through the ceremonial greetings and expression of deference and declarations of sincerity and friendly feeling that they had gone
through yesterday. Clark had Baptiste flash back his similar declarations. Baptiste knew that there was no way to
hurry an Indian through this.

Then came the first bit of substance. The chiefs
promised for both their peoples, and all the tribes and
bands of both peoples, their everlasting allegiance to the
Red-Headed Chief. Clark explained to them through Bap-

tiste about the greater White Father, the one in the great village on the Salt-Water-Everywhere many sleeps to the east, the father who was chief of all the white men. This confused the chiefs. They had been told about another chief of all the white men who lived on the other side of the Salt-Water-Everywhere to the east. Clark cussed the Britishers—the Oregon question wasn't yet settled—and had Baptiste tell them that the White Father he spoke of was their chief. They may not have understood, but they pledged their allegiance. They promised peace as long as the sun shone and the water flowed. They promised never to fight with their white brothers. They promised to befriend those of their white brothers who came into their country, to give them shelter, to feed them when they were hungry, to give them the skins of animals. They begged their white brothers to come to them.

Baptiste figured they were trying to get trade—must be needing guns, maybe to fend off the Blackfeet again. Clark had said the Blackfeet were well armed by the Hudson Bay Company, damn John Bull. And maybe these chiefs were wanting some big gifts to make them everlastingly friendly.

Clark, though, knew that was enough for the day. He summoned the chiefs to a meal, and asked Baptiste to come again the next morning. Hell, Baptiste thought, he still wants to initiate me into what he thinks is my natural career.

AUGUST 19: Baptiste's diary: "I spent the morning again in finger converse with the chiefs and General Clark. The affair is outrageously stupid, and would try anyone's patience. The afternoon more satisfactory: I sneaked into Coco's room when everyone was out and dallied in bed with her. The enterprise, though, was taken at great risk to us both, and it would be unwise to repeat it."

AUGUST 24: "Coco and I attended the dance *chez* Labbadie, and much enjoyed ourselves, to the unspoken consternation of everyone present. Our public demeanor, however, is impeccably impersonal. We had to part without touching."

AUGUST 26: "Prince Paul sat in on one of our meetings with the chiefs. Afterwards I explained the entire affair to

him, somewhat to his amusement. Coco and I managed to
slip away this afternoon to ride, and ride, again."

The hotel clerk handed Baptiste an envelope of heavy
brown paper: It was from New York.

New York, New York
August 1, 1829

M. Jean-Baptiste Charbonneau
In the care of General William Clark
Superintendent, Bureau of Indian Affairs
St. Louis
State of Missouri

M. Charbonneau:

Harper & Brothers are pleased that you have thought
of our firm in connection with the publishing of your
projected book. We are receptive to seeing your completed manuscript, or to seeing any part of it that you
may at present have written.

Sincerely yours,
A. J. Gurney
Editor

"Goddamn," Baptiste grinned. He showed the letter to
Paul, who declared himself happy for his protégé; Baptiste
begged for three or four days to do some writing so that
he could send off a part of the manuscript to New York
before they set out upriver. Paul consented.
Baptiste's manuscript:

In the summer of 1829, after an absence of nearly
six years from the shores of North America, *le
sauvage naïf* returned to the United States with
Prince Paul. Because of his wide experience of the
world and his university education, he considered
himself well fitted for a substantial post in commerce
or any other post that might be open to a young man
of twenty-four years of comparable knowledge and
experience; yet because of his too intimate acquaintance with the prejudice of whites against
"breeds," he also feared that few or no avenues
would be open to him. Therefore he was partly recep-

tive to the arguments of his old benefactor and
friend, General Clark, Superintendent of Indian Affairs, that he should enter the service of the U.S. government as an Indian agent: General Clark declared
convincingly that the young man, having the languages and the knowledge of both peoples, could
render great service to his red people and promote
understanding between the two races.

Fate, however, sometimes take a determining hand
in these matters. Just as Charbonneau was giving
heed to the General's well-intended words, an event
transpired, with an irony that seemed Providential, to
close his mind to such a possibility forever.

In August, not long after Prince Paul and Charbonneau's arrival in St. Louis, five chiefs of the Flathead and Nez-Percé Indians lifewise entered the
city; though they had come only half the distance in
miles, they had ventured from a place much further
from St. Louis in other ways—from their home on
the western slopes of the Rocky Mountains in the
Oregon Territory. They had made this journey, in-
comparably difficult for them, a wayfaring into the
mysterious and unknown, 'as a kind of pilgrimage:
They said they had come for the white man's book,
the Bible.

These Indians, living in one of the least accessible
areas of all the West, the mountains where Lewis and
Clark made their arduous crossing of the Continental
Divide, have had almost no contact with the white
man, much less than the warlike Sioux and the infa-
mous Blackfeet. Yet they heard from British and
French-Canadian fur traders of the Bible; and they
wanted to discover the medicine hidden in this great
book for themselves. Therefore they made a long
journey from their homes through unfamiliar country
to find the Red-Headed Chief. (They remembered
Clark with trust and affection from nearly a quarter of
a century earlier, and recalled the promises of friendship and assistance he had given them.) Hearing that
he was in St. Louis, they did not heed that the way
was long and hard and led through the lands of tribes
hostile to them; they resolutely took the trail east-
ward.

On arriving in St. Louis, they found that no one in

that city accustomed to Indians spoke their language. They were obliged to explain their pilgrimage to Clark through primitive and unclear sign language. (Clark, wanting to baptize his Paump in the responsibilities of Indian agents, asked your Charbonneau to assist in interpreting.) First there was much smoking of the ceremonial pipe, and many repetitions and elaborations on both sides of the friendship and loyalty both white and red had for each other. When the chiefs turned to the substance of their mission, General Clark could scarcely believe the words of the interpreter; he himself watched the hands of the chiefs carefully several times over while they repeated what they wanted. Were they indeed asking for the white man's book that told the secrets of the white man's God? The Bible? Even General Clark, wise in the ways of the Indians through his long experience, was inclined to see here the evidence of the hand of God, the sign of a miracle. What, other than the mysterious ways in which God works, could lead benighted Indians to seek the salvation of their souls through Jesus Christ? However, he remained uncertain that he understood them and continued the parleys.

General Clark could not easily give them the Bible anyway. They had no knowledge of writing, much less of the languages in which the Bible is printed. He had it in the back of his mind to report this extraordinary event to the various missionary societies that were beginning to clamor for the conversion of American savages to Christianity, but he took no action yet except to continue talking with them. It was during these extended talks that Charbonneau came to realize what great goal the chiefs had come to St. Louis to achieve.

Indian medicine, that is, religion, is the source of Indian power in this world, rather than the source of his salvation in the next. The Indian assuages and implores the forces around him with his magical chants, songs, dances, and prayers; in that manner he believes he gets what he needs to live. When he wants rain, he appeals to the gods of thunder and the west wind. When he wants meat, or blankets, or hides for his tipis, he does a buffalo dance. When he wants great strength, he prays to the grizzly bear, perhaps even eats some of the fur of that bear. He gets the necessities of life through his medicine, his religion.

When these Indians saw the white man's guns, his watches and compasses, his brass buttons, his clothing, his saddles, they were amazed; they had no knowledge of manufacturing and therefore assumed that the white man got these marvellous objects through his religion, through prayer and the conjuring of his God. It must be a powerful God, they concluded, who dispenses such gifts on the people who pray to him.

Charbonneau, observing that the chiefs recurrently mentioned the white man's book and the goods that they wanted, in close relationship, as though connected, at last realized that there was a connection between the two in the Indians' minds: They did not seek the Bible to cleanse their souls against Judgment Day; they sought it so that they could pray to God and magically get guns and other trade goods. They wanted to own for themselves the goose that laid the golden eggs!

Charbonneau urgently pointed out to General Clark what he believed to be the key to the chiefs' thinking. General Clark confessed that he was beginning to surmise the same. Then the extraordinary event: General Clark averred that he could see nothing to do but tell the chiefs that he would try to send them, in due time, someone who could tell them about the white man's medicine as taught in the white man's book; and he felt obliged to report the Indians' plea for Christianity to the churches.

Le sauvage naïf, feeling more than ever *naïf* and somewhat outraged, protested emphatically, to no avail.

Why, he demanded rather too peremptorily of General Clark, could the matter not be suppressed? Why could the chiefs not be told that the white man's *science*, and not his *religion*, produces the wonders that the Indians coveted?

"Paump," said General Clark, using still the affectionate name by which he knew me as an infant, "we must not cavil about these things. Perhaps the Indians ask to know our Lord for the wrong reasons. Our Lord has used even stranger means to bring lost souls to the light. My conscience could not rest easy if I did not at least inform the missionary societies of this appeal. I might be responsible for souls lost that could have been saved.

"Even if I wanted to stop the missionary movement to the Indians," he continued, "I could not. This summer Bill Sublette has taken wagons to the Rocky Mountains. Organizations are being formed to promote emigration to Oregon, and in ten or twenty years white settlements there will be substantial. The duty of the government is to protect the lives and property of its citizens: That means that the wagon route to the Pacific Coast must be made safe; it means that the Oregon settlements must be protected from Indians. It means that the Indians of the West must learn to live with the white man. All that is inevitable, Paump. Perhaps missionaries can help to persuade the Indians to be peaceful; if not, then the U.S. Army must pacify them. The missionaries are the more kindly means. And," he added pointedly, "the whites will make every effort to convert the Indians anyway."

It is the old story, thought Charbonneau: First the traders, then the missionaries, then the soldiers.

It was a classic case of two races, two peoples of different cultures, misunderstanding one another. The Indians do not want salvation in the next life; they want material goods in this life. They have asked for goods, and they will be misunderstood, with cause, by millions of Americans who cannot know what the Indians really want. In good conscience these Americans will offer them a terrible delusion which will in time lead to terrible disillusion. It will also lead to the further subjugation of the American Indian.

This event was a crossroads for Charbonneau. Whatever thoughts he had entertained of entering government service to promote understanding and peace between the red and white peoples, both of whom are his blood kin, he now abandoned. It seemed to him that the U.S. government, for all its stated benevolence, was embarked on a course detrimental to the Indian; it also seemed to him that the gulf of misunderstanding was too wide to be bridged without prodigious effort. It is the sincere hope of the author that this may contribute something to the mutual understanding now so sorely wanting.

Baptiste included a letter with this piece of manuscript:

St. Louis, September 3, 1829

Mr. A.J. Gurney, Editor
Harper & Brothers
New York, New York

Dear Sir:

I thank you for your letter of August 1. Enclosed for your perusal is a section of my manuscript relating a recent event. I choose it because it seems to bring into bold relief the misunderstanding of the red and white races, each of the other, the same misunderstanding which I humbly hope partially to alleviate. I should add that while the *theme* of my book is the nature of two different, even conflicting cultures, its specific matter is a series of improbable and colorful adventures of a member of both races, myself.

Prince Paul and I set out for the Rocky Mountains tomorrow. On this expedition I hope to deepen my knowledge of Indian culture for the sake of my book. Correspondence will either be carried to me by courier in Indian Territory or held for me in St. Louis until my return.

Your humble servant, &c.,
Jean-Baptiste Charbonneau

Coco was stretched on the damask linen among the spiky weeds, the sun full on her face. Her eyes were closed, and her mouth was on the verge of a smile: He imagined that she was watching the shifting, yellow-red glow the strong sun made on her eyelids—she liked that sometimes. Her hair, still an outrageously bright red, twirled behind her head in patterns more intricate even than the twilling of the damask; the sun glinted on both.
Baptiste, looking down at her face, and sometimes looking the length of her nude body, very white and very freckled, wondered how he might describe this feeling if he were to put it in his book. The only words he could think of were *full,* or *complete.* He put his dark wrist

against her shoulder to see the difference in tone, and smiled. She opened her eyes into his face.

"I'll be back in May, I think," he said. They had not spoken of the fact that he was leaving on the morrow, and they had not spoken of the future.

A strange look, sad perhaps, flickered in her eyes and passed. She put a hand on his hoop, dangling from his neck through the open shirt and rubbed the stone with a forefinger. "Baptiste," she said, "in May, if things work out, I will probably be engaged to be married. I may be married. I must." She drew him down gently by the stone and kissed him lightly on the lips.

DECEMBER, 1829: This Kenneth MacKenzie seemed more than hospitable. He'd put Paul and Baptiste up in part of the apartment he'd built for himself in Fort Union, and invited them to a dinner they "wouldn't be accustomed to in this country" that night.

They had ended up here at Fort Union because their traveling was by courtesy of the American Fur Company. They had gone by steamboat up to Fort Atkinson at the mouth of the Platte; Paul had spent some time with the Sioux there, giving Baptiste a chance to improve his Sioux-speaking skills. Then on by horseback through Sioux country to Fort Kiowa, with a small American Fur party, and on to the Arikara villages and then the Mandan villages. It had all been familiar to Baptiste, homecoming more of curiosity than enthusiasm. Paul had been fascinated by the Mandans, who lived in big circular huts made of grass, and had developed a complex ceremonial society. They both took copious notes for their respective books on the graded orders of Mandan society—Fox, Foolish Dog, Half-sheared, Make-mouth-black, Dog, Crow, Buffalo Bull, and Black-tail-deer for just the men alone—on their elaborate ritual dances, and on their colorful symbolic dress.

To winter on the plains, to get some shelter against the blizzards, the ferocious winds that swept down from Canada, and the sub-zero temperatures, they had accepted the offer to go on to Fort Union at the mouth of the Yellowstone, the headquarters of Kenneth MacKenzie, the King of the Missouri, and the chief ambassador for John Jacob Astor in the West.

MacKenzie was expansively gracious that evening.

Though the fort was only a year and a half old, by now he had the accoutrements of civilization. He offered them wines, apéritifs, brandies, and fine cigars. The meal was a handsome affair in several courses served by beautiful Assiniboine girls. Baptiste had already heard that he dressed his Assiniboine mistress in the latest fashions St. Louis had gotten wind of from New York, though he hadn't seen the lady. Clearly, MacKenzie was a man of style.

And of ambition. He expounded his ambitions over dinner. In the first two summers at the fort they had accomplished great things: They had driven cows and hogs from Missouri to the Yellowstone, and were getting the butter and cheese and bacon Paul and Baptiste were now enjoying. They had planted the first corn crops this far west. MacKenzie had even brought up a still that he used to produce corn liquor. Before long, he indicated, he would have turned Fort Union into a burgeoning oasis of civilization on these vast, sun-burned plains.

And he would make it pay. American Fur already had the river trade well in hand—they'd been trading with the tribes along the Missouri for beaver pelts for years—but the mountains were the gold mine. The mountains, still several hundred miles to the west, where Ashley, Henry, and the others had found untrapped country and had been harvesting it alone. You had to send trappers instead of traders there, MacKenzie explained. He would be sending some next summer to the mountains, and he intended to do what the Ashley bunch had never been able to bring off—build a fort in the heart of Blackfoot country and open trade with the most hostile Indians in the West. Mr. Crooks—Ramsay Crooks, the head of the fur end of John Jacob Astor's empire—believed in the mountains and the West. MacKenzie would justify Crooks' faith.

Paul inquired about the customs of the principal Indians of the area, the Assiniboines. MacKenzie knew nothing about that.

Baptiste wanted to know whether the trappers who worked the mountains found it profitable.

"They do," MacKenzie said, "they certainly do. A good trapper brings a high wage. But they never get to spend it." He smiled a little. "When Ashley brought them to the mountains, he thought they would stay a year or two for the money and then get back to the settlements, out of harm's way. But they don't. They stay in the mountains. They live like Indians, like savages, and they enjoy it. The money just sits in a bank in St. Louis, what of it they don't spend on whisky."

When Paul and Baptiste retired for the night, one of MacKenzie's aides told them quietly that if they would only say the word, girls would be made available to them. Paul seemed embarrassed about that. Baptiste laughed.

MacKenzie treated them well that winter—he was aware that his firm was host to a prince. Paul and Baptiste were fascinating guests for MacKenzie. The prince, aside from lending a certain distinction by his mere presence, was interested in commerce. The King of the Missouri talked with the Prince of Württemberg for hours about MacKenzie's dreams for the area—dreams that reached beyond the fur trade and amounted to a virtual empire. Paul noted that MacKenzie would be giving the Indians useful employment, and approved. Baptiste seemed to MacKenzie to be a moody young man, but he was still intrigued by the slender, handsome breed who spoke half a dozen languages, could read and write and quote the Latin poets, sometimes reminisced about European courts, and had had the shrewdness to make himself companion to a king. MacKenzie admired shrewdness.

In the long evenings of the northern plains, around a huge fire that prodded back the cold, Baptiste would sometimes play his harmonika. He would play American country dance music, which MacKenzie liked because he could take a turn or two with his favorite Assiniboine girl, and sometimes Baptiste would even play the compositions of one Beethoven. MacKenzie had not heard of the composer, but he knew that the music lent a touch of class to his crude drawing room, an aura of courtliness to the primitive palace of MacKenzie's empire.

JANUARY, 1830: An Assiniboine meat-making party, following some buffalo tracks that a scout had found, was ambushed by a larger Blackfoot party and virtually wiped out. Two braves made their way back to the tipis clustered around Fort Union to tell the story. The Assiniboines promptly held the largest and most elaborate war-dance ceremonial that Baptiste had ever seen.

He was singing the songs aloud again, so that he could

copy down the notes as well as the words for his book,
when MacKenzie walked into the apartment.

"What in hell are you doing," MacKenzie asked, not
meaning to be unpleasant, "getting worked up to attack
the fort?"

"Noting down Assiniboine songs for my book," Baptiste
laughed. He explained a little about the project; MacKenzie didn't seem particularly sympathetic.

"Your Herr Beethoven may be a discovery of worth,"
MacKenzie judged, "but I doubt that the compositions of
Watery Eyes will get a following." That was MacKenzie's
nickname for Sky-Blue-Eyes, the young warrior-leader.

"But they have more of a place in my book."

"Here's a letter for you," MacKenzie smiled. It was
from Harper & Bros. in New York. "Courtesy," MacKenzie elaborated, "of the U.S. Postal Service by steamboat to
St. Louis, the U.S. Army by steamboat to Fort Atkinson,
and the American Fur courier by horseback and snowshoe
from there." He waited for effect. "You're lucky. I get pa-
pers from Chouteau once a winter."

New York, October 2, 1819

M. Jean-Baptiste Charbonneau　
In the care of General William Clark, Superintendent
Bureau of Indian Affairs
St. Louis
State of Missouri

Dear Sir:

We are in receipt of your letter of September 3
and of your partial manuscript.

I fear that in our opinion the completed section
does not augur well for the book in its entirety. In
this section you deal both with the policy of our government in regard to the proper treatment of Indians
and with public sentiment about their conversion to
Christianity. It seems to us that your own attitudes in
these matters are perhaps more radical than would be
acceptable to the American public, and your expression perhaps gives not enough judicious consider-
ation to the views of others. In brief, it seems to us
that you hold attitudes which the majority of your
readers would find unacceptable. Harper & Brothers
could not at this time consider a manuscript which

flies in the face of the very public on which Harper &
Brothers is dependent for its support.

We are aware, of course, that a partial manuscript
may misrepresent the whole, and remain open to con-
sideration of your efforts.

Sincerely yours,
A.J. Gurney
Editor

"Efforts without balls," Baptiste said.

Two trappers wandered in during late January with
horseback loads of furs and settled down to wait for
spring. One, a bent fellow who called himself Old Bill
Williams, didn't have much to say except that he'd got
tired of freezing through the winter with the miserable
bunch of Crows down on Powder River, and he reckoned
he'd have a look at what MacKenzie would give him for
his plews. Williams worked alone, apparently, which astonished Baptiste. MacKenzie gave him a handsome price. The
King admitted to Baptiste that it was mostly a ploy to get
Williams' business—American fur would take a loss on
these plews—but the money went a long way toward keeping Old Bill's thirst quenched and his tongue loosened.

Bill was called by other names, he confessed, Parson
Bill and Old Solitaire and some others as were discompli-
mentary. He was an educated man, for a fact, and he had
been a Baptist preacher when he was nigh seventeen. Next
he'd carried the Word to the Osages. He'd taught them to
worship the white critturs' God, sure enough, but they'd
taught him to worship their gods too. He'd ended by
chucking the whole thing, layin' in some powder an' lead
an' baccy and pointin' his old mule toward the mountains.

Bill was gray, but he could have been almost any age.
His face was tanned to the roughness of buckskin from
years in the sun and wind. His eyes were slits from squinting into strong light, and crow's feet forked out from
their corners like the branches of a tree. His nose bent like
a hawk's beak and threatened to play footsie with his chin.
His back humped about halfway up, thrusting his head
forward, and he walked in a slouch. With an old Hawken
rifle, .55 calibre, that he shot with an odd wobble, he let

fly at some chunks of firewood in competition with Paul, an expert shot; Bill could shoot with the prince.

The traders had heard stories about him. He was supposed to be a loner, working the small creeks in high mountains by himself while the other trappers marched about in brigades. He had had a string of squaws to keep his blankets warm and his lodge tidy, but he turned them back as often as he got them. He was said to be ornery and mean. The word was that in starving times it wasn't a good idea to ride a trail in front of Bill Williams.

He didn't really talk about himself, but he told stories. One night, late, when they had both drunk too much, Baptiste asked him what kind of wives squaws made.

When Bill got started, Baptiste knew better than to interrupt:

"From Red River, away up north among the Britishers, to Heely in the Spanish country—from the old Missoura here to the sea of Californy, I've trapped and hunted. I knows the Injuns and thar sign, and they knows me, I'm thinkin'. Twenty winters has snowed on me in these hyar mountains, and a niggur or a Spaniard would larn some in that time. This old tool," he tapped his Hawken, "shoots center, she does. And if thar's game afoot, this child knows bull from cow and ought to could. That deer is deer and goats is goats is plain as paint to any but a greenhorn. Beaver's a cunning crittur, but I've trapped a heap. And at killing meat when meat's running, I'll shine in the biggest kind of crowd.

"For fifteen year I packed a squaw along—not one, but a many. First I had a Blackfoot—the damnedest slut as ever cried for foofuraw. I lodgepoled her on Colter's Crick and made her quit. My buffler hoss, and as good as four packs of beaver I gave for old Bull-tail's daughter. He was head chief of the Ricaree, and came nicely round me. Thar wasn't enough scarlet cloth nor beads nor vermilion in Ashley's packs for her. Traps wouldn't buy her all the foofuraw she wanted. And in two years I'd sold her to Cross-Eagle for one of Jake Hawken's guns—this very one I hold in my hands. Then I tried the Sioux, the Shian, and a Digger from the other side, who made the best mokkerson I ever wore. She was best of all, and was rubbed out by the Yutas at Brown's Hole. Bad was best, and after she was gone under, I tried no more.

"Red blood won't shine anyways you fix it. And though

I'm hell for sign, a woman's breast is the hardest kind of rock to me, and leaves no trail that I can see of."

MARCH, 1830: It was a bitter winter. After a few days of sun in late February which made them think the thaw was coming, it turned cold and snowy for another month. Baptiste walked out with Bill on some days to relieve the boredom. It was high plains country, rolling, for the most part, and covered with flat white to each horizon. Walking in the primitive snowshoes Bill had made—willow sticks lashed with thongs—was awkward and laborious. Baptiste sweated in his heavy capote, and his brain swam sometimes with fatigue. After a while he saw colors on reflecting white surface.

Bill showed him the broken cottonwood trees, where the cold had got so sharp that it split the trunks. He showed him the carcasses of buffalo stuck solid in the ice of the Missouri. The damned Indians, Assiniboine or Blackfeet one, had got them running and herded them off some bluffs above into the river and they'd drowned. Damned Injuns slaughtered them that way and didn't even take all the meat—did it for fun. Bill showed him how to survive a subzero night on the plains: Up under the boughs of a tree that didn't shed, if you could find one, and in a deep hole in the snow to keep the wind off if you couldn't.

One afternoon, when the sun was so bright off the snow that Baptiste could barely see, Bill cut buffler track. The crittur couldn't be far, Bill opined, as they didn't move much in the deep snow. The two waddled along the tracks and found them in half an hour—a bull, a cow, and a yearling cow pawing at the snow for what little they could get.

Baptiste was not over being awed by buffalo. This bull stood about six feet at the hump, went ten feet long, and might have weighed out at a ton. He was yellow-haired about the hump and shoulders, darkening to brown at the rump. He could have tramped Bill and Baptiste with scarcely an effort. But he didn't, mainly because he didn't see, hear, or smell them. Buffalo were stupid; mountain talk for "dimwitted" was "buffler-witted."

They crawled to within easy range. Bill always carried his Hawken, but Baptiste didn't have his. A buffalo was a hard shot. In all that mass only a ball placed just behind the shoulders and barely above the brisket would bring one down, and even when hit there, it might run half a mile. Bill picked the yearling as the most tender, waited patiently, and hit her true. She took a couple of steps, dazed, then braced her legs well apart for the on-slaught. The other two looked around, seemed to notice nothing, and went on grazing. The young cow began to sway and stamp as though she had delirium tremens. She rolled her head, and blood gushed out of her mouth and nostrils. After she shook a little more, she crumpled to her knees and rolled onto her side.

Bill yelled and waved at the others to shoo them away. He reckoned he wasn't interested in supplying meat for the whole damn fort.

Bill turned the cow onto her belly, made the two long slits that form the sign of the cross, pulled back the skin to use as a tablecloth, and went to work at the butchering. When he got to the liver, he cut off raw slices, dipped them in bile for a sauce, and shared them with Baptiste. Baptiste heard that the Indians ate it raw, but he had never seen it or tried it. His mind wrenched at the thought of what he was doing, but his tongue put a tentative OK on it.

Then Bill cut out the boudins—the guts—and offered Baptiste one end. Baptiste declined, so Bill started sucking the boudins down, apparently without chewing, and push-ing the contents out with his hands as he went. Baptiste went queasy, then upchucked the fresh liver on the snow.

Bill grinned without stopping. When he had finished, he said "You act like a *mangeur de lard,* boy." Literally, it meant "pork-eater," and figuratively a man who was not used to mountain diet, a man who was green.

Bill told Baptiste to cut the tongue out while he took the boss, the hump, and the hump ribs. They carried the meat back to the fort in the buffler skin—Bill wanted the hide for a blanket.

That night they invited Paul to an open-fire feast—hump ribs roasted on a spit, hump roast, and, at the very end, the tongue baked slowly under the coals. Baptiste had recovered his stomach and told Bill it was a superb meal. "It does shine, don't it?" Bill agreed. Even Paul seemed to think it a treat of a sort.

Mostly though, that March, Bill used his time to drink and play cards. Baptiste became a first-rate euchre player during all-day sessions with Bill. They amused themselves from time to time by trading a few beads for the services of a squaw—always briefly, though sometimes it was a lot of fun. Baptiste listened to Bill's bottomless well of stories, some of them fantastic but probably true, others entertainments that strung the believer along until the last line that was outlandish and made him feel foolish for having listened seriously.

Baptiste spent his time watching spring come to the plains, the snow sagging first into tiny rivulets of melt, then backing up to show clumps of dead grass here and there, then melting into the ground and coming back in the pale yellow of early grass and the lively colors of wildflowers.

APRIL, 1830: MacKenzie struck the match, put it to the cigar, and blew out the smoke in quick little puffs. "You've not been doing much on the book," he said to Baptiste.

Baptiste waited a moment while the Assiniboine girl reached around him for the dishes. "Not much," he admitted.

"Giving it up?"

"Just letting it slow down."

"Would Your Highness object," MacKenzie asked, "if I made your retainer an offer?"

"Not at all, he's a free man."

"We can escort you back to St. Louis by boat with an experienced and well-armed crew. You wouldn't be stranded if you lost him." He turned to Baptiste. "You've said the normal avenues weren't open to you in St. Louis commerce. No such prejudice exists at Fort Union." He drew deeply on the cigar. "Stay here with me. You can be extraordinarily valuable. You not only have the languages and the understanding of the Indians, you are yourself an Indian. Indians will trust you, and through you will trust us. You can make a great contribution to American Fur, and you can benefit the Indians as well through our trade." He paused to see what effect he was having on Baptiste. "I will make you my righthand man."

"No," Baptiste said.

"It's a handsome offer. The Company will take care of all your needs—food, lodging, horses, clothing, everything—and will pay you three thousand dollars a year."

"No, I'm sorry."

"Do you want more money?"

"The money's generous. I don't want to do it."

"Do you mind telling me why?"

"I don't like what you're doing here. I think it's ruthless."

MacKenzie eyed him for a moment. "Well, my boy, it's meant to be," the King smiled broadly. He had just dismissed Baptiste from his mind as a valuable employee, and as a possibly successful man. He rose, announcing the end of dinner. Prince Paul and Baptiste started toward the door.

"By the way," MacKenzie called after him, "what do you intend to do?"

"Go to the trappers' rendezvous with Bill Williams. It'll be fun. Then we'll see."

Baptiste had not mentioned this plan to Prince Paul; the more serious problem was that he hadn't mentioned it to Old Bill.

"Take ye?" Bill crackled in his squeaky voice. "Does this child look like he's narsin'?" He stalked off, his legs moving like boards linked by rusty nails.

Baptiste had to get an outfit. With his own horse and equipment, plus the $700 he had coming in wages from Paul, he traded for a buffalo horse, a packhorse, another set of buckskins, some buffalo robes as blankets, horns for powder and for beaver medicine, a pouch for bullets, a skin sack for possibles, several more pairs of moccasins, and some pemmican. From MacKenzie he bought six traps at $20 apiece, tobacco, some whisky, cooking gear, a pistol, a Green River (the preferred mountain man's knife), powder, and balls. He was surprised that in the mountains everything cost five to ten times and more what it cost in St. Louis. But he didn't care.

Bill pretended to pay no mind to what Baptiste was doing. He took to saying once in a while that he was a loner, and to telling stories about when the damned Shian had got Lew Marcus, or the Blackfeet had cut Old Pierre into a lot of little pieces, or Jed Smith had lost two dozen men in two massacrees on the way to Californy and back. He recalled how the Pawnees tortured men by tying them to poles, jamming sticks into their skin, and setting fire to the sticks. He remembered Baptiste the imagination the Blackfeet brought to torture, and the vehemence the women showed in chopping up the bodies afterward. Baptiste just listened. He had a feeling Bill was watching him.

APRIL, 1830: On a fine morning without a cloud from far
horizon to far horizon, Bill started grumbling about how
lazy he was, how late he was, how the beaver could swim
to St. Louis before he did anything about getting them
there. By mid-morning he was packed and ready to ride.
Baptiste's one horse was packed and the other saddled
next to Bill's. Bill said nary a word as he mounted. "I'll
track you if I have to," Baptiste said. Bill eyed the pack
on Baptiste's horse for a moment, said nothing, and set
out.

Living came first, he found out, and trapping second.
He learned to poke in the driftwood along the west bank
of the Yellowstone for Jerusalem artichokes the gophers
had stored there. He learned to pick hips off the wild roses
regularly, because they alone would keep away scurvy. He
learned to find chokecherries and serviceberries to spice a
stew with, and maybe some wild onions. Bill brewed up an
aromatic tea from pine needles, which Baptiste thought
at least the equal of India tea; when Baptiste brewed it,
though, he steeped it and ended up with something that
tasted like oil. Bill also taught him to eat pine nuts, and
how to make kinnikkinnik from soft, shredding bark to
replace tobacco. When Bill got tired of jerky and pemmican, he killed a deer. They ate the heart, tenderloin, and
liver immediately just a turn over the fire away from being
raw, and shared the ribs and large roasts that night. Bill
gave Baptiste a lesson by putting away what looked like
ten pounds of fresh meat—said he made a habit of eating
high for a couple of days and then going nearly hungry
for a few days. Since the next morning was sunny, they
spent the whole day jerking deer meat in the smoke, sun,
and wind. They were having so much fun living that they
didn't get around to trapping for quite a while.

Trapping turned out to be an arcane skill. Bill didn't let
Baptiste trap—said he would only mess things up for Old
Solitaire—but set Baptiste's traps along with his own. After they started up Powder River, Bill began to work the
cricks coming out of the mountains to the southwest. He
would ride up a crick watching for slack water, beaver
dams, and other beaver sign. When he found it, he set a
string of traps in likely spots. He would walk downstream
from the spot and wade back up, to kill the man smell.
Then he would drive a heavy float stick deep through one
end of the trap chain and into the bottom in deep water.

The trap he snapped open and set in shallow water. Then the seductive touch. Bill kept a horn full of secretion called castoreum that he took from the scrotums of beaver he'd trapped. He didn't know why, but he knew that beaver were intrigued by its smell. He dipped a little stick into the castoreum, and planted the stick next to the trap. The point, he said, was to get the beaver to come to the medicine, stand up to sniff it, and put his foot where he shouldn't. Once he did that, the float stick would keep him from dragging the trap into the bank and gnawing his own paw off to get free. So he would head for deeper water, and would end up drowning.

The days' routine was relaxed. Bill and Baptiste checked the traps at daylight and dusk. Bill crabbed every morning that he was stiff from wading up to his thighs in the damned cricks; getting bad joints from the cold water, he was. In the morning Bill supervised, puffing on his pipe, while Baptiste skinned the beaver and scraped and stretched the skins—even a Frenchy had to do something to pay his way, Bill judged. In the afternoons they loafed and gathered some greens for the night's meal—growing all around ya, all ya got to do is stick your hand out to eat, Bill said. Just before dark they ran the trapline again. And then they'd have boiled beaver tail for dinner, finest eatin's Bill knowed of anywheres, he said.

Sometimes Bill smoked at night while Baptiste applied himself to the skinning again. Sometimes he told stories. He had a favorite about the time he was up to the head of the Yallerstone, fust time he ever was, whar was b'ilin' springs and hot clay, and the water shot out of the ground like God spittin', and he seen an elk standing still grazin' more'n twenty-five yards away. He knelt right down and let fly with his Hawken, which wasn't this'n but another'n what also shot center, and the elk didn't move. Didn't fall, didn't run, didn't do nothin'. Bill couldn't figure it out so he powdered and patched and rammed another ball home and primed and let fly again. Still nothin'. Bill was beginning to wonder if that elk was a statue made of bronze by some fancy fellow back to St. Louy. But he crawls up to ten yards away and lets fly the third time. Still nothin'. So he says, Goddam it, this child'll make you know he's hyar, even if you're a damned divil. So he ran up to the niggur holding his Hawken by the barrel, meanin' to club the crittur over the head. Just as he was about to swing, something knocked him flat on his withers. He got up, cautious-like, and begun to feel around with his fingers. Pretty soon he figured it out. Thar was a glass mountain, clear as a mountain crick, 'atween him and that elk, and it was actin' like a telescope, makin' that elk seem close when actual it was twenty-five mile away on the far side of the mountain.

Bill didn't stay anywhere long. After no more than three days in the same camp, he'd decide to pick up and move on. Didn't want any Crows to get a bead on him, and there were plenty of them around. Real civil fellows when they met you in a brigade, but right unfriendly when they caught you alone or in twos and threes. So the two would pack up and move south over a little divide to another crick, work down it for three days, cross another little divide onto another crick and work up it.

Bill always led them into new areas by ridges. He rode slowly and silently; Baptiste had to learn that jawboning was forbidden on the trail. As soon as Bill topped a ridge, he turned himself into a bundle of nerve endings, all eyes, ears, and nose, picking up the minute signs of what was going on in that vicinity. If he saw a duck swimming down a crick, he could tell whether it had been frightened by human beings above or was just looking for food. He registered without thinking whether a stick had fallen into the water or had been knocked in by a hiding Indian. He could tell by the way a deer stood whether its enemies were nearby. So when Bill kicked his mule to the crest of a divide, everything he could see, hear, and smell was an encyclopedia of what had been happening in the area, what was happening, what was about to happen. He would sit quiet for a few minutes, absorbing, then ride slowly on, being careful not to silhouette his party against the sky, soaking in all the information he could. He explained to Baptiste once that a coon didn't think about that, didn't do it consciously, just did it. That was how come Bill didn't get caught by the Injuns, and a lot of beavers was gone under when he was still aboveground.

In that fashion they worked their way up the length of Powder River, crossed the Big Horn Mountains above its source, trapped west across the Big Horn River and into the Absaroka range. They never saw Indians. Bill saw plenty of sign, and knew where they were often enough, but he and Baptiste slipped around them. Bridger and Sublette and them critturs liked to travel in brigades, Bill said, big bands of fifty and sixty. No need for it. It would pass if you wanted to outfight the Indians—and some of them liked to kill Blackfeet, he guessed. "But this child don't want to fight 'em. Jist ease around 'em."

JUNE 29: Baptiste's journal: "Old Bill told me last evening a saying of the Indians which he is fond of, and evidently much given to quoting: They say that once a man drinks of a streamlet in the high mountains, one of those fledgling rivulets that will assemble later into wild, turbulent mountain rivers and still later into the more stately rivers of the plains, the cold, clear, pure water must inevitably draw him back to that place to drink once more before he dies. The saying is expressive of the idea, more generally, that the high Rockies exert a mysterious force on people that, like a magnet, must pull them back to the mountains. I can believe that. The white man insists on claiming the arable plains of the Ohio River Valley for himself, and on assigning to the red man these vast reaches of mountain and desert. In doing so, he may have ironically ceded the most remarkable land of this continent to those whom he wishes to see disinherited. If those eastern lands have more of value for commerce, these may have more of value for the spirit.

"Poesy is full of tributes to mountains; yet the verses of even the greatest poets suggest a gentle and idyllic clime suitable for the musings of the gentlemen and gentlewomen. Here unfolds a virile, masculine poetry: The stony ridges rise unadorned by plant or tree above the pine forests, arrogant in their supremacy; even the *rough-and-jumble* of rocks draws their boulders, each chaotically shaped in itself, into a larger rhythm; they rise toward the sky like melodies, with many intricate variations, but united in the universal motion of ascension. Yet these melodies do not impress with their sweetness, their charm, or their wit; rather they awe with their nakedness, their jaggedness, the immensity of their upward thrust. Perhaps the poets do better to leave these mountains alone; for, truly represented, they are no suitable subject for lyric muse. Poor words do not do justice to their thunderous poetry, nor to their drama: for in their majesty they are capable of a fierce hostility to the men who dare travel them, and can dispense death with a terrible and swift unexpectedness.

"Again no words are appropriate to them because scribbling draws back the mind from their immediacy. 'Old Bill' is even now chuckling at his companion for putting down these words; while *le sauvage naïf* (!) scribbles and keeps his eye on the pen and page, 'Old Solitaire' lets his eyes and ears reach out to the amazing world around him, recording, experiencing, being. A man who chooses to write about these mountains puts himself at one remove from them; the men who understand them best write nothing, but merely live among them. Perhaps they have a secret of which *civilization* knows nought."

He closed the journal and put it away; he wondered whether he would be troubling much longer with pen and page.

JULY, 1830: The Crow touched the medicine object at his neck, a small hoop with four eagle feathers and a lock of hair; he closed his eyes and uttered two little piercing cries, falling in pitch. Then he smiled at Baptiste and rolled his eyeballs. He tossed the piece of bone, carved into the shape of a tiny war club, between his hands four times. He clasped his hands together, the bone between, wrung them for a moment, then stuck them out in Baptiste's face. Baptiste touched the right hand. The young Crow opened the left, showing the bone, and gave a series of little whoops.

Baptiste slid the blue beads in front of the Crow, clapped his hands to get the fellow's attention, and put down a mirror. The Crow pushed the beads out and started the ceremony again. Baptiste had already lost twenty dollars in trading goods to this damned puppy, and he was mad. He lost again. He figured the crittur must have got the cloth for his red sash and his cap with rolled ermine tails at this damn game. He quit.

Joe was tellin' again about the time last winter when he'd got lost and wandered into Yallerstone, and the place reminded him of Pittsburgh. Baptiste had heard it. He was about to plop down next to Joe when they heard shooting—a lot of shooting—down to the south of camp. They saddled up, with four or five other trappers, and rode down to have a look.

It was Bill Sublette come with the supply train to the rendezvous of 1830 on the Wind River.

Sublette's packs were full of what the trappers and Indians had been waiting for, so they got straight down to business. Sublette's men set up the bar first thing—selling whisky that had been watered down with water from the Sweetwater River a ways back and was spiced with tobacco, molasses, red peppers, and ginger. It went through a considerable mark-up, from about five dollars a gallon to twenty dollars a pint, but nobody gave a damn. It was the only drink in town, and it sure topped pots of coffee made for the third time from the same grounds. Besides, Elkanah over yonder in those aspens, already getting bleary, needed to forget about the time two good beavers had gone under up at the Three Forks and he'd run like a divil-chased mule hisself. Adam was glugging at it to forget the letter he'd written home last rendezvous about coming home rich, and to help him decide whether to write another pack of lies. Jamie, sitting opposite Adam and looking scarcely old enough to drink, was still trying to warm his toes from the frostbite he'd got on the Judith—the things were still tingling and a little numb. Old Frapp, prone in the cottonwoods, was trying to get rid of the memory of the taste of crickets he'd et on the lava plains around the Snake River last autumn during real starvin' times. And they all were trying to get drunk enough not to notice the mountain price of Sublette's St. Louy-bought goods this time; they knew he'd charge as much as two thousand percent of what he paid for 'em.

Joe's friend Long Otter, a Shoshone, begged Joe and Baptiste for some firewater. Joe grinned at Baptiste and dumped his tin cup over Long Otter's head. Long Otter instantly considered himself insulted, grew very solemn, asserted that he was a made-to-die, and challenged Joe to mortal combat. Joe laughed and fumblingly explained to Long Otter, with signs and his few words of Crow, that he meant to make a joke, such as Crow clowns make. Robedo, who spoke better Crow, confirmed what Joe said. Long Otter was uncertain, but since Baptiste was laughing hard, he seemed to agree to be pacified at the cost of a full cup for himself.

Joe was handing the cup to Long Otter when Robedo reached out with a stick and knocked the whisky into Joe's face. Long Otter started laughing hysterically. Joe slapped Robedo as hard as he could. Robedo, still laughing, kicked Joe in the thigh, and Joe knocked him down. Baptiste and Long Otter jumped onto Joe to tear him off Robedo, but the fight had started. Someone Baptiste never saw thumped him so hard on the back of the head that he nearly lost consciousness. He rolled to one side, lay still a moment, and watched the brawl. Long Otter had gotten out of it too. Joe and Robedo were tussling on the ground. Five or six trappers were having at each other—sometimes standing stock-still to take a bone-shivering blow, recovering, and then giving one back while the other fellow stood still, sometimes wrestling, throwing each other over shoulders, all the while whopping and hollering like Injuns in a battle. Baptiste gathered it wasn't serious—no biting, no eye-gouging, no knife-play. The boys were just having fun.

Joe got some the best of Robedo, who was a smallish French-Canadian. The fellow looked dazed. Joe helped him up. "Robedo," he said, "no hard feelin's." He clasped his arms around Robedo's shoulders. "You're a good beaver, and I recollect when you saved my skin that time I fell asleep on watch. Ye've got the ha'r of the b'ar in ye. I surely am sorry."

"Sorry? Son of a bitch, he says he's sorry. I buy you a drink, to make up for next time, when I lodgepole you."

Joe saw Baptiste stretched out off to the side, relaxing. "Don't cotton to a little scrap, John?"

"It might spoil my complexion," Baptiste said.

"Onliest way to keep out of fightin' around here is thar whar ye are, knocked out, or passed out."

Robedo brought them both a drink.

Late the next afternoon a huge tribe of Crows rode by the main camp at a respectful two hundred yards. Baptiste had never seen anything quite like it. The Crows were on what General Clark would have called dress parade. The braves led, in large groupings. Robedo explained that the Crows had societies within the tribes, units of warriors in friendly competition, sort of like clubs. Each of these societies was putting up a kind of show. The braves galloped forward, stopped abruptly, reared the horses prancing lightly in neat files. What surprised Baptiste was the next maneuver, a curvet in which the riders persuaded the horses to leap with both front feet off the ground at once and make little half circles as they landed. The Crows were the best horsemen in the mountains and on the plains, and these were making their best show.

Their dress was likewise spectacular. Baptiste couldn't really distinguish the societies by their dress—he didn't know the religious emblems—but all the men were hand-

somely decked out. Some of them were roached, others
had half-shaved heads, others yet wore roach headdresses
or ermine caps. Robedo pointed out that some of them
held long straight staves and some curved staves, signify-
ing different positions of honor. The staves were decorated
with eagle feathers or rolled ermine tails or otter skins.
Some braves were draped in big red sashes—that was why
the cloth was in demand, thought Baptiste—and others
had belts of kit-fox skin. All of them carried buffalo-skin
war shields, and most had ornamented rattles. Robedo said
that though they were too far away to see, every brave
had a medicine object, one that had been revealed in a
dream as his personal protection, around his neck or tied
to his buckskins. Baptiste reminded himself to note it all
down that night for his book; but he didn't get around to
it.

After the braves came the women and children, walking
or riding in travois, following drably in the dust of the
show horses and bearing the belongings of the tribe.

"Them squaws won't be so meek later on," grinned Joe.
"Just wait till they get slickered up."

The squaws did not show up for some time, as they
were obliged to take care with their toilette. They made
their long, black hair glossy with porcupine-tail brushes.
They perfumed their hair and bodies with herbs, grasses,
pine needles, and flowers. They put finger-spots of vermilion on their foreheads, cheeks, and noses, and a streak
of it where their hair parted. They put on dresses of doe-
skin that they had beaten thin and. whitened; the skirt
might be fringed with tiny bells, the bodice decorated with
colored quills and ribbons. And they would be looking,
when they did get to the main camp, for a trapper who
would give them more foofuraw to bedeck themselves
with.

They came in the twilight, the splendiferous braves and
their wives and daughters of age, to launch their bargaining. They had some furs to trade to Sublette and his partners, Jed Smith and Davey Jackson; and the ladies were
prepared to make buckskins or moccasins for any trapper
who needed them. But, mainly, they intended to trade, for
the slightest of trifles, the sexual services of the ladies. In
return they wanted the great medicine that the white man
conjured, the cloth, knives, beads, vermilion, mirrors, and
all the rest. Foofuraw, the trappers called it—frippery. The

Crows were amazed that the trappers would give so much for so little. Some of them figured their must not be any white squaws.

"Ye'll be buying ye a dose of the clap," scratched a high-pitched voice. It was Old Bill, sidling up between Joe and Baptiste. He stood with them for a minute to watch the circulating squaws. "Ye make the damnedest friends. This Joe Meek hyar, he believed me last year when I told him that whisky would kill the clap. But he drank it, 'stead of puttin' it on his pecker. He don't know what way the stick floats."

"I seen how you done with the whisky," Joe said, keeping his eyes on the squaws. "You guzzled till you couldn't get it up. That did keep the clap away."

"I do believe I druther play euchre tonight," Bill squeaked, and wandered off. Baptiste had scarcely seen him since they got to rendezvous, as Bill had kept to himself.

"Lookee thar," Joe observed. "That un's flirtin' with ye." It was a Crow girl, no more than fourteen, and not bad looking. The Crow women were not particularly beautiful, being tall, broad-shouldered, and flat-faced, like the men. But this girl wasn't grown.

"See how she gapes." The girl was glancing up, shyly, it seemed, at Baptiste from time to time while her father was bargaining with another trapper. "If they don't keep their eyes to the ground, they're practically invitin' ye," Joe explained. "Their manners don't allow women to look men in the eye."

Baptiste watched while the other trapper shook his shoulders, started to walk away, acted reluctant, and, in general, whittled the price down. When he walked away with an older squaw, maybe the girl's mother, Baptiste stepped in. He knew better than to talk to the girl directly, but it was easy to reach an agreement with her father. Trappers liked the Crows because they were always friendly to whites; their way of being free with their women was part of being friendly.

Baptiste felt a hand on his shoulder, and was instantly awake. "Easy," someone said. "I heard you was here." The big black face grinned. Under the eagle-feather headdress and behind the gaudy red sash Baptiste could still recognize Jim Beckwourth. "Long time, John," Beckwourth said, and shook his hand. The girl stirred uneasily on the blanket beside him. They walked aways from her to talk.

"Damn, are you a Crow?"

"Been living 'mongst the Crows for two years. I'm a sort of chief."

"Chief? Shit."

'Wall, a kinda war chief." He said he was a made-to-die in the Fox society.

Jim had a long story to tell. He had gone to the mountains the year Baptiste went to Europe—Baptiste knew that. He'd been an Ashley-Henry man, and then had trapped for Smith, Jackson & Sublette. He'd done some fearsome things—set fire to a thicket once where eighty Blackfeet was holed up and burned 'em out, killed nearly all of 'em. Niggurs'd killed and sculped some Shoshone women. Lived up with the Blackfeet once, like no other mountain man had ever done. Jim Bridger—did Baptiste remember Jim, that shy, skinny little kid?—was up there with him. Beckwourth had married—wall, not really married, naturally—the daughter of the chief, and had axed her for disobedience. Then the chief give him the other daughter for his bed. Meanwhile, the first girl rose from the dead and come back to his blankets, so he had two. He was full of other stories, too.

How come he'd turned Crow? Baptiste wanted to know.

Crows liked him, mainly. When he'd first come out, they was excited about his black skin, though they'd seen another of what they called the black white men. Still, it made him popular, particularly with the squaws. Which was a change from the settlements. And then old Ezekiel told them a story, at the rendezvous of '28, about how many Blackfeet Jim had killed, and it was true he'd killed a many. But Ezekiel concocted a tale about Jim being born part Crow and getting kidnapped by the Blackfeet, so the Crows welcomed him as a long-lost son. And Jim, wall, he just went along with it. He had a good thing with the Crows. Soon American Fur would be stepping up their Crow trade, and Jim was in a position to deliver it to MacKenzie and make himself a lot of money working for American Fur among the Crows.

He didn't have no special love for this Smith, Jackson & Sublette anyhow.

The race thing? Baptiste asked.

Naw, that didn't figure too much out here. Once you

fought Injuns with a beaver and shot the meat he et and stood watch while he slept, he didn't give much of a damn what color you were. The trappers hated Britishers more than they hated blacks or breeds. Every color and nation of man amongst the trappers anyway. Naw, it was just that Jim and the other trappers didn't always get on too good. He didn't toe the line with them trappers who'd just do whatever the company said, and buy trade goods at whatever price the company wanted to charge, which was gettin' more every year. Them hosses couldn't think for theirselves. Jim was setting up to outdo all of 'em, and keep his independence while he was at it.

Baptiste discovered during the next few days that Jim had a reputation as something of a daredevil, as something of a rascal and double-dealer, and as the biggest liar in the mountains.

Jim showed him around the Crow camp that afternoon—the Crows Jim had come with the day before were by far the largest tribe at the rendezvous—and he explained something of the Fox society he belonged to. They elected officers every spring for the hunting and fighting season. Some braves were named leaders, two men hooked-staff bearers, two more straight-staff bearers, two rear men, and one or two named the bravest of all. Jim was one of these. With the title he got privileges like getting to choose his meat first at a feast and getting to eat before anyone else started. Plus the privilege, of course, of catching the most hell in any kind of skirmish.

These officers had definite duties: The leaders spearheaded the society into battle, the staff-bearers planted the staves and were obliged to stand by them and refuse to retreat, the rear men had the job of facing off the enemy in case of a retreat. The bravest-of-alls did everything. All these officers were made-to-dies which was as high an honor as a Crow could aspire to. Still, some years no one seemed to want to be an officer, especially if they were expecting trouble with the Blackfeet.

Most Indians were pretty chicken-shit about fighting, Jim said. When he'd come to the Crows, they were just doin' the usual Indian crap, an occasional ambush of the Blackfeet or sneak-thievin' Blackfoot ponies. Never a head-on confrontation of parties matched in size. Injuns figured that they'd lost the battle if one man got killed, no matter how many of the other side went under, so they wouldn't fight on equal terms. But Jim had got 'em shaped up some. His Fox society was some mean band of fighters now, and had given the Blackfoot what for more than once.

Wall, Jim was glad to see Baptiste in the mountains. Shinin' times out here. Man didn't have to obey no laws nor listen to no preachers nor kowtow to no sheriffs nor get penned in by no rules. He was good as the next beaver if he had the savvy to stay aboveground, his color no matter. And Jim had a good set-up. Why didn't Baptiste throw in with him? The Crows would take Baptiste on Jim's say-so.

Baptiste said he'd think on it.

Bill fetched Baptiste out of a game of Old Sledge that afternoon. Said he wanted Baptiste to meet the boss man standin' next to him, Jed Smith. "John hyar's more'n a no good *vide poche*," Bill said. "That's how come he figures to go back down to St. Louy with ye. He's a'scribblin' at a book." Bill cackled as he creaked off.

Baptiste knew about Jed Smith. With Jim Bridger and Tom Fitzpatrick, he was one of the trappers that all the men agreed had the ha'r of the b'ar in 'em. Smith was probably the most yarn-spun of all. He located South Pass and led the trappers to the western slopes of the mountains and the desert beyond. He found the way to Californy and all the way up to Fort Vancouver on the Columbia and back. He was a fierce fighter and a savvy brigade leader who'd brought his men through some lean times. But he was a strange figure in the mountains, not only an educated man who was making maps of the whole country, but a Bible-reading man. More than once he said prayers over a trapper who'd gone under. No one else in the mountains done anything like that.

"A book about the mountains?" Captain Smith asked.

"No, about my own life," Baptiste answered. They sat cross-legged on the ground, Baptiste lit a pipe (which Smith declined), and Baptiste told his story. Captain Smith was a good listener: He offered only an occasional word of response, but he looked at Baptiste directly, in a way that made Baptiste feel that he was absorbing each word. "But I don't know that I'll write the book, or go to St. Louis."

Smith raised his eyebrows.

"The publisher I wrote indicated that there's no room for a breed's perspective if it runs contrary to what the whites already think."

"You fight that," Smith said.

"And the settlement don't take to folks what have Injun blood," Baptiste added ironically.

"You fight that, too."

"I'd rather fight the Blackfeet. It's cleaner."

"I've been in the mountains for eight years," Smith declared, "and I've done well. I've loved the mountains—loved them maybe too much, like a pagan, forgetting my Christian duty. I've seen things—seen too many men killed, led too many men into getting killed. Seen too much drunkenness and lewdness. The mountains turn something loose in a man that's wild, like a beast." He thought for a moment. "In me too.

"So I've made some money now and have some capital. I'll start a business in the settlements and take care of my family and make a contribution, and serve my God." Baptiste had the sense of something private, and sad, that Captain Smith wouldn't talk about.

"I don't put much faith in the white man's God."

Smith put it simply, and with an air of finality. "I'll give you a job. I don't know what business I'll go into, but it doesn't matter. You're intelligent, and you'll fit somewhere. Think on it." He raised his long frame and walked away.

"I'll stay in the mountains," Baptiste called after him. Smith smiled a little, not happily. "Then come with me. You'd better meet Old Gabe."

Old Gabe was Jim Bridger. He was only twenty-six, but one of the most respected men in the mountains. Smith had given him the nickname because Jim always looked as solemn as the archangel Gabriel.

Gabe was glad to have Baptiste. He and Broken Hand Tom Fitzpatrick had just gone together and bought out Smith, Jackson & Sublette, who were quitting the mountains. Old Frapp and Baptiste Gervais and Milton Sublette had gone in with Gabe and Broken Hand too. They could use a man what could read and write to keep records with the brigades. Hell, three of the new partners, countin' Gabe himself, couldn't read or write. They'd give Baptiste three hundred dollars a year plus pay him for half his plews at three dollars a pound.

Baptiste accepted. He gave his notebooks to Jed Smith to carry to General Clark. The man who had tried to avoid the fur trade was a fur trapper.

Chapter Six

1831

1831, August: Nat Turner led a Negro insurrection in Virginia.

1831: Cyrus McCormick invented the mechanical reaper.

1831, APRIL 25: James K. Paulding's *The Lion of the West* introduced the frontier man as a comic type in American literature.

1832: The Illinois militia effectively ended the Black Hawk War with the massacre of Black Hawk's tribe, including women, children, and old men.

1832, FEBRUARY 6: The first printed call for a transcontinental railroad appeared in a weekly newspaper in Ann Arbor, Michigan.

1833: Noah Webster brought out his bowdlerized edition of the Bible.

1834: Thomas Davenport constructed the first electric motor.

1835: Samuel F.B. Morse invented the telegraph.

1836: Texas declared itself an independent republic.

Eighteen Hundred Thirty-One

JANUARY, 1831: It was a rough winter on Powder River. On the high plains there was almost nothing to break the gales, so they battered the camp night and day. Baptiste learned to be grateful for the days it snowed, for the wind eased and the temperature rose. The clear days were cold and wind-blistered. The men kept to their lodges—large tipis made from buffalo hides—and always had a pot simmering. The pots were full of meat for most of the winter because Powder River country seemed to be thick with buffalo that season. The men couldn't get around well in the snow, and were half-blinded by the glare, but the buffalo had the same handicaps, and, being buffler-witted besides, fell regularly to their Hawkens.

Winter camp was mostly lazing and yarn-spinning and card-playing, for no one cared to stir. The lucky trappers now were the ones who were squaw men. Their women kept the lodges warm, tidy, and dry, mended their clothes, made their buffalo robes cozy and told the tales of their people, those little mixtures of legend and fantasy that the Indians handed down from generation to generation as philosophy and history.

Baptiste heard for the first time that winter of '31 the Osage story of the origin of death. A squaw had twin daughters, mere infants. She would leave them in the tipi sleeping, unwatched. But when she came back she sometimes found signs that they had been walking around and maybe even fighting. So one day she sneaked up on the tipi and listened to hear what they were doing. They were arguing. One was saying that mankind was nasty, corrupt, plague-ridden, weak, vain, and altogether unworthy of life. The other was answering that mankind was noble and fair and strong and good and should be entitled to live forever. The squaw listened to this quarrel for a few minutes, one

186

child arguing for obliterating the human race and the other for granting it immortality. Then the squaw walked into the tent and scolded the twin sisters for squabbling. And that was how death started, because if the squaw had let them finish the argument, either there would be no men, or men would live forever.

Baptiste shared a lodge with Joe Meek and Joe's friend Doc Newell. When Baptiste had told Old Bill his decision, Bill reckoned that this old bull druther be away from the herd, so he'd go down along the Front Range (in modern Colorado) and amble on down to Taos. Beckwourth had shaken his head at Baptiste's throwing in with Rocky Mountain Fur when he could have gone with Jim, and went back with the Crows. Baptiste had joined up with Bridger's brigade, a big one, run like an army because it invaded Blackfoot country. That many trappers in a bunch intimidated even the Blackfeet, though, so Gabe was able to lead a good hunt from the Three Forks east to the Powder.

Joe and Doc were free spirits. Both had been in the mountains only a year, and both were younger than Baptiste, but they took to the mountains naturally and got into trouble only from having too much fun. Gabe, who was always solemn and understood the rascality of the Blackfeet, chafed at them for thinking that trapping was a game.

The three were hunting one day with a trapper named Doughty, when they came on grizzly tracks in front of a cave.

"Scratch my ass," yelled Doughty, "lookee thar for b'ar meat. This child'll climb up above thar"—pointing to the cave—"and shoot the niggur. Which of you boys'll go in and run him out?"

Doughty was a little chagrined when all three of them volunteered.

The cave was plenty big to stand in. They eased off to one side, out of the stream of light from the entrance. When their eyes adjusted to the dark, they saw that the cave was about six yards square. They also saw not one but three grizzlies, all looking at the trappers. The bears were growling, not loudly, and they weren't moving. Baptiste guessed they were half asleep and didn't know what was happening. The three crept forward.

Suddenly Joe bolted out and cracked the biggest bear on

the head with his wiping stick. Joe whooped—he'd counted coup. The bear turned and ran out the cave. They
heard Doughty shoot, but the bear only wheeled around
again and charged back into the cave. All three of them
let fly with their Hawkens at once. The bear dropped.

Damn, Baptiste thought, none of us has a ball in. The
three of them, disarmed, turned slowly to face the other
bears. The bears didn't seem to be moving, just standing
there looking at the trappers. Baptiste caught the eyes of
Joe and Doc, and they all grinned. "Damn," said Joe, "we
are three Daniels in the lions' den and no mistake."

As soon as he had reloaded, Baptiste calmly walked up
to one of the other bears and whacked him on the head
with the wiping stick. Doc and Joe cheered. Baptiste had
to hit the crittur again before he ran out. This time
Doughty threw him cold.

"Go at 'im, Dan'l," Joe said to Doc. So Doc ran up to
the third bear and began to thrash him on top of the head.
Evidently mystified, the bear made to run out of the cave.
At the entrance he was dropped by three simultaneous
shots.

They whooped and whooped. "Daniel was a humbug,"
Joe shouted. "Of course it was winter and the lions were
sucking their paws! Tell me of no more Daniels. We be as
good Daniels as he had the gumption to be! Hurrah for us
Daniels!" When they got back to camp with all the bear
meat, even Old Gabe seemed to smile at their prank, at
least with his eyes.

OCTOBER, 1831: Baptiste had not eaten for a day and a
half. Last night he had watched while Joe and Doc held
their hands in an anthill until they were covered with ants
and then licked the critturs off. Baptiste had not been able
to eat the ants. He still felt sick from the night before.

The three had joined up with Milton Sublette in that
autumn of 1831 to trap out toward the Humboldt River
and then go north toward the Snake. Partly, Milton had in
mind to see just what was out there.

He found the poorest land any child of them had seen,
a barren waste of sand, sagebrush, creosote bushes, occasional junipers, and scarcely a plew. The land even served
up the poorest Indians they'd seen, miserable, naked ras-
cals called Diggers who lived in holes in the ground and
ate mostly insects. Baptiste judged that if ever man was an
unaccommodated, poor, bare, forked animal, the Diggers

were. The mountain men laughed at the Diggers until the trappers found themselves eating ants for dinner. Two days ago they had finally trapped some beaver and had roasted what flesh there was. But it was poisonous—the damned country didn't give the beaver anything to eat but wild parsnips—and half the men got sick, including Baptiste. That was when Milton picked up and headed for Snake country.

But it was a long, dry drive northward, with almost nothing to eat or drink. Baptiste just held himself in the saddle that first day, aching, half blinded by the sun off the dust and sand when he opened his eyes, mostly keeping his eyes closed and unable to get his mind beyond his hurting anyway. He ignored his pack mule completely. That day he did nothing but hold on and let his horse follow the brigade.

The second day he was in agony. His tongue swelled in his mouth, cracked, and threatened to split down the middle. His stomach raged for food, twisting angrily inside him. That night the men feasted on crickets pounded with rocks into a kind of mush. Baptiste got about three bites. It only made the hunger ache more. On the third and fourth days he felt weak and sinking, barely able to go on, and constantly nauseated. He lived in a dream world of floating memories and fantasies colored red on the insides of his eyelids by the sun. That night Joe bled Doc's mule, taking about a pint from a cut in his ear, and the three shared the blood.

The next day Baptiste felt wild, jumpy, feverish with energy, cannibalish. He thought of nothing but what he might eat that night, beast or man. He was passed out on the sand that evening when he smelled roasting meat. *Saunt-den-tickup, hintz,* Joe said in Shoshone—"Good meat, friend." Milton had cut the throat of a mule which was dying, and the brigade stuffed its stomachs.

They killed another mule the next evening, and Baptiste began to feel almost human. But he wanted a decent drink—not blood, and not the brackish stuff that seeped up from holes in the sand—clear water.

Late the next afternoon the horses and mules, more famished and thirsted than the men, started trotting forward and then broke into a gallop. The trappers hung on. Gear was strewn all over the plain. The animals had smelled water and were going for it.

They plunged in without stopping. The men were glad to get soaked, and didn't give a damn about the equipment. They lolled around in the Snake, dipping their heads to drink and letting their pores absorb the water. That night two horses died from drinking too much.

JULY, 1832: The rendezvous in Pierre's Hole, on the west side of the Grand Tetons, looked to be as fat as last year's rendezvous had been lean. Last year Tom Fitzpatrick hadn't shown up with the supply train for rendezvous at all. The free trappers and the hired hands like Joe and Doc and Baptiste had had to ride back into the mountains without having any whisky to wet their dry, without foofuraw, with damned little DuPont powder and Galena lead, and without enough traps. They'd gone cussing, and the Indians had ridden away muttering too. This year they were getting two supply trains—Bill Sublette was bringing one for Rocky Mountain Fur, which was Gabe and Broken Hand and the boys, and Lucien Fontenelle was bringing one out for American Fur.

Joe and Doc just grinned about that. Another company in the mountains should mean shinin' times for them. Instead of trapping for RMF and paying monopoly prices for their outfits, they could work as free trappers, sell their furs to the high bidder, and buy their goods from the low seller. The tale was that American Fur meant to get the trade by buying high and selling low. Well, Baptiste thought, MacKenzie is an ornery man.

American Fur had gotten into the mountain trade in a big way during the last year. Its brigades were inexperienced and had green leaders, but they'd hit on a shrewd plan. Vanderburgh and Drips, the partisans, had lit out on the trails of the RMF brigades. Since they didn't know the mountains or mountain ways, they intended to learn them from the beavers that did know. Old Gabe, Fitzpatrick, Milton Sublette, Frapp, and Gervais had become unwilling guides for American Fur during the last fall and spring hunts. Naturally, those partisans hadn't liked taking American Fur through Rocky Mountain College, and as canny a coon as Bridger had shaken his followers for a while. But Vanderburgh and Drips were dogged; they kept cutting Gabe's trail and catching up with him. RMF had most of the plews—they got to every crick ahead of the Company—but they were riled just the same. They were afraid that if Fontenelle won the race to rendezvous, the Company would get all the trade of the free trappers and most of the plews. And Fontenelle, coming from Fort Union instead of St. Louis, had a headstart.

Bill Sublette was too wily to be outdone by a newcomer like Fontenelle, of course. He got up the Missouri, up the Platte and Sweetwater, through South Pass, across the Siskadee River (later called the Green) and the Snake River in record time. At mid-morning on July 8 a hundred rifles volleying from the south of the Hole told everyone that Sublette had outstripped the Company and that RMF's mountain wisdom still counted for more than John Jacob Astor's money.

And so the carouse was on—brawling, drinking, fornicating, gambling, lying, gypping, and the other favorite mountain pastimes. This year Baptiste got to chuckle at some greenhorns, greener than he had been two years before, trying to get the hang of mountain life. One Nathaniel Wyeth, a Boston ice merchant, had come to make his fortune in the fur trade. Wyeth was a clever man, hardheaded, quick to catch on; he'd already figured out, riding with Bill Sublette on the way out and paying for the privilege, that his ideas about the trade were naive, and he'd already begun to adjust them to realities. He'd brought nineteen fresh hands for the job.

"D'ye eye them *mangeurs de lard*, boy? D'ye eye 'em now? Wagh! But ain't they some? One of them could make a buffler look right smart."

Baptiste handed Bill a twist as greeting after not seeing him for two years. In fact, Baptiste had heard the Arapahoes had lifted his hair down at Bayou Salade.

"Ye see these greenhorns to the mountain country? Apackin' their bacon and flour, I swan. You mind, they'll be splittin' rail and puttin' up fences out here mighty quick. An' then they'll be totin' women out here. Great Jeehosephat."

"Missionaries, Bill. Missionaries'll come before women. You used to be one of those yourself, as I remember."

"Wagh! This child did, too, but he growed up."

"We're as independent as hogs on ice for now," Baptiste said. "You think it'll change?"

"Change? *It* won't change, it'll change them greenhorns. They's a rattlesnake coiled around every sagebrush out here, and passes in them mountains ain't nothing but a marmot crossed since the mountains riz up—nothing but a marmot and this child here. And they's the wind to dry their faces and the sun to split their lips. They ain't gonna preach no sermons in this country. They ain't gonna be able to talk none.

"Aside, this child knows cricks and valleys and basins ain't no beaver seen. Ain't nobody gonna find this child with no sermons and skirts."

The boys constructed a special amusement or two for the Bostoner's greenhorns. Ike Davies screwed a Shoshone squaw within five yards of a bunch of them, and invited them to follow, which they declined. Some of the boys started playing Seven-Up using a dead trapper for a table. That turned the newcomers a bit greener around the gills. Black Harris doused a red-headed trapper, a lanky fellow, with pure alcohol. Someone put a burning stick to him, and he lit. Joe and Baptiste pounded out the flames, but the poor fellow damn near died anyway.

And the boys had a few stories to tell them. One green fellow asked Black Harris if he hadn't been over a good deal of the country. Harris was a wiry man, hard and sinewy as a blacksmith, whose face looked like tanned leather with gunpowder burned into it. He was a specialist in the midwinter express—long trips from the mountains to St. Louis alone or with one companion, made in bludgeoning weather. He had been about the country more than a good deal.

"A sight this coon's gone over, if that's the way your stick floats," he started counting his coup. "I've trapped beaver on the Platte and Arkansas, and away up on the Missoura and Yaller Stone. I've trapped on the Columbia, on Lewis's Fork, and the Siskadee. I've trapped, Mister, on Grand River and the Heely. I've fought the Blackfoot, and damned bad Injuns they are. I've raised the ha'r of more than one Apach', and made a Rapaho come afore now. I've trapped in heaven, in airth, and hell, and scalp my old head, Mister, but I've seen a putrefied forest."

"A what?"

"A putrefied forest, as sure as my rifle's got hindsights, and she shoots center. I was out on the Black Hills, Bill Sublette knows the time—the year it rained fire—and everybody knows when that was. If thar wasn't cold doin's about that time, this child wouldn't say so. The snow was about fifty foot deep, and the buffler lay dead on the ground like bees after a beein'. Not whar we was, though, for thar was no buffler, and no meat, and me and my band had been livin' on our mokkersons (leastwise the parfleche) for six weeks. And poor doin's that feedin' is, Mister, as you'll ever know. One day we crossed a canyon and over a divide and got into a peraira [prairie] whar was green grass and green trees and green leaves on the trees, and birds singing in the green leaves, and this in February, wagh! Our animals was like to die when they seen the green grass, and we all sung out 'Hurrah for summer doin's.'

" 'Hyar goes for meat,' says I, and I jest ups old Ginger at one of them singing birds, and down come the crittur elegant, its damned head spinnin' away from the body, but never stops singin', and when I takes up the meat, I finds it stone, wagh!

" 'Hyar's damp powder and no fire to dry it,' I says, quite skeered.

" 'Fire be dogged,' says old Rube. 'Hyar's a hoss as'll make firewood.' Schruk! goes the axe agin' the tree, and out comes a bit of the blade as big as my hand. We looks at the animals, and thar' they stood shaking over the grass, which I'm goddamned if it warn't stone, too. Young Sublette comes up, and he'd been clerking down to the fort on the Platte, so he knowed somethin'. He looks and looks, and scrapes the tree with his butcher knife, and snaps the grass like pipe stems, and breaks the leaves a-snappin' like Californy shells.

" 'What's all this, boy?' I asks.

" 'Putrefactions,' says he, looking smart, 'putrefactions, or I'm a niggur.' "

"Putrefactions?" asked the greenhorn. "Why did the leaves and trees and grass stink?"

"Stink?" said Harris. "Would a skunk stink if he was froze to stone? Nosir, this child didn't know what putrefactions was, and young Sublette's tale wouldn't shine nohow, so I chips a piece out of a tree and puts it in my trap sack and carries it safe to St. Louy. A Dutch doctor chap was down thar, and I shows him the piece I chipped out of the tree, and he called it a putrefaction too. And so, Mister, if that warn't a putrefied peraira, what was it? For this hoss don't know, and he knows fat cow from poor bull, anyhow."

Gabe added his story about the time he was alone in

that same country and the damned Ricarees was chasin'
him and he got away from them by jumping his horse
over a canyon half a mile wide, on account of the law of
gravity was putrefied too.

Old Ed Rose, someone said, the half-black, half-Injun
who'd gone under on the Yaller Stone, had ridden through
that putrefied forest once on his way to Fort Atkinson. He
picked up a couple of them stone birds and perched them
on his felt hat to hear the singin' as he rode. They done fine,
but when he got to the fort, his buckskin shirt was covered
with bird droppin's—which war stone.

Baptiste found Bill sitting with three *mangeurs de lard*
and Doc Newell around a stew pot and wagging his head
at them like he had antlers. Baptiste knew this routine. Bill
was explaining to them that when he went under, he
would come back as an elk. He was teaching them the set
of antler signals he would use to show them that what
looked like an elk was Old Solitaire, so they wouldn't
shoot him. The greenhorns were laughing at Bill's put-on.
But Baptiste knew it wasn't a put-on. When Bill shed his
white religion, he picked up a lot of red religion to replace
it. So he was serious about the signals, and pissed off at
their ignoramus laughter.

These recruits of the Boston ice merchant were more
than a little puzzled by what they saw at that rendezvous
of 1832. The mountain country seemed to them majesti-
cally beautiful but savage. The mountain men seemed at
least as savage. They had not started out as an elegant
bunch—they were often enough men on the run for breaking some law, runaway slaves, runaway bound boys, freed
blacks, half-breeds, outcasts, men disgruntled with the settlements. The man who had hired one of the first bands
said that Falstaff's battalion was genteel in comparison; the
trappers had not gained any gentility in the intervening decade. Some of them, of course, were simply men with a
taste for adventure. Of these quite a few were educated
and more than one trapper carried a copy of Shakespeare,
the Bible, or *Pilgrim's Progress* in his possible sack. In
fact, Tom Fitzpatrick was an Irish aristocrat; so was Bill
Sublette's partner Robert Campbell. It was a contradictory
society, and Jean-Baptiste Charbonneau, the half-breed
trapper with the education and manners of a courtier,
caught the contradictions succinctly. John gave the trapper jigs and square-dance tunes regularly on his harmon-

ika. One evening toward the end of rendezvous, when the men were tired of drinking and brawling, he improved their minds around the fire with a little *andante cantabile* of Mozart.

It was a good rendezvous for Baptiste, Joe, and Doc. All three were graduate mountain men now. And though Lucien Fontenelle never did show up at rendezvous with supplies, it was clear that American Fur would be competing with Rocky Mountain Fur for plews. It would pay a man to go independent, so that's what the three decided to do.

Fur-trapping had its caste system. On the bottom were the camp-tenders. On the next rung stood the trappers who hired themselves to one of the companies, working for wages or giving a percentage of their plews for goods. These men had to take orders from the brigade leaders. Above these trappers stood the partisans or booshways (*bourgeois*), the men who commanded the brigades, and their immediate lieutenants—Gabe, Fitzpatrick, Frapp, Milton Sublette, and the like. But at the top of the heap were the free trappers, the men who traveled with brigades or rode off on their own as they pleased, answered to no one, and bargained for their plews at year's end as independent agents. These were the cocks of the walk. So now Baptiste, Joe, and Doc promoted themselves to the rank of free trapper.

SEPTEMBER, 1834: Bill was nursing his Nez Percé pony, a fine new Appaloosa, slowly upwards. Baptiste, Joe, Doc, and Mark Head were easing along behind him with their pack mules. They didn't know just what he was doing—he'd gotten quiet—but they followed without a word. Old Solitaire didn't always travel with other trappers; when he did, he was the leader. Besides, they were on a fork of the upper Yellowstone, and he knew the country best. He swung away from the crick, made a wide circle for half a mile, and came back to it.

"Do 'ee hyar now, boys?" Bill squeaked. "Thar's Injuns knocking around, an' Blackfoot at that. But thar's beaver, too, and this child means trappin' anyhow." He didn't say what he had seen or heard, and none of them knew.

Well, they were willing to try their luck if Bill was. They camped that night without a fire.

The next morning Bill stayed to guard the camp and the

others split up in pairs to trap. Baptiste and Mark Head set their traps in the dawn light, six each, spread out over a couple of little cricks. As they were riding back to camp, they saw three lodges on the edge of a meadow. Baptiste turned his horse back into the trees.

"Hell," said Head, "they's nobody home. They've left it to us." And he kicked his pony straight across the meadow toward the tipis. When nothing happened, Baptiste followed.

Head reached into the pot and fished out a piece of meat. "A little feedin' on the peraira," he grinned. He looked at the medicine bag in front of the lodge, a piece of skin hanging from a stick tripod with the brave's totem objects in it. "Shit, we'll make this coon askeered to fight—askeered to live," Head said. Baptiste stayed on his horse. Mark opened the bag. "Lookee here, a hawk's claw. What you reckon this does for him? Wall, it . . ."

The arrow hit the lodge skin with a ri-i-ip just past Head's shoulder. Baptiste saw the niggur who let it fly fifty yards off. There were three of them, and they were leading their ponies. He rode like hell for the trees. When he got there, he looked back and saw Mark whipping his pony the other direction with the damned Blackfeet right behind him.

Baptiste moved slowly on a roundabout route back to camp, not wanting to stir up any more. He was easing up on the camp when he heard a horse clattering up from the other direction and then Bill's voice. "Do 'ee feel bad now, boy? Whar' away you see them damned Blackfoot?"

Baptiste got close enough to see. Mark's face was covered with blood, and an arrow was poking out of his back.

"Well," Mark puffed, "pull this arrow out of my back, and maybe I'll feel like telling."

"Do 'ee hyar now? Hold on till I've grained this cussed skin, will 'ee? Did 'ee ever see sich a damned pelt, now? It won't take smoke anyhow I fix it."

Baptiste sat his horse forty yards away, unseen, while Mark waited and fumed.

While Baptiste and Mark were telling their story, and Bill was cussing Mark for being a damned fool, Joe and Doc rode up in a hurry with scalps swinging from the barrels of their Hawkens. Bill looked at the scalps and said, "This coon'll cache, he will." He threw his saddle onto his

Appaloosa, tied on his pack, grabbed the lead of his pack mule, spurred up a bluff and disappeared.

The four didn't try to keep up with him, as they knew he would cuss company. Forgetting the traps, they rode uphill, parallel to the creek, toward the distant ridge. Somewhere on the other side of this mountain would be safer. They kept down below the edge of the bank when they could. When the bed narrowed though, they kicked up the slope. On this exposed ground the horses walked as quickly as the grade allowed; the men touched them along the route most covered by trees; their eyes flitted about the countryside, picking up tiny pieces of information and transferring the pieces wordlessly into the movements of their hands on the reins and their knees on flanks. They rode like that all day, until well after dark, and made a fireless camp in a thicket in a deep cut of the creek.

Baptiste sat up, wide awake at the first yell, his Hawken cradled in one arm as he slept. A ball spewed tiny sticks into the air three feet from him. In one quick move he was sprawled behind a bush, peering up at the rock wall above. Doc was next to him. He heard Joe and Mark getting cover facing the other side of the cut.

From the yelling, Baptiste judged there must be a hundred of the coons, hot for blood and sure of counting coup. He waited. In the half-light he couldn't see a single Injun up on the rocks, a hundred feet above his head. Flashes from their fusees showed that they were shielded by boulders up there. Fusees were lousy old guns, and Blackfeet got all excited when they shot, so Baptiste didn't figure to go under from their fire. He did wonder how in hell the four of them would get out of there.

One niggur was stirring up the dirt around him and Doc pretty well, though. Before long the fellow overplayed his hand. He leaned so hard on the boulder he was behind that it toppled over the edge and left him open. Doc was quick and shot him center. He body came bouncing down the cliff and into the bottom.

Mark, who was a daredevil, jumped out, ran to the body, made a savage arc with his knife, and whooped as he held up the scalp. Half the Blackfeet must have shot at him, and a dozen exposed themselves in their eagerness. Baptiste shot one in the chest, and he came tumbling down. Doc got another. They meant to show the coons how to make shots count.

But taking a chance on getting shot was not the Blackfoot idea of a fight. Suddenly they began to run like panicked sheep, showing their backs. All four trappers fired,
and three Blackfeet dropped. Maybe that would keep them
running for a while.

Baptiste walked over to the brave he had shot. The man
was dying but not dead. He was hit in the lungs. For the
first time Baptiste was sure that he had killed a man. He
looked down at the face, an ugly face with a flat nose and
unfocused eyes. He just watched it for a long moment,
aware of Joe's eyes on him. Then the brave saw him. The
lips pursed to spit at Baptiste, but the man coughed instead and light, frothy blood oozed out. Baptiste knelt
down, took the man's top knot firmly, and looked the man
in the eye as he cut a small circle around the knot. Then he
put his foot against the man's head and jerked the scalp
off with a pop.

"Thar's smoke," Mark yelled. It was coming up through
the thick bottom downstream. Ordinarily they would have
set a backfire to stop it, but the wind was coming strong
up the gorge, and they might not be able to put out the
backfire. The flames were coming like a thirsty horse to
water. They packed as fast as they could, rode a little up
the creek, and spurred their ponies up the steep bank onto
the open plateau above.

The Blackfeet were waiting. They charged on horseback
and stampeded the pack animals immediately. Baptiste
was nearly jerked out of the saddle by the lead line when
his mule bolted. More Blackfeet were riding up from below.

"Break," Joe yelled. "Break and cache!"

Baptiste drove his mare straight back into the smoke
toward the creek bottom. When the smoke got thick, the
mare fought him, twisting her head and tearing at the
reins. He forced her to go forward. The water of the crick
calmed her a little as they crossed, but she panicked from
the fire smell on the far side and got her head enough to
run a hundred yards upstream.

When Baptiste finally got her around the fire and downstream, he cached for two days in the thicket, building no
fire, not hurting, sitting completely still. Then he rode
back uphill, over the ridge, and down into another valley.

He had no idea where his friends were. He had lost his
traps and his dried meat and his possibles. Well, at least he

had his Hawken, his pistol, his Green River, his powder and lead, and he wasn't afoot. Things could be worse.

He turned west. It was the middle of October already. Bridger and Fitzpatrick were trapping Blackfoot country to the east and would likely winter far over on Powder River. Milton Sublette was trapping Salmon River country to the west. Old Gabe and Fitz would probably have been easier to find—they were closer right now—but Baptiste would have to ride alone through Blackfoot territory to cut their trail; he hadn't any stomach for Blackfeet at the moment. The route to Salmon River country lay through Shoshone country. Shoshones were invariably friendly to the trappers—Gabe reckoned they were the best Injuns in the mountains, honest and dependable. Baptiste knew the Shoshones, not his mother's band which was shy and stayed in the mountains, but the large nation that roamed the Great Basin. He'd rather throw his luck with them, if he had to meet any Indians.

Baptiste leaned in the saddle to pick some rosehips. He was hungry, having had almost nothing to eat for the two days of hiding out. Riding toward the headwaters of the Gallatin, he dug some camas roots that first night. The second evening he sat by a dam and at length shot a beaver, which he'd never done before. He ate not just the tail but all the flesh. The third day he was lucky; he killed a small doe. He sat around a fire for three days while he jerked the meat—thin strips of it laying on wooden racks above a low fire, drying in the smoke, sun, and wind. He ate all the fresh meat he could. And he walked around quietly.

He had never spent much time alone in the mountains. Now he was not purpose-ridden. He was idle, waiting for the elements to do their work.

He had camped on the edge of a big meadow stretching away to pine-studded hills on both sides. Little creeks, some no wider than a man's stride, criss-crossed the meadow, run-off from the snow that already covered the peaks. He sat on the grass sewing himself three pairs of deer-hide moccasins—he'd lost his others. He stretched the skin to use as a ground cloth—the nights were cold, and he had no buffalo robes, just his capote. He watched his mare munch the plentiful grass; he listened to squirrels chattering; he noticed the calls of the grouse.

At night he lay on the deerskin and looked a long time

at the stars; through the thin alpine atmosphere they were as thick as gravel in the sky. He smelled the clear, cold air. And he played his harmonika—not the jig tunes he was used to playing for the trappers, but his Beethoven, Mozart, and von Weber, sending the fragile melodies out into the cold night. The second night he doodled on the harmonika with tunes of his own. Tunes were already running through his head—graceful little themes with a hint of plaintiveness, most of them—and he found the notes and began putting harmonies to them. He must have played his own melodies for three hours that second night. He was damned cold by the time the yearling black bear came wandering into camp to see who he was. He shot it. He was already impatient with shivering all night.

He rode slowly on west for the next several days. He saw no reason to hurry. He was sure he wouldn't see any Indians in this country—it was too late in the season and too cold and the game was thin. He didn't have to worry about food, he'd jerked over fifty pounds of meat off that doe, which reduced to half that behind his saddle. He doubted he could find Milton before winter camp, and that would be in December. He couldn't trap. So he just rode, wandered, and absorbed, through the piney country that drained its waters down to become the Three Forks and the Missouri River. He saw a little spring trickling from between some rocks and stopped to drink from it. He spent two hours at midday stretched out on a grassy knoll looking at the immense sky and the circle of ridges that held it in shape. He watched beaver play at diving and swimming behind a dam. He got off his horse and walked to a ledge. A little stream of water was falling off the rocks above, and he stood for a moment, mouth open, with his head in the spray. He observed a water spider shooting magically across a clear pool. He found a hot spring, steam rising where it flowed into the cold crick, its smell of sulphur strong, and bathed in it, luxuriating in the warmth. At night he fooled with his tunes. He got one worked out, a sort of song except that it didn't have any words, just a series of different musical sequences like verses and a chorus that repeated itself after every verse. It had a pastoral feeling to him, and he called it "Lone Mountain Song."

The life seemed good. It struck him one evening that he had no reason to go on. He could set up a lodge here—

even build a shack if he wanted to—and simply stay. He doubted anyone would ever disturb him. There was good water, good wood, plenty of meat for one man, lots of roots, and all the berries he could gather in the early summer. But he would have to go to rendezvous sometime for powder and lead and another horse or two. And riding with the boys was fun—trapping, carousing at rendezvous, swapping stories. He believed he'd go on.

The next morning he was sure he'd go on. These mountains were too cold. He needed buffalo robes. So he started watching to the south for a pass. On the third day he saw a way—he might find some snow up there, but nothing he couldn't ride through easily enough. He cut toward the pass, and came out of the mountains two days later onto the plains. And smack into a band of Shoshones.

He rode up on them before he saw them, three braves on horseback. His best chance was to brazen it out. He held up his hand in the sign of friendship, and told them in his bad Shoshone that he came in peace. They motioned him into the camp a hundred yards away. He rode in without hesitation, for a show of confidence. Since there was no sense in taking chances, he went straight to the biggest lodge, the council lodge, dismounted, and stepped inside. If their hearts were bad or their faces blacked against the white man, parley would slow them down.

Four braves came in quickly, seeming a bit excitable, though he wasn't sure of all they were saying. Then the chief walked in with the pipe, and he felt his throat tighten. It was Mauvais Gauche—Bad Left Hand, the only Shoshone chief with a reputation for malice and double-dealing. Baptiste had picked himself one.

Gauche (pronounced Gosha) lit the pipe, saluted the earth, the sky, and the four cardinal points, and passed it to the left. Everyone was seated around the fire, in descending order of importance from Gauche's left; Baptiste was on his immediate right.

When Baptiste smoked, he declared that he was a friend to Gauche, to his band, and to the Snake people.

Did he bring presents? Gauche wanted to know.

He regretted that he did not. He had presents—plews, tobacco, and beads—but some evil Blackfeet, who were his enemies and the enemies of the Snakes, had stolen the presents and his other horses. He did have one humble gift for Gauche, the scalp of one of the Blackfoot thieves. And he handed Gauche the Blackfoot scalp that was tied to his belt.

This pacified Gauche some, but it wasn't enough. The Frenchman (the Shoshone name for all whites) was hunting on Shoshone land, feeding on Shoshone meat, drinking Shoshone water, riding under the benevolence of the Shoshone gods who gave all good things to this country. Did he expect to take what did not belong to him without tribute? Such was typical of Frenchmen, who made Shoshones poor without recompense.

Baptiste started to apologize again for coming empty-handed when he heard a woman's voice outside the lodge. One of the braves jumped up and stopped her from coming in. He could hear them talk for a moment. The squaw was insisting that they take the Frenchman in as a friend and give him the hospitality of their lodges; the brave was arguing with her. Baptiste was astounded. He had never heard any Indians pay attention to the council of a squaw, even to the extent of bothering to deny it. After a moment all the braves left the lodge, tying him up first, and held council with the squaw outside the lodge.

There was no sense in getting heated up about the whole thing. No place to go anyway. Equably, he set about working the rawhide off his hands. After a few minutes he freed them, listening always to the deliberate palaver outside, following it loosely, thinking how odd the squaw's voice sounded; he undid the rawhide on his feet without making it look untied. Just as he was finishing, he heard some angry words outside, someone jerked back the hide flap of the lodge entrance, and a middle-aged woman stepped in, talking over her shoulder. She was a slender woman, wirily strong, with gray hair and eyes that seemed too large for her tiny head. She had a knife in her hand.

When she looked at the prisoner, she hesitated oddly. Baptiste stood up, almost tripping from the ties still partly around his feet, and tried to find the right words. He saw her recognize his medicine-stone necklace. The words felt strange, and doubly strange in Shoshone: "Hello, Mother."

She stepped in, put her hands on either side of his face, looked long, then buried her face in his chest. He held her. When she raised her head, she was not crying, though her eyes glistened. The braves were gathering around in the tent, standing off, uncertain. He pushed her head against

him again. She came barely to his shoulders. He looked at
Gauche and the other men. "This is my mother," he said.

There were stories to tell, of course. Sacajawea would
not tell her own until she had heard about the rest of his
years in St. Louis—about his meeting with the prince
(which made her puffily proud), about the great house
that rode the salt-water-everywhere, about the wooden-
shoe white men, about Africa—everything. He thought
that he would stupefy her, but she absorbed it evenly. She
asked him questions and questions. The most important
was: "Do you have the secret of the marked-down signs?"
He chuckled. He had been able to read and write when he
last saw her.

Her story was briefer, cryptically told, for she was only
a woman. When she ran onto the plains that night west of
the Ree villages, she had wandered for two days. Then a
Pawnee war party, out raiding the Sioux, had found her
and taken her to their village. The man who kept her,
Jerked Meat, had given her five children, and she had been
contented. But he died several years ago, and his brother
then treated her as a slave. That she would not endure.
She took her daughter, then less than two, and ran away.

She walked up the Platte and the Sweetwater, seeking
her own people. Some trappers helped direct her, for she
was past the age of child-bearing and of no interest to
anyone. She found the Shoshones near South Pass after
the rendezvous of 1830. True, she did not find her own
band—they had dwindled and dispersed.

She might have been an outcast, wanted by no one, except that she discovered among them her son Bazel—the
son of her dead sister whom she had adopted when Lewis
and Clark had met the Shoshones, and whom she had
never seen again. Bazel was a good man. He gave her a
lodge and a fire and meat. She had an honored place in
his household.

And did she always argue with the braves in council?
Baptiste laughed.

Well, she knew that she was only a woman. But she had
done things beyond a woman—she, had been to St. Louis,
she had lived with the white man, she knew his ways, she
knew his heart. Sometimes, when bad Shoshones wanted to
leave the trail of friendship, she told them they were fools
and cowards. She would always be a friend to the white

man. The Red-Headed Chief was the best friend she had ever had, and the best man she had known.

They talked long into the night by the stewpot in Bazel's lodge. Baptiste evaded some of her questions. Did he understand the white man's god? He could not tell her that the white man's god was false, as her own gods were false. She glowed when he said that he did. Would the white man send medicine men to show them how to make the marked-down signs? Baptiste said he thought so.

He lay beside her that night. He fell asleep thinking how much he hated the white man.

Bazel was a stout, affable, cheerful man, a little older than Baptiste. In the morning he declared solemnly that he welcomed Baptiste as a brother; as a sign of his friendship he would give his brother two horses. He added the hope that Baptiste would stay with the tribe, as his experience would enable him to give wise counsel.

"My heart is grateful for the horses," Baptiste responded in his awkward Shoshone, "for I come to you poor and have need of them."

Sacajawea, who was rebuilding the fire under the pot in the center of the tipi, spoke up promptly: "I hope that you will stay with us a while, after these many years. But he must go back to the Frenchmen, Bazel. He is an important warrior among them. He can win their friendship for our people." Bazel nodded.

Baptiste was relieved. "I will stay for a time before I go," he said. "I know too little of my own people. I will sit at your feet for now as a learning child."

Baptiste, who thought of his mother and foster brother partly as children, was surprised at how much there was to learn. This band was on the move. It had come to the mountains as protection against the summer heat; now it was meandering for a final hunt before the snows came, laying by meat for the long winter. It would join most of the Shoshone nation, with more people than there were needles on a pine tree, for the big winter encampment near Soda Springs on the Bear River.

Every step of this march was ordained by the spirits. Tipis were pitched with their flaps facing east, so that on awaking in the morning the people would be aware of the rising sun and give thanks to the One-who-created-all for its light and warmth. The first puffs of smoke from the morning fire were dedicated, with looks and little prayers, to the spirit that lives beyond the clouds, the smoke carrying the prayers to him.

Buffalo Horn, the medicine man, and Buffalo Cow, a squaw, had had visions of buffalo when they were small, and therefore lived under the power of that animal. Each of them made calls every day to bring their brothers near the band so that the people might have enough meat to eat and skins to keep them warm. The buffalo pair was consulted every four or five days, when the band moved, on the direction to take to find their brothers.

Once every day Bazel sang prayers over the medicine bundle. He took the bag off the tripod in front of the tipi and spread the objects on the skin. There were several—a sacred pipe, four golden eagle feathers tied together, a bear-claw necklace, a small piece of onyx, a tuft of bear hair.

As a boy becoming a man, before his first battle, Bazel had sought a vision. He needed this vision as a guide to his course in life and as protection against his enemies. So in May, after the winter camp and when the tribe was preparing for its hunt and its wars of the coming season against the Blackfeet, he walked into the mountains alone to fast.

He went humbly, on foot, taking nothing but a bow and a few arrows. He followed a small creek up into the mountains. The first evening he heard a bear in the darkness, but it stayed away from his fire. The second afternoon he came into a small glade, with grass for some distance around the creek, then forest stretching away. It seemed a good place. He sat cross-legged by the creek that afternoon and all the next day, taking nothing but the clear, cold, sweet creek water for nourishment. He ignored the aching of his stomach, looked at the huge blue sky, and waited for the spirits to speak to him. That night spirits teased him nastily, but he could neither see nor hear them clearly. He wondered whether the NunumBi, the elfin men who waited in the rocks, were tormenting him with their arrows of misfortune. On the fourth day he felt listless and stupid. Instead of sitting, he sprawled on the grass by the creek; he forced himself to be patient for whatever might be revealed to him.

And that night the bear appeared to him, the magical bear that had visited his camp and must have watched him ever since. Though the bear seemed to say nothing at the time, he heard its meaning without words. Sometimes it had the head of an eagle, and he understood that he must emulate the eagle's high-flown daring. And he understood that he must seek the stalwart fierceness of the bear. He was disappointed at the time that it seemed to teach him no dance or song.

But when he returned to his tribe, he purified himself and then called them together to tell them of his vision. He discovered then that he knew somewhere inside himself the dance that the bear meant him to have. The people joined in it solemnly. Then the shaman told him that he must kill a bear and eat its heart to gain courage, and eat its hair as well, and keep the hair and claws as sacred objects, and trap an eagle for its feathers. Then he must revere these objects for the rest of his life in tribute to these animal spirits who put their sacred power in his keeping. That he had done so, Bazel explained, was the reason for his good health and fat belly and many horses, and the reason he had not been wounded in battle.

The entire movement, the routine, the very existence of the tribe, bound, as it was, inevitably to the mountains, canyons, creeks, trees, grass, and the animals, was a kind of tribute to the powers of these creatures; for all were creatures and none inanimate objects. The band's reverence expressed itself in ritual that governed every detail of their hunting, migrating, cooking, eating, and sleeping; it governed their lives as a slow and stately dance, a dance that embraced every waking and sleeping moment.

Baptiste found the ritual irksome and unnecessary in some ways; he thought it had more to do with airy magic than with concrete topography. But he found the spirit behind it, in a way, beautiful.

He imitated the sacred songs on the harmonika. His new friends were charmed and fascinated, but they wanted to hear his own songs, the songs revealing the magic he had learned from the white man. So he played for them his arrangements of some Mozart airs and Beethoven sonatinas and his own "Lone Mountain Song." Though he could see that the music made no sense to them, they listened in rapt attention, with the deference due an appeal to sacred invocation. Then they promised, when the season came, to teach him the Wolf Dance, and the Buffalo Dance, and the Sun Dance, exchanging their greatest secrets of power for his.

NOVEMBER, 1834: The bands came in to Soda Springs one by one, setting up their lodges in tribes, in the sheltered places close to water, about a dozen tribes of two to four hundred people each. The people made Baptiste welcome. It was good that he was son to Canoe-Launcher, who had traveled with the Red-Headed Chief. It was better still that he was friend to Old Gabe, the Blanket Chief, whom they all knew and respected. Was not the Blanket Chief husband to the daughter of one of their chiefs, Hawk in Hand? Was not the Blanket Chief their son, and his children their children? Baptiste was an honored man in camp.

A cut of light brightened the tipi for a moment as the girl slipped in. She stood there, between the flap and the fire, looking shy and confused. Sacajawea realized that she couldn't see in the darkness after the glare of sun on snow, and did not notice that the old woman was sewing in the shadows. The girl stooped and felt in the half light for Baptiste's buffalo robes, put a pair of moccasins on them, and bolted out.

When he came back, Baptiste turned the moccasins over and over in his hands. They were quilled and beaded— Sunday-go-to-meetin' moccasins. He looked quizzically at Sacajawea. He had never been proposed to before.

"Running Stream is set apart for Spotted Horse," Sacajawea said quietly.

He hardly knew Running Stream. She was fourteen or fifteen, the late-in-life daughter of Mountain Ram, once a warrior leader and now a graying councillor. She was a tall girl, rangy, broad-shouldered, with the easy movement of a natural athlete. Report had it that she was envious of the boys' duties and bored with women's work. Baptiste was sure that Mountain Ram had taught her a proper Shoshone squaw's obedience, but apparently she had a mind of her own. He grinned. She sure did—set down for Spotted Horse but proposing to Baptiste.

"Spotted Horse staked three ponies for her," Sacajawea said, "at the start of winter camp. He heaped honor on himself last summer against the Crows. It is thought a good match. Mountain Ram will reply soon."

It was just as well. She was comely enough, he'd

watched her, but she wasn't worth a feud. Besides, for a
rover like him it wasn't suitable to have a squaw in tow.

But Running Stream did have a mind of her own.
Shoshone women were accorded more respect and independence than the women of other plains and mountains
tribes, and Running Stream took advantage. She openly
eyed Baptiste. Once she went so far as to smile at him.
She lingered around Bazel's lodge when she could find
an excuse. Finally she topped it off by giving him an
elaborately decorated buckskin shirt. It was downright embarrassing. And Spotted Horse was starting to fume
openly, and to mutter obscure threats.

Bazel told Baptiste one afternoon that Spotted Horse
was preparing himself—painting himself, chanting incanta-
tions, putting on his medicine objects. So Baptiste made
sure to keep his Green River and his pistol about him.

He heard it just soon enough to duck sideways. Spotted
Horse's stone ax hit him on the shoulder. It ached like it
was broken. Damn, so Spotted Horse had meant to kill
him right off. But by this time Baptiste had spun off and
was facing the bastard. Spotted Horse was screeching to
whatever his medicine was. That meant he was scared.

"You are a child," Spotted Horse cried. "Your bowels
run cold as winter rain. You are a woman, you would
rather weep than fight. You have the blood of a Shoshone
squaw in your veins, but none of a Shoshone brave. The
spirits scowled on the day you were whelped. I will spread
your blood on the dust, and from now nothing will grow
there. But I will not eat your heart, because it is yellow. I
will not let my dogs eat it. I will throw your flesh to the
ravens, and they will scorn it."

Baptiste growled fiercely and faked a head-on charge.
Spotted Horse jumped back. Baptiste had proven his point,
and grinned mockingly.

Spotted Horse was ashamed. He marshalled his courage
and charged, swinging the ax at Baptiste's head. Baptiste
jumped to the side, and the ax changed direction, hitting
him on the left arm without force. O.K., Spotted Horse's
charge was wild. Baptiste grabbed his own arm with his
right hand, as though hurt. Spotted Horse was quick. The
ax arced toward Baptiste's head. Baptiste grabbed it and
used the momentum to pull it past him, closing on Spotted
Horse. He kneed Spotted Horse violently in the groin.
When Spotted Horse doubled up, Baptiste brought his fist

and the shaft of his Green River down hard at the base of his neck and his knee up into his face. It didn't work. The neck was not broken. But Spotted Horse crumpled.

Baptiste pounded on him, rolled him onto his back, and jammed the point of the Green River at his throat. It would only be decent to kill the bastard. They glared at each other. Baptiste moved the knife tip down to Spotted Horse's chest. He made a long, thin cut down the breast bone. Then he crossed that cut low down on the ribs. "I have cursed you with the sign of the white man's God upside down," he said. And he walked away. Now the niggur would be afraid to come back at him. Running Stream, he saw, had been crying, and he heard her wail during the fight.

He walked to Mountain Ram's tipi and took away Spotted Horse's three ponies. Then he thought about it some. Sacajawea made the trip to Mountain Ram's tent to summon Running Stream. The girl came in with her head down, still crying, and wilted to the ground far to Baptiste's right. Sacajawea sat behind her in the shadows. Baptiste moved close to Running Stream and lifted her face so that he could see it in the firelight. She could not look at him.

"I fought for you," he said. She cried more freely. "I fought for you to be my woman. You will go away with me." The girl nodded yes. No one would deny his right to her now. He looked at Sacajawea, back at Running Stream, and added, "Tonight."

"It is right," said Sacajawea.

Later he thought what Joe and Doc and Bill would say, seeing him womaned. If they were aboveground to say anything. Well, hell, he could always trade her for a good buffalo horse.

The elopement was easy. Mountain Ram and his squaw were expecting it, so Running Stream openly tied her belongings into skin bags, said her good-byes, and waited at the entrance of the lodge a while after the moonrise. Baptiste brought his six ponies, two of them carrying jerky, pemmican, robes, and lodgeskin. He strapped Running Stream's light pack onto a third, mounted without a word, and set out.

No one had asked him where he meant to go. Probably they figured that, since winter was setting in, he would pitch their lodge in one of the nearby Shoshone camps, more of a gesture at elopement than the real thing. But he intended to find Milton Sublette and the RMF winter

camp up on the Salmon. In present weather that was ten
sleeps away. With heavy snow, it would be much longer
or—well, he didn't want to think about it. Too many
mountains between here and there.

It was a clear, cold night, the sort that comes after
snowfall. The snow lay thin on the ground, crusted to ice,
and the horses' hooves crunched as they walked. The moon
made the plateau nearly as light as day, and the cold hurt
his lungs a little. It made Baptiste feel good. The girl said
nothing at all. When Baptiste figured they had covered ten
miles, he made a fireless camp in the lee side of a big over-
hanging tree, where the ground was bare.

He thought Running Stream would be withdrawn, shy,
remote—still suffering the aftershock of the fight and the
elopement. But as he watched her standing silhouetted
against the white sheen of snow, she slipped off her buckskin dress and came to the buffalo robes with him naked.
She teased him a little. Then she kept him awake for a
couple of hours, dog-tired as they both were, making love
and playing and making love. Damn, she has fun with it,
he thought as he drifted off.

The next day he forced them thirty miles, and the day
after that they made a freezing ford of the Snake River.
Running Stream never complained, and did whatever Baptiste told her to do quickly and efficiently. The snow held
off as they crossed the lava beds. When they reached the
mountains and set out down a wide valley between parallel ranges, the snow was still not deep enough to trouble
the horses, and Baptiste thought they would make it.

They made camp under the boughs of a big fir tree.
Running Stream gathered wood for a fire and brewed tea
from the needles. He drank it almost boiling hot. As they
were finishing their pemmican, she told him the most obscene joke he had ever heard. While he was still guffawing,
she reached out to play with him. He started to come over
her, but she pushed him onto his back, held him down,
and then showed him he could enjoy being passive. That
night Running Stream demonstrated that she had imagination as well as enthusiasm in the buffalo robes. The next
morning he told her that he must give her a French-
woman's name for the other Frenchmen to use: Sophie.

The snow did fall for one day and one night, a windless
time with huge snowflakes falling and drifting on the air
like the leaves of maples back in Missouri. Baptiste took

his leisure that day, noticing how snow curled over the lips of small cricks, watching two deer nibble at the ends of branches, listening to the big, soft silence that falling snow creates. He played songs into the silence, and Running Stream listened reverentially. The next day, though, he had to hurry on, to find graze for the horses.

He opened his eyes and caught Sophie leaning over him and examining his necklace. Her eyes fell. "It's all right," he said. "It is a piece of a star that traveled here from the far heavens, a stone of many stones. It came with me when I traveled far across the salt-water-everywhere. But I no longer travel among strangers." She smiled like a child.

He came on Milton and the brigade just below where the North Fork flows into the Salmon, in the big canyon where the snow never stayed on the ground all winter long although the high ranges around were completely impassable. The boys didn't remark much on his squaw, but they did seem to think she had a way with a story.

Baptiste had to sign some notes for what he wanted—a fine saddle decorated with silver brought clear from Taos for Sophie, and every sort of trading goods for Mountain Ram. When he finished bargaining, and trade goods were even more expensive than they would have been at rendezvous, he'd spent almost all of what Prince Paul had given him. Well, what did dollars matter in a country where there were no grocery stores anyway? He surprised Sophie with the saddle, and delighted her. The boys reckoned that Baptiste was a little gone on that squaw.

JULY 1836: The whole camp was grumbling. First Gabe and Fitz, the White-Headed Chief, had give up, the summer before, and throwed in with American Fur. Independents just couldn't compete with the Trust, which baited them with money and then gobbled them up. So the boys had to buy and sell with the only store in town, which meant selling low and buying high. Baptiste thought MacKenzie must be gloating back at Fort Union. But he wasn't. The fickle people in St. Louy and New York and London who had kept the demand for beaver up for a couple of centuries, doffing hats made of nothing else, had suddenly decided that silk was better. The price of plews dropped like a stone into a well, and broke when it hit bottom. "In the old days," Luke Habber declaimed, "it was three dollars a pound, old 'un or kitten." Now it was a dollar a pound for fine plews only. The boys were in the squeeze. And so were Kenneth MacKenzie and American Fur, for whatever consolation that brought.

But the price of living didn't go down. Baptiste still had an outfit to buy, and some foofuraw for Sophie, whose high spirits called for a certain sartorial flair; and Jesus, there were her relatives to take care of. Since Baptiste had carried fine gifts to Mountain Ram, back in the spring of '35, that particular bunch of Snakes never missed a rendezvous. Of course, all Baptiste's in-laws expected presents from their rich relative; Bazel was like a child when it came to presents, and Sacajawea had some coming; on top of that, it seemed that Running Stream's near relations amounted to three dozen Shoshones.

So Baptiste was gladdened, with all the other boys, when the sound of rifles down the Siskadee below Horse Creek signaled the supply train and a chance for a bust-out. Baptiste jumped onto his fastest pony bareback to race a dozen other trappers to the train. He saw Fitz, the White-Headed Chief, at the head of it, with another Irish aristocrat, Bob Campbell, alongside him, and behind them—Baptiste couldn't believe it, so he rode right up to make sure. Some child must be buffler-witted. For next to the missionary doctor, Whitman, sidesaddle, was a handsome blonde woman in full skirt and stays. And behind, bumping uncomfortably on a wagon seat, came a solemn-looking fellow and another woman, scowling. The first white women had set foot in the Rocky Mountains.

Wall, it was at least cause for a celebration. The boys painted themselves up like Blackfeet on the warpath that night and treated the missionaries to an actual Blackfoot war dance. Truth was, so many good beavers had gone under to Blackfoot balls in the last year that the dancers meant it. The Shoshones, sparked by the notion of making Blackfeet come, joined in. Dr. Whitman, who had seen it all the summer before, thought the spectacle a high time, though he wondered whether he ought to. His lovely, buxom wife, Narcissa, delighted in it openly. The Reverend Henry Spalding was appalled by the white men who made themselves as low as savages. His self-righteous spouse, Eliza, retired to their tent at the start of the dancing.

Some of the men thought Narcissa a fantasy come true. Hadn't they dreamed and even sung about the girls they'd left behind across the wide Missouri? And warn't Mrs.

Whitman a picture, with that red-gold hair piled on top of her head and them fine tits parading out front?

The Indians welcomed them too. After all, these missionaries were the answer from the white man to the plea that had gone to the Red-Headed Chief seven years before. Some Nez Percés were in for rendezvous, and immediately begged the missionaries to live with them and teach them the true way. The Snakes were heated up to learn it, too. Besides, the squaws were fascinated by the dresses with all their fancy stitching and embroidery.

Old Gabe just shook his head. He knew they warn't long for that country. How could them ladies get by whar the sun would parch thar skin and the wind tan it to leather and the alkali water turn their bowels to water? Wagh! But he was obliging. As the head chief and host, he entertained them with yarns: About the river he'd found what run so fast downhill that it was hot at the bottom from friction. About echo canyon, whar the walls that threw a child's voice back at him was so far away that it took six hours for the echo to get back whar it started; Gabe used the echo for an alarm clock, he did.

Baptiste was disgusted. He had some idea of how much they knew about what they were getting into—about as much as that first missionary who'd come two years ago, alone, and who thought that Flatheads were Flatheads because their mothers bound their heads as children and deformed them. He'd given that preacher credit, though. He'd cleared out of the mountains, moved on to Orgeon, and eventually had gone back to the States and told everyone that the Indians couldn't be made Christians until they were made white men. Which was right. Were these damn fools come to make them white? No chance in this country. Why the land itself said no. The mountains and the plains would defy anyone who meant to divide them up, fence them, and farm them. Nature would say no to God.

Campbell liked Baptiste. The Irishman had come to the mountains for his health a decade before: he became a graduate man, and then turned for profit to supplying the rendezvous. He hadn't lost his sophisticated tastes; Baptiste was the only Indian he'd ever met who'd even heard of Shakespeare, and the only Indian he knew who spoke English, French, German, and Spanish, and bore himself, even in buckskins, with the grace of a courtier.

As cavalier to Narcissa Whitman—he disliked Eliza

Spalding—Campbell took Baptiste by to call. Narcissa was emphatically religious, he told Baptiste on the way to the Whitman tent. The report was that she had married principally to get to the mission fields; and for a fact she had worn black at her wedding, presenting herself as the bride of death.

For such a bride she seemed full of life. She served tea on her canvas-topped veranda, on an actual white tablecloth and in proper cups. She was full of curiosity about the trappers, and pealed with laughter at the stories of their lives—especially one Baptiste told about Milton Sublette climbing a tree to get away from a grizzly and ending up with a bear hug on the trunk two feet off the ground. At mention of mountain marriage she blushed a splendid crimson which only made her look more alluring, he thought, and seemed to mask fascination rather than disapproval. Baptiste entertained her graciously with anecdotes of Europe and Africa; he did not mention his dalliances. He was just thinking what a splendid, high-spirited woman she was when Old Bill creaked up and unceremoniously sat on the ground. He was, Baptiste judged, tanked up but coping nicely.

"Mrs. Whitman," offered Baptiste, "permit me to introduce you to the most considerable man I have met in these mountains, variably known as William S. Williams, Master Trapper, Old Bill, Old Solitaire, Parson Bill, and the old so and so."

Bill looked like he wanted to spit fire at Baptiste, but he said "How de do" without touching his felt hat. Narcissa greeted him graciously.

"This rheumatic, ornery, canny old coon has been my personal master and genie in learning mountain life," Baptiste went on devilishly. "Despite his uncouth appearance, he is an educated man, deciphering letters as well as he reads Blackfoot sign, and parsing both Latin and Greek as well. I doubt that he is suitable for your company, though, as he is a fallen angel. He was once a preacher and a missionary. He has declined into a thorough savage, regrettably, even to the point of putting faith in Indian superstitions."

"Is that so, Mr. Williams?"

"It is, Marm, though that scalawag would say so if it warn't. This child has preached to the Osages, away back to Missoura, and he's put the fear of God into a many.

And he's sent some Injuns to the other place, too, if I do say it myself. But this child has larned some'p'n, Marm, he has. He knows pore bull from fat cow, and he has kept his ears and eyes op'n, he has larned some about religion from the Injun, damned as they be."

"They are damned, Mr. Williams, because they do not see the divine light. Dr. Whitman and I hope to help them to see." Narcissa was still smiling.

"Wall, Marm, this child doesn't but think thar's some the Injuns could help any white man to see, meanin' no disrespect."

"Do you believe in Indian religion then, Mr. Williams?"

"No, Marm, this child don't. He's no damn fool of an atheist now, but he don't cotton to no set religion. This child has seed his own religion. But white folks could larn some from the Injuns, yet. They could larn that thar's the One-who-created-all, as the Injuns call him, everwhar they look. In Horse Crick right over yonder, it's what makes the water sweet and cold and run downhill. It's pushed up them Grand Tetons up north of here, and put Jackson Lake right smack in front of 'em, whar a coon'd want to set down on his haunches and gawk and never stop gawkin'. And it's what makes them columbines poke thar heads up right after the snow melts to water 'em. And it's in the grass and the pines and the rocks and the buffler and the elk as same as it's in man. The Injuns know that."

"And still they're sinners, Mr. Williams, and lost in the sight of God."

Bill looked at her hard. "Wagh! This child don't doubt that they be, Marm, but he knows what he does know. It's sin as'll spile this hyar country, and it's missionaries as you what be bringin' sin out hyar."

Campbell interrupted. "It's too fair an afternoon for heresy, Mr. Williams."

"No," said Narcissa, "I want to hear what he has to say."

"Since ye ask, Marm, this child'll give tongue to his thoughts. 'Ee recollect the story of Adam, what was set down in paradise and then sp'iled it all? Why, we is set down in paradise again, right hyar. So we be.

"A man was born to be free and nat'ral. Even the critturs know that. But over the centuries them Britishers and Frenchies and Dutchmen and Eyetalians, why they did mess things around. They got theirselves kings to boss around men as were born to be kings on their own. They got theirselves priests and told 'em what war nat'ral war wrong. They got theirselves a bunch of laws as to corral 'em. It war agin nature, Marm, but they done it.

"But the One-who-created all, he done give us a fresh start. He opened up this New World. And folks give it the monicker New World on account of it war a chance to get rid of them kings and priests and laws and things what put ropes around a man.

"Right off some fellers tried to start up with that old stuff agin, but it didn't shine. Too much land. If a beaver didn't take to all them stake-ropes, he could walk over yonder hill and be whar thar warn't none. That's how come my pap crossed the Cumberland Gap and settled in Kentuck'. And lots of other beavers too. Meant to be thar own kings on thar own place.

"Right quick them as like to regalate everbody else, why they followed on with thar damned, beggin' yer pardon, laws and thar churches. But we just come further west. We walked out of thar reach. And we mean to stay out, Marm, these children be free men"—he took in the whole camp with his hand—"and this airth ain't seen many free men. What we be is Adams. Adams in a new Eden: American Adams, that's what we be. Whelped in Original Goodness.

"Now 'ee missionaries kin ride out hyar and tell the Injuns to mend thar ways. 'Ee kin try to tell us beavers what know better. Wagh! But it don't shine, Marm, and it ain't gonna take. No way to pen a man up when over yonder ridge be a valley whar no coon kin find him, nor rule him. Set your eyeballs upon the land, Marm. The country hyar be too wild and fierce and just too damned big, beggin' yer pardon, Marm, for any man to fence it up, parcel it out, make it go by no rules. This be an Eden, Marm, what war true made for Adams. Sin ain't got no place hyar."

Narcissa beamed. "You should have kept your calling, Mr. Williams, for you are an eloquent preacher. I fear, though, that you are lost to the cause of Jehovah. And from your smile, Baptiste, I fear that your mentor has led you astray as well."

Narcissa, who had read the great romances, told Dr. Whitman that night in their tent that Baptiste and Bill were a veritable Lancelot and Merlin. But they and their fellows, she added, were as much in need of divine instruction as the Indians.

Chapter Seven

1838

1838: The Underground Railroad was by now well established.

1837, MAY 10: New York banks suspended specie payment, precipitating the Panic of 1837 and a seven-year depression.

1838: Joseph Smith and followers fled to the Far West, near Kansas City, Missouri; after a conflict with the Missourians, the Mormons would relocate to Nauvoo, Illinois, before making their emigration to Utah.

1840: During the 1840s the temperance movement gained such impetus that fourteen states adopted prohibition.

1841: The first wagon train crossed the plains, the mountains, and the deserts to California.

1841: Ralph Waldo Emerson's *Essays* (first series) appeared.

1841: New England Unitarians and Transcendentalists founded Brook Farm.

1842: Charles Dickens visited America to great adulation.

1843, MAY 22: Over 1000 settlers left Independence, Missouri, for Oregon, beginning the Great Migration.

1843: Lt. John Frémont's second Far West expedition explored the Oregon Trail, the Great Basin, and California.

Eighteen Hundred Thirty-Eight

JANUARY, 1838: Baptiste was riding with the Bridger brigade for American Fur now. Trapping had fallen on lean times, and Old Gabe wanted Baptiste and Kit Carson for his lieutenants that year for a big hunt in Blackfoot country. Hell, Baptiste would rather have been out on his own, but with the price of plews so low, he couldn't get a dollar for his possible sacks. And Gabe was offering handsome wages, wages that would let Baptiste set something by for the child Sophie was carrying. She'd be light in the spring.

The hunt was trouble from the start, skirmishes with Bug's Boys all along the way. The brigade spent more time in secure camps than out working the cricks. Just before winter set in for sure, the scouts reported a lot of Blackfoot lodges down the Yellowstone a little way. Carson, who'd come to the mountains a year after Baptiste and was younger, clearly had the ha'r of the b'ar in him; he was always ready for a fight. So were a lot of the boys: Too many of their friends had gone under because of Blackfeet; besides, times were bad and spirits festering. So little Kit led half the brigade downstream, set up in a good spot behind some rocks, and made thirty of the critturs come before dark spoiled the fun.

Gabe moved camp a ways up the Yellowstone and settled in for the winter on a spot between a steep bluff and the frozen river. He had sixty men, enough to make even riled Blackfeet wary of a fight.

But he kept a weather eye out for trouble. And one afternoon in January he thought he'd found it. Ten miles to the south a whole plain was swarming with Blackfeet, his scouts said—more than they had ever seen assembled in one spot. Jim ordered a six-foot breastwork of tree trunks thrown up around the three exposed sides of the camp. He

218

had Baptiste and Kit hand out the DuPont and Galena he'd kept in his packs. He sent men to keep watch on the bluff. And he waited.

The next morning Baptiste led a small party to take a look at the Blackfeet. They laid less than half a mile off and watched them for an hour. "Gabe," Baptiste said when he got back, "there's more'n a thousand of 'em. Their faces are blacked, and they're dancing for war."

"Druther they came on, John." Most of the trappers would rather they came. Some of the squaws, there in the middle of the camp, singing softly their songs designed to ward off injury and death, weren't so sure.

That night the sky gave a lurid show—a spectacular display of northern lights, flashing red and green and yellow for a couple of hours, then settling into a huge expanse of blood red covering the northern half of the sky. Some of the trappers were superstitious enough to wonder if it was a bad omen.

Morning broke brilliantly clear and bitter cold. At dawn the men could hear the sharp crack of cottonwoods popping in the sub-zero temperatures. From the bluff the watch could see nothing. At mid-morning a few Blackfeet crept to within three hundred yards and let fly some useless, silly sniping. Gabe changed the watch. This was the biggest force the Blackfeet or any Injuns had brought against mountain men. They surely didn't mean to stop at snipin'.

At noon the watch reported the whole Blackfoot army on the march, coming up the ice and the banks of the river. This was it. The trappers spread behind the breastwork, primed, and thought on what the Blackfeet might do. Gabe, Kit, and Baptiste were to have their men fire alternately, so that part of the brigade would always have its Hawkens loaded. It was simple: If the Blackfeet had the gumption for a charge, the brigade would go under, every man, woman, and child. But probably the niggurs would decide a direct charge was too expensive.

When the Blackfeet pulled up in ranks, out of range, a chief held up a white blanket. With two other chiefs, well armed, he walked toward the breastworks. Gabe waved to Kit and Baptiste, and the three walked out to meet him. At fifty yards the chief with the blanket stopped, laid down his gun and his knife, and walked forward again.

Gabe did the same. Baptiste knew it was a ruse. What he couldn't figure out was why the Blackfeet were stalling for time.

"Bad medicine," signaled the chief. He spread his arms toward the northern sky, back toward the Blackfoot camp. Baptiste couldn't hear whether Gabe and the chief were talking, but he could see the signs.

The chief smacked his left fist into his right palm, sketched a medicine pipe in the air with both hands, and pointed his right arm into the distance. Sign language for: Friendly. Smoke pipe. Leave.

Gabe sat with the coon and blew smoke in the ceremonial tribute to the earth, the sky, and the four winds. When he got back, he permitted himself a grin. "Queersomest thing I ever seed," he allowed.

DECEMBER, 1838: The Bridger brigade settled in this winter with the Shoshones. It had been a poor spring hunt, a dispirited rendezvous, and a poor fall hunt. Beaver was scarce. The price for beaver was still low. Eight more missionaries—four couples—had come to rendezvous. Even some of the fun was dwindling: The trappers' favorite enemies, the Blackfeet, had been nearly wiped out by smallpox the previous spring. So the boys didn't have many good scraps to liven things up. Old Gabe, when he found the Blackfoot lodges filled with infected bodies, reckoned that the chief had been right, that them northern lights were bad medicine after all.

Winter camp was a quiet time, with no one stirring much. Occasionally some braves and trappers would make meat; but mostly they sat it out around the fires and stewpots in their tipis. Baptiste and Running Stream—their child had been stillborn—sat many long afternoons in the lodge of Mountain Ram. He was old now, half blind, and knew that he did not have long to live. He liked to spend the days with his daughter and his son-in-law, though he would have been more pleased if they had children. He liked to spin tales for hours on end—tales of coup he had counted, tales of wonders he had seen, tales of how he had outwitted an arrogant neighbor, tales of how Shoshones outmaneuvered the fierce Blackfeet. His mind turned even further back, to the peculiar blends of history, myth, legend, and fantasy that made up Indian history and was handed down from generation to generation. One after-

noon he told Baptiste the story of the origin of the dance
of the buffalo calves:

A man married a buffalo. She ran away and re-
joined her herd. He followed her. The buffalo chief
came galloping up to him as if to gore him. But the
man stood fast and declared he would not depart
without his wife. The chief retired, and another came
up in the same threatening way. Four times this happened. Then the chief said, "If you can identify your
son four times among the dancing calves, you may
have him and your wife." So the man entered the
camp.

His son secretly came to him and said: "In the first
dance one of my ears will be drooping, and so you
will know me. In the second I shall have one eye
closed. In the third I shall limp." So three times the
man identified his son. For the fourth dance, however, he had no sign. He could not tell which calf was
his son. He made a mistake. The old buffalo there-
upon stampeded and trampled him to death. There
was nothing left of him. The buffalo went away.

With his father the man had left his medicine-robe,
a buffalo-skin with the horns attached. This he used
in curing the sick. He had told his father why he was
going away, and if something happened to him his father would know it by the robe. Lying on his pallet,
the father heard the rumbling bellow of a buffalo. He
said to his wife: "The robe has made a noise. It
means that something is happening to our son. He is
killed. Let us look for him." He had the small hoop
and shafts used in the game *itsiwan*. They made
ready for a journey. After four motions he threw the
wheel to the ground. It rolled away. They walked
beside it. Sometimes it would stop where the young
man had stepped in water. The man would throw it
again. Whenever the young man had stepped in water
or stopped to drink, the wheel stopped. At last it
stopped in a place where the grass over a large space
had been trampled by buffalo. The old man picked it
up and threw it down with four movements. It went a
little way and came back in a circle to the center of
the plot. Four times it did this. Then the man knew
his son had gone no farther.

He searched for some sign, and at last found a bit of hair and a long-bone partially covered with earth. He said: "Let us see what we can do for our son. Give me the robe." He spread it on the ground and wrapped the hair and the bone in it. He laid the bundle down. He raised it, and called his son, "Aiakatsi (gambler), we are going to gamble!" He spat on the hoop, and with four motions dropped it to the ground. It rolled in a circle, and the robe stirred. His son got up, alive. He told them that the buffalo had said if he could defeat them in a fight, he should recover his wife. So he was going to fight the buffalo. He covered himself with the medicine-robe. He threw himself on the ground and rolled like a buffalo and grunted. He stood up, a buffalo. He pawed the earth. They saw a large bull coming. Behind him was the herd. The two bulls charged. Neither could succeed in goring the other. After a long struggle the young man was weary. Just then he recognized his wife standing by. He implored her help. She ran up and gored her buffalo husband, making a long gash in his flank. He retreated, and Aiakatsi ran forward and gored him to death. The buffalo chief told him that since he had won he could take his wife and his son home. The buffalo became a human woman, the calf a boy. They went home, and the young man founded the Horn society, to perpetuate the dance of the buffalo calves.

When Mountain Ram was not telling stories of old times, his squaw was telling obscene stories and jokes, in the bluest language Baptiste had ever heard. He wished the missionaries could hear it.

Or he spent days sitting with Bazel and Sacajawea. She liked to listen to his music, so he would work on new songs in the long evenings, not songs about objects or places, but songs that brought up moods, songs of feeling that he remembered and associated with various places in the mountains. Sacajawea made a singular audience. He could never have gotten an impression of whether she liked the music—the notion of liking or disliking a song was utterly foreign to her—but he got her solemn attention, her reverence in the presence of something mysterious, sacred, and powerful.

He was developing new impulses in his own songs. They had a sliver of the four-voice Protestant hymns of his childhood, a sliver of the Catholic liturgical music of his puberty, a piece of the square-dance and boatmen's tunes of his adolescence, a large piece of the Haydn-Mozart-Dittersdorf-Hummel-Beethoven he had heard in Europe, and a piece of Indian music laid over the whole. It would have driven a musicologist batty. But Baptiste had an idea now why Indians spoke of being given songs in dream-visions: He heard songs in his head, involuntarily, any time he was willing to listen—when he was riding quietly, or waiting for a deer to come out of the brush, or looking into a fire or relaxing after making love to Running Stream. When he paid attention, interior music made an inexhaustible accompaniment to his life.

One afternoon he asked Sacajawea whether he should not have a Shoshone name. Most of the American trappers called him John. Some of them, especially the French-Canadians, called him Baptiste. Some Crows called him Long Foot, because of the time he got his horse killed and made a seventy-mile walk into rendezvous; some Snakes called him Wooden-Shoe-White-Man. But neither Indian name had stuck firmly. And Baptiste felt his separateness from his wife's people, his mother's people, halfway his own people, when they called him by his white name.

Sacajawea summoned Thunder Cloud, the tribe's medicine man, who had been given, as a sickly teen-ager, a great vision that came from the thunder gods of the west. She gave him three buffalo robes, and Baptiste added a pony. Thunder Cloud promised to divine Baptiste's name.

He listened for hours to the story of Baptiste's life. Sacajawea told of the bitter, stormy winter day when he was born with red and white blood. She told of the long journey with Lewis and Clark, and of the way the infant Paump charmed Clark with his dancing. Baptiste told of his early education by two tales of the white man's god, of his years spent east of the salt-water-everywhere, of his return to the white man's great village on the Mississippi, of his journey to the mountains, of his decision to stay in the mountains as a trapper. He explained to Thunder Cloud the medicine of the hoop-and-stone necklace Sacajawea had made for him.

Had any bird ever spoken to Baptiste? Thunder Cloud

wanted to know. Or any other animal? Or rock or tree or cloud? Baptiste said no.

Had Baptiste had any dreams in which power was revealed to him? Had he received in dreams any deeds he must do? No. Any dances? No. Any sacred words? No. Any songs?

Baptiste considered and said yes, sort of. He supposed that tunes that ran in his head were something like that.

Thunder Cloud was primed now. Would Baptiste sing the songs for him, so that he could feel Baptiste's medicine?

Baptiste grinned as he showed Thunder Cloud his harmonika. Thunder Cloud had no idea what it was. Baptiste started with "Lone Mountain Song," then "Riding Song," then "Swift Creek Song," then "Song of the Fire." He took time between songs to notice that Thunder Cloud was puzzled, maybe dumbfounded, that he could find no string that might untie the strange bundle of this music. But they said nothing. Thunder Cloud listened in utter, trance-like concentration while Baptiste played "The Song of the Running Buffalo" and "Aspen Grove Song."

When Baptiste stopped, Thunder Cloud sat still, eyes lowered, for a long time in respect for Baptiste's medicine. At last he said that it was difficult medicine, elusive, perhaps beyond Thunder Cloud's ability to enter and partake of. Thunder Cloud would think on what he had heard, and then dream on it, and return tomorrow. Then perhaps he could give Baptiste his name.

That night Sacajawea came to Baptiste's lodge to eat and sat long with them around the lodge-fire. She liked to tell, as Mountain Ram did, the ancient legends of the Shoshone people, the stories Baptiste would have been raised on if she had not taken him to the Red-Headed Chief. This particular night she told another version of the origin of the dance of the buffalo calves, and a long story about the wily, pranksterish coyote god. Then she started telling the story of the first Shoshone.

He was a coyote, and he ran on the plains and hunted like the other coyotes. One night in a dream he saw a two-legged creature he had never seen before. He thought that having two legs was a disadvantage—clearly the creature could not run as fast as a coyote. The creature was also poorly armed, for he had no fangs and only short claws. Yet the two-legged creature stood tall and could see

around him, over the tops of the sagebrush. He had hair-
less skin, and that seemed to the coyote very beautiful.
The coyote himself wanted to be so beautiful.

In his dream then the coyote accidentally touched his
own skin, and to his amazement it felt smooth. He woke
up. He crawled out of his lair in the brush to go to the
water, and felt that he was standing on two legs. Looking
down, he saw the skin and long legs and arms of the creature in his dream. He was amazed. At the creek he looked
into the reflection of his own face, a man's face, and
thought that it was fair.

"This Paump," she said, "ran off the next morning
to . . ."

"What did you call him?" Baptiste interrupted.

"Paump," Sacajawea said.

Baptiste looked puzzled.

"First-born sons are called Paump after him," Sacajawea said. "The one. The Shoshone. The head man."

"So I was called after the first Shoshone," Baptiste
grinned. And then he laughed out loud.

"Your name is not yet revealed to me," Thunder Cloud
said the next morning. "I fasted last night, but my dreams
were troubled, and I saw nothing clearly." He paused and
considered a long while. Baptiste, Running Stream, and
Sacajawea waiting respectfully. At length Thunder Cloud
went on: "You are a man of two dreams, a man split by
two dreams. Half of you is white, and it has a white man's
dream to guide you on the earth. The other half is
Shoshone, and it has a Shoshone dream to guide you on the
earth. Perhaps you are as a man split, and that is why my
dreams are uneasy and unclear."

Baptiste let time pass to indicate a respectful hearing.
"Thunder Cloud," he began, "with your permission I
would like to choose my own name."

"Perhaps you alone can divine it."

"I choose Paump." The women shifted where they sat.
"I know it is a child's name, to be shed at manhood." He
thought for a moment how to angle his tiny deception.
"However, it means the first Shoshone, and I am the first
Shoshone white man. In the white man's language it
means the first man, who lives in a new and abundant
garden. Such is this land. Thus I choose Paump."

Sacajawea and Running Stream looked at Thunder

Cloud for an answer, afraid he might think his medicine offended.

"I trust to your wisdom," Thunder Cloud said, "and I shall tell the people your name."

Baptiste said silently to the image of Old Bill in his mind, "By God, I am an Adam, you old bastard."

JULY, 1839: Rendezvous just wasn't fun anymore. Baptiste had trapped Snake country in the fall and the Three Forks in the spring with Gabe; but the brigade was half the size it used to be, the plews were few, and the Company had gotten tight with its wages and its liquor. Beaver didn't shine, plews didn't bring a price.

Black Harris brought the supply train in to Horse Creek on July 4—a pitiful sight, just nine men and four mule carts. Jim Beckwourth came riding with it.

"Wagh, John!" he said as he swung off. "These days be pore bull, don't they?"

So they had a pipe together and swapped stories. Beckwourth had finally left the Crows because they turned on him. Their plews and their loyalty to the Company didn't bring much beads and firewater any more, so they blamed Jim.

"Ye heerd the words of it?" Jim asked. "This child lost his job with the Crows so he come to rendezvous thinkin' he'd jine these coons and set the old traps. But it won't hold. Company ain't gonna outfit any more brigades. They say the dollars ain't in it no more. No more brigades, no more rendezvous. We is shot in the lights."

"Unemployment comes to the wilds," Baptiste said wryly.

"The fellers'll shit when they hear tell."

When Baptiste got to circulating, he found what he liked even less: The strangers Black Harris had brought to rendezvous were a preacher, a scientist, and something entirely new—a band of emigrants headed for Oregon and Californy. The sign was getting plain enough for the most buffler-witted to read: Ordinary folks—civilized folks—were moving west.

The camp simmered with grousing that night. Wall, the boys declared they weren't ready to pack in their traps yet. They might not be able to thumb their noses at any war parties—they'd have to slip through the mountains in twos and threes, hoping that no Injuns saw them. They'd have to tote their plews to the forts which had been springing up, not only Cass and Union, but Fort Laramie at the mouth of the Sweetwater and Bent's Fort down on the Arkansas on the trail to Taos. There wouldn't be any more rendezvous. But on the whole they weren't inclined to quit. In the mountains they were their own bosses.

Gabe wasn't ready to knuckle under either. He wasn't about to slink through mountains where he'd captained an army. He made up his mind to go back to St. Louy, collect his back wages, find some more money, and outfit his own brigade.

Paump and Jim were at loose ends. Well, hell, they knew plenty of places between them where they could lay hands on twenty packs of beaver. They'd just have to go higher into the mountains, up smaller cricks, into places a whole brigade couldn't travel. They thought they'd give it a try down to Bayou Salade (South Park in Colorado) and to Taos for the winter.

SEPTEMBER, 1839: Paump, Beckwourth, Kit Carson, Long Hatcher, and two more trappers are riding south on the plains between the South Fork of the Platte and the Arkansas. It is a hot, dry, late-summer noon. Burned, dusty hills stretch in all directions to the horizons, as big and wide as the perfectly blue sky. Heat waves shimmer on the ground, blurring features and minds. The next water is nearly fifty miles away.

All the trappers seem to notice them at once—a band of Comanches on the top of a low rise, painted for war. Screeches cut through the dry air. There looks to be no cover, not even a deep gully, for miles. The Indian ponies start moving.

Carson is quickest; he jumps off his horse and drives his Green River into the neck of his mule. "Get the goddamn animals down for a fort," he yells. In moments each man slits the throats of his horses and mules and throws them into a crude breastwork. Paump and Jim lie side by side facing the charge. The others spread in a circle. "You first," says Baptiste. No one needs to say that half will fire, half hold, so that some Hawkens will always be loaded. Each man is focused on the Indians, coming forward at a trot. Each knows that he is likely to go under. Each thinks only of the job at hand.

At a hundred yards the Comanches break into a canter.

The trappers wait. Finally, at thirty yards, three Hawkens jump. The front Comanche and two just behind him fall to the ground and are trampled. The column splits in two and sweeps past on either side of the smelly fort. The trappers say nothing at all. The Comanches are regrouping.

Twice more the same pattern—the charge, the center shots, the sweep by. The Comanches take time to talk things over.

"They'll come straight over this time," Carson warns. The dust is acrid in Baptiste's nose and eyes. The stink of blood from the animals is thick and nauseating. Hell of way to go, he thinks.

The Comanches are coming straight over. At the last minute three of them drop, and their horses go crazy— rearing, whinnying, trying to turn back into the charge. For long moments chaos: Horses bumping into horses, braves hurtling out of saddles, men and animals screaming, a melee in which Baptiste can see almost nothing.

Then some riders skirt the mess and bear down on the fort. "Let fly," yells Carson. Two more drop. Now all the Hawkens are unloaded. If the Comanches keep charging, rifles won't help. Maybe the pistol fire will keep them off.

Four more get through the turmoil. Beckwourth and Baptiste stand up, exposed, and kill two of them with pistols. But the others hold fire: The horses are refusing to come closer. Ten or fifteen yards away the horses slow, turn off, and take the bits in their teeth, terrified. Some Hawkens are reloaded now, and the trappers drop two more. But chaos has changed to flight. The Comanche ponies are turning off and running away. In moments they're gone.

Carson is shaking his head. "The blood," Baptiste says. "The smell of blood is spooking the critturs."

The trappers lie behind their putrefying fort all afternoon in the brutal sun, ready. The Comanches never come back. After dark the six of them, unscratched, pick up what they can carry and start walking to water. All make it. Four days later they hoof into Bent's Fort. They have to buy new outfits, of course, mostly on credit. Each has lost nearly all his worldly goods. But hell, it's all part of the fun.

Bent's Fork was full of bullwackers and greenhorns on the way to Santa Fe or, sometimes, just out for a lark. The boys told them a few yarns, doubling the size of every war party and the length of every rattlesnake, and got on with them well enough, but they didn't cotton to them. Greenhorns. Emigrators. Fellers as was safe back in Boston, Massachusetts, when the mountain men were living in the Rocky Mountains.

"This child hates an American," said Long Hatcher on the way back to the mountains, "what hasn't seen Injuns skulped or doesn't know a Yute from a Shian mok'sin. Sometimes he thinks of makin' tracks for white settlement, but when he gits to Bent's big lodge on the Arkansas and sees the bugheways, an' the fellers from the States, how they roll their eyes at an Injun yell worse nor if a village of Comanches was on 'em, pick up a beaver trap to ask what it is—just shows whar the niggurs had their brungin' up—this child says, a little bacca ef it's a plew a plug, an' DuPont an' G'lena, a Green River or so,' and he leaves for Bayou Salade. Damn the white diggins while thar's buffler in the mountains."

JUNE, 1840: Paump, Beckwourth, and Old Bill are camping in a grassy meadow in Bayou Salade. Running Stream and Yellow Leaf, Jim's new squaw, are smoking deermeat over open fires and converting the skins into clothing. They pound them with stones, wash them, stretch them, pound them, stretch them. Bill and Jim heave big rocks into a small crick to block it and form a pool. Walking a ways upstream, they step in and clomp down toward the rocks, splashing as much as they can. When they've pinned the trout in the pool, Jim peers into the water and neatly grabs one with his hands and tosses it onto the bank. While he keeps catching them, Bill stands knee deep in the crick, splashing and cussing about how the cold makes his old bones ache.

Baptiste, having pocketed a quart of berries, walks on up high, climbing up from one basin into another narrower basin. Here the ground is covered with dandelions from rock wall to rock wall—thick, healthy dandelions a foot and more tall. From a few yards away the ground looks solid gold. He takes a drink from the litte stream— the water is cold enough to hurt—looks at the sun, and judges that he has three hours of daylight.

He wades on through the dandelions to the upper end of the basin, climbs the boulder field, and then starts clambering up the rocks on the west wall. Before long the going gets harder. He climbs on small holds for his moccasined toes and his fingers. Just below the spiny ridge the rock seems almost vertical. At length he grabs a rock with both hands, pulls up, lets his legs swing, and mantles onto the ridge.

For a while he sits and looks around. The looking isn't purposeful. It is absorbing, smelling, drinking in rather than looking. A greenhorn would have thought it useless, wasteful. He sees a bighorn sheep over on the eastern ridge. The sheep seems to look straight at him for a while, unmoving. Then, with ease, it bounds up a vertical wall for twenty feet and disappears.

As the sun begins to set, Baptiste starts playing his harmonika. He has a new song, "Alpine Sundown," that he plays two or three times.

The sun is almost down. Paump watches the red rock of the eastern ridge. In the last hour of daylight, when it catches the reddening sun, it seems to glow, as though it did not reflect light but radiated its own light, a soft, rose-colored emanation, the phenomenon called alpenglow. He has no thoughts. He simply absorbs.

In the twilight he hurries down the ridge and walks through the basin, gathering some dandelions to add to dinner.

They have a guest for dinner, a child who calls himself Elkanah. Elkanah has arrived at a good time, not only fried trout and fresh greens and berries for dinner, but biscuits made from flour Jim has saved for weeks. They swap news—who's gone under, what plews will bring to Taos, where the buffler are, what Injun trails they've cut—and then they swap yarns. They recollect the old days.

Elkanah, sitting cross-legged in front of the fire, the light showing his browned and reddened face and his glints of eyes, nearly closed from years of sun, sounds the old theme:

"Thirty years have I been knocking about these mountains from Missoura's head as far sothe as the starving Heela. I've trapped a heap and many a hundred pack of beaver I've traded in my time, wagh! What has come of it, and whar's the dollars as ought to be in possibles? Whar's the ind of this, I say? Is a man to be hunted by Injuns all his days? Many's the time I've said I'd strike for Taos, and trap a squaw, for this child's getting old, and feels like wanting a woman's face about his lodge for the balance of his days. But when it comes to caching of the old traps, I've the smallest kind of heart, I have. Certain, the old state comes across my mind now and again, but who's thar to remember my old body? But them diggins gets too overcrowded nowadays, and it's hard to fetch breath amongst them big bands of corncrackers to Missoura. Beside, it goes agin' nature to leave buffler meat and feed on hog. And them white gals are too much like pictures, and a deal too foofuraw. No, damn the settlements, I say. It won't shine, and whar's the dollars? Hows'ever, beaver's bound to rise. Human nature can't go on selling beaver a dollar a pound. No, no, that aren't agoing to shine much longer, I know. Them was the times when this child first went to the mountains. Six dollars the plew—old 'un or kitten. Wagh! But it's bound to rise, I say again. And hyar's a coon knows whar to lay his hand on a dozen pack right handy, and then he'll take the Taos trail, wagh!"

He knocks the ashes out of his pipe and gazes about at Baptiste, Jim, Bill, and the two squaws. "Well," says Baptiste, "beaver may not rise. I know those civilized folks who used to wear beaver hats. They say silk is all the fashion. And they are fools for fashion."

"Wagh!" says Bill, "they be."

Baptiste and Running Stream spread their robes on a soft, grassy spot thirty feet from the fire under a sky clustered with stars thick and big as columbine in June.

"Paump," she asks, "why do dollars matter to him?" Baptiste looks at her in the dark. Running Stream usually doesn't ask questions.

"Just to buy possibles and trade goods," Baptiste says.

"They don't matter," she claims. "Everything you need is here. My people have lived here since before the memories of the grandfathers of the oldest men. The One-who-created-all has provided everything for us here. You need no dollars. The white man is crazy for dollars, and he makes the Indian crazy for them."

Sometimes he thinks she is a lot more than a squaw.

MAY, 1841: Two sleeps from Fort Laramie Baptiste, Bill, Jim, and Long Hatcher were making camp on the South Fork of the Platte. They heard footsteps. "Speak up," said Baptiste, "or you go under." Two Indians walked into the penumbra of the fire and made the sign for peace. "Sit and talk," Baptiste told them in their own language.

The talk was the usual, effusive expressions of friendship and good intentions. After ten minutes the trappers found out what it was about—Bill's mule hee-hawed, and then hooves clapped on the hard earth. Bill had his Hawken against the chest of one of the critturs before they could move. Jim and Baptiste ran into the dark.

"Mind to steal our ponies, do 'ee? Wagh! We'll steal your topknots if 'ee try. This child'll steal your cocks"—he mimed it with his Green River—"and deliver 'em personal to your squaws."

"Bring back the horses," yelled Baptiste somewhere in the dark, "or we kill the hostages."

The movement off in the brush stopped. Then a voice called for time to consider.

Back around the fire Bill and Long Hatcher had the hostages trussed up. "Do ye hyar?" said Jim, "it's the critturs or your scalps. Tell them," he said to Baptiste, "that we burn 'em alive unless we get the animals back."

Baptiste did. The Arapahoes immediately began to sing their death songs, calling for divine protection. "That won't help," Baptiste said. "Call out and tell your friends that they bring the horses back or we throw you on the fire."

One of the braves got hold of himself enough to yell the threat in a quavering voice into the darkness.

"Wait and we talk," called a voice from maybe thirty yards out. There was no sound from the horses, so the Arapahoes must have eased them further away.

Bill tripped one of the braves and shoved him face down into the fire. The man screamed and rolled out. The other brave pleaded with his friends to trade the horses for their lives.

After a couple of minutes a voice shouted that they would give two horses for the two prisoners. They had stolen eleven horses and mules.

"No deal," Baptiste yelled. A few more minutes passed. "The niggur must be palavering with his buddies," Jim said. Long Hatcher slipped out into the dark.

"Two horses for two men," the same voice yelled.

"May the One-who-created-all curse you," Baptiste yelled, "and give your children club feet."

They heard the horses begin to move far out in the

dark—moving away. Someone screamed out there. A moment later Long Hatcher walked into the camp with a fresh scalp. "He won't do no more parleying," Hatcher observed.

All four men built up the fire. The two Arapahoes went into a kind of trance, lifting their death songs.

Bill and Hatcher heaved the first one onto the fire and pinned him there with long sticks. They ignored his screams. After two minutes he stopped thrashing. Baptiste and Jim put the other one in the fire.

"They heered it," Bill said. "Mebbe that'll larn 'em."

After three days the trappers caught up with the whole band. They slipped into the herd at night, knifed the guard, cut out eighteen head, and led them away undetected. Jim was furious, though, because in the dark he hadn't found his buffler horse.

JULY, 1842: Baptiste and Jim, returning to meet Sophie and Yellow Leaf with the Shoshones on Black's Fork, were riding through South Pass. The July afternoon was almost unbearably hot. The pass was a twenty-miles breadth of sagebrush flat and parched buffalo grass. The plain shimmered with heat waves, and the distant hills seemed to be detached from the earth. There was not a breath of air in the pass.

Ahead they thought they could see figures above the sagebrush, but in the shiny blur they couldn't be sure. Figures, sure enough. A man and a woman, the man flopped on the ground, the woman bending over him, the horses drooping nearby.

"Afternoon," Jim offered, "need some help?"

The woman looked a little scared. A breed and a niggur who look as rascally as Indians, Baptiste thought. She probably thinks we'll scalp him and rape her.

"Water," croaked the man. "I'm dying from lack of water." A lot of words from a dying man, Baptiste thought.

Jim swung off his horse. "Don't got no water," he said, "but hyar's some whisky." They had been parceling out the whisky all the way from Laramie. Jim held the man's head up and started to tip the kettle.

"What's that ye say?" the man asked. He had just gotten a load of Jim's black face.

"Whisky. Drink."

The man turned his head out of the way of the pouring stream, and it dribbled off his cheek onto the ground. "God save me," he sputtered, as though he'd actually gotten some in his mouth, "no spirits. I won't partake of alcohol. I'd rather go to my Savior now."

Jim looked at him disgustedly.

"You aire somteeng," Baptiste spoke up for the first time. "You lay zere and die. *Idiot!*, and go to hell. No wan weel miss you." Jim was grinning. "What about your wife? Standing here in ze sun? She ees not pretending to die. She is not yellow-leevered. She is fine, spirited woman, fit to leeve and make children. You go ahead and die. We take her with us."

Jim grabbed her and helped Baptiste get her up behind him. She looked terrified. Baptiste gave his horse a kick and trotted off, him right behind. She was wailing in Baptiste's ear about being left to die with her beloved, about being consecrated to him as though to Jesus. A quarter mile away Baptiste looked back and saw the fellow standing up in the sagebrush.

Down on Big Sandy Creek late that afternoon they caught up with the main party. Baptiste handed Mrs. Jones down with a polite flourish.

"Where's Brother Jeremiah?" a big fellow asked.

"Left dying of thirst by the pass," she said, crying only a little now.

The greenhorns found him halfway to camp. By the time the missionary got to camp, having guzzled Big Sandy refreshment, he was prepared to give Jim and Baptiste a proper chastising, and to turn them over to the local authorities. But they were gone on, having little tolerance for the company in the neighborhood. If the Reverend Jeremiah Jones saw hellfire in their eyes, they saw prissiness in his.

JUNE, 1843: Baptiste pulled Pilgrim up short. Pilgrim snorted impatiently, eager to move. Old Bill, Jim, and Joe Meek rode up alongside him and saw why he stopped. Their mules bore thick packs of plews; their swing through Pierre's Hole, Jackson Hole, and the Absaroka Range had made a fine spring hunt. Idling their way toward Laramie for a good pay-off, they thought that trappin' was shinin' again. But there, reaching in front of them from above Independence Rock down past Devil's Gate, spread a huge

litter of white tops. The wagons were winding up the
Sweetwater in a long, slow, sinuous crawl like the verte-
brae of a snake.

"This child reckons it's a thousand emigrators," Bill
wheezed. They just looked for a long time—at the river, at
the mountains that rose, aloof, to nine or ten thousand
feet to the south, at the cleft where the Sweetwater suddenly plunged down into the turbulent hell of Devil's Gate
for a quarter mile, at the land that changed through the
seasons without ever changing, and at the wagon train inch-
ing up the valley. Baptiste figured there were more white
men in that single train than had ever come into the
mountains before. He kicked Pilgrim forward.

Baptiste saw Dr. Whitman riding in front of the lead
wagon, and pulled up. "Where to?" he asked, sweeping his
hand over the length of the train.

"Oregon, Baptiste, mostly the Willamette Valley. Hello,
Joe, Bill."

Bill grunted. "This ain't fitten, Doctor."

"You're a reactionary, Bill, an amiable reactionary. And
a sinner. Come to Walla Walla and be reborn."

"Wagh! I'll be reborn, sure." He made antlers with his
fingers. Whitman laughed.

"What's the weather ahead?" Whitman asked.

"Quiet," Baptiste said. "Shoshones to Black's Fork. Old
Gabe's built a fort there. You can do some trading and
smithing. Crows are mostly away up north. Utes were up
a while back, and were raiding Shoshones, but they're
chased back south. Should be peaceable to the fort."

"Thanks," said Whitman. He looked at Jim as though to
introduce himself, but apparently thought better of it.

"Preachin' bastard," Jim said as they rode off.

"Mark my words, boys," cried Bill, "these fools is thumb-
in' thar noses at nature. The mountains ain't fitten for
women and children. One day Colter's hell ull open and
swallow 'em up. Let 'em stay on *God's* side of the Missouri River."

"Welcome," Baptiste called down from his horse, "back
to Atlantis."

Robert Campbell strode across and shook his hand
warmly.

"What be Atlantis?" Jim asked, shaking likewise.

"The one-time home of the gods," said Campbell. "I believe Baptiste is suggesting that the mountains will soon be the one-time home of you one-time gods. May I offer the gods a drink?"

They swung off. "Whew," said Joe, "mighty fancy."

"I want you to meet someone," Campbell smiled, and led them toward the main tent.

"Captain William Drummond Stewart of Her Majesty's Army," Campbell announced. He was a friendly looking man of military erectness, with a splendidly bristling mustache and a beard of more recent cultivation. He wore riding breeches and high leather boots, but had shed his coat. After the formalities Campbell explained: "Captain Stewart is a Scottish baronet, proprietor of Murthly Castle. He's here to shoot some mountain critturs and take back some trophies."

Baptiste laughed out loud. "I hope you're not planning to take any Indians to the Sahara desert."

Steward looked dumbfounded. "Would you care to explain that over a glass of wine?" he smiled.

Running Stream and White Pebble—Jim had lodgepoled Yellow Leaf up at Pryor's Gap and sent her home—took the pots to the Sweetwater, and set about making camp while the men drank. Captain Stewart, it turned out, had brought along in his wagon a generous selection of wines, brandies, whiskies, cigars, and various delicacies. He offered a Rhine wine cooled in the river and some smoked oysters. While Jim muttered about the sissy wine and spat out the oysters, Baptiste told Stewart about William Clark and St. Louis, Prince Paul, Stuttgart and King William, the University of Württemberg, France, England and North Africa.

"Hamlet's university, eh? It is a good joke. My own lands include the Wood of Dunsinane. Wrong play, right author." He considered. "It's quite fantastic. The course of your entire life has been altered, incredibly altered, by chance encounters with two famous men."

"Perhaps," Baptiste answered. "But when all is said and done, I am still here, in the mountains, trapping—just where anyone would have predicted the son of a squaw and a fur trader would end his days. And that is not chance, but choice."

"You have a somewhat richer perspective, I suspect, than your fellow trappers."

Jim set down his empty wine glass impatiently. "Got any whisky?" he said in a mock growl.

"My friend's palate is less than refined," Baptiste smiled. "But what can you expect of a rude, uncouth trapper?" Stewart reached for a bottle. Baptiste stalled the pouring until he could pick some mint for juleps.

"Where to, gentlemen?" Campbell asked.

"Black's Fort," Baptiste said.

"Old Gabe's built hisself a fort thar," Jim elaborated. " 'Pears he's a mind to set up at storekeepin'."

"Gabe?" Campbell was amazed. "The king of the mountains tending a store?"

"It's bad times, Bob," Baptiste said. "Half the boys are leaving the mountains."

"Yes, I saw Fitz and Kit guiding a Lieutenant Frémont above Ash Hollow."

"And some of them are nursemaiding the emigrants across to Oregon and Californy, meaning to set up as farmers when they get there," Baptiste said. "The rest are just caching their traps. *Tempis fugit.*"

"He talks funny and he wears lace panties," Jim said.

"Meet your squaws' people at Bridger, and then what?" asked Stewart.

"Hunt for the Snakes a while," said Baptiste. "Our squaws are Snakes. And then this child'll trap, I guess."

"Boys, there'll be a rendezvous this summer. I know the rendezvous has gone under, but for old time's sake. We've brought kegs of whisky, and there'll be prizes for riding and shooting. Whole thing's on Captain Stewart. He wants to see one."

"Wagh!" grunted Jim. "A rendezvous on the peraira? You be flinging the dollars about."

"Somewhere in the Wind Rivers," added Campbell, "I'll send a man to Fort Bridger to leave word where."

"Tell all the trappers you see," said Stewart. "And come yourselves. We'll have some fun."

"One last bust-out," Baptiste said reflectively.

A young man walked up to them, but before Campbell could make the introduction, Baptiste recognized the red hair.

"Jefferson Clark," he smiled, and stuck out his hand. They hadn't seen each other in twenty years. "Jean-Baptiste Charbonneau."

Baptiste shook his head in embarrassment. "I am delin-

quent in writing your father—he's damn near *our* father.
Will you carry a letter to him?"

"He died, Baptiste. Three years ago."

Baptiste examined the young Clark for a long moment.
"He lived an honest man," Jeff nodded.

"Paump," Running Stream began as she lay down
beside him the next night, "I may not go to the Wind
Rivers, and I don't want to go on a fall hunt. I want to
stay with my people. My time will be before winter."

"You want to be near Crippled Hand?" Crippled Hand
was the principal midwife of the tribe.

"Yes, and my father. He does not have many moons
left."

He held her for a moment. He was glad that she was
with child again; he'd been afraid that the first child, born
dead, had somehow damaged her insides.

"Sure," he whispered, "we'll travel with the Shoshones
this fall and make winter camp with them." He smiled at
her. "And since it's free, maybe we can get the tribe and
half the Shoshone nation to come to rendezvous."

She was convinced that their son had died because she
had not stayed with her people; the old women of the
tribe, who knew about such things, had not been there to
isolate her from the men and sing their sacred songs and
help with the delivery. This time she would get what she
wanted. "Everything will be OK," he said, and rolled onto
his back.

"Maybe not," she said. She put a hand on his shoulder.
"The trapping will end soon. There are no more dollars in
it. Is that not so?" He nodded. "You must make a choice.
You must go back to the settlements, or go to California
or Oregon, or live with the Shoshones, must you not?"

He was surprised that she spoke up like this. But then
she had surprised him before. "I might keep trappin'. The
dollars don't matter."

"It is finished, Paump. I do not want to go to live with
the Frenchmen. I want to stay with my people on our
land. I want for us to raise our son among the Shoshones
and teach him as he should be taught."

"I'll think on it," he said.

She knew the sign to quit. As he lay there, agitated
now, and unable to sleep, he figured that she was probably
right, all the way around. Still, he'd butt up against all that
when the time came.

JULY, 1843: Paump did persuade a few Snakes to come to rendezvous—Bazel and his squaw and three teen-age children, Sacajawea, Mountain Ram and his older daughter Spotted Deer and her man, Big Belly, and two other lodges—a dozen and a half in all. He might have gotten more, but he had to tell them that not many trading goods would be there.

He was disappointed that the young chief of the entire Shoshone nation, Washakie, refused. Washakie seemed to Baptiste to have an inner calm and wisdom that set him apart, and he was a remarkable orator. The Shoshones had a well-earned reputation for unbroken peace with the white man—which was handy for the whites, since the Snakes controlled the area of the Oregon Trail from South Pass west far beyond Fort Hall. Washakie, who had become chief about the time the first emigrants started coming through, was a determined advocate of strong bonds of friendship with the white man.

Baptiste and Jim led the small band from Fort Bridger up the Siskadee to the mouth of the Big Sandy, a way up the creek, and then due north for East Fork. Old Pierre, back at the fort, had said rendezvous would be up at East Fork Lake.

Just above the mouth of Big Sandy, Baptiste saw a huge congregation of wagons a quarter mile ahead; the emigrants were making no preparations to move on. He wondered how far the stragglers were strung out behind them—clear to South Pass, probably.

Little Bear, Bazel's teen-age son who fancied himself a warrior, gave his horse a kick and came past Jim and Baptiste; Mountain Ram was right behind him, the silver-haired old man waving his lance and shouting. It was the old trick of riding up on a party fast, as though you were going to attack, and stopping dead at the last minute to shake hands, clap backs, and laugh. All right, why not a little fun? Everyone except the two horses dragging travois galloped toward the wagons. Baptiste and Jim fired their Hawkens into the air.

A couple of men did reach toward their rifles, but there was no real chance of being misunderstood—there must have been four or five hundred whites to a band of less than twenty Indians, counting women and children.

"Mornin'," the old fellow who walked out said to Jim.

Baptiste laughed: He himself must look so Indian that the fellow took a black as the one who spoke English.

"Whar to?" asked Jim.

"Fort Bridger, Fort Hall, and then some to Oregon and some to Californy."

"Zat is zee first fitting place," Baptiste spoke up. "Oregon or Californy."

"This country is God-forsaken," the old man, looking around edgily.

"It's quiet ahead," Jim said, "no trouble nowhar. That Oregon does shine."

"We air just passing by," said Baptiste, and nudged his horse. No sense in palavering all day.

The next noon, just before they started up the West Fork of Big Sandy, Baptiste and Jim saw a half-dozen dark dots against a hill a mile off to the right: Buffalo.

"Damned emigrators is ridin' right by 'em," Jim said, "didn't know what they was."

"Let's go," Baptiste grinned. Some more robes and meat would be fine for rendezvous. "Mountain Ram," he called, "we'll catch up."

"I said what would happen if you went foolin' after them darn buffalo," Eliza whined, "I surely said it." Five-year-old Julie, on her lap, wailed louder. Rube Applegate, ignoring his wife, clucked at the oxen pointlessly.

Ike Reed flicked his roan a few yards ahead. He had sworn yesterday that if she started in again, he's stuff her mouth with dust and cactus needles. His brother Frank eased up alongside him. "Well?" He meant what about moving on, leaving these bickering blunderers to muddle through, or not muddle through, on their own?

"Not yit. The train'll wait up afore long." Ike and Frank were eating the Applegate and the Olafsson's grub in return for helping drag and push the wagons through the bad places. Ike figured they ought to stick with the job. Frank figured his brother just liked being picked on.

Ole Olafsson was dreaming on the seat of the front wagon. He had opted out of the quarrels among the Applegates and the nastiness between the Applegate and the Reed boys ever since the two wagons lost the train a week ago. His own wife, who had dysentery, spent most of the day lying in back with the children. He just tried to keep the oxen moving. He noticed more and more, though, that his mind floated away from this land of dust, buffalo grass, cactus, and dry washes to his childhood—to his sister's wedding, to the first months of his marriage—to anywhere but where he was. He refused to quarrel. But he kept letting the oxen wander into the worst places, getting the wagon stuck, and then the Reed boys would curse him disgracefully. His only defense was staying eight thousand miles away.

"What the hail?" Ike yelled.

Ole snapped to. Goddamn: Injuns riding down on them hard—an old man waving a lance in front and two more right behind, all of them screeching. Ole looked quick at Ike and Frank, who were doing nothing on their skittish horses but looking edgy. That sight struck sheer panic through Ole. He had to do something. He lifted his cap-and-ball rifle off the seat, pointed it toward the old men, and jerked the trigger. The old man's horse stumbled, and he pitched to the ground.

Oh shit, Ike thought, now it's a fight. Two of the Injuns pulled up, but another came around them yelling and waving one hand. Ike leveled on the redskin, and noticed only as he pulled that it was a girl. She jerked backwards. Ike could shoot and hunt with anybody.

Bazel lifted Mountain Ram to his horse; the old man's leg was bent funny. Spotted Deer helped Little Bear get Running Stream onto his pony; she was shot in the stomach. Big Belly fired once at the whites to cover the rescues—it was the only rifle the party had. He heard a ball whiz by him, and whooped when he realized it had missed. They turned their backs to ride away, pulling the travois, which slowed them down, but the whites didn't shoot any more.

"Goddamn it, you bastard," Frank yelled at Ole, "that warn't no war party. You wanna get us all killed?"

"Ware was he wen he had to shoot?" Ole yelled back, pointing at Rube. With Eliza screaming and clinging to him, Rube hadn't even managed to get his gun from behind him.

A few minutes later Ole heard gunfire somewhere off to the north. He was already driving the oxen in a cold fury; he drove them harder.

Baptiste and Jim made a long cut across where the trail should have been, but they didn't find it. They had angled north to catch up with the band. Finally, they started backtracking toward where they had last seen the others. The horses were loaded with skins full of fresh meat.

The sounds of wails came to Baptiste's ears across the scorched plains, faint and mournful, like the cries of doves. He sucked in his breath deeply as he let himself know what they were, and then gave Pilgrim a kick. Jim was already several strides ahead of him.

All he got from Little Bear's babble was Mountain Ram and Running Stream, Mountain Ram and Running Stream. She was stretched out on a deerskin in the shade of one bank of the wash. Her knees were up and her legs spread wide. Blood had been scraped away from the dust between her legs, and scraps of human tissue were here and there. A long shudder started and convulsed his body. He cut it off. The bone-chill stayed.

He slipped one hand behind her head, and she opened her eyes. They were glazed, and he was not sure whether she recognized him. She looked old, incredibly old and haggard.

Sacajawea pointed, and he saw the wound. It was on the right side just below the ribs. No digging for it, no cauterizing, nothing to do. He crossed his legs and sat down, her head still cradled in his hand. She looked like she might be asleep.

"John, let's go. They got to be the stupidest niggurs in the mountains, and murderin' bastards asides."

Baptiste cut him off with one hand. "Maybe later," he said. Jim looked at him hard, then strode off toward his horse. Baptiste guessed that later the revenge would be over.

"You must not," declared Bazel. "You must not. It was our mistake. A misunderstanding. Stupidity."

"That kind of stupidity can get a man killed," Jim said. "It damn well oughta get a man killed." Big Belly, who had already promised to get the man who did it, was mounting up.

"Face-Always-Black," called Little Bear, "let me go with you."

"No," Bazel said. "You may not go."

"He's old enough to larn," Jim told Bazel.

"My son stays here. Mountain Ram would say you all stay here. Washakie would say the same."

"Mountain Ram is a fevered old man with a broken leg. Washakie is a fool. So long, Bazel."

They walked their horses slowly, since they would wait until dark to do the job.

> Hy-ee-ah!
> Hy-ee-ah!
> *I am a made-to-die.*
> *Today is a good day to die.*
> Hy-ee-ah!
> *I am a made-to-die.*
> *Today is a good day to die.*

Jim shook his head. Big Belly had already told him that nothing could hurt him today. His magic had turned the ball fired at him by the gray-hatted Frenchman, and today it would turn all that might do harm. But he kept singing the damn song talking about dying. In Jim's experience, lead had a way of cutting straight through magical words. He'd damn well shut Big Belly up before they got close.

"You sure you know what ones done the shooting?"

Big Belly nodded emphatically.

> Hy-ee-ah!
> *Today I take many scalps.*

Jim didn't know what this crap about scalping was. He'd already told the crittur that they'd ease up in the dark, pick out the two who done the shootin', kill 'em, and clear out before all the son of a bitches got to chasing.

They sat perfectly still in the sagebrush. They had waited twenty minutes, and Jim was willing to wait however long it took to get the best chance. He wanted them all sitting down around that pitiful little fire they were trying to make out of sagebrush. The men and boys kept wandering into the dark to get something more to burn, but it didn't look like they would cross the little wash between them and Jim and Big Belly.

The damned Snake kept mouthing his prayers and fingering his piece of onyx and his antler tip. He wasn't making any sound, but Jim was sure that his mouthing would somehow carry across the watch and spoil the job.

Finally they all settled down. One of the two young fellers, the one who was Jim's, sat where Jim couldn't get an angle at him. The red-headed niggur, the one that talked funny, leaned against a wagon wheel, an easy shot. Jim had picked the young feller for himself because he and the other carried pistols in their belts—them new Colt guns. The others didn't bother.

They crawled around to where Jim could get a clean shot. "Wait till I shoot," he told Big Belly.

He laid his pistol on the ground within easy reach and got up on one knee, to be sure of clearing the brush. He held his sights on the man's chest and squeezed. The bastard flew backwards like a kicked can.

Bazel jumped up, whooped loudly, and snapped off a careless shot. The red-headed fellow just stood there, untouched. And the idiot was still standing there, like he was frozen. Jim stood up, leveled the pistol with both hands, and shot him center.

But Big Belly was already halfway into camp. Since he'd missed, he must mean to take the bastard with his knife. And then probably wait around to scalp him. Jim ran for his horse. He heard a pistol shot and Big Belly's scream. He kept running. After a moment another shot and scream from Big Belly. Jim figured he might as well lead Big Belly's horse back to camp.

Near sundown Running Stream seemed to get better. He had been wiping her face with a damp cloth; and the fever seemed to go down, and she stopped tossing and grimacing.

Her eyes lifted open, slowly, and this time she knew who he was. Her lips started to move. "Don't talk," he cut her off. "Rest." She understood and said nothing, but she kept looking at him. Once in a while her eyes went blank, and he knew that she was unable to see from the pain. Every few minutes he gave her a sip of water.

He knew the change was coming; he could feel it in her body. "I'm cold," she murmured. He put a finger on her lips while Sacajawea pulled a buffalo robe over her. She shivered for long minutes, holding his eyes with hers. Then her own eyes glazed. He waited for the pain to pass so that she could see again. After two or three minutes Sacajawea put a hand on his elbow. Running Stream was dead.

Sacajawea began to croon her mourning song; in the near-darkness others heard, and their voices joined hers. Baptiste lowered Running Stream's head, stood up, and walked out among the creosote bushes. He put his face in his hands and cried.

After a few minutes, he walked through the chanting mourners and knelt by her body. He took off his necklace, slipped the thong around her neck, and centered the hoop and stone on her chest. In his mind he said, "For your journey."

They had to make camp no more than an hour or two from East Fork Lake. The moon had not risen, and it was too dark to travel. Baptiste was irritated about that. He had moved all day long on a tide of impatience: At rendezvous they could stop dragging Mountain Ram along on the travois, bearing the bumps to his splinted leg in silence. At rendezvous they might get some better medical help for him. At rendezvous they might trade for the Hawkens that Stewart and Campbell had brought to sell or to give away as prizes—the Shoshone needed them. Besides, Baptiste could get some whisky. He couldn't remember when his dry had so wanted some wet.

"Paump," Sacajawea said quietly. She sat down next to him in the dark, ten yards from the fire, and waited for his attention. "Spotted Deer is your squaw now."

He looked at her like she was crazy. "She's what?"

"You know this, Paump. Spotted Deer is your squaw. Not because Running Stream is dead. Because she is Running Stream's sister and her brave is dead."

"Jesus Christ," he swore in English.

"She did not come to you last night because you were deep in your grief. But she will come tonight. She belongs to you."

"I don't want her." He was a little surprised that he didn't feel as adamant as he sounded.

"It is your duty. Mountain Ram will expect it. Everyone will expect it."

"No."

"If you do not want her, you may trade her to someone else, which would humiliate her. In the meantime she is yours." Sacajawea stepped back to the fire.

"Tell her not to come tonight." He had halfway noticed that she had been doing things attentively for him since yesterday, but he'd forgotten the custom for the moment. He put down his blankets far out in the dark, and she did not come that night.

Rendezvous was petering out by the time they got there. Baptiste did hallo some old friends—Gabe, Joe Meek, Doc Newell, Black Harris, and Mark Head had come in. But Carson and Fitzpatrick were off playing nursemaid to Lt. Frémont, Bill Williams and Long Hatcher were gone to Bayou Salade, and others were scattered across the landscape, gone to Oregon, or gone under.

Campbell traded him three new Hawkens and some Du-Pont and G'lena, but warned him against stirring up the Snakes, which would only shed more blood. He managed to pick up two more used rifles.   ·

Captain Stewart cultivated him. He was intrigued with the paradox of Baptiste. The second evening he made an offer: "Bob and I are going to do some hunting up in the mountains," nodding toward the Wind Rivers. "Why don't you guide us?"

"Naw," said Baptiste, "Bob knows 'em."

"He hasn't been there for ten years. He says you know them better."

"Mebbe."

"I'll give you a hundred dollars for the month. Your people can stay here at camp."

"Don't that shine? Why didn't you say so right off?"

He told Jim to come along and split the hundred. At least this was a way to keep the situation from getting sticky with Spotted Deer. And he had something in mind other than guiding.

He stopped Pilgrim, when they rode into the bottom of the high basin surrounded by the Cirque of the Towers, just to drink it in for a moment. The basin undulated gently toward its upper end. The floor was a mossy, spongy, tundra-like grass; they had left trees behind a thousand feet below. Tiny streams hatchworked the floor, some no wider than a man's hand, some several feet across, all running with the coldest, clearest water a man would ever expect to drink.

At the head of the basin the grass, so green it hurt the eyes, gave way to a glacier; the glacier angled up toward the peaks, a band of white dividing the region where plants and animals can live from the region where they cannot; the peaks jutted up from the glacier into an immense circle of nine high towers, huge slashes against the sky. The towers were slabs on slabs of perfect, unbroken, gray granite, laid behind each other as neatly as playing cards. They rose in an assault on the blue, as though the rocks had been blasted from the earth by some huge energy, and had been frozen at the top of their flight.

The Indians had named the highest and most jagged tower Lightning Peak. Probably it got its name because it attracted lightning; Baptiste thought it looked itself like lightning stilled and fixed.

In fact only a few Indians had ever been there, and Baptiste had come only once before. He had camped, looked, played songs, and done nothing that first time. This time Stewart's desire for a bighorn sheep, found only in remote places, would provide a good excuse to do it again.

"What's this—Orpheus?" Captain Stewart cried. Baptiste put down his harmonika as the horses and mules clattered up to camp. He guessed everyone would be in high spirits: Two bighorn sheep were draped over pack mules, a considerable day's work. "A little minstrelsy?" Stewart repeated.

"A little music to soothe the *savage* breast," replied Baptiste.

Stewart swung off. "But not savage enough to enjoy a little hunt. A fine trick splitting the work and the fee with Jim here. Did you see?" He grabbed one of the sheep by its horns and stared it down. The huge, curling horns dwarfed the head—it was a splendid specimen.

Stewart's best came out that night, Scotch whisky and Drambuie. Stewart tried the meat of the sheep, but it was stringy and they ended up having hump ribs instead.

"Baptiste," asked Stewart, "what were you playing this afternoon? Can you give us some music? The party needs some livening."

Baptiste had not played from the night of Running Stream's death until that day. Entirely alone, he played his own songs, and even toyed with an idea for a new one, a kind of *rondo* with a principal theme suggesting the Cirque of the Towers and nine themes for the individual towers. But he felt too private about his own songs right then. "You have a choice of Mozart, Beethoven, backwoods American, French-Canadian, and Indian."

"Leave out the weighty ones and let's have the rest."

It was a cold night, there at more than ten thousand feet; clouds had spit a little snow that afternoon; the men were crowded close around the fire, front sides scorching and back sides freezing—Stewart, Campbell, Baptiste, Jim, and the three muleteers. Baptiste tossed off a boatman's ditty, which Stewart applauded heartily, and then a new song, "Across the Wide Missouri," which, without lyrics, seemed to miss. *"Mes Voyageurs"* went over because Antonine, one of the muleteers, knew the words.

So Baptiste decided to take a risk. "This is a Navajo song, an invocation of the most sacred powers, an appeal for their blessings." Throwing his head back, looking at the glacier and the granite walls and the reaching towers and the remote sky, he chanted with all his force:

Tsehigi.
House made of dawn.
House made of evening light.
House made of dark cloud.
House made of male rain.
House made of dark mist.
House made of female rain.
House made of pollen.
House made of grasshoppers.
Dark cloud is at the door.
The trail out of it is dark cloud.
The zigzag lightning stands high upon it.
Male deity!
Your offering I make.
I have prepared a smoke for you.
Restore my feet for me.
Restore my legs for me.
Restore my body for me.
Restore my mind for me.
This very day take out your spell for me.
Your spell remove for me.
You have taken it away for me.
Far off it has gone.
Happily I recover.
Happily my interior becomes cool.
Happily I go forth.
My interior feeling cool, may I walk.
No longer sore, may I walk.
Impervious to pain, may I walk.
With lively feelings, may I walk.
As it used to be long ago, may I walk.
Happily may I walk.

Happily, with abundant dark clouds, may I walk.
Happily, with abundant plants, may I walk.
Happily, on a trail of pollen, may I walk.
Happily may I walk.
Being as it used to be long ago, may I walk.
May it be beautiful before me.
May it be beautiful behind me.
May it be beautiful below me.
May it be beautiful above me.
May it be beautiful all around me.
In beauty it is finished.

A hush lingered among the men as the echoes of the chant died away.

Finally Stewart, as though taking responsibility as leader, spoke up: "By God, the Indians do love the earth, don't they?"

"Would you play one of those 'weighty ones,'" Campbell said, "just to satisfy my curiosity?" So he gave them a lovely *adagio assai* of Mozart, which may have bored everyone but Campbell. "Baptiste," he said seriously, "you're a virtuoso on that thing. With the mouth organ and the Indian music, I believe you could have had a concert career. Don't you think so?" he asked Stewart.

"The public in Britain and Europe would flock to hear that music."

"I might have liked that," Baptiste said. "I also compose my own songs."

"Play us one," Campbell asked.

Baptiste considered. "Not tonight," he said. "An Indian must keep his magic to himself, lest others borrow it."

Stewart called Baptiste into his tent while the others were breaking camp. It was snowing lightly for the second straight day, and a nasty wind was up. He handed Baptiste a cup of hot coffee and poured some Scotch in.

"I have a proposition for you, and I want you to take me seriously. I hear that when you first came to the mountains, you were planning to write a book." Baptiste nodded. "About the Indians?"

"About my own life as an Indian and a white man."

"I don't know whether you're still interested in it, but if you are, I'd like to help you."

"Go ahead."

"Come back to Scotland with me. You can live at Murthly Castle. You'll have a sinecure for life. For life. Isn't the trapping at an end anyway?"

"It's dwindling."

"You can write your book, which will be much more colorful now. I may be able to help you place it with a publisher, and the income will be yours alone."

"Interesting."

"You might also give some concerts," said Stewart. "I know nothing of that world, and have no judgment about what is possible. Whatever my support is worth, you will have it."

Baptiste just looked at him. He was partly overcome with an impulse to burst into laughter at the coincidence of having two European aristocrats invite him to be members of their households. But that wasn't the point.

"What do you think?"

"I'll put it under my hat for a while," Baptiste said.

"Would you like another drink?"

"Does a bear shit in the woods?"

They chitchatted for a while, but let the main subject go. Baptiste didn't mention what was heaviest on his mind. William Stewart, baronet, was taking back live elk and buffalo to roam his ancestral Scotch estate. Would Jean-Baptiste Charbonneau be his live, souvenir Indian?

Back at the main camp Spotted Deer moved in with Baptiste without asking. Apparently his interval of mourning was considered over, and regardless of what he ultimately wanted to do with her, she was his property for now.

He liked her well enough. She was not a beautiful woman—her features were too strong and blunt for that—and she was thirty-five or forty. She was tall—strapping, in fact—and had a hard, wiry body that looked cut out for hard work. Like Running Stream she had mind enough of her own to talk back to him; she was full of common sense, and would sometimes make jokes that made him wake up in the night laughing. Well, she wasn't keeping him from taking a second squaw, if he wanted, so why not?

He noticed one night that the fact that she was lying down nearby had the simple effect of making his cock stand up. So he took her. It turned out to be a treat—she was athletic—and Spotted Deer seemed very pleased about it. He didn't mind it himself; for however long she belonged to him, he thought he'd keep it up.

Stewart's party rode with the Snakes all the way to Fort Bridger on Black's Fork, since Stewart wanted to see Gabe again before he moved toward St. Louis and ultimately Scotland.

The morning before they got to Fort Bridger, Stewart approached him after breakfast.

"Have you decided?"

"Yes. I'll stay here."

"You feel attached to the Shoshones?"

"I feel attached to this land."

Stewart let his eyes run in a wide circle over the scorched plains and the high mountains beyond them. He thought maybe he understood.

JANUARY, 1844: Washakie had agreed to have the big tribal council start in two days. The Shoshone nation was spread out through the Cache Valley, along the Bear River above the great rapids that rush it toward Salt Lake. The chiefs and principal warriors of all the tribes would come from their winter camps to sit at Washakie's council circle; Washakie had a huge lodge made especially for this meeting, and sent his hunters for enough meat to last several days. It would be the biggest council since the fight with the Crows on the Wind River three years earlier, when Washakie had persuaded the chiefs that the Shoshones must drive the Absaroka people from the Wind River Mountains and claim those hunting grounds for themselves. When it came to other Indians, Washakie was a warrior.

Paump had his work cut out for him. In the autumn he had made a long ride alone through the Salmon River Mountains to think it through. He spent more than a month wandering through that country. He rode over the big east-west divide, through a succession of wide alpine meadows full of deer and laid out like immense parks, to the head of Middle Fork, then down that river—the swiftest and most violent he had ever seen—all the way to its mouth at the main Salmon. He loved the country: The river canyon was too deep and narrow a cut ever to permit wagon traffic or any sizable party through; it abounded in grouse, deer, elk, bear, mountain-goats, and bighorn sheep; he had never seen so much game; the canyon would stay warm in the winter, and the animals would be forced down to the river; it was an ideal spot, far too wild for any white men and for most Indians; he marked it down as a vacation spot. And he caught glimpses of the Sheep-Eater Indians, relatives to the Shoshones, who were too man-shy to come even to him. He saw their ancient paintings on rock walls. There were only a few of the Sheep-Eaters; they had probably seen white men, but not even trappers had seen them. Aside from riding and hunting, he played the harmonika, lay on his back on the grass, and thought. When he came out, he had made up his mind what to say to Washakie.

Now he had to persuade the council. He spent the last two days before the parley politicking—talking to Bazel and Sacajawea, to Mountain Ram, who was now crippled, to Broken Hand, Little Eagle, Fat Bear, Buffalo Horn, Crazy Eyes, to every man who would attend the council. He had no idea whether he would get support from anyone but Jim.

Washakie puffed, then saluted the earth, the sky, and the four winds. "Our brother Paump has asked to me to call this great council," he began. "We will speak of what we must do concerning the Frenchman, who now comes as many as the locusts—who drinks the water, burns the wood, and kills the buffalo of our hunting grounds, so that the Shoshone people may one day have not enough to eat. Paump has lived among the white men and knows their hearts. Therefore do not be offended that I have invited him to sit here beside me and to speak to you his heart about the Frenchman."

He passed the pipe to Paump, who puffed ceremonially. Ordinarily, the first speeches would have been preliminary skirmishing, but he decided to pitch straight in.

"My brothers, the white man wants your land, your game, your water, your wood, your children, your minds, your hearts, and perhaps your lives.

"Before the memories of the grandfathers of the oldest men, the Frenchmen came across the salt-water-everywhere to this land. From the beginning they fought with the Indians and took the land where they had lived since the time before the memories of the grandfathers of their oldest men. First they pushed the red man away from the salt-water-everywhere, beyond the first range of mountains, and took their land for themselves. They promised, however, that the red man would have the land beyond those mountains to live upon as long as the grass shall grow and the sun shall shine.

"Then the white men themselves crossed the mountains and began to take the land. When the Indians fought them, they sent the long knives with many guns to drive the red men far to the west or to kill them. They killed many, and stole the lands of the others. Only fifteen years ago they declared that all the land west of the Missouri River shall belong to the Indian as long as the grass shall grow and the sun shall shine. They herded all the red men of the east together and drove them in herds like tamed oxen to the west side of the Missouri River. Even to the Frenchman that march is now known as the Trail of Tears, for many died of weariness, of hunger, and of sorrow.

"Now, however, they wish to use the land for themselves which they promised to the red man for as long as water shall run downhill. They wish to make a great trail to the salt-water-everywhere that lies to the west. Last summer wagons came thick as grasshoppers across our land, scavenging all that lay in their path and leaving it barren. Last summer the long knives sent out a band to mark the trail. Soon the long knives will come to guard the trail with their rifles, and the long knives will live in the forts and feed off the land.

"My brothers, the Frenchmen are many. The Great White Father alone rules a hundred villages each with as many Frenchmen as there are braves, squaws, and children in the Shoshone nation. And for the Frenchmen in those villages there are ten more living in smaller villages. Many more white men live across the salt-water-everywhere, and now they come to increase the number swarming across our lands. They outnumber us as the flies outnumber the buffalo.

"They will come as thick as mayflies if we permit it. They have the boat that moves driven by mist, as you have heard, which carries many people. They also have a wagon that is driven by mist; it pulls many more wagons behind it, so that together they stretch farther than the highest lodgepole pine. This wagon travels many sleeps in a single day. Many will come to our country on that wagon and will spread like plague through our land.

"My brothers, they are many and they are strong. Perhaps they are too strong for us. But we must fight like made-to-dies. If we die now, that will be better than living to be toothless old men, starving as we wander the earth because we have no lands. Perhaps, however, we can in our brave fight stop them. For the land is on our side.

"The Frenchmen who cross our land in wagons do not understand it and do not love it. Therefore they come in fear and quake in their sleep. They are poor hunters, nearly starving in a land of plenty. We can use their fear, their lack of skill, and the land.

"All the wagons that cross to Oregon must come through South Pass. The next pass over which oxen may draw wagons is many sleeps to the south, further far than any Shoshone has traveled. The land there is a desert, without water or game. Few white men can cross it without perishing.

"Brothers, we can close South Pass to the wagons. Its western side belongs to us. It is narrow, and our braves can hold it against many guns. The eastern side of South Pass belongs to the Crows. We can ask them to join us in blocking the pass against the wagons. Against the Shoshones no Frenchmen will get through. The Crows will make the Shoshones even stronger, and we will no longer help the Frenchmen by letting Shoshones kill Crows and Crows kill Shoshones.

"Brothers, until now the white men we have seen have been men of good heart, and they were few. They took only the beaver, which we did not need, and they gave us guns in fair return. The Frenchmen who now come in wagons on the great trail are many, and they are not of good heart. They take our buffalo, our deer, our elk, our wood, our water, and give us nothing in return but misery. Brothers, we can force them to a halt, and we must."

As a sign that he had finished, Paump passed the pipe to Mauvais Gauche. He hoped he'd done right spitting it all out at once like that.

It would be a long process now, for every brave who wished to speak would be heard in full, and none cut short. He would not know what had been decided until the pipe went full circle to Washakie, and then perhaps full circle again and again. Aside from the chiefs and the principal warriors who sat in the circle, many braves and even squaws sat and stood behind them listening: some of those braves would speak and be heard.

Mauvais Gauche supported Paump, except that he would not go in league with the Crows but would kill everyone he saw and curse their grandchildren. One Eye said that the Frenchmen were too many, and perhaps the Shoshone should demand payment for the crossing of their land, because they could not keep the wagons away. Buffalo Head agreed with One Eye, Fat Bear with Mauvais Gauche; Bazel said that he believed that the Frenchmen would be brothers to the Shoshone and teach them their great medicine; Crazy Eyes called for the closing of the pass. And so it went, hour after hour. Opinion seemed split, except that all were against making a pact with the Crows. Damn, Paump thought, they'd rather raid their old enemies than save their lives and their land. The pipe had circled nearly two full times when they quit for the day, but Washakie had said nothing.

The next morning it went the same. Paump had no idea what they would decide. Jim, sitting in the place of least honor on Washakie's right, helped with an impassioned plea for war against all whites. He reminded everyone that the whites had made slaves of the black men—braves, too, not just squaws—and had bought and sold them like horses. They would do the same to the Shoshones, he said, if the Shoshones did not fight like made-to-dies. Baptiste saluted him with an eyebrow.

It was time for those sitting in the rear to speak. Mountain Ram was first. He said simply that the whites had killed his one daughter and his other daughter's brave without cause, and he would see their blood in the dust even if he, an aging cripple, had to kill them himself. Three more braves called for war on the Frenchmen: If Paump, who had lived among them many years, said that their hearts were bad, it must be so. Baptiste thought maybe the ayes had it.

"Fathers and sons"—it was Sacajawea's voice—"I also know the Frenchman's heart, and know it to be good." Damn, he couldn't believe she would speak up in council, being a squaw. Washakie did not interrupt her. "I lived near the white man's big village St. Louis for two summers and two winters, and visited there many more times. Always they treated me with sincerity and respect, and my children also. Furthermore, I have the word of the Red-Headed Chief that the Great White Father holds us as he holds his brothers and sisters and sons and daughters. This

I believe, for the Red-Headed Chief always spoke the truth to me. The Shoshone must never black his face against the Frenchmen."

That hurt. Baptiste looked at his knees while he listened to Washakie sum up. He invoked open hands for the Frenchmen, blackened faces for the Crows. It was settled.

"Whar you went cockeyed, John, was askin' 'em to jine up the Crows. Wagh! If Frémont come back with fifty men, the Shoshone would give him five hundred warriors to help kill Crows, and fork up the know-how besides. The Crows 'ud do the same against the Shoshones, or the Blackfeet, or the Sioux. And t'other way. John, they druther kill each other than the U.S. Cavalry."

"Looks like it."

"What ye gonna do?"

"Stay here a spell. The time isn't yet."

"It will be, afore long."

Epilogue

SUMMER, 1847: The spearhead of the Mormon migration crossed the Wasatch Mountains and neared the Great Salt Lake, in country hunted and disputed by the Shoshones and the Utes for generations. Brigham Young announced, by the authority of divine revelation, that this territory was ideal for the cultivation of crops, for settlements, and for the Saints' way of life; back up the trail a ways, Jim Bridger had announced the same to Brigham Young, by the authority of a quarter-century spent learning the whole interior West. Brigham exhorted his people to the stalwart courage and determination to succeed that would be needed.

1848: Paump, having observed the impassioned and inspired efforts of the Saints' first year, and also having noted the astonishing numbers of Mormons who kept bumping into the area in wagons, decided that a little distance from them would be a tonic. By then he had a second squaw, a teen-aged girl named Aspen whom he thought remarkably beautiful. He packed up Spotted Deer, Aspen, and their year-old daughter, and rode north for Salmon River country. He promised Sacajawea that he would be back next summer to trade for supplies at Fort Hall.

Brigham Young's representatives promised the Shoshones that they would teach them how to tend the soil so that they would have food, and how to tend their souls so that they would be saved. Washakie and the other chiefs, aware that their people were beginning to go hungry from lack of game, pronounced themselves grateful.

Paump sets up this lodge beside a swift-running creek seventy miles below the mouth of Middle Fork, in the upper part of the river's deep canyon. Between his lodge and the river stretches a grassy meadow about a hundred yards

257

wide. That winter he shoots an elk, a bear, and two deer, and could shoot as much in any week of that season. He builds a second lodge to use as a smokehouse.

1850: The Shoshones began to distinguish between "Americans," whom they liked as good friends, and "Mormons," whom they did not like.

Paump builds a log cabin. After living in it two months, he decides to travel to the plains to get buffalo hides for another tipi. And he presents to Sacajawea that summer, at the tribe's camp on the Siskadee, now better known as the Green River, another grandchild, this time a son.

1853: Washakie, angered by a slight from the captain of the Green River ferry, shouted at the Mormons who owned the ferry that he would kill every white man, woman, and child he found on the eastern bank of the river the next morning. The Mormons spent the night getting ready to defend themselves. At sunrise Washakie came back with fifteen warriors and declared his people to be the good friends of the white man.

Paump's year has evolved its own seasons: The winter he spends by his meadow in the canyon, where the animals join him for shelter against the deep snow and zero temperatures of the surrounding mountains. When the snow melts away from the bottom of the rocks and trees, and then from the meadows, and the brown grass begins to green and the wildflowers bloom, he moves slowly up the river. After a couple of weeks the salmon run, and for a few days he catches the huge fish on hooks made from pins and smokes the meat on wood racks above open flames. The squaws gather rosehips and every imaginable berry as they travel, for drying and for use in pemmican. All summer they camp above a savage set of falls near the mouth of the river, in a series of meadows that unfold as broad, flat, green, and gentle as any country estate in England. He spends his days on long walks or long rides, for here the country is high, cool, and truly alpine, the hills covered with pine, spruce, and fir, the water plentiful, the temperatures cool. Sometimes he spends whole afternoons inventing new tunes on his harmonika; sometimes he spends whole days sitting still in the forest watching, listening, drinking in. And in the autumn, when the aspens begin to turn color, he makes a circle through the mountains back to his meadow in the canyon. So he has a summer home in the high alpine plateau, a winter home low in the warm canyons, and a spring and fall of traveling.

1854: Brigham Young sent missionaries to Washakie with the *Book of Mormon*. The chief whiffed on the pipe, then passed it and the book left around the council circle without comment. Every brave puffed, fingered the book, and pronounced the book good for the white man, no good for the Indian. After the book had made the circle over twenty times, without a word being said in its favor, Washakie upbraided the councilors for their stupidity:

"You are all fools, you are blind, and cannot see; you have no ears, for you do not hear; you are fools for you do not understand. These men are our friends. The great Mormon captain has talked with our Father above the clouds, and He told the Mormon captain to send these men here to tell us the truth, and not a lie.

"They have not got forked tongues. They talk straight, with one tongue, and tell us that after a few more snows the buffalo will be gone, and if we do not learn some other way to get something to eat, we will starve to death.

"Now, we know that is the truth, for this country was once covered with buffalo, elk, deer, and antelope, and we had plenty to eat, and also robes for bedding, and to make lodges. But now, since the white man has made a trail across our land, and has killed off our game, we are hungry, and there is nothing for us to eat. Our women and children cry for food and we have no food to give them.

"The time was when our Father, who lives above the clouds, loved our fathers, who lived long ago, and His face was bright and He talked with our fathers. His face shone upon them, and their skins were white like the white man's. Then they were wise and wrote books, and the Great Father talked good to them; but after a while our people would not hear Him, and they quarreled and stole and fought, until the Great Father got mad, because His children would not hear Him talk.

"Then he turned his face away from them, and His back to them, and that caused a shade to come over them, and that is why our skin is black and our minds dark. That darkness came because the Great Father's back was toward us, and now we cannot see as the white man sees.

We can make a bow and arrow, but the white man's mind
is strong and light.

"The white men can make this [picking up a Colt's
revolver,] and a little thing that he carries in his pocket,
so that he can tell where the sun is on a dark day, and
when it is night he can tell when it will come daylight.
This is because the face of the Father is towards him, and
His back is towards us. But after a while the Great Father
will quit being angry, and will turn his face towards us.
Then our skin will be light."

Paump is tramping, this summer, across a steep hillside
above the mouth of Middle Fork; he moves slowly and
keeps his eyes roving after rotten logs. He walks over a
mile, stopping at seven or eight logs, before he finds what
he is looking for: Hidden in the decaying wood, on the
shady side of the log in marshy ground, grows an alpine
orchid, pale burgundy tinged with violet. He picks it
gently. It is his second of the day—one for each squaw.
He smiles at the thought of the speech he has long since
stopped giving them, about how they are getting free what
only queens can afford to buy.

1856: One of them does move a little—just the quick jerk
from freeze to freeze that birds make with their heads—
and Paump has them. He's carrying his Hawken, as always, but he also has a four-foot club in his right hand.
He stands still for a moment and watches them, three prairie chickens perched stock-still on the ground underneath a
big fir tree. He wonders if, when he stands still so long,
they forget he is there, or can't distinguish him. Then he
bolts. He clubs the first one before it moves at all, and gets
the second after the short step it takes before it flies. The
third sits stupidly on the lowest limb of the fir, not thirty
feet away. But he doesn't shoot it. It's by not shooting often, and never missing when he does shoot, that he keeps
his trips to the fort for trading down to once in two or
three years.

1859: Spotted Deer raises up from the ground, the newly
pulled camas roots in her hand, and freezes. A hundred
yards across the meadow, green with spring, Paump realizes
something is wrong, then sees what it is: A grizzly, probably not long out of hibernation, is inspecting her closely
from twenty yards away. No telling what the damn thing

will do. He walks slowly toward Spotted Deer, his rifle in one hand; he doesn't want to shoot it, because he doesn't need the meat. It still doesn't move. He passes Spotted Deer, who retreats to hold the horses, and yells at it: "Hey! Horse turd! Wake up! Get out of here!" The bear just blinks. "Move your ass! Clear out!" The bear doesn't budge. It is stupid. He looks back at Spotted Deer, who is mounted and has the reins of the second horse. All right, OK, he'll see what happens. He slides his wiping stick off his Hawken. Slowly, step by careful step, he eases toward the bear, which is on its hind legs. It's just a yearling. Maybe it's thinking of settliing in with his little family and teaching them a new dance. He raises his wiping stick.

Just then the bear drops to all fours with a growl and charges. Paump drops the stick and the gun and runs. Shit, the bear's almost on him. He zigs hard to the right, stumbles, rolls, and is back on his feet running. Damn thing's on him again. He zags toward some rocks. Hell, no choice. He turns for the edge of the rocks, shouts "God-damn it!" when he sees it's twenty feet to the ground below, and jumps.

When he begins to get his breath, the damn bear is on its hind legs up on the rocks roaring at him. "Get out of here!" he yells. "You've got bad breath." His damn shoulder hurts where he rolled on it. Spotted Deer comes up leading his horse, and nearly breaking in two with laughter. He gives her the evil eye, which only makes her laugh harder, and climbs on.

1862: No gifts had come to the Shoshones from the Great White Father for five years, despite many promises. Impatient with Washakie's peaceableness and willingness to wait, the tribe was ready to fight. The long knives were not so many now, because most of them were gone to fight a war between the white men east of the Missouri River. Pash-e-co, who was warlike, won the hearts of most of the Shoshone and displaced Washakie as supreme chief. In March he mounted a huge and devastating campaign against the whites. It ended, the next winter, when General Connor massacred Bear Hunter's band on the Bear River.

Paump and his son Paump are walking by the edge of a marshy place. Out in the trees they can hear a sow squirrel chattering as she hops through the trees. Her litter is squalling for food, sending its little shrieks from the hole of a tree twenty feet out into the slough left by the heavy rains. The sow squirrel flies from branch to branch and from tree to tree, ranging wide in her mission, all the while calling back that food is on its way.

The father points out to the son a black snake slithering into the water. It swims to the base of the slender tree and winds upward to the hole. The litter squawks a new signal—high, more piercing—just before the snake's head slides into the nest.

The boy goes rigid before his eyes pick up the sow, charging through the trees in huge bounds. In instants she is at the hole, her hind claws dug into the trunk and her head ready to strike. Once, twice, three times the sow's head whacks at the snake. The third time it holds, then cocks again, its teeth sunk just behind the snake's head. The sow shakes it violently, shakes it again, and then lets the snake drop into the water. She disappears into the hole for a moment; then she darts down the trunk head first; holding on with her hind legs, she dips her nose and paws twice into the water.

The man and boy wade to the base of the tree and retrieve the dead snake. The man holds it against the trunk, slits it open, and shows the boy that there are no tiny squirrels inside.

1863: At the big treaty council at Fort Bridger in July, Washakie accepted the government's terms for peace with the Shoshones: The Indians granted safe passage to emigrants, the right to settlements as way stations for them, the safety of the mail and the telegraph, and permission for the railroad to cross their lands. In return they got a ten-thousand dollar annuity for twenty years, and their claim to the Wind River country was recognized.

1865: After the death of Aspen, Paump agrees with Spotted Deer that the two children must learn something of their people. The family joins a segment of Washakie's band on a journey across the Bitterroots to the eastern side of the Continental Divide, where the buffalo are not yet so thin. Young Paump is given the name Mountain Goat by Sacajawea, and he kills his first buffalo. Paump gives his daughter to the brave of her choice, Three Hoops, and tells him with a grin that he may not find her as submissive as other squaws.

At Pierre's Hole, on the way back from the hunt, Mountain Goat asks his father for permission to join the tribe, and it is granted.

Paump, now with only Spotted Deer as a companion, returns to his winter home on Middle Fork. He is sixty years old. On the long trail ride home he and Spotted Deer scarcely speak, and he plays the harmonika for long hours.

1868: The Great White Father did not pay the dollars he promised to the Shoshones; the people were restless, and Washakie was on the verge of anger. At a great treaty council at Fort Bridger the Indians and whites made a new agreement: The Shoshones would give up their nomadic life, settle down in one place, and learn to till the soil. For this purpose they were given a reservation in the Wind River Mountains; the head of each Indian family would be entitled to 320 acres of land, which he would own as long as he continued to cultivate it. It would be a sea-change in Shoshone life.

Washakie, though, did not look back enviously on the old way. He said instead:

"I am laughing because I am happy. Because my heart is good. As I said two days ago, I like the. . . . Wind River valley. Now I see my friends are around me, and it is pleasant to meet and shake hands with them. I always find friends along the roads in this country, about Bridger, that is why I come here. It is good to have the railroad through this country and I have come down to see it.

"When we want to grow something to eat and hunt, I want the Wind River Country. In other Indian countries, there is danger, but here about Bridger, all is peaceful for whites and Indians and safe for all to travel. When the white men come into my country and cut the wood and made the roads, my heart was good, and I was satisfied. You have heard what I want. The Wind River Country is the one for me.

"We may not for one, two, or three years be able to till the ground. The Sioux may trouble us. But when the Sioux are taken care of, we can do well. Will the whites be allowed to build houses on our reservation? I do not object to traders coming among us, and care nothing about the miners and mining country where they are getting out gold. I may bye and bye get some of that myself.

"I want for my home the valley of the Wind River and lands on its tributaries as far east as the Popo-agie, and want the privilege of going over the mountains to hunt where I please."

Paump also hunted as he pleased. He had opted out of the momentous struggle of the Shoshone against the white man. With Spotted Deer he lived the balance of his life in the wild and inaccessible Salmon River Mountains, moving with the weather, hunting and trapping and fishing, watching the seasons change and then change back, making his music. Later, the Shoshones, when they told tales about him, said that nothing happened to him the rest of his life. He would have said that what mattered to him happened every day of his life.

AUGUST, 1876: The old man awoke in the pre-dawn light. He felt it, sometimes, like this; he could sense that in a few moments the sun, like a bubble of air that has risen from the bottom of a lake, would burst silently over the ridge to the east. He got up quietly from the buffalo robe, not disturbing the two squaws who slept nearby, and walked to the flap that always faced the rising sun and looked out at the eastern sky. His sense had been right, as it had been right on most mornings since he had come to live here in this wide grove beside the Salmon River. He looked at the distant ridge across the river where the sun would appear, this time of year, to the right of three juniper pines just below its flat top. The sky was not yellow or red—the sun had been above the earth's horizon for more than an hour already. The sky was instead the crystalline, cornflower blue of mornings in the mountains. The spot where the sun was aiming turned a brilliant white, and then the first edge of the yellow globule flickered above the ridge.

The old man stood facing it, as he did every morning, naked in the cool air.